FROM THE GATES OF AKSUM

Frontispiece: Procession of the Scald Miserables in 1741. Mackey

FROM THE GATES OF AKSUM

Gérard A. Besson

www.pariapublishing.com

Typeset in Poliphilus 13 point by Paria Publishing Co. Ltd. and printed by Lightning Source, U.S.A./U.K.

ISBN 978-976-8054-97-5 (softcover)
ISBN 978-976-8054-98-2 (hardcover)

Cover engravings:
Assemblée de Francs-Maçons pour la réception des Apprentifs.
Entrée du Récipiendaire dans la Loge. (1745)
Map of Venezuela and Trinidad. Published by the Dutch cartographer Willem Blaeu in Atlas Novus (Amsterdam 1635). Photo by N. Staykov (2007) (istockphoto)

Books in print by Gérard A. Besson:
The Book of Trinidad (with Bridget Brereton)
Folklore & Legends
The Cult of the Will
The Voice in the Govi

In memory of
Clifford Sealy and Lionel Seemungal,
without whom this story would not have been told.

PREFACE

This is a Caribbean and South American historical novel of high adventure. It is set in the period of the French Revolution as it swept through the Caribbean and in that of the Wars of Liberation on the South American continent.

The idea for the book was first suggested to me by Lionel Seemungal in 1980 when I was helping with Michael Pocock's *Out of the Shadows of the Past*, a work on the history of some of Trinidad's French colonial families.

In *From the Gates of Aksum* I try to enter the imagination of the people of those times, the age of the Enlightenment, as it expressed itself in the Americas and in the Caribbean. I attempt to capture the atmosphere of Simón Bolívar's victorious armies, the terrifying depredations of the revolutionary Victor Hugues, Trinidad's early slave society, the smell of hot molasses, and warm rum of the plantations and the howling winds that drive the protagonists to Europe, the Middle East, and to the high plateaus of the kingdom of Aksum in ancient Ethiopia.

I must say thanks to Angela Lewis, to Beatrice Caballero y Calderón, and my wife Alice Besson, as they each in turn inspired me to write this story. I am grateful to Georg Cantor for the insights gleaned from his 'set theory' and to Robert Temple for his inspiring thoughts.

Grateful thanks to Raymond Ramcharitar, Simon Lee and Jannine Horsford for their invaluable help in the editing and the proofreading of this book. V.S. Naipaul's *The Loss of El Dorado*, Augusto Mijares' *The Liberator*, Gilberto Jaimes Correa's *Trinidad Through the Eyes of Francisco de Miranda's*

Correspondence, Anthony de Verteuil's *Corsicans in Trinidad,* Laurent Dubois' *A Colony of Citizens,* E.L. Joseph's *Warner Arundell: The Adventures of a Creole,* Gaylord Kelshall's *Trinidad & Tobago, The Gateway to South America,* and the Abbé N. de Montfaucon de Villars' *The Comte De Gabalis* were all valuable sources. Thanks to Rowena Tindall, who lent me O. J. Mavrogordato's unpublished manuscript *Our Ancestors,* and most significantly to Lionel Seemungal, historian and archivist, who tirelessly strove to conserve Trinidad's early Masonic memory. As for Clifford Sealy, occultist, bookseller and antiquary—perhaps he only pretended to die, as in the way of the philosophers of long ago, who feign death in one place only to transplant themselves to another.

GÉRARD A. BESSON

"Tall Stories," Cascade
April 21st, 2012

ix

CONTENTS

In the Beginning
xiii

BOOK ONE

"Princes shall come out of Egypt; Ethiopia shall soon stretch out her hands unto God."

Psalms *68:31.*

G

IN THE BEGINNING

Sirius, the Dog Star, hung like a beacon in the golden dawn, soon to be absorbed into the glory of her father Ra. There is a mystery in the legend of the Sun behind the Sun, as there is a mystery of Egypt being the daughter of Ethiopia.

GEOMETRY. *Geo*, meaning earth, *metri*, measurement—earth-measuring. Geometry is a branch of mathematics and is concerned with the questions of the shape, size and the relative position of figures, and the properties of space. Geometry is one of the oldest mathematical sciences, and one could say that it was fundamental to the creation of the civilisations that achieved hegemony in the *Outremer* at the start of the early Bronze Age, circa 4000 B.C.

Geometry gave birth to the scientific discipline of geodesy; this enables the denoting of the shortest possible line between two points on a sphere, which facilitated the establishment of degrees of latitude and longitude. Geometry is older than Time itself, for it was geometry, together with geodesy and astronomy, which were employed in the reinvention of Time—which had become lost to mankind in the aftermath of the calamity of the great flood which had been occasioned by a hail of meteors colliding with the earth.

THE AXIS MUNDI. In the 480th year after the Great Initiate Moses liberated the Hebrew people from the bondage of slavery in Egypt, there ruled a great king whose name was Solomon. King Solomon, faithful to the promise made to his father, King David, proclaimed, "I propose to build a house unto the name of the Lord my God, as the Lord spake unto David my father, saying, 'Thy son, whom I will set upon thy throne in thy room, he shall build an house unto my name'." The time having come to fulfil that promise, King Solomon caused to be built the Temple at Mount Moriah in his capital city, Jerusalem, so as to house The Name of God.

The sciences of architecture and geometry had been taught to the Hebrews by Moses, "who was learned in all the wisdom of Egypt and was mighty in words and in deeds." *Acts 7:22.* This wisdom inspired King Solomon to create the designs for the building of the Temple, and enabled him to devise its dimensions and proportions and to design its entablature, decorations, and its accoutrements. When the time was deemed appropriate, King Solomon called upon the friend of his father's youth, Hiram, King of Tyre, for the materials to undertake this great work, whose purpose was revealed to him by the God most high, the very same deity whose name it was to house.

King Solomon said unto King Hiram: "I am now building a house for the name of my God. Send me a man skilled in the use of wood, stone, gold, silver, iron, bronze, scarlet, crimson, violet, the art of engraving too, for he is to work with my skilled men."

Hiram, King of Tyre, replied: "I am sending to you Hiram Abif. He is the son of a widow of the tribe of Naphtali; his father was a Tyrian, a bronze worker. He is skilled in what you desire and in the execution of any design."

This most famous of temples was built of stone, by, it is said, tens of thousands of Maçons. In the ancient charges of the Guilds of Stonemasons are classified different areas of knowledge. In these it is said: the fifth science is geometry, also known as Masonry. "It is the art of measuring everything on earth and in heaven."

What did the master builder, Hiram Abif, build? It was an edifice of smooth and gleaming stone, completely lined inside with cedar wood brought from the Lebanon and decorated with high reliefs of cherubim, pomegranates and open flowers. Its distinguishing characteristic was the quantity of gold that covered its floor, walls, reliefs and ceilings. The whole building was aligned from east to west, with a single entrance at its western end, in whose porchway stood two enormous bronze pillars that were cast by Hiram Abif and named in turn by him Boaz and Jachim.

In the volume of the Sacred Law, the Temple is described as an oblong building, consisting of three compartments: the porch, the great chamber for worship, and the *Kodesh Hakodashim,* the Holy of Holies, also known as the *sanctum sanctorum.* The Holy of Holies was an empty space that measured 20 cubits long, 20 cubits wide, and 20 cubits high, as it is described in the *First Book of Kings 6:20.* It formed a perfect empty cube.

In geometry, a cube is a three-dimensional figure that contains six square faces, facets or sides, with three meeting at each vertex. The cube can also be called a regular hexahedron and is one of the five Platonic solids. It is a special kind of square prism, of rectangular parallelepiped and of trigonal trapezohedron. The cube is dual to the octahedron. It has cubical symmetry, also called octahedral symmetry. It is special by being a cuboid and a rhombohedron.

The key to the science of the Hebrews—as received from the Great Initiate Moses, who was learned in all the sciences of Egypt, as written in *Acts 7:22*—was made manifest in the cubical empty space of the Holy of Holies. In this cuboidal space, upon its square floor could be demonstrated the ratio between the circumference and diameter of a circle with the numerical value of this relation expressed in integrals such as 22 over 7, or—Pi, or 3.14159: infinity, known in the Hebrew language as *Ein Sof* "the Endless One," that is, *she-en lo tiklah,* the Infinite. Thus, the Holy of Holies indeed "housed" The Name of God, which is infinite no-thingness. For the Hebrews the relation of diameter to circumference became a supreme concept expressed in the Tetragrammaton, the four-letter name of the One Infinite God. *Yod Hay Vav Hay.*

Geometry was the epitome of science at King Solomon's court, as the Holy of Holies' sole purpose was to house the One, infinite, absolute Name of God. The Hebrews with this knowledge were able to arrive at a profound appreciation of the fundamental nature of reality and of existence.

Pi, infinity, established for them an elemental truth, which was that there can only be One infinity. This idea thus became for millennia the significant achievement of the human condition. Giving birth to the concept of monotheism, which was to be celebrated with human-kind's highest tribute, it became a religion, being the belief in and the worship of a superhuman controlling power.

"Hear, O Israel, the Lord is our God, the Lord is One," declared the *Book of Deuteronomy 6:4–9,* thus establishing what was to be perceived as a universal truth, and that is: there can only be One infinity.

❖

FROM THE GATES OF AKSUM: As the sun cleared the summit of Har Tzion, her caravan that had travelled through the night descended into the Holy City. Several miles long, it was a wonder to behold. Thousands of camels, donkeys, magnificent Arab steeds festooned, and gorgeous palanquins laden with precious stones, diamonds and sapphires, with antique gold, spikenard for the anointing of kings yet unborn, and frankincense for the glory of The Name of God.

She herself rode before all this grandeur, in the midst of a clamorous horde of warriors, upon a giant Bactrian camel whose harness and flanks were decorated with enormous magenta tassels bound in gold. A thousand golden trumpets sounded and the royal herald declared: "Makeda, daughter of Africa, having heard of the fame of King Solomon concerning The Name of God, is come to pose him hard questions." And King Solomon received her and gave unto the Queen all she desired, whatever she asked, besides which the king also gave unto her of his royal bounty.

At their parting, King Solomon presented her with a gold ring which was to be given to their son upon his majority, so that he, who would be born to her, and be known to the world as the Prince Menelik, when come of age, would be made known to his father, the king.

Queen Makeda thus returned to her own country. That night, King Solomon was visited by a dream in which the genie of the dream caused to rise before him a vision in which he beheld the sphere of the sun in glorious array. Then, to his great consternation, he saw the sun depart from the land of Israel.

The royal youth, Ebn Melek, their son, was raised a prince in the Kingdom of Aksum. He was presented, as a boy, with a beautifully crafted mirror and encouraged to regard his handsome countenance so that he would recognise his father the king upon attaining his majority. When that time arrived, he ventured to the Holy City and there recognised his father the king, who had taken up a position amongst his warriors and courtiers, and presented him with the gold ring, and so received from his father's hands his consecration.

Prince Menelik, as Ebn Melek became, was anointed by King Solomon in wonderful magnificence, Sovereign of an empire that extended from the river of Egypt to the west, and from the south to Shoa, thence eastward to India.

It is written in the *Kebra-Nagast, The Glory of Kings* that in departing the Holy City, Prince Menelik and twenty of his chosen companions, the sons of Zadok, nobles of Israel, the Levites, priests of The Name of God, entered the great Temple that King Solomon caused to be built at the very centre of the Holy City and penetrated to the *Kodesh Hakodashim*, the *sanctum sanctorum*, the Holy of Holies, that empty space where only the High Priest might enter just once a year.

There the sons of Zadok, the Levites, priests of The Name of God, demonstrated to Prince Menelik that the *Kodesh Hakodashim* was a cube that measured 20 cubits long, 20 cubits wide, and 20 cubits high and that the Holy of Holies was compliant with the Law that commanded in the *Book of Deuteronomy 5:6–21*: "Thou shalt not make unto thee any graven images, or any likeness of anything that is in heaven above, or is in the earth beneath, or that is in the waters under the earth; you shall not bow down thyself to them, nor serve them." And, as such, the Holy of Holies contained neither idol nor effigy, but was designed as an expression of pure scientific thought in keeping with the relative position of figures, and the properties of space in which the One infinity may be demonstrated and realised.

The sons of Zadok, the Levites, priests of The Name of God, then guided Prince Menelik into a secret place, a vault that lay beneath the foundation stone of the Holy of Holies, which would, in time to come, be known as the Well of Souls. This vault contained a beautiful alabaster obelisk upon which was placed a large, crystal-like object, ingenuously crafted and mysteriously inscribed. It was formed from tchãm, a glass-like substance known solely to the antediluvian inhabitants of this world, similar to crystal, in appearance like golden glass, found only in the interior of meteors.

This crystal stone awaited a distant time and place, Prince Menelik was informed by his priestly conductors, as its shape, form, facets and inscriptions spoke in an antediluvian language, one that when deciphered and placed in the service of the future dwellers of this planet-world that we call earth, will provide the keys to the comprehension of yet another infinity, an infinity of infinities existing parallel to the one demonstrated in the Holy of Holies above. This advancement, he was told, would enable mankind to identify itself with the consonance of the spheres, that is to say the suns, our own star and another, the most brilliant in the night sky, and in so doing achieve the ultimate promise of spiritual symbiosis with a cosmic intelligence beyond contemporary mankind's capacity to appreciate, but one that would in a far-off future, aided by the scientific achievements of that time, provide the mechanisms for shaping a common humanity and the ultimate goal of mankind's destiny. Which is to be in harmony with The Name of God.

This crystal stone they removed from its place upon the alabaster obelisk, and carried it away with them from the Holy City. Crossing the Red Sea, the company journeyed inland into Ethiopia to arrive at a mountainous plateau and there entered the fastness of Shewa, in the Kingdom of Aksum, which was founded by Cush, son of Ham, the brother of Mizraim. They came eventually to the ancient city of Sheger, located at the foot of Mount Entoto, a sacred mountain, a place that would overtime become home to many monasteries and be known as a great centre of learning. This place, in the centuries to follow, would be called Addis Ababa, the capital city of the Empire of Ethiopia. It is a city that lies $10°$ north of the Equator. All this is recorded in the *Kebra-Nagast, The Glory of Kings*.

Littais L'Eau, Frère Servant, M.M., D.G.C. $14°$

Caracas, 1857.

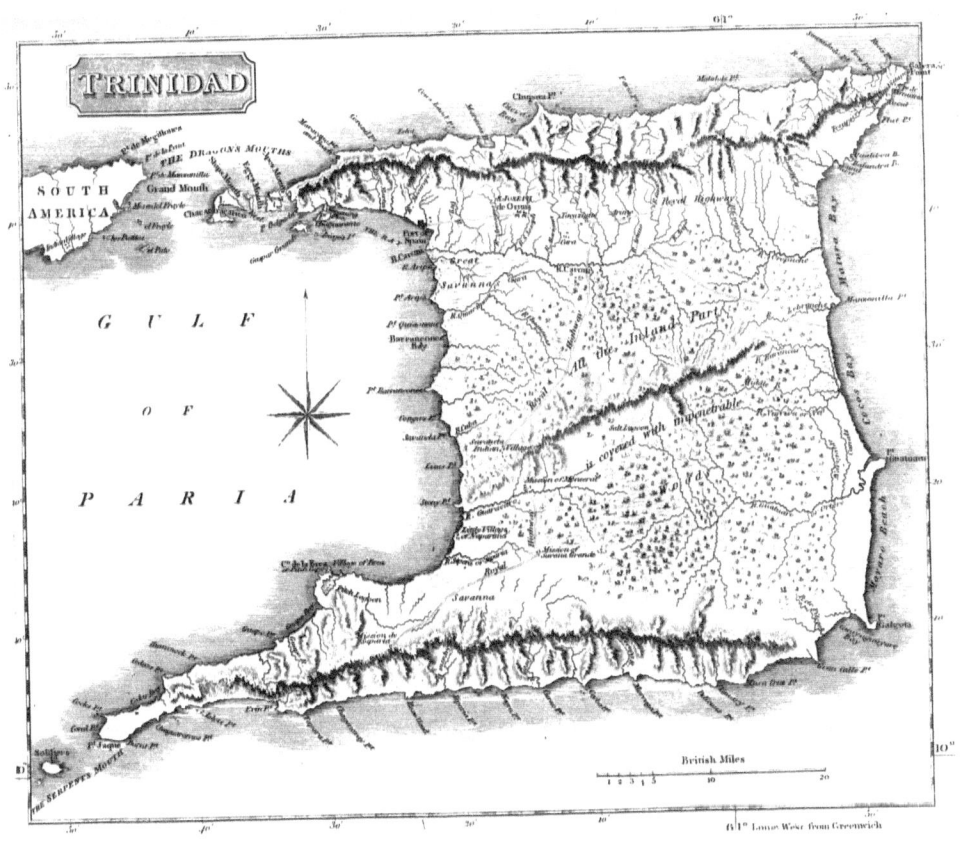

Thomson Map of Trinidad, 1816

BOOK ONE

1:

1787–1795.Victor Hugues,

Les Frères Unis.

They say he was a red-skinned man of mostly French but also of African descent; that he was born in Marseilles in 1760. His father was a baker, they say. He was apprenticed in the town of La Ciotat, or perhaps Aubagne, to a hairdresser. He possessed a natural affinity for learning and yearned to travel. He shipped aboard a merchantman as a cabin boy sailing the trade routes on the Atlantic run. He often wintered in the French Antilles, enjoying the wealthy mulatto lifestyle of the parvenus and the debaucheries of the harbour towns.

A raucous man of huge sexual appetite, he tended to attract the young, naive and impoverished whites. A thirst for knowledge and an instinct for the changing times, coupled with the pursuit of belonging, made him seek membership in a pseudo Masonic order, called *Societé d'Harmonie*. He established a *comptoir* at Port-au-Prince, dealing in an assortment of goods variously acquired: some traded, others of course stolen, or pilfered off the dead, or collected from the detritus of the pirates.

Saint-Domingue was the New World's first real crucible for the transmigration of souls. To produce vast quantities of sugar, the source of its wealth, Saint-Domingue, like all the islands in the west, was turned into the burial ground for the bodies of the hundreds of thousands who were chained to plantations scattered across the Caribbean archipelago, with Saint-Domingue as the largest, most prolific and valuable sugar-producing slave colony, ever, in the world. A wide variety of Africans, representing an array of peoples, religions and cultures, arrived at this place after a horrendous journey. Here they experienced life and death so hideous that to attempt to describe these would be altogether too distracting.

This was where men lived out their most macabre fantasies. A hedonistic, rapacious society beyond the Papal Line of Demarcation, where almost everything lay outside the purview of the Law. This island's plantocracy, *les gran blancs* lived in extravagance, tinctured by fear, in the midst of sumptuous wealth. Great fortunes were founded on those chattel slaves who were sold out of Africa, dying daily by the thousands, fostering an inexpressible anger and nursing desperate hopes for retributive revenge. "One day, one day, Congo's day": this was the source, of course, of the slavocracy's fear.

A conspicuous product of all this was the bewildering array of the mixture of European and African strains, *les gens de couleur*. A terribly beautiful new race of people conceived in bondage by women not in command of their wombs. These were immediately and universally despised as well as loved, and yes, desired by both the Africans and the Europeans. From this element would arise new and original animosities, divisive relationships, bitter disappointments, fierce jealousies and eventually the patricidal uprisings that would herald the New World's first Armageddon.

In his youth, blinded by his physical appetites, he could not care less about the miserable blacks, nor the wealthy or aristocratic whites. As for the mulattoes, quadroons, octoroons, sacatras, marabous and mamelouques, and others of his kind in their thousand-and-one varieties, he dismissed them for their intransigence and abused their insecurities, their hopelessness and what he considered to be their manufactured belief in their own victimhood; he felt no sympathy for their plight. But, as he grew older, his envy of the rich and privileged Europeans who scorned him yet used him at their convenience filled him with self-disgust, envy and eventually with hatred.

But this theatre of the macabre was tottering, destined to collapse, not be maintained for even another night's performance. All this was apparent in the fractiousness of the planters, the recalcitrance of the enslaved, the spread of abolitionists' sentiment in Europe as expressed in the *Société des amis des Noirs* and, the call for a revolution, which commenced in France in 1789. Thinking people knew that it would find a furious reflection of itself in Saint-Domingue. It did. *Les petit blancs,* the poor, envious and suffering whites flocked to the revolution. "Listen to the voice of Liberty, which speaks in the hearts of all," was the rallying cry of all the oppressed. The Declaration of the Rights of Man and of the Citizen was adopted on 26 August 1789, by the National Constituent Assembly. This produced a state of contagious panic that swiftly mutated to mass hysteria. The eruption of the mulatto war in 1790 did not surprise him. The Negro insurrection which followed frightened him.

The cacophony of conch shells that sounded through the length and breadth of Le Cap-Haïtien, loud enough to raise the dead, had summoned the fearless. He hadn't heard them. The uprising of the blacks in August 1791 swept him aside by its violence. The swarming mob destroyed his *comptoir*. The men in rage bellowed above his talk. He hid in the cellar of a burnt-out public building, with looters living above him, not daring to breathe. This gave him time to think.

He saw the city's great houses burn in Port-au-Prince; fires blazing in the night, red, a brilliant cadmium yellow, behind white lace curtains. The old monsieur, dead, his sons too. Their wives, already roasting like turkeys upstairs. The slaves are butchering the horses, the domestic servants, the blood hounds, the mulatto bastards. Down the mansion's marble front steps comes the *Da*, the black nurse. She holds Madame's big silver jewel box tight against her copious chest. Her small round head, tightly tied in white, is bowed. A man of blood, blood streaming down the arm that is holding high a cutlass, rushes past, snatches the jewel case and runs screaming into the night. The woman walks briskly into the devastated garden. The planter's little boy and his sister are running too, stooping beneath the nurse's wide skirts. She saves the children and herself, together with the gold and jewels that are sewn into their clothes. They board a ship bound for the distant island of Trinidad, to windward, *Barlovento*. Much in this manner, in a variety of circumstances, would that island acquire its population.

Hunger drove him from his hiding place. In the dark and blazing night, he saw the madness of the slaves, the terror of the rich pleading pardon for transgressions too enormous to be expiated, exonerated; retribution, immediate, was executed, severing the past. This was when he heard of his brother's death at the hands of the marauding slaves. He, with certain death trailing him, just managed to escape by swimming into the roadstead where a brigantine was making ready to catch the falling tide. At first, they fired on him. He commanded them to hold, and they, responding to the authority in his voice, hauled him up the side as she heaved to, leaving a wide wake, a white line that caught the flaming town, tingeing it to blood red.

That was where I, Littais L'Eau, met Victor Hugues. We sailed the Atlantic for ninety days in a pounding sea. The grey-black sky appeared to shatter with lightning that illuminated the clouds with phantasmal forms, accompanied by peals of thunder, a veritable orchestra playing the prelude to a disastrous climax. He told me he would return, his time had come. He was not escaping. He was in search of a mandate.

We parted at the port of Bordeaux, where the sea, exhausted, could barely lap the shore. He left as we dropped anchor as he had came, overboard, and made his way to Paris to find the centre of the storm, the vortex of the revolution, to match his rage with theirs, to out-rage them. I later heard that he was now a member of an extreme faction of the Jacobin Club, a group known as the Mountain, so called because they occupied the high back seats of the Convention Chamber. He became one of the *Enragés*. The *Montagnards*, as the Jacobins sitting high on the left called themselves, established their control of The Convention on June 2nd, 1793, not by vote, but by fear, a fear that sent many of their fellow revolutionaries fleeing for their very lives. Several, too afraid to leave, sent their sons abroad, some of these eventually came to Spanish Trinidad, whose government was attempting to create an instant population of armed and militarised planters by the issuance of a *Cédula de Población*.

The "Incorruptible," Maximilien Marie Isidore de Robespierre, recognised a kindred spirit in the zeal expressed in Hugues' hatred for the cursed race of Kings, the debauched clergy, the degenerate aristocracy, and immediately appointed him public prosecutor at La Rochelle. There, in the courthouse, I heard, he placed a guillotine, so as to facilitate the quick turnaround of justice. Such were the revolutionary credentials of this soon to be most fearsome terrorist.

After the emancipation decrees of Léger-Félicité Sonthonax and Étienne Polverel in Saint-Domingue in 1793, the Committee of Public Safety declared the end of slavery in all French territories in February, or *Ventôse,* as that month was renamed by Charles-Gilbert Romme in the new French revolutionary calendar. Victor Hugues was named civil commissioner to Guadeloupe in 1794.

He returned with the mandate he desired. The mandate was simple: kill all the aristocrats and royalists and free all Negroes in a state of slavery. Guadeloupe had been a French colony since 1635. An indication of Guadeloupe's great value to France as a sugar producing island was demonstrated in the Peace of Paris of 1763, where France, defeated in war, agreed to abandon its territorial claims to Canada if the English returned Guadeloupe, which they had captured in 1759. Imagine, an island far smaller than a country estate exchanged for almost half of a continent.

Universal war against republican France had commenced in February 1793. Plans were laid by the English government to recapture the islands that they had ceded to France in 1763. In 1794 an English force landed in Guadeloupe. It was welcomed by the French royalist planters, who were now made terrified by the execution of Louis XVI and the immediacy of revolutionary justice. Some royalists left for North America; several others found their way south to Trinidad.

That very year, 1794, Victor Hugues also landed an army in Guadeloupe and attacked and captured Basse-Terre. Under the banner "Law, Liberty, Equality" he proclaimed the end of chattel slavery and recruited the former slaves into his army. He erected the first guillotine ever seen in the New World at Pointe-à-Pitre, executed hundreds of French royalists, People of Colour and others suspected of being uncooperative to his regime, and imposed revolutionary law, which sent many more scampering for their lives to the safety of Trinidad. In Sainte Lucie, where I, Littais L'Eau, lived at the time, we received horrendous anecdotes of death and valour. Major General Thomas Dundas, a professional soldier, a man who saved the lives of many, was in command of the English forces that captured Guadeloupe on April 21st, 1794. We heard that in June of that year, the army under his command was attacked by the republican forces, aided by local insurgents under the control of Victor Hugues. Dundas died on that day, in that spot where he held the breach at Fort Matilda. He was buried that night, the soft bloody earth a womb to receive him, whale oil lanterns barely giving a misty glare to the burial party. From the distance came the sounds of a fierce battle being fought at Pointe-à-Pitre.

Hugues routed the English and continued the slaughter of the French royalist families. It is related how some were shot, others guillotined. Young women were auctioned off to the brigands. Other ladies were used as gambling chips in lunatic card games played by their former slaves. Hugues, this man of blood, this Robespierre of the colonies, like a man possessed, marched on the ruins of Fort Matilda and exhumed the body of Major General Dundas and threw it in its decomposing state into a nearby field, where it was eaten by feral dogs.

In a proclamation Victor Hugues wrote: "*Liberté, Égalité, Droit et Fraternité.* This ground, restored to liberty by the valour of the republicans, was polluted by the body of Thomas Dundas, governor of Guadaloupe for the bloody King George the Third."

A pamphlet that still circulates reads:

"The republicans erected a guillotine, with which they struck off the heads of fifty of them in the short space of an hour. This mode of proceeding, however, proving too tedious for their impatient revenge, the remainder of these unhappy men were fettered to each other, and placed on the brink of one of the trenches which they so gallantly defended: the republicans then drew up some of their undisciplined recruits in front, who, firing an irregular volley at their miserable victims, killed some and wounded others, leaving many, in all probability, untouched. The weight, however, of the former, dragged the rest into the ditch, where the living, the wounded, and the dead shared the same grave, the soil being instantly thrown in upon them."

Hugues informed the English that for every republican killed by them, of whatever colour or condition, he would kill two English prisoners. He mobilised the malcontented of these islands, energised old hatreds, and activated the seven devils, the princely rulers of the deadly sins. Lucifer: Pride, *superbia*. Mammon: Greed, *avaritia*. Asmodeus: Lust, *luxuria*. Leviathan: Envy, *invidia*. Beelzebub: Gluttony, *gullia*. Satan: Wrath, *ira*. Belphegor: Sloth, *acedia*. Servants rose up against their masters, servants murdered servants, mulattoes made pacts saying "I will kill your father, you will kill mine," brothers killed each other, sisters betrayed everyone, and life-long friends stabbed each other in their backs and shot and killed one another on battle fronts across the Caribbean Sea. It was the end of that world. Hugues exported the incubus of vengeful murder to the neighbouring islands of Dominica, Saint-Martin, Grenada, Saint Vincent and to Sainte Lucie.

Sainte Lucie, from where our story takes root, unlike other colonies in the French Antilles, at first was able to absorb the shocks and dreadful tremors of the revolution with no more severe consequences than internal social strains. Some Sainte Luciens, men of substance, were far-sighted; they identified with the higher principles of the *Lumières* or the Enlightenment as it became, and, although, they were all slave owners they were inclined towards the humanitarian impulse expressed by Jacques-Pierre Brissot, founder of the *Société des amis des Noirs*. This was reflected in the erection of three Ateliers, that is to say, Masonic Lodges, in as many years. These were Le Choix Réuni in Port Castries in 1784; L'Harmonie Fraternelle at Choiseul in 1787; and Les Frères Unis at Micoud on Wednesday the 27th of June 1787. They embraced and enthusiastically received the news of the revolution. The National Assembly in Paris was moved to designate Sainte Lucie "The Faithful," and authorised it to send a deputy to France. On the orders of the National Convention, a Colonial Assembly was instituted on the island.

But within a short time, the mood of the place became increasingly threatening. Its residents were overwhelmed by refugees from the neighbouring islands. Some came, fleeing the massacres they witnessed, with frightening stories of slaughter, of appalling violations, separations, loss of all and everything, shocking incidences of random killings, rapes, and of betrayals. A deep sense of fear took hold throughout the island's otherwise serene society.

Others arrived triumphant, spoke of "liberty" and talked of old scores settled, the manner in which revenge was sought and obtained, and how "equality" was achieved. All blood, they shouted, was red; they related spectacular massacres, told of rivers of blood, of conflagrations, boasted of their new state of compassionlessness as though it was a virtue, newly hatched, freshly minted, yet to be further expended and explored. Proud of their proficiency in the murder of old persons, they boasted of their success in achieving "fraternity" by the number of women, girls and religious they had violated and strangled, of boys beheaded, and of former masters hacked to death. Power, after generations of being powerless, became a narcotic, addictive, captivating, possessed of an impetus that became an all-absorbing lust.

Republican agents, dispatched to Sainte Lucie, compelled the monarchist governor, Monsieur Jean Zénon André de Véron de Laborie, to flee for his life. Late the following year a Captain La Crosse appeared in the capital, Castries. His stated purpose was to radicalise the radicals with the newly perfected doctrines of the revolution, inasmuch as it had now achieved a fresh velocity in Paris.

The rabble throughout the French islands now seized control of the revolution. The pirates and brigands, the criminals, the lunatics, many mulattoes, even slaves and the inevitable opportunists, all spoke eloquently of "the rights of man," with no notion of its meaning, or shouted one of the several revolutionary mottoes going about; "liberty, equality, fraternity" which, to many meant, "be my brother or I'll kill you." Terror filled the hearts of brave men who could no longer look their sons in the face. There was no place to hide, and very few could leave. The rule of law collapsed. General Gabriel Ricard was the next extremist to arrive in Castries with a directive from the Committee of Public Safety to enforce the abolition of slavery.

In February 1795 the colony descended into hell. Victor Hugues arrived with a motley "army" of desperadoes. A reign of terror was introduced that matched the one in France. Seven-eighths of the habitations were destroyed by fire and sword. Eight of the eleven parishes were laid waste. People fled from their homes into the mountains. A guillotine was introduced. Hugues' men slaughtered, after raping the women, more than eighty-five families of all colours and opinions without even sparing the babes, the sucklings.

This was immediately followed by an attack and subsequent capture of the island by English forces under the command of Lieutenant-General Sir Ralph Abercromby.

The remnant republican army, insurgent Free Coloureds, slaves and irregulars, took to the mountains and, from the high woods, terrorised the English and everyone else whenever and wherever they could. It felt as if war would never end. A creature of Hugues' returned to the island, his name was Jean-Joseph Lambert. Formerly a captain in the National Guard, he was familiar with the leading men, the planters, the men of affairs.

Jean-Joseph Lambert also knew who were the philanthropists and the Franc-Maçons, those who previously joined together and appealed to the Grand Orient de France for Charters to establish Maçonic Ateliers in Sainte Lucie. Jean-Joseph Lambert was instructed by Victor Hugues that the thinking with regard to the Franc-Maçons was now reversed by the Committee of Public Safety in Paris. The Craft was now perceived as counter-revolutionary, and Franc-Maçons were now the enemies of the revolution, condemned as backstabbing opportunists, traitors and cowards in waiting, contriving the return of the monarchy.

The ideals of Franc-Maçonnerie, expressed as "Brotherly Love, Relief, and Truth," which had once captured the imagination of the originators of the Enlightenment, the philosophers, the *encyclopédistes*, and had been so quickly embraced by the orators, pamphleteers, the *sans-culottes* and the proponents of the revolution in the Jacobin Clubs for the purpose of the overthrow of the throne, the altar and the aristocratic society of Europe, were now betrayed, debunked and refuted, in writing, by the Committee of Public Safety.

Within one week, thirty-seven Maçons were murdered in Sainte Lucie, some as they slept, others ambushed, hacked to death as they went about their business.

A former slave on the La Tille habitation by the name of Marinier, together with a party of armed brigands and slaves, attacked the town of Micoud in the middle of the night. With the town ablaze and the people fleeing the butchery, the twenty-four-year-old Frère Terrible and Secrétaire of Les Frères Unis, Benoît Dert, was just quick enough to run to the Atelier's newly erected temple, snatch its Charter certificate off the wall and flee, making his way over the mountains to Soufrière where he sought out Vincent Patrice, François de Gurvand and myself, Littais L'Eau, all Brothers in the Craft, and together with de Gurvand's son Adhémar and daughter Adèle, we boarded a privateer bound for Trinidad, where Benoît's brother, Dominic, owned a coffee plantation.

Many years later, I, Littais L'Eau, read the obituary of Victor Hugues in *Memorial de la Barrèrelais,* reproduced in the *Port-of-Spain Gazette*. In part it stated:

"To what extent Victor Hugues' presence pushed Don José María Chacón, Knight of the Order of Calatrava, the last Spanish governor of Trinidad, into easy surrender to the English in 1797, may only be guessed at. The fact is that the tens of thousands of those who walk the streets of Port-of-Spain today came here because of the displacement of ancestors to these shores by Victor Hugues."

But this account is not about Victor Hugues. He is but one parent—the other is fate. The fate of two men, friends, Brothers, who, in pursuit of their own ambitions, with purposes in mind known only to themselves, boarded a ship bound for Port-d'Espagne in Spanish Trinidad, as Sainte Lucie burned. But it is also about the revolutions that changed the course of the history of the world, and about a secret, one which would herald the birth of a new and different civilisation, if it is ever discovered, deciphered and of course revealed.

Having lived to this great age and being amongst the very few left alive of those who were consumed with sentiments of the deepest patriotism, I now commend this true account to you, dear reader, in the hope that the valour of the brave will be remembered, and also that the doors of Time be unlocked so that humankind might select the future that will fulfil its sacred destiny.

2:

1795–1797. Littais L'Eau,

Le Frère Servant.

He fell from the place running. That place where he had found friends, a home with Brothers. He could still feel the shame and remember the pain, he would know forever the meaning of the experience, and tell of it, vividly, when he was eighty years old, with the memory of other tragedies and disappointments still wild rumours in his mind.

A Knight Kadosh as Le Frère Terrible, robed in flowing black silk, wearing the spotless white gloves of the innocent, his face in a mask of antique silver with a smile sardonic, with eyebrows raised in exclamation, had pointed him out and demanded his expulsion, as the Brethren mourned, and called a chant for the dead. He was struck across the face. Le Frère Terrible then bound his right arm painfully with a leather strap that was soaked in sea water about the wrist, this arm was pulled violently upwards behind him and the strap tied around his neck.

An ancient Past-Master had stood forth to extinguish his candle by turning it over wick first, on the tiled black and white checkered floor.

They had sentenced him to die two deaths, one in this world and the other in the past. He was to have no future.

He staggered down the Rue des Trois Chandelles choking, pariah dogs howling at his shadow. The leather strap tightening, his every breath felt like his last.

"Sé mèyè kouwi kon on gwan kapon ki mouwi kon on gwo kouyon."

She was so old she could remember when this island was devastated by the raids of the Corsairs. Their captain, one Teach had burnt the town and carried away the golden Zemi, the effigy of Yúcahu Maórocoti, the deity of cassava, all this as a result of the blasphemous impiety of the inhabitants.

"I did not *flee* as a coward!" he croaked.

"Why you do this thing?"

"I was drunk."

"Then you is a ass of a fool."

She cut the strap and he fainted. She felt the humerus, thinking that it was broken. It was not. She straightened the cramped and twisted limb and massaged the sprained muscles and torn ligaments of his back, shoulder and arm with warm camphorated oil, to which was added a tincture of opium, and bound his arm tight, close to his body. He mumbled and whimpered. She had given him a *tisane* concocted with the drug. That night she closed her eyes and sang "Oh Joe Joe, Congo Joe" and put some food out for them at the foot of the back steps. She had not done that, or asked "the old people" for anything, not even when she had carried a cannon ball chained to her right leg for a year and a day for cuffing the old white woman to whom she once belonged, long ago, on the island of Grenada.

❖

The heat of the day lingered past the setting of the sun. Upon arriving at the Atelier I noticed Símon Agostini's petulant frown. He fanned himself using a small square of plaited cane as he went about his chores; for an instant he looked like a plump somewhat unhappy cherub, particularly so when he unsuccessfully sought to adjust his crooked *toupé* upon his incipiently bald head. Símon was a person of Mediterranean temperament and stature, thus much concerned with his appearance. He adorned his small feet with high-heeled, Boudrie patent leather buttoned boots, even when riding out to supervise his alembic which was located on the south-eastern edge of the town, La Basse as it was called, where he made certain that his products were neither consumed, stolen nor evaporated.

"No compassion," he muttered to himself, frowning and shaking his head, slipping a silver watch back into the pocket of his red and aubergine striped sateen waistcoat as he continued the preparations for the lighting of the three tall brass lamps which stood upon a round wooden table before him. He had said to me that he regretted the sad event that we had witnessed. His words, and I dear say his thoughts, fell readily into the dialect of his native village of Camera, Cap Corse, which he had never lost or attempted to lose. *"Cuesto povero bambino, povero* Adhémar. He is young, and it was too much. He needs his arm."* Adhémar de Gurvand's father, François, with whom Símon did business, was until recently the Master of Les Frères Unis where Símon served as Frère Trésorier.

Símon lit the last lamp, then with great care, hung it on a hook in the narrow upstairs gallery and sighed, "Ah well." It now made three; the lamps cast hardly a glow on the street

18

below, where pale pools of filthy water absorbed the ruts of wagon wheels, the tracks of boots, of horses, and those of the *gallinazo*, called *corbeaux* here, the large black carrion birds without which the town would have been an even unhealthier place.

Símon's house, with its high-pitched roof, was two-storied, wooden and covered from top to bottom with walabar shingles. It was one of the more substantial in Port-d'Espagne; it actually looked almost like a house. It stood on the north-western corner of Calle del Infante, much later to be called Duncan Street, and Calle San Louis, then called Rue des Trois Chandelles, which would become Queen Street. It served him as a place of business, his family home when in Port-d'Espagne, and was, from the time of its arrival in Trinidad in 1795, the location of the Atelier Les Frères Unis.

Now in his thirty-second year, he had come to this island some ten years before in the company of several of his fellow countrymen, all escaping the wars of attrition that would decimate their generation on the island of Corsica. Last week's work did not please him. The punishment the boy Adhémar de Gurvand had received at the hands of Benoît Dert as the Frère Terrible was very harsh, the circumstances surrounding it, iniquitous.

"*Mamma mia*, they have unleashed the beast," he muttered. "The beast of the inferno itself."

A windy drizzle commenced. Blowing in from the south-east, it brought with it flying ants, the smell of rancid whale oil and the smoke of a hundred coal pots, that filled him, he said, with nausea. Or was it fear, I wondered out loud.

The three lamps hanging in the upstairs gallery of the Atelier Les Frères Unis burned brightly despite the battering of the flying ants, the pervasive damp and misty evening air that was enveloping Port-d'Espagne, a dismal place on an almost uninhabited island occupying the eastern edge of a vast, virtually unknown continent. A place in waiting, surely, on the wheel of history.

Vincent Patrice, as the Vénérable Maître of Les Frères Unis, rose to his feet and, with one rap of a heavy black marble mallet called the Lodge, or as it was known in those times, the Atelier, to order. He looked about him, the hooded shapes of the assembled Brethren casting wavering shadows on the black and white checkered floor. Without change in demeanour he rapped again twice, summoning the Premier and Deuxième Diacres. Almost soundlessly, with slow and deliberate movements, these separated themselves from the others. Their long, white, wide-sleeved dalmatic tunics whispering softly, tall, black measuring wands at their sides, with heads bowed and hooded, they stood before him.

The Atelier, which met in the space beneath the high-pitched roof, was draped in dark blue cloth spangled with small silver stars, as was the canopy above the throne of King Solomon, the altar, and the pedestals of the Deuxième and Premier Surveillants. The temple's floor was illuminated by twenty-one large wax candles, placed in three tall, heavy, intricately worked brass candelabra each standing at about four feet. These were arranged about a picture that was painted upon a white cowhide laid out flat on the checkered floor. The picture, in vivid colours, depicted the four cardinal points: in the east, on one side, the shining sun in a blue sky, and on the other in the west, the moon with seven stars was captured in a little bit of night. The whole glittered with tiny gold-leaf stars.

On a line between the north and the south was illustrated a pair of golden compasses, a board for tracing, a trowel, a compass, a plumb, a square, and a rough ashlar. In the south-east, a hammer, a chisel, a level and a polished ashlar. In the south-west the two pillars marked J and B, and between the two pillars, the mosaic pavement and a drawing of the seven steps leading to the porch of the temple of King Solomon.

"Frères, assist me to commence the *Ars Magna* of this Atelier."

Vincent rapped three times, signalling that the Atelier was now at work. The door in the north-eastern corner opened and the *Elus*, gowned in blue, white and silver, entered, followed by the *Maître Ecossais*, robed in green and gold, then the *Chevaliers de l'Orient*, in white capes hooded in red velvet. These were followed by the *Chevaliers de Rose Croix*, robed in red silk, bearing drawn and naked blades that caught the flames and reflected these upon their stern faces. All took their seats in the long benches against the eastern wall, on either side of the throne of King Solomon, before which stood the Maître Vénérable, robed in red silk. The assembled sang the opening ode, 'Hail to the Craft.'

"Frère Sablich," intoned Vincent in the shuffling silence that followed, the young man, startled, started to his feet. "What is the primary intention of assembled Franc-Maçons?"

"To see the Atelier close tiled."

Vincent regarded him, he was the acting Frère Deuxième Surveillant this night, the son of a German immigrant, a commission agent of the town.

"Direct that duty to be done."

"Frère D'Argenté, you will see the Atelier close tiled." The command, directed to the Inner Sentinel, was given in a shrill

nasal voice in imperfect French with a German accent, was
not convincing.

Jacob D'Argenté, the Inner Sentinel, turned towards the
Atelier's main door, and brought the iron knocker down with
the velocity of a rifle shot, to which I, Littais L'Eau, on
the outside, as Frère Servant, Tuileur and Outer Sentinel,
answered equally, and then, with the enthusiasm of a gaoler,
he locked and bolted everything. Through the peep-hole I
glimpsed Vincent's magenta silhouette back-lit against the
nine lights burning in the east behind him.

Vincent, I knew, appeared enigmatic in the eyes of Símon
Agostini, who I could see, from the desk of Frère Trésorier,
was also regarding the Vénérable Maître closely that night.
An *arriviste,* Símon once said of him, a self-made scamp. A
man without a past. Agostini knew very little about him, this
Frenchman, Vincent Patrice. I did. Patrice was a Creole of
Sainte Lucie, a merchant, something of a mechanic, educated,
with a knowledge of Latin and Greek. He had come to
Trinidad in 1795 from Sainte Lucie together with François
de Gurvand, Benoît Dert, myself and some others with the
Charter certificate of Les Frères Unis, just managing to escape
the massacre of Franc-Maçons inspired by Victor Hugues on
that unfortunate island.

Vincent Patrice possessed an inborn authority, a feel for
command. No aristocrat, in fact no one that I have met, was
endowed with such a presence. Patrice, was about forty years
of age, sallow complexioned, he wasn't particularly tall, his
head was too big, it appeared out of scale, his forehead and
bushy bony brows were prominent over his piercing jet-black
eyes, his nose, fine, was long and beak-like, his thick hair,
black and receding, was worn long, his jaw jutted forward,
massive hands, imposing, punctuating his speech. Patrice gave
the impression of being too large for this small island.

"Frère Sablich, the Atelier proves close tiled."

"Vénérable Maître, the Atelier proves close tiled."

"Frère de Cayeaux, what is our next care?"

"To see that none but Franc-Maçons are present."

"Frères, to order as Franc-Maçons."

In the shadow of his hood, returning the sign, Vincent glanced about him at the Brethren standing to order in the First Degree. I knew well the thought that crossed his mind. "There be traitors here."

"Frère Premier Surveillant, how many officers constitute an Atelier of Franc-Maçons?"

"Eight, namely Le Vénérable Maître, le Premier Surveillant, le Deuxième Surveillant, le Récipiendaire, l'Orateur, le Secrétaire, le Trésorier, le Frère Sentinel, or Frère Servant."

"The situation of the Outer Sentinel, the Frère Servant?"

"Outside the door of the Atelier."

"What is his duty?"

"Being armed with a drawn sword to keep off all cowans and eavesdroppers," answered the Frère Deuxième Surveillant, his voice echoing in the silence of the temple, "to see that candidates come properly prepared and to see that none shall pass or re-pass without the permission of the Maître."

The Atelier, called to order, was thus opened according to ancient custom in the First Degree, and commenced its night's work.

Outside the door of the Atelier, hidden in its recesses, I, Littais L'Eau, Frère Servant, stood sentry. Hooded, my face hardly visible beneath a wide-brimmed, black, felt hat pulled low, with a dark cape thrown over my shoulders that smelled of wood smoke, I was armed with a loaded French flintlock pistol, a dagger and an épée, the hilt of which I caressed gently. A short while before, I had observed a shape detach itself from a shadow down and across the street, and move silently to the foot of the stair below.

"Come to me, come," I breathed, "now there," in a whisper. I held the small frame.

"Ha, a spy, a pretty little spy?"

"Oh Master . . . ."

"Yes?"

"Master, *pardonnez,* have pity!" She had felt the blade. "I bring a message for *M'sieu* Patrice!"

"Tell it!"

The child hesitated, once, then murmured the French Patois into my lowered face.

"The English are coming, my grandfather will pilot them."

"When?"

"I don't know. Mamy Fijonel say so—she say tell Massa Vincent, *vite,* she say, he want to know! So I come."

I released my grip and the girl slipped away, her pretty eyes and little round mulatta nostrils catching the light from the lamps, a smile flashing in her round face. "Sharper's granddaughter is growing into a pretty one," I thought.

Sharper, the Muhammadan Mandingo, belonged to Monsieur Jesse Noel. Sharper was a fisherman and knew the tides and the *rémous* that run through the Dragon's Mouth. He had disappeared from his master's yard two months ago, drowned, it was said. No. Gone to the English, that's what.

I could see clearly the inter-island schooners, a slaver and a merchantman turning at anchor with the falling tide. The moon, full, appearing enormous, high above the Laventille hills, illuminating the Gulf of Paria to quicksilver, charging it with an ethereal brightness that found reflection on the undersides of low-hanging clouds.

The town, actually a wattle-and-daub hamlet, had languished, since Raleigh burnt it to the ground, almost two hundred years before, inside of a vast mangrove and manchineel swamp. Gigantic *ceiba pentandra* or silk cotton trees, a veritable forest of them, descending from the surrounding hillsides, stood about it and beyond it towards the west and along the mangrove shore. The Carib Indians used a word for the place, something like Coo-mu-cu-rapoo, "the place of the silk cotton trees." It contained about a hundred-and-fifty, perhaps less, buildings constructed of undressed local hardwood, half of which were two storied, framed, even decorated in many instances with flotsam and ship's timbers and superstructure. These nautical embellishments lent a sort of style, albeit jerry-built, that suited its designation, a port of Spain. Some were roofed with thatch, others with wooden shingles, a few with locally made clay tiles. There were another hundred or more *ajoupa* houses, built of wattle-and-daub on the ground level, also roofed with thatch or *tirite* palm leaves, some actually attached to, or built into, the ceiba's high buttress roots. These houses, the majority of which were on the eastern edge of the place, straggled along six unpaved streets running south to north from its Plaza, which fronted the sea, and were intersected at right angles by three short streets going east to west, everything ending in either the swamp or the surrounding jungle, except for the Plaza, from whence the King's Road commenced. This travelled east to the ancient capital, San José de Oruña, founded by Don Antonio de Berrio y Oruña in the 1580s.

The entire place returned to swamp yearly when the spring tides coincided with the rainy season, and rain in the mountains caused the Rio Santa Ana to rise and breach its banks, resulting in the melting of the *ajoupa* houses. The streets were empty now. The town lay in its own smoky, slowly encroaching shifting shadows, superintended by millions of mosquitoes and assiduously picked over by packs of bulgy-eyed feral dogs.

In the distance, those around the Eastern Market howled a doleful chorus that seemed to accompany a quick, repetitive and insistent drumming coming from the wooded Laventille hills. The drumming appeared to pose and repeat an urgent question, which was answered, inconclusively, by several other drummers from closer, across the *Savane Ceduine*, an open grassy area that sloped down to the Dry River on the eastern edge of the town. From there came the cry of one possessed. Speaking in the voice of a deity, he demanded adulation for the sacred incantation that he was bellowing, to the echo, in the French Patois of these islands. "Slaves in heat," I thought. "Soon there will be changes, the English will either find a way to own them, or, like the French, free them. They may already know of the impending invasion."

My reverie was broken by the Inner Sentinel's sharp knock, to which I responded. The Atelier was to be passed to the Second Degree. A quick glance through the peephole revealed the Vénérable Master interrogating the Frère Deuxième Surveillant.

"Frère Deuxième Surveillant, are you a Fellow Craft Franc-Maçon?"

"I am, Vénérable Maître, try me and prove me."

"By what instrument in architecture will you be proved?"

"The Square."

"What is a Square?"

" . . . . ?"

Too long, that could end badly. I closed the peephole.

Things had changed already—I had watched my "Brother" Benoît Dert, as the Frère Terrible, at his work. I saw him strike young de Gurvand twice across the face, then wrench his bound right arm around and up his back, and wrap the leather thong about his throat. Adhémar de Gurvand had choked, and with his left hand, tried to relieve the choking by pushing up on the elbow of the right. He cried loud hard harsh howls as he struggled not to suffocate. The small ante-room could hardly hold his anguish.

His consciousness appeared to leave him; Vincent had loosened the strap. The young man caught himself, gasping for air, for life, he had soiled himself. Then they threw him out into the street. That night they performed the ritual for a dead traitor. Traitor? My eye. Vincent, together with Benoît and Dominic Dert, had surely created the circumstances in which Adhémar de Gurvand had made a fool of himself.

Oaths of secrecy define the Craft. The workings of the first operative masons who built the great cathedrals held, in truth, many trade-secrets. There had always been a secret within the secret. The symbolic workings of the Craft conceal secrets about a secret that is hidden by yet another secret, of which you become, whether you are conscious of it or not, the custodian. Can you keep a secret that only another secret can reveal? That is the true test of character of a man of honour. The power of the secret is not its content, as much as it is the act of will, the moral strength of the individual that binds him to the oath. That is what all this is really about. Secrets? What secrets? The boy knew nothing. A password, a token, of an Entered Apprentice, common knowledge on the streets of Paris these days. The real secret of the ancient Craft is that there is no secret. The library of the Grand Orient de France had been literally put into the streets of Paris by the mad men of the Convention. The reign of the Terror has ended The Age of Reason. There were no more secrets left in this world. Vincent's action was meant to create schism in Lodge Les Frères Unis.

The revolution had disowned all French Freemasons, and proceeded to murder them in France and in these islands. This Lodge, this Atelier, was no longer chartered to the Grand Orient de France. That institution had ceased to exist. Les Frères Unis was now independent, chartered to no one, answerable to no authority.

Vincent, the brothers Dert and others, the Corsican traders who were seeking office, they were talking about establishing Les Frères Unis as the Grand Lodge of a liberated South America. Independent of Europe. Their aim was to make contact with rebels on the Mainland through the Corsican families who were thriving there. The Venezuelan rebels, self-styled republicans, in Güiria and at Angostura, had raised the flag of revolt. Vincent's faction in Les Frères Unis had found a new revolution and new financiers.

But François de Gurvand, the Immediate Past-Master and his circle, would have none of that clique, nor support Vincent's intention. His son Adhémar de Gurvand had been tricked to disgrace himself by revealing some trifle, tricked to break an oath—ah, it was the oath, the sworn oath, that the word—"the word, the Maçon's word"—must not pass our lips, not even to a Brother. All that to break what power that was still in the hands of François de Gurvand, the boy's father, in this Lodge.

The fellowship of the Order, the Brotherhood, is meaningful to Adhémar. His father François was the one who brought the Charter of Les Frères Unis to Sainte Lucie from the

Grand Orient de France. In Paris, it was placed in his hands by the Grand Maître Maçon himself, Louis Philippe, Duc d'Orléans, at l'Atelier *Les Neuf Sœurs*. François returned with a manuscript copy of La Franc-Maçonnerie, *écrasée*, dated 1746, the instrument, the master plan for the great revolution of 1789. He also brought all the regalia, the antique implements, the working tools, the complete drawings for the entablature of the new temple. The designs for the horizontal continuous lintel which the two columns support, drawings for its architrave, frieze and cornice and many crates of books; the writings of the metaphysicians, of the physicists and geometricians: Euclid and Sir Isaac Newton; the works of the philosopher and mathematician René Descartes, and a printing press, which we just managed to get aboard the privateer that sailed under the very guns of Hugues' fleet from the Bay of Soufrière in Sainte Lucie to Trinidad.

For us, in Sainte Lucie, the Atelier *La Loge des Neuf Sœurs* in Paris signified the true home of our Order. We thought of her as our mother Lodge, the birth-place of the revolution. Benjamin Franklin sat on her benches during his time in Paris. And so did Voltaire, the conductors at his initiation were Benjamin Franklin and Antoine Court de Gébelin. He, Voltaire, was one of the great minds of the Enlightenment, as were Montesquieu, John Locke, Jean-Jacques Rousseau, and Émilie du Châtelet.

Their work and their ideas as Freemaçons and philosophers, men of the Enlightenment, influenced the important thinkers of the American and French Revolutions, and perhaps will shape the one taking place in Saint-Domingue at present. And if Vincent has his way, the revolution in the south Americas.

Mirabeau was a Past-Master of *Les Neuf Sœurs*. He was its Frère Orator. He was poisoned in Paris in 1791. Condorcet also was made a Maçon there. His ideas are held to embody the very ideals of the Age of Enlightenment. With death facing him in 1794, his friend, Pierre Jean Cabanis, procured for him a poison, he used it. Georges Danton sat on her benches, he became the first President of the Committee of Public Safety. He was the force in the overthrow of the monarchy and the establishment of the First Republic. He was guillotined during the Reign of Terror. Jacques Hébert, another Past-Master of *Les Neuf Sœurs*, was the founder and editor of *Le Père Duchesne*, he faced the guillotine, but, supported by the *sans-culottes*, the Convention was forced to order his release. He died two years ago. The French Revolution eats its parents. It will also eat its children.

The Inner Sentinel's knocks again brought me back from my musing. The Lodge was now to be raised to the Sublime Third Degree.

"Frère Deuxième Surveillant, what is the first care in an Atelier of Master Maçons?" demanded Vincent, an edge sharpening his voice.

"To see the Atelier close tiled," shrieked Frère Sablich.

I closed the peephole. Tragic, very tragic. I thought of young de Gurvand again. The same could have happened to me. What action would his father now take? As I looked over the quiet water of the Gulf of Paria, my heart quickened. *"Rappelle-toi de mourir,"* I muttered. "Remember to die." For a moment, my own test passed before my eyes. That night, yes, my eyes covered with the hoodwink, with my left hand's fingers splayed upon a pulsating heart. "Now," said the Hierophant, and I plunged the dagger. I felt the hot blood spray across my face. Was it a dumb beast or a man?

The rituals of death characterise the Craft. That rite that marked my elevation to the "Higher Degrees" took its origins from the days of great danger for the Craftsmen. It remembered a time when an interloper or eavesdropper, when caught, would die quickly.

"*Rappelle-toi de mourir,*" the Hierophant whispered the password of that Degree, "guard it with your life."

Inside, a trio of fine bass voices was singing the closing lines of the Third Anthem . . .

> "*Time shall their glorious acts enrol,*
> *While love and friendship charm the soul.*"

I opened the peephole to see Vincent interrogating the Frère Deuxième Surveillant, Frère Sablich: "What is a centre?"

"That point within a circle from which every part of the circumference is equally distinct."

"Distant! Distant! Damn it. You dimwit! Say it again!"

"That point within a circle from which every part of the circumference is equally dimwit?"

Not everything translates.

In 1781 Trinidad escaped the calamity of an English invasion. A hurricane that swept through the Lesser Antilles, ravaging Sainte Lucie, from whence it was to be launched, thwarted the English plans.

Spain, alerted to the intentions of the English to seize the continent, and knowing that this island was the key that fitted into the lock of the Orinoco delta, the gateway to their Empire in South America, was persuaded to make the awesome choice of exchanging Gibraltar and the control of the straits, for Trinidad. The English now control the Mediterranean Sea, and they will take the key to all of South America. In such a manner empires are created.

The Spaniards, aware of their tragic lack of manpower realised that their only option was to invite settlers here, arm them, and proceed with the creation of a militia strong enough to hold this place against the inevitable English invasion. All men, including the Free Coloureds the majority by far on the island, of military age, are compelled to serve in the Spanish militia. Each European, and there are about one thousand, on arrival receives thirty-two acres of land, with half that amount for the Free Coloureds, and sixteen acres per slave, but the bureaucracy is tedious. Entire extended families arrive daily with their chattels, the more slaves they bring in, the more land they are granted. There could be sixteen thousand slaves now, perhaps more.

The legend that Philippe Roume, the Grenadian adventurer, moved His Most Catholic Majesty to grant a *Cédula de Población* in 1783, is a yarn spun out by the French royalists so as to establish and reinforce their credentials in this, a Spanish colony. Roume pushed on an open door, anyone might have served. They, in the Cortes, used him to convince and recruit the planters in the French islands, then forgot about him. There are five or six thousand Free Coloured people here, all of them French-speaking. Many hold lands and slaves. A few are felons, condemned to death on other islands, others are incorrigible rogues, poor and idle. Increasingly the republicans come. All slaves speak Creole French, or at least respond to it.

The wretchedness that all this generates is astounding. People pay clever rogues whatever is asked to live in shacks all over the swamp and on the hillsides. The old Spanish families remade their fortunes with land they pretend to own; the French emigrés pay in gold. Quickly the coastal areas along the shore of the Gulf of Paria are opening up; it is now lined with habitations. Truly, I have seen much cruelty done to the Africans.

Our graves, but mostly those of the blacks, fertilised the plantations.

Men would defend their property and their families to the death. Spain's dilemma might have been solved in holding Trinidad from the ambitions of the English, except that the world is overwhelmed by the events of the French Revolution. Spain sent out an honourable naval officer to be governor here, Don José Chacón. He is very pious. It is unfortunate that so many ignorant planters regard the governor with disfavour and seek his undoing.

So, now, finally, the English are to come. In truth, the English have been here for years, cruising the Gulf of Paria with impunity. In February of this year they acted with determination: a squadron led by *HMS Zebra* under the command of a Captain Fitzowen Skinner, destroyed a fleet of Victor Hugues' privateers in Chaguaramas Bay. These were supplying arms to Julien Fédon, Hugues's creature, in Grenada. A few months later one Captain Vaughn, in command of the *Zebra's* sister ship, the *Alarm* landed an armed detachment in Port-d'Espagne following a fracas in Mrs. Murphy's bordello. This led to Spain's declaration of war on England, which could mean the end of Spanish dominion in South America.

The Inner Sentinel's knock alerted me that the Lodge was conducting the ceremony of closing the Third Degree. I glimpsed through the peephole. I saw Vincent draw himself up to his full height and address the Frère Deuxième Surveillant in a voice booming and senatorial. "Frère Deuxième Surveillant, whence come you?"

"From the, the . . ."

I closed the peephole, the Deuxième Surveillant had obviously lost his way.

The militia is yet to be formed in strength. Now everything has changed. The governor has very few resources, hardly any troops, no fortifications. There is no real gaol, barracks, or armory magazine, nothing built in stone. In fact, he has left all to the good faith of the public—and this public is made up of individuals from other nations, with the least number being the Spaniards themselves. As a consequence the people are disunited by mutual discords, through differences of traditions, they are rivals and enemies. Many pursue vendettas, killings are common and in public. There is about the place a febrile quality, a heat that could last for generations, perhaps forever.

In response to the Inner Sentinel I gave the appropriate knocks for a Lodge of Entered Apprentices. Through the peephole I saw Vincent moving through the motions of preparing to close the Atelier quickly. It would not be elevated to the four Higher Degrees of the *Rite Français* that night.

The Inner Sentinel, with a great clang and clash of bolt and iron bar, flung open the doors. From where I, Littais L'Eau, stood I could see Vincent in the east peering over the heads of the milling, hungry crowd. I caught his eye and gestured with my head, "outside." He nodded. How he dealt with young de Gurvand's father, François, became the center of interest to all the Brethren, and influenced the future of the Atelier.

3:

1797. François de Gurvand,

Des Lumières.

Day break. Port-d'Espagne looks better at night. In the daylight, its squalour appalls. It swarms with an ever-increasing number of the destitute, and jabbers with an extraordinary orchestra of voices. From the grass market beneath my window the coarse enticements of touts rival the cries of vagrants demanding breakfast of passersby and those of sellers of deadly medications, in at least three languages, possibly four. All mingle discordantly with the interminable babble of the slaves—which could bring the number of languages to seven, or eight, or nine. These blend with the incessant hollering of market women, shrill *marchandes* and hucksters of all shades from the French islands, who shout in a variety of vernaculars flavoured by an instantly invented slang which, combined with that of the slaves, the Venezuelan peons and the Warahoons, creates a Patois, already the lingua franca, altering and changing daily, a restless language that shapes raucous humour and feeds inborn antagonisms begotten in forgotten calamities.

Words are the key to understanding a culture. The French language shapes the origins of this colony and will inform its future. This shiftless population, particularly the Coloureds, are devoted to Rabelaisian amusement, the creation of illusion, fantasy, satire, the love of the grotesque, of bawdy jokes and loud drumming, singing, dancing and rum. All this is amplified against indecipherable undertones, whispered innuendo, languid syllables, shrieks of laughter, hissing sibilants, the gurgling of dismay, even death. Shouts from the depths of subterranean nightmares and cries of pain, moans of pleasure even in the middle of the morning, the silence of anger and the grinding teeth of hate. Yes, language is everything.

This farrago of the most gaudily overdressed is concentrated in just eleven short streets, and forms the backdrop to a frenzy of activity, a lot of it pointless. Grog shops overflow. A crowd is gathering, someone has discovered a corpse. People die here daily in the appalling violence that characterises these islands and from a host of ailments, most of them unknown to science, all of them terrible.

Most persons who come here will have to overcome a ghastly illness, the rum, the heat, the diseased women: then there are duels, matters of honour, naturally. Those deadly distractions I must avoid.

Just yesterday Vincent Patrice and his clique handed down their barbaric sentence to my son, who now lies abed drugged into a stupor. That act was nothing less than a vile manipulation of trust, a dishonourable action directed at me that has angered me, but one that I must deal with cautiously, having far more crucial concerns here than Vincent's depraved machinations.

I had regarded him, Adhémar, that morning as he dressed. He was standing before the long mirror in my bedroom. He seems, to me, at times to linger in his childhood. I have come to believe that this characterises young men in the Antilles. Although he could, as they say in these islands, stand fire. As

36

a lad of just twelve or thirteen, I had tested his nerve, as is the custom here, by placing a pineapple on his head and shooting it at fourteen paces, he hadn't flinched.

"Today, Adhémar," I had said to him that morning, "we arrange for the letters of credit—we no longer possess Richmond and Balthazar in Grenada."

I closed the ledger. The money from the sale of the estates represented the land, the buildings, the factories and the proceeds of the year's crops. That money and the slaves in my possession would be used to maintain ourselves on this island. Trade, in any form, is out of the question of course. The old regime is gone forever, we knew it would be over soon than later. I must be well-placed to assume responsibilities when the time comes. Indeed, the very reason for us being in Trinidad is a challenging one, in that I, François de Gurvand, am the precursor, one could say, for the commencement of a new dispensation, the New Order. This constrains and shapes many of my actions. Not the least of them being to deal with Patrice.

The harbour fort, on that fateful day, had just fired the morning gun, signalling sunrise. It was an hour late. "*Un garçon, pas un homme,*" I had murmured to myself, looking him over. He was tall, fair-complexioned, and broad-shouldered. His dark brown curling hair, his mother's, full upon his head. That day it was tied at the back with a dark ribbon. Handsome, yes, certainly gentle, possibly brave. He is hardly French, really, I thought, he is a Creole of these islands. How will he acquit himself when his time comes?

All colour here is lurid. Below, the noise of iron-wheeled traffic as slaves from the town's households pile bales of para-grass onto wagons and hand carts. I see the town's gentry stroll or ride in the cool morning air, to regard one another, still alive, to bow or grimace. There passes an officer of one of the Spanish regiments, and ladies and young women, as well-dressed as in Europe, they walk on wooden planking towards a linen market set up on the Plaza. A party of newly arrived Frenchmen with powdered hair, white silk stockings and buckled shoes attempt, in vain, to avoid the filth. *Peninsulares* in black with much lace and shiny gold buttons cast lecherous looks at the gorgeous mulâtresses, displaying their wealth. An old Spaniard, Farfan, disapproving of such a display. Two ladies in a fine carriage. Quantities of domestics, mostly idling, laughing, joking, shouting familiarities, insults, going about their own business. A convoy of ox-drawn wagons bearing hogsheads of rum, of sugar, making its way to the quay-side close to the fort, passing to the lee of the small wooden white-washed church that serves the faithful, which sees five times more deaths than baptisms. In its courtyard, the white-haired parish priest, Father Magneval, is overseeing an ancient female blackamoor, she is slaughtering a ewe.

"Angel's birthday party at Mrs. Murphy's tonight. Eh?" I had called out to Adhémar that morning. Mrs. Murphy is an enormous Irishwoman who runs an establishment on the Plaza del Marina and lives in a suffocating medley of perfumes, vapours used in defence of those that emanate from the nearby fish wharf, "Stinking Corner," they, of course, have named it. He had tightened the wide belt at his waist and drew the Ferrara rapier from its scabbard, its fine blade caught the morning light. I had glanced at it, held lightly in his hand. It once belonged to my father. I had taught him its benefits, being, for a time, a pupil of the school of Jean Baptiste le Perche du Coudray myself. Adhémar at twenty-two was a swordsman of some skill.

"Adhémar, you go today to La Pamplona, *n'est-ce pas?*"
"*Oui,* Papa. I will spend this fortunate day in the company of

Marie Sophie, Marie Eugénie and Ninon, the three graces." He had made a playful bow and smiled.

Marie Sophie and Marie Claire, called Ninon, were the daughters of Hippolyte and Clothilde de la Barrère; Marie Eugénie was the only daughter of Pierre-Louis Roget and his wife Jeanne. The de la Barrères lived at Moka in the upper reaches of the Maraval valley, and the Rogets lived just over the ridge described as the "Saddle" in Santa Cruz. Their property, La Pamplona, occupying most of the Santa Cruz valley, was this island's most productive habitation.

"These letters are for Pierre-Louis. See that you hand them to him upon your arrival. And this is for Jeanne."

It was a small wooden box that contained a miniature portrait of her on the inside of a shell. I had made it to amuse her, she was our cousin.

We had departed our fair Brittany, and established ourselves in Grenada, in 1761, where my father held the very modest post of *procureur du Roi*. I was later commissioned a Lieutenant in the Militia, and married, in my late teens, Anne de Laval, the daughter of one of our *compatriotes* in Les Chambrés. In 1763 the island was ceded to England. Adhémar was a still a boy that day in July of 1779 when Saint George's was bombarded by the French fleet. This altered our lives: we were all in the smoky kitchen of our townhouse, Adhémar sitting on a chair that had crossed the Atlantic with us, together with his grandfather, his mother, my dear wife, Anne, his sister Adèle and younger brother Alain, when a loud explosion shook down the house, catching it on fire.

Mayotte, his *Da*, had grabbed him by the arm and stumbled through the door into the courtyard. The cannonade, like rolling thunder, was echoing and re-echoing in hills around.

"*Mon dieu, le bébé!*" Mayotte had screamed and plunged back through the crumbling burning house, to emerge seconds later with my little girl, Adèle, in her arms. The bombardment of Saint George's almost completely destroyed my family. Admiral d'Estaing, after the Battle for Grenada was won, offered to me his sincere condolences for our loss. Mayotte saved Adèle's and Adhémar's lives. It was she who had tended his injuries the other night.

I was reduced by the loss of my wife, son and father, who all died during the attack. My family, our family, almost came to an end, my son and I may now be the last of our people. I know not the fate of our other relatives in revolutionary France. My life, it felt to me, was ended, I was haunted by the memories of my gentle Anne, imagining her presence in the early hours of the morning and in all familiar places. I felt that I must leave Grenada so as to engage another reality. We moved to Sainte Lucie, together with Mayotte and five domestics, and I commenced, in ernest, the role that my family's destiny had ordained for me. I became a Franç-Maçon at Lodge Parfait Union in Saint-Pierre—it suited my purpose, Les Chambrés' purpose, to do so—and travelled to France in the last anguished years of the *ancien régime* to receive the Constitution of Les Frères Unis from the Mâitre Maçon. Circumstances in Sainte Lucie served to quicken the purpose for our being in the Caribbean, which was to settle ultimately in this island, Trinidad. This was facilitated by the Cédula of Population that was being promulgated throughout the Antilles. We moved here and set up house in this ramshackle building bought from Jean de Boissière, a fellow Franc-Maçon. Les Chambrés was now established on this island in the furthest west.

After the death of my dear Anne, I did not consider remarrying, bearing in mind what the future might hold for me.

I stayed apart, except for my activities in the Lodge, from the town's society, paying particular attention to the small property at Mon Repos in the Sainte Anne valley and La Prosperité at Blanchisseuse on the north coast of the island. My relationship with Néolise, a young, perhaps too young, coloured girl from the Mon Repos estate produced a son whom I christened Jean-Paul de Gurvand. When the boy was one year old, I gave to Néolise and to her mother their freedom and adopted the boy as my own. Néolise's father, Albert Danguard, the Welsh foreman on the Sainte Anne property had fathered her with one of my field slaves, Julienne. Julienne, Néolise and Jean-Paul lived at Sainte Anne in the little village of Sainte Elisabeth, on the property of Gabriel Gomez that bounded the Coblentz Estate.

"Take care on the way back," I had cautioned that morning, never imagining that my warning should have contained a caution to be wary of strangers. "It will rain this afternoon, and the Maraval river will rise at La Seiva."

"*Oui,* Papa, I will be back in town by sunset and Cocoutes will come with me. All will be well." Adhémar naturally understood my concern. The loss of his grandfather, my father, his mother, and his brother in the tragedy of war had aged me before my time. Thank god for Néolise and the birth of little Jean-Paul. "*Au revoir,* Papa!" I had heard him call from the street. I stepped onto the small wooden balcony that ran the length of the house, and thoughtfully watched my son, accompanied by his servant, ride up the Rue d'Eglise. Little did we know that on that very evening, an ignorant and malevolent hand would reach out to strike us.

A dog is caught in a barking cramp. I resist the temptation to shout "shut up." The morning's sea air, invigorated by an eight o'clock shower, is followed by the reemergence of the sun.

Heat causes the ground to steam and emit older stenches, these to blend with the newer vapours. I close shut the windows and sit at my desk. My poor boy. This is a vile place.

Death is carried on the warm moist air. Yesterday there was the odor of human flesh being roasted. A Reign of Terror is here as well. From below continue the shouts of the carter-men and vendors, the incessant crowing of a rooster, the hammering of carpenters and the rattle of arriving anchor chains. From the back of the grass market, where that very morning, quite early, came the ring of the blacksmith's anvil, mingled with the wailing cries of female slaves being flogged, there now arises a fine baritone voice singing the aria from the opera, "The Power of Love and Hatred" by Francesco Prata.

I have been exposed to the sight and to the practice of terrible severities. We are all tarnished by this evil, which will grow worse, with the collapse of sugar production in Hispaniola, this as a result of the revolt of the Blacks, is driving up its price. England benefits because of holding Barbados and Jamaica. I would leave these islands if it were not for the foggy web of destiny in which I am caught. I would have returned home, to Brittany, notwithstanding the revolution. I can survive under the Directory. There is Father Magneval now beneath my window with an earnest expression. No, no, not today, I will not receive him. "Mayotte. Tell him not today."

It was once our custom, when the children were young, that on an evening Adhémar and Adèle would find themselves fitted snugly at my side in the lamplight and I would read to them from the stories of La Fontaine, the Holy Bible, the Fables of Aesop and from the *The Cornucopia* by the Abbé de Morim.

Adhémar was already becoming familiar with my own modest library. I am, in truth, grateful for the kind ministrations of that priest, Father Hubertus Magneval, who became a regular visitor. We both sought to guide the children through the shock and the grief of our loss, towards the comforting distractions of writing and reading.

Learned we are, I suppose, in this, a town of soldiers and farmers, pirates, imposters and impersonators of heroes now dead on other islands. Our avid discussions would pass away the hours. These discussions, I am sure, have served to enhance the education of young Adhémar, as he sat and listened, often ignored, but gleaning oddments of history and general information on topics that he would quiz me on after Father Magneval had returned to his presbytery. Father Magneval and I spoke, at times, of the wars in Europe, which was always exciting for Adhémar; of princes, Black Virgins, bishops, knights, queens, damsels, dragons; of Saladin, "Salah ad-Din Yusuf ibn Ayyub," Father Magneval would correct; of Saint Louis, the King—"Can a King be a saint?" asked Adhémar. No one answered this. We were already discussing the San Graal, le mort d'Arthur, Richard Cœur de Lion, and other ancient kings, those who grew their hair forever and married their sisters.

"Their sisters? Ugh!"

The conversation could then move on to the church's irrevocable views on several subjects, which, I would mischievously pretend, confounded me: "What of slavery in these islands, Hubertus? Surely as disgraceful a portion of history as the whole course of time has known, why no condemnation? As the condemnation of scientists, mathematicians and astronomers as heretics, for example?" His insistence that papal encyclicals condemning "unjust" enslavement alleviated suffering did make me laugh out loud. "*Just* enslavement, Hubertus, is still accepted!" Then we spoke of saints, popes, martyrs, sinners, the reincarnated and the damned.

"This naturally is your area of expertise. Not so?"

"No, Hubertus, I would imagine it would be yours," I laughed, changing the conversation to the mathematics of the Greeks, to the Byzantines, the Persians, to the Golden Hoard.

"Try a little Armagnac, Hubertus, it's good for the numbed member." The conversation turned to the fabled Atlantis, the lost continent written up in Plato's *Timeaeus*.

"The lost word," said Father Magneval, meaningfully, his face like crushed velvet.

"The arithmetic of Archimedes," I replied. "Eureka! I have found it!" I exclaimed and laughed—this became for Adhémar a favourite turn of phrase for a while. Once he heard of Ahasver, the Wandering Jew. The idea fascinated him and me as well.

"Not a Jew at all," said the priest. He was a strong, rugged-faced, stocky, bowlegged man from the Alsace, of middle height, prematurely grey in his late thirties or early forties; seen by most as irascible. "The name was adapted from Ahasuerus, the Persian king in *Esther*, who was not a Jew at all, and whose very name among the medieval Jews of Eastern Europe was an exemplum of an idiot. We must discuss these enigmas, François."

"I am afraid that I have never heard of him, Hubertus. Sample a little of the liquid from the coco palm, it is grown on the Bande l'Est at Mayaro. It is very good with rum, medicinal, I am told."

Adhémar listened as we spoke of the seven wonders of the world. Father Magneval said, "the hanging gardens of

Babylon, the statue of Zeus at Olympia, the temple of Artemis at Ephesus, the Mausoleum at Halicarnassus."

"Remarkable," I said.

"Yes, the heathens were quite, quite . . ."

"Erudite."

"Yes. Thank you François. But you know all this, don't you François?"

"No, Hubertus, I can't imagine, I am not as informed as you are. You must be a student of the great *Encyclopédie*."

"Oh no, my friend, the Systematic Dictionary of the Sciences, Arts, and Crafts is beyond my purse."

Adhémar and Adèle heard that the stars in the night sky that turned above the little town on the edge of the great jungle were named for the gods of ancient times. "Not gods, no, no, not at all," said the priest, "just folklore."

In this manner our conversations meandered, at times possessing an uncomfortable tension that I was aware of and of which the children, particularly as they grew older, became conscious. Father Magneval probing, and I, evading. We found no end to our contentions, and long ago decided to perpetuate them, as well as the ongoing disagreements which were designed to entertain and to surprise ourselves through the interminable evenings of asphyxiating boredom of the little town. His interrogations, not always subtle, were always amusing.

I had brought an agent of change—a printing press—with me from France, first to Sainte Lucie, and then to Trinidad. It was important that I appear to be an avid republican Freemason. It occupied the back room of our home, a startling contraption in the eyes of many, a dangerous tool in the opinion of some, a voice that spoke the language of freedom in my opinion, and the work of the devil in the priest's mind.

I taught Littais L'Eau, the Frère Servant, the use of the printing press. Littais L'Eau, a tall, thin, at times parsimonious man with small black beady eyes, a shock of unruly auburn hair, and a long nose that manages somehow to express disapproval, is a Creole of these islands. To my surprise he actually appreciated the essence of the age of the *Lumières*—the social changes that we, in western Europe, were experiencing. An equinox, if you like, of the human condition. A time when one interpretation of the past was giving way to another.

"A shift in moral values," he called it. L'Eau, the product of generations of master locksmiths, was a Huguenot. Educated at the University of Fribourg in his father's city of Fribourg, Switzerland, where he, for a while, read Law and then History. He had been born on the island of Sainte Lucie, where his mother's people, the Canisius family, had sugar plantations.

This shift in moral values, we agreed, had commenced in the 17th century when what was witnessed were two significant, fundamentally different revolutions taking form, altering, shaping the features of the unfolding of the Enlightenment.

These were first the social revolution that took place in England in the 1650s, which left behind a residue of thought, republican thought, that was nurtured by the likes of Baruch Spinoza, this eventually militarised the Enlightenment, producing the American, French and other revolutions now in the making. And the other revolution, less bloody, was equally profound in that it could be described as the scientific revolution. It achieved an impetus with Copernicus' *De revolutionibus orbium coelestium,* which generated an intellectual metamorphosis that produced Newton's *Philosophiæ Naturalis Principia Mathematica.*

These two revolutions put into place the intellectual mould of the radical Enlightenment that was taking place at present.

Littais L'Eau was convinced that they in the Caribbean, and by they, he meant, I was sure, the Creoles, the local-born, too were experiencing a Caribbean Enlightenment that expressed itself with the work of men like the Haitian Toussaint L'ouverture, the Grenadian Julien Fédon, the South American republican de Miranda and even what has been accomplished by Philippe Roume, the Grenadian French Creole idealist and adventurer with the Cédula of Population of 1783 for Trinidad. A most remarkable document in his eyes, because it not only saved the lives of thousands of people in the Caribbean, European and Free Coloured, but slaves as well. He believed that it was a constitution of sorts, typically New World, a liberal philanthropic and enlightened document, if there ever was one. Littais L'Eau was an original thinker with a highly developed critical faculty. He too had a sense of adventure, I had to say, for a Creole.

Our first printed pamphlet proclaimed:

"Liberty! The Philosopher's Stone that turns all metals to gold. Look at the inhabitants of the North of our America. You will see that Nature delights in populating the fields of liberty, and looks otherwise, with regret, on the growth of slavery, an institution that is contrary to her laws. Deserts, solitude and silence are the fruits of tyranny." To which I added as a footnote;

Màs vale tarde que nunca.

Le Patriote. Le front encore paré des fleurs de la jeunesse,

O vous, jadis l'amour de Rome & de la Grece,

C'est trop long-temps languir dans un honteux repos;

MUSES, reparoissez, & chantez nos Héros.

Vos accords, autrefois, consacrés aux grands hommes,

Resteroient-ils oisifs dans le siècle où nous sommes?

These I have secretly dispatched to Caracas. "It is so typical of the Spaniards not to possess a printing press in Caracas," I said to Littais L'Eau one evening. "A university they have, but no printing press. They fear the written word. Language is everything."

4:

1797. Domingo Antonio Vallecilla,

The Poisoner.

Domingo Antonio Vallecilla y Gomez was dressed in black from head to foot when he stepped ashore at the Mole. His breath smelled of decay, and there was a look of gaol about him, even though he had been released from La Guaira prison more than six months before.

He was, he said, an antiquary, born in the Valle de México and taken by his grandmother to Salamanca, where she was employed in the household of the mother of the last Marquis Herrera y Menénz de Avilés.

Lucky for him. Little Vallecilla was taught to read and write at the old palace on the Plaza del Corrillo, adjacent to the Plaza Mayor. He read the classics at the University of Salamanca and, by imitation, acquired something of the manners of the drawing room. In that city he became a member of the clandestine Masonic Lodge, *Lascia ch'io pianga,* The Triumph of Time and Truth, named for the oratorio by Georg Friedrich Händel.

Padre Juan Camilo, the Capuchin, distrusted him upon seeing him and was not at all surprised when Felipe, his boy lover and a pupil of Vallecilla, told him lispingly of the extra-mural activities conducted in the small house with the blue courtyard on Salamanca's Street of the Taylors, where Vallecilla ran a school for poor boys. The worthy cleric felt compelled to report Vallecilla to his superiors.

Thus it was discovered that Vallecilla was not only a Franc-Maçon, but that his school provided the camouflage for his pederasty. In 1792, Domingo Antonio Vallecilla y Gomez was condemned to death, but again he was lucky: the old Marquesa, in whose service his grandmother was bound, saved his skin. He was sentenced to be transported to Panama for life and there to receive one thousand five hundred lashes. Some six months later, he arrived at the port of La Guaira on the Spanish Main in chains.

La Guaira on the Caribbean coast was the home of the trading monopoly the Compañía Guipuzcoana de Caracas and as such bustled. It was also a haven for the flotsam and the jetsam of the Caribbean, and was one of several crucibles for revolution in South America in the 1790s. It was peopled by rabid republican, opportunistic anarchists, dreamy philanthropists, right-wing royalist extremists, government spies, spies in general, conspiracy enthusiasts, castaway Spaniards, a surprising quantity of Corsicans, all with connections to Trinidad, French republican revolutionaries recuperating after exhausting wars of extermination, the inevitable Antillean Negroes, retired pirates and the remnants of the vice-regal aristocracy, impoverished from the previous century, in search of the opportunity to marry into the newly created wealth possessed by parvenus so as to continue the maintenance of hauteur. Incredibly, their descendants walk that city still.

A frigate was expected to take Vallecilla to Panama; in the meantime it was gaol. The gaol was the most imposing building in the province. It boasted walls four feet thick and was built of stone imported at great cost from the limestone quarries of Margarita.

Pedro Emmanuel de la Rosa, the gaoler, hailed from Santa Cruz de Tenerife. He was a large man, very red, with an enormous head, and, due to his generous temperament should never have been a gaoler. Vallecilla saw this at once, and sensing the potent currents of republicanism that filled the air which, on windless afternoons, was so hot that paralysed birds fell dead as they flew, filled his gaoler's head with stories of utopian paradises, of harems of women with precious stones hidden within their orifices, there for the taking. Liberty and equality and a free house for everybody, all goods to be held in common, everybody to own everything and nothing.

De la Rosa's wife cooked for him in the hope of putting some flesh on his skeletal frame and to alleviate the melancholy of his rheumy eyes. He got a brand new mattress. The frigate bound for Panama came and went.

He befriended the parish priest and strolled about the port, his gaoler now his guide. He found the atmosphere in La Guaira pregnant with subversion, and the names of Manuel Gual, Manuel Carlos Piar and José María España in everybody's mouth. In the gaol, he met the San Blas conspirators, an anarchist cell transported from Spain, which had contemplated the overthrow of the Spanish Crown. When uncovered by the Spanish authorities, they were tried and sentenced to deportation and were in La Guaira en route to Panama to serve life sentences punctuated by inquisitional torture. Thus, Vallecilla made the acquaintance of Juan Bautista Piconell, José Lax, Sebastián Andrés and Manuel Cortés Campomanes.

Vallecilla, in pursuit of companionship, eagerly entered into their compulsion to conspire and plot. Their circle, at whose hub was Juan Bautista Piconell, was enthusiastically joined in their excursions into the town by Manuel Gual, and José and Manuel España. Vallecilla's Masonic affiliation proved advantageous, as Manuel Gual was also a philanthropist, an eminent Maçon and an ardent republican. All together they planned an uprising for early July. In their enthusiasm they told everyone they met.

The authorities bided their time and two months or so later struck all the conspirators with one shot. Twenty-four people were arrested. Amongst those who escaped was Manuel Gual, as did José María España and Juan Bautista Piconell. Piconell fled to Guadeloupe and, eventually, to Texas where he continued his ardent revolutionary activities against the Spanish Crown.

Domingo Vallecilla was arrested and tortured by the espionage police. He confessed everything he knew, which was very little. It was thought by the police that Vallecilla could become useful to them, inasmuch as he knew Manuel Gual, who had evidently escaped, most probably to Trinidad, and that Vallecilla might be able to reach Gual in Trinidad. He was promised money, immunity, rehabilitation and exoneration of his previous sins and crimes if he was successful in murdering Manuel Gual. He, to fulfil his mission, agreed to be starved and made pestilential and be put aboard a windjammer, where he spent several days sleeping in the bilge, and arrived in Port–d'Espagne looking like a refugee, feeling damp and feverish and smelling like a scavenger.

Almost by instinct he made his way to the jumble of wooden and wattle buildings roofed with decaying thatch opposite to the town market, on the Calle de Santa Ana, which later would be called Charlotte Street. This place was occupied by a Spanish government agent known as Enrique. Enrique was tall, fat, balding and unshaven. He had lost an eye while arranging the transshipment of Madeiran prostitutes to Puerto la Cruz some years before and displayed a disfiguring scar across his pate, which he disingenuously described as a bite. He was master of most of the human trafficking in the Eastern Caribbean. He transported with impunity and invisibility entire coastal tribes to be enslaved in Hispaniola, freshly arrived cargoes of Negroes kidnapped from the Kasanje kingdoms of Angola and stolen or ownerless second hand Negroes from the devastated French islands, whose wholesale value was on the rise.

His contraband connections moved shipments of sparkling wine, stables of Andalusian horses, sarcophagi laden with gold stolen from the graves of the Chibcha priest-kings previously bound for the royal mint at Cartagena de Indias, simple household utensils and dry goods to be bartered with the anthropomorphic inhabitants of the Orinoco delta, men whose heads grow beneath their shoulders, in exchange for pearls as large as your eyeballs, hermaphrodite brigantines mysteriously abandoned, discovered adrift on the wide Sargasso Sea. He had recently arranged the rescue of a party of not so intrepid explorers. They had been captured in their quest for lost cities in the upper reaches of the Rio Mata by man-eaters, who were fattening them up in wicker baskets suspended from gigantic Brazil-nut trees.

Enrique and Vallecilla descended immediately into an underground cavern beneath the premises. This commodious excavation reminded Vallecilla of the catacombs beneath the city of Salamanca, possessing as they both did the distinct odour of corpses.

"You are very safe here," Enrique said to Vallecilla, placing at his disposal a steaming mug of Oronoke coffee, laced with

Jamaican rum, a package of papilones, molasses-sugar cones of a dark-yellowish-brown, a pipe, a quantity of black Trinidada tobacco and a thick slice of tasso from a long-ago slaughtered ox, smoky smelling, hard but pliable. The bunker held a wide assortment of goods, some dry, some liquid, and quite a few still alive. There was no denying that.

"Make yourself at home. I will contact the ones who will give you access to Manuel Gual. Do not mention his name. Rest. And wash. Eh." Enrique indicated a deep zinc wash basin, a bar of blue carbolic soap and a round divan upholstered in tattered crimson velvet, decorated in gold-leaf and bearing the imperial arms of Spain, having once formed part of a vice-regal establishment of New Granada at La Fria in the high Andes.

"And later, when refreshed, you may take comfort from anyone of these that you can catch. Eh." He raised his lantern, its pale light exposing two wild-appearing Negresses, shackled to a mahogany table, and an adolescent Carib boy, attached by a chain to an iron ball embedded in the earth, who clutched an obsidian knife, bared his teeth and hissed—a sound that reminded Vallecilla of some kind of feline, hopefully extinct.

His weariness amazed him. It was more overwhelming than his apprehension of Enrique's weird cargo, and he fell asleep after downing the steaming cup of coffee and almost losing a tooth on the tasso.

Some nights later, Vallecilla, following instructions, kept an appointment.

"Enter now," said the voice at the back of the gate. "He is within." A soft yellow light appeared and broadened into a doorway. The Spaniard entered with a changed demeanour and stood like a supplicant in the semi-darkness.

"Brother Vincent?" he ventured.

"Yes." The voice was so close that he jumped.

"Brother."

"Be calm." A shadow detached itself from the dark and struck a flint, a wick in a bowl of castor oil flamed, the low room wavered into view.

"Tile him."

Dominic Dert, a tall, thickset person with small features, a medieval haircut and a smile full of ill-natured irony, as Frère Sacrificier, would now examine him to verify Vallecilla's claim to membership in the Brotherhood. He took the Spaniard through all the steps, signs, tokens, grips, and passwords of the seven Degrees of the *Rite Français* worked by the Spanish Grand Lodge. Vallecilla, faint with fear, was covered with a cold sweat by the end of the interrogation.

"Sit." They sat across a large, old table. He looked about. There were two others in the room. Another light was brought, on the table were a long poignard and an antique silver mask with an unnerving expression. The others ignored him, speaking amongst themselves in a Basque dialect that he could not comprehend. It did not matter to him, he felt he could be dead by morning. These three, he thought, are utterly ruthless, every one of them a murderer. He hung his head.

"He escaped with Manuel Gual and some others from the La Guaira crackdown, he may be of use to us," said Vincent.

"I do not trust that one," said Benoît Dert, stepping forward from the corner dressed in what appeared to be a shroud, and smelling of incense—the type burnt in churches when the Holy Sacrament is exposed in a golden monstrance. He was a large, dark man whose features indicated a shrewd slyness. He picked up the mask; it was, for the time being his brother's as Frère Terrible.

"Quite so," Vincent Patrice caught his eye. "Quite so. But he is a stranger, a *coquin*, a rogue, and if anything goes amiss . . ." The small black eyes under the huge forehead, topped with a big white wig, looked long and hard at Domingo Vallecilla.

"Vallecilla," Vincent said softly, "we have an errand for you, for which you will receive a handsome *douceur*." Vallecilla looked up with what he hoped was an expression of enthusiasm. "Adhémar de Gurvand is a newly-raised Master Maçon. He is the son of François de Gurvand, who is a Knight of the Order of the Temple amongst other things. Adhémar is a simple boy, just twenty-two. He is honest and dedicated both to his father and to the Craft. It has been decided that the Brotherhood begin to take a more active role in the political events taking place on Terra Firma. Adhémar de Gurvand has to be tested, he must be made to break his Masonic pledge. He must be made to turn from this," he gestured about him, "idyllic life and has to be encouraged to take an active and heroic part in the coming events. He must seek to redeem himself after his betrayal. He may seek to take your life when he realises the role that you have played. In any event he has to be outcast, rejected, broken, then reinstated, remade and redirected." Vincent moved closer to Vallecilla, regarding him with interest. "In this undertaking he must not know that you work for my intentions."

Vallecilla was about to ask something. Vincent raised his hand. "Adhémar, of course, knows nothing. All you need to do is have him reveal his passwords and his tokens. We will do the rest and you will be paid, and go your way."

"Why do you do this?" Vallecilla felt compelled to dare this inquiry.

"It is a test," replied Dominic Dert, the younger of the two brothers Dert.

"To see whether he would come back," said Benoît Dert, putting the mask to his face. "To test his love and devotion to the Craft. No matter what." His voice held a hollow ring behind the shining wicked thing. This man, thought Vallecilla, is malignant for the sake of malice.

"Make him drunk. You make him drunk," said Vincent, his voice a little raised, "and you make him talk," he repeated more softly. "You inquire and he in his youth, in his trust for you, a Brother, he will tell you what he knows and what he has seen and done on the square."

"And for this? How handsome a *douceur*?"

"For less, Vallecilla," Benoît Dert drove the dagger into the table. "For much less." He said, taking two *real de a ochos* from a leather pouch, "Sixteen reales perhaps, when the job is done."

They stood side by side, almost identical, brothers of the knife. Holders of the Masonic offices Frère Sacrificier and Frère Terrible. This, he understood perfectly, described them.

Benoît Dert let Domingo Vallecilla out by another exit. The Spaniard, upon leaving, farted several times in relief, spat like a cat and left behind a rancid smell that lingered as a shadow. He crossed the street, looked sideways, and continued, glancing about in the lonely moonlight as he headed through the drizzle towards the excavation that contained the live cargo.

5:

1797. Adhémar de Gurvand,

Les Frères Sacrificier & Terrible.

Life at La Pamplona achieved and maintained *bon ton*. The Roget de Belloquet would insist *haut ton, à la Française*. So sternly was it disciplined. It was in its hey-day, one could say, as I rode towards it that bright hot morning, my father's letters to Pierre-Louis in my pouch together with his little gift for *Tante* Jeanne. Its kitchen never closed. Meat and game were perpetually in the process of being skinned or buccaneered, smoked or seasoned, stewed, roasted or baked. Vegetables, washed, chopped and cooked, peas shelled, bread and cakes baked, fruits preserved, cordials and juices made and rum cocktails shaken. All this, prepared and served with the appropriate style at appointed hours, designed to promote great ease, and sumptuous graciousness, *à la beau monde* in the *Antilles*.

I loved it. It was big, over 560 acres, grew sugar, cocoa, coffee, citrus and tobacco. There were drying houses with moveable roofs and storage sheds; cottages for managers, overseers, foremen and craftsmen. There were acres of plantains and ground provisions, food for the two hundred and eleven slaves. These lived in the barrack ranges built close to the foot and hand stocks and the punishment cage, the branding irons and whipping post in the yard, kept in readiness, always waiting for the recalcitrant.

The blacks were called to labour here at four sharp by the bearded head overseer, an inspiring Scotsman called "Antipode" Mac Ivor, standing in the courtyard of the quarters, cracking his seven-foot-long horse whip, giving rise to the popular saying "the crack of dawn."

In the stables slept the grooms and ostlers, a coachman and some stable boys, who, by custom, were so privileged. At the house were the *chef de cuisine* and *sous-chef de cuisine,* two Gasconese who would leave their mark, red hair, for generations in the valley. Five young maids there were, and three *Das,* mulâtresses, estate-born, all pretty, to look after the children—*un véritable Bourg Mulâtresse* here in Santa Cruz. There were washerwomen and seamstresses, black as pitch, one disdainful Maltese butler, and two white indentured Barbadian footmen trained for domestic service who stood and waited and served at meals. These were liveried in dark blue with shiny brass buttons, wore white gloves and periwigs and went barefoot, as did all the Negroes.

I could see him, old Pierre-Louis, sitting on his front gallery, he was listening to his cocoa growing. A favourite pastime of the planters. In the distance, there, a mill driven by mules and a boiling house. If Pierre-Louis were to glance to his right, he would appreciate his cane in arrow, waving in silent reflection of a hot wind coming across his valley. The hot wind carried the voices of sixty-seven praedial slaves, his, raised in industrious work-song, as in unison they slashed, like a forceful machine arrayed across a field almost half-a-mile wide, the full-bodied Bourbon cane, thick as a man's forearm. Pierre-Louis' sugarcane stretched from La Canoa Road to the boundary of La Regularda Estate, which belonged to la Famille de La Rouveyre. It is we, the French *colons,* who built this colony.

This hot wind carried the fragrance of warm rum, poured from copper ladles into massive oaken hogsheads. This estate distils its own blend, a hellish, fiery affair, drunk with a degree of risk. The hot wind was redolent with the aromas of the wet brown sugar, called muscovado, and those of boiling molasses, all this enriched by that of the freshly turned earth and the smell of rain, high in the virgin forest that covered the surrounding mountainsides.

Pierre-Louis Roget could see, beneath a spreading samaan tree, large for its young years, the family graveyard. It contained the remains of his father, his son Andrés, his daughter Isabella and those of the sixteen slaves who had accompanied him during the Brigand's War, men with whom he had once shared life and death, whom he buried there, next to his children. He had led such an adventurous life.

Pierre-Louis possessed slaves to work his crops, to feel his lash, to be locked in his stocks, to warm his bed, to cook, to clean, to serve, to be silent, to fan his feet in his sleep, to wake him gently, to help him into his pantaloons, his shoes, his coat, to pass his hat, his cane, his whip, to hold the door, to close the door, to drive his carriage, to curry his horses, to bow before him, to bow after him, to whisper even in his absence, to rise, to wake, to sleep, to die for him. He was born to be the master of men. And so, I supposed, was I.

The Great House of La Pamplona Estate was the fulcrum for a variety of lives. It was large, too large, a wooden, two-storied labyrinth built by slave labour, by slave masons, slave carpenters, wood-carvers and plasterers: all these had been bought by him in Saint-Domingue. Habitation La Pamplona was named by him for the kingdom of Navarre, his one true love, as he once told me.

That hot wind brushed his clean-shaven cheek but hardly moved his great gray mane, gathered in a queue at the back and tied with a jet-black, velvet ribbon.

His Jezebel, she would bend gracefully before him as she placed a silver tray, upon which was arranged in a tasteful manner his breakfast, on a low table. She did this slowly so as to allow him to admire her young charms, tipped a darker hue than she. He was old-fashioned and preferred the young female house slaves to serve him half-naked. So would I.

Jeanne Roget, my father's cousin, being brought up *bienséance,* preferred not to be served by the women, and did not appreciate the custom entertained by her husband and his friends of having them go about with their breasts exposed.

There were, at the time of my arrival, two other families, passing a prolonged sojourn at La Pamplona. Jeanne Roget was happy for the company. The house, with its commodious offices, sitting, dining and withdrawing rooms, was surrounded by a wide, shaded terrace, and the bedrooms, upstairs and downstairs, could sleep twelve or fourteen people with comfort.

Dejeuner was served on the terrace, after which, at about half-past two in the afternoon, the company retired, the ladies to doze in hammocks slung in the doorways, the men to smoke cigars and fall asleep and snore so loudly that the servants would sometimes appear, believing that they had been summoned.

I kissed my cousin Marie Eugénie on her lips and felt her small mouth open to receive me. We were in the stables surrounded

by the warm smells of animals and fodder. I caressed her face
and looked in wonder at her fine eyes, golden and green. We
kissed again and I felt her soft round body against my own.
My breath quickened as I smelled her own. We would meet
like this since we were children, exploring each other, knowing
even in innocence that our bodies could fit together as perfectly
as two silver spoons. We never found it necessary to talk of
love. We had kissed and touched each other, looked at and
admired the nakedness of each other, talked and shared and
danced and laughed, sometimes to tears. We knew that we
were meant to marry, live in a house like this, work a great
habitation, own land and slaves and raise children. Marie
Eugénie kissed my eyes and face and held my hands, both of
them, in her own. She looked into my smile and loved the way
the sun lit up my hair. I knew this. She was tall. She could
see right into my eyes, and me right into her soul.

"Maman showed me the little painting your Papa sent. It is
so beautiful!" I caressed her lips with the tips of my fingers.

"Let's marry, Marie," I murmured, "marie-moi Marie!"
She laughed and kissed me fully on my mouth and caressed
my back.

"Yes, my love, let's marry. Let's, yes." But already she was
drawing away, knowing that I would want to take her in the
stables on the ground, and she would want me too. "Go, my
love, before Maman sends for me, or Boy O comes to see you
off. Go, come on Saturday."

"I want you, Pony." I called her by one of our secret names,
my voice hoarse with passion. "Let me touch you."

"No, my love. Not now. I have the curse. It will be gone by
Saturday. Come early!" She was already slipping away.

"I will talk to your father, Marie!"

She laughed. "He will expect you to. Now go and say *au revoir*. Maman will be in her room, you know she would be glad to see you." I hugged her tight and smelled her hair. To me, it always smelled of sunshine.

As my father predicted, the sun took an early retirement that day. By four o'clock, it vanished behind dark, rolling clouds, and the intermittent downpour of the tropics descended on the Northern Range.

Keeping my father's warning in mind, I left the Great House at a trot. Cocoutes and the mule were dozing beneath a patriarchal grove of Sandbox trees near to the habitation's cemetery.

"Come, Cocoutes! Make haste. Look, it's after four!"

"Ah coming, ah coming, Massa Adhémar! Dis dam mule like he want to lie down!" Under the Law of the Indies Cocoutes was a complete person. If called upon, he could say that he was from Port-d'Espagne, from parents who belonged to François de Gurvand's father in Grenada, and that he lived in the house across the street from the grass market as a consequence of belonging to me, Monsieur Adhémar, to whom he was bequeathed by deed of gift. As a boy he thought that the oil paintings of my grandfather and others that hung on the wall of the house were alive and even kept an eye on him. He felt the same way about the old clock. He learned to pray. The priest taught him many prayers. He sometimes sold this talent. Cocoutes kicked the mule into a quicker walk. We were already ascending the series of bends and curves that wound their way through the high forest, which would take us over the Saddle and into the Maraval valley.

The surrounding forest, thick with gigantic trees, was decorated with magnificent orchids. There lived timid deer and huge morocoys that moved with prehistoric slow-motion, and delicious armadillos, big iguanas and the deadly mapapire zanana. The forest teemed with bird life that flew in flocks or perched or soared in solitary splendour, the most amazing of these were the iridescent humming birds, their phosphorescent jeweled flight vibrating the spectrum, motionless, mercilessly covering wanton hibiscus, magenta vulva, erect pistils. Fornicating with flowers. I laughed out loud. Overhead the immortelles were in bloom, and bright vermilion blossoms, fallen from the trees, stood out sharply against the green moss and thick ferns that grew along the path. Above and ahead a bellbird called to its mate. Like the sound from a distant cloister, she answered.

"Bells for us, Marie," I smiled to myself. "Bells."

Cocoutes and I were drenched by the downpour before we arrived in Port-d'Espagne. Later that night, in high spirits, I visited Mrs. Murphy's establishment on the Plaza del Marina opposite to Fort San Andrés, a small battery of two or three guns built by Governor Chacon on a tiny rocky island a few score feet from the high water mark that was accessed by a Mole. I was in company with Angel Caballero y Calderón, a young Spaniard, just a little older than myself. That night we dined with Joseph Maingot de Surgères and another young Spaniard, Juan Basanta. Maingot was a surveyor and had been encouraged to come to Trinidad by Don José Chacón. Both Basanta and Angel Caballero were to take up positions in the governor's service.

The night was cool. The air, completely purified by the afternoon's rain and cosmographic bolts of lightning, was refreshing and smelled of the sea and resounded with the bellow of amorous bullfrogs whose bulging eyes at water level in the surrounding mangrove reflected the wavering flambeau that decorated the entrance to Mrs. Murphy's grog shop and brothel. Constructed entirely from debris, it was all of three floors and was the tallest structure on the island. An amazing contraption, surrounded by mangrove, it was devised mostly from the remains of a Spanish galleon's forecastle, together with other marine flotsam, huge whale vertebrae and undressed planking. Decorated with fishnets holding crustaceans, and the enormous teeth, saws, spines and jaws of the as yet unidentified inhabitants of the Gulf of Paria, it was by far the most popular watering-hole on the Caribbean coast.

We were in shirtsleeves and drinking Portuguese wine, made from the *Tinta Adhémarela* grape, which Mrs. Murphy kept cool in a large stone jar buried in a tub filled with coarse salt and sand on her back step. The conversation turned from the weather to the crops and, with contagious happiness, to the coquettes, the present generation of daring young mulâtresses and chabines, certainly occasions of mortal sin, dressed in starched embroidery, wearing enchanting madras turbans and cosquel foulards which hardly covered their delicious décolletés. These immediately took one's absolution away. We all agreed. After hovering for a moment in the mists of lust, our talk then turned to war and revolution.

What commenced in the North American colonies as a war for independence, in France, in 1789 turned to a revolution. Its fierce reverberation was felt in Saint-Domingue and rapidly spread to the French islands of the Lesser Antilles, possessing the promise to resonate in South America in the coming decade.

"In Saint-Domingue the slaves were manipulated!" shouted Basanta above the noise that filled the room. "Manipulated!"

His voice was thick with wine, his animated youthful face rosily illuminated by the whale-oil lamps.

"By whom, Manuel? By whom?" Caballero called.

"By whoever controlled Toussaint! The stage was set by Boukman Dutty, the Jamaican wizard. They say he lives in the forest to this day." We were all speaking, shouting, mingling both Spanish and French, laced with the vernacular of the Caribbean coast.

"Republican Negroes, made free by revolution, mulattoes, made free by their fathers, all assertive, rude and out of place," I said to no one in particular.

"The ideology of revolution has jumped from island to island. It is now here in your midst, in Trinidad," a coarser, minatory voice responded. A stranger, speaking Spanish, had joined us.

"Who are you, Señor?" demanded Basanta. I turned on the bench and regarded the bony-faced stranger in the flickering lamplight. I sensed something unhealthy about this man. Turning to Maingot, who sat at my left, I remarked: "The evening takes a turn."

"My name is—" The stranger appeared to hesitate. "Domingo Vallecilla." Vallecilla bowed slightly, displaying a somewhat mocking parody of the courtly gesture. "I am merely a traveller in these waters."

"In search of?" asked Basanta.

"Knowledge."

"You won't find that in this house!" several voices shouted. The conversation turned to Victor Hugues, the revolution in the French islands—Captain Skinner's raid. How Hugues had been dispatched by Robespierre to terrorise and murder the royalists.

"A mulatto, not so?" I asked.

"A hairdresser, I understand," remarked Maingot.

"A ship's captain," said Basanta with authority.

"A strategist," said Domingo Vallecilla.

"He captured Guadeloupe from the English and the royalists with merely one-thousand-five-hundred men, although outnumbered by more than three-to-one," said Vallecilla. "He dug up the dead body of the English General and left it for the dogs and the corbeaux." He drained his cup. "But come, let us speak of other, more enlightening subjects."

Caballero called for more wine and Basanta pressed a silver coin into the hand of an amazing gold-complexioned mestiza with frizzy, yellow hair and a smile like a barracuda's.

"Ask Dominga to play, and you dance." The woman smiled again, revealing a row of teeth all made of solid gold.

Soon the tavern was full of music, the clapping of hands and stamping of feet to the fandangos of *entremés el novio de la alana* and shouts in Spanish, French, Corsican, and even German. We dined upstairs. Later we were joined by the mestiza with the frizzy yellow hair and her sisters Dominga and Conchita, they appeared to me in the shifting light as Harpies from some fantastic odyssey. The shouted conversation again turned to the politics of the region. Vallecilla was saying: "Jean François was a slave who took his freedom in Haiti with Toussaint. He fought with the Spaniards on that island against the French. I understand he has offered Governor Chacón a battalion of former slaves to garrison this island." The others laughed. It was absurd.

To me it appeared not so strange. The administration, as everyone knew, was hardly in control. Most of the time there were no police, order seemed to disappear at the least provocation.

Most times the island appeared French, not Spanish at all. All classes and colours fought amongst themselves, murders, at times disguised as duels, were common. Blacks and mulatto bastards and masterless men wore the tricolour cockade and sang the Marseillaise. They should be shot. In the ever-increasing uncertainty, I must say I felt a sense of surety in my father, his friends and of course the Craft. The Julien Fédon uprising in Grenada just the year before had sent terrified French *colons* to this island, many mourning their dead parents, wives and children. They arrived to live cheek by jowl with the men who murdered these, as was the case with refugees from all the French islands. I shook my head. Trinidad is where everybody ends up. I glanced up from my meal. The Spaniard was looking at me attentively.

"We have not met," he said, and put out a sallow, bony hand. I felt for a moment a sense of revulsion, but took the offered hand at once. I felt the familiar grip. Taken by surprise, I withdrew my hand rather swiftly and immediately felt embarrassed.

"No need to feel beside yourself, Brother," said the Spaniard and added casually, "Boaz is to Jachim what Jachim is to Boaz."

I was alarmed. To speak these words, which belonged to another place, so openly, so casually, was out of character for me.

I looked at the stranger with surprise.

"Sir, this is hardly the place."

The Spaniard smiled and then laughed, his thin elongated features and melancholy eyes transformed into a comic mask. He shrugged his wide and bony shoulders and drank from a tumbler brimming with *noyeau*, a heady liqueur concocted from brandy, flavoured with a variety of kernels of tropical fruit, some found only at altitudes of above one thousand feet.

"The Craft is a living thing, my Brother, Adhémar." He leaned back in his chair and regarded me. "It possesses both an inner and an outer character. It may illuminate a life, or it could take one. It has always been the custodian of knowledge and the keeper of the secret seals. It is eminently a benevolent institution. It has many names and conceals many names. It deals with the arithmetic of life itself."

"Indeed, Brother Vallecilla," I said. "But tonight our purpose is to celebrate with our friend Angel. Ah, Angel, how does it feel to be now a quarter of a century old?"

"Poor," answered the other, planting a kiss on the lips of the voluptuous Conchita. "Poor, but ever hopeful." The others laughed and Vallecilla took the guitar from the table. He played with considerable skill an Andalusian fandango first, then a soulful bolero, and then a spirited flamenco dance. Castanets appeared and furious hand-clapping. The gathering, red faced in the light of the flambeaux, soon revolved around the music as the women danced upon the tables in the rising heat. Other voices and guitars joined them, and the late evening, turning into night, assumed the nature of a joyful fiesta, carrying all and everything along with it. For a few hours, we forgot our uncertainty, lost our fear of living in these phantasmal times, in this small muddy town, now one of the more dangerous places on earth.

Later, the exuberance of the night overflowing the upper rooms, I, accompanied by Domingo Vallecilla and Joseph Maingot, the surveyor, sought the fresher air of the waterfront. We were joined by Don Manuel Sorzano, who was the Alguacil Mayor, the head of the police.

"So, Angel's birthday celebration has become a fiesta?" enquired the police captain.

"In truth," said I, sitting upon a low wall next to the unsorted cargo awaiting shipment to La Guaira in the morning.

Sorzano shifted his weight from one foot to the other and regarded Vallecilla.

"And you, Señor, *rara avis in terris?* I see that you have made the acquaintance of the young blades of the town at, from what I can hear of it, is quite a celebration. What brings you to these parts?"

"Si Señor, I am perhaps a rare bird in this land, but not as graceful as the black swan." His gesture theatrical, was made ironic by the slight tilt of his head. "The pursuit of opportunity brings me, Señor," continued Vallecilla. "The town is growing, emerging from the backwardness of former times. It now has commerce and trade, agriculture flourishes and families are thriving. A school, an academy of learning for boys, is my purpose."

Don Manuel regarded the Spaniard. He had responded well to the reference found in the work of Juvenal, educated, but somehow he did not seem to be a professor. There was a look about him—he searched for a word in his mind—depravity? Sorzano had been notified of Vallecilla's arrival. He claimed to have sailed from Sainte Lucie, then to Grenada, and eventually arrived aboard one of John Black's ballahoo schooners, the *Crispin Wayne*. But Sorzano suspected Puerto La Cruz or Cumana. He was seen a week before hurrying through the night rain on the Calle de Santa Rosa, which would one day be called Prince Street, with little more than an old bag. No luggage, no books.

Suddenly, shouts from the tavern distracted his train of thought. A fight had ensued, a crowd was gathering, Negroes running towards them. "A man dead! They kill de man!" shouted the foremost. He carried a lantern, the whites of his rolling, wide-open eyes were illuminated in its glow. The four men swiftly walked back towards the tavern. Already there were two alguacils in uniform on the scene, attempting to make the crowd fall back. All fell silent with the arrival of the Alguacil Mayor, us two and Vallecilla. In the muddy road lay the body of Angel Caballero y Calderón, his shirt bloody from a single wound to his chest.

I stood stock-still at the corpse's feet in the red and wavering torchlight, looking wide-eyed at the bloody stain that grew so quickly to cover almost the whole of Angel's upper body, emerging from beneath him to trickle away into the pools of stagnant filth. Around me, my friends, their dislocated faces shocked out of drunkenness. A muffled cry rose in my throat, I could not take a breath. I heard a confused unbelieving cry that I realised was mine. I clutched the hilt of the rapier. Then, of a sudden, my mind a blank, I swung around, and strode away. "Oh highest wisdom, with what art you rule in heaven and earth and in the world of sin." I heard these words, or maybe I said them. Or did I hear someone else speak?

The burial service for Angel Caballero y Calderón took place early the following morning, as was the custom in the tropics, in the small wooden whitewashed church on the Plaza del Marina, the interment in the Campo Santo, the burial ground, to its east. I, like all of the other participants of the previous night's celebration, stood at the grave in my best clothes, black crêpe around hat and sleeves. I was saddened by the loss of one who belonged in our midst, and felt great anguish at the grief expressed by the young man's parents.

As the mourners threw blossoms, together with handfuls of black earth, on the lowered coffin, I became overwhelmed and

71

was relieved when the funeral was over and rode in solitude up the almost dry Santa Ana riverbed. It was a hot and overcast day, the dry season was ending, and blue-grey thunderheads were practising with the velocity of cannonades in the mountains above the Fondes Amandes valley. Angel Caballero perished in a mindless act. He was stabbed to death by a French sailor, who was acting in revenge for a crime committed by another Spaniard on a different island at another time.

"A most fatal consequence," Father Magneval remarked. His words at the funeral service came disconnectedly to me. "In the midst of life—ashes to ashes—in the sweat of thy face shalt thou eat bread, till thou return unto the ground; for out of it wast thou taken: for dust thou art, and unto dust shalt thou return . . . grant him eternal rest, oh Lord, and let perpetual light shine upon him, may he rest in peace. *Kyrie eleison; Christe eleison; Kyrie eleison. Amen.*"

"The rituals of death punctuate our life," my father said in consolation. "But life is forever. We are but forms, expressions of existence that come and go. The Great Architect has built a temple that contains all that is created and all the uncreated. Life moves, as it were, from one room to another, gaining always from having experienced the light." My father's words, my father's face, my father's sadness.

"Bless us, oh Lord, bless us," I clutched the reins tighter, whispering, as the animal threw up her head in surprise, danced sideways on the river stones and almost threw me. She snorted, I sensed her wanting to rear, as I just regained control. Domingo Vallecilla, dressed in black, sat on the riverbank, his own horse tethered close by in the shade of a grove of cocorite palms.

"Señor Vallecilla, what brings you?" I asked.

"Ah, Adhémar, *mi hermano.* You too seek the comfort nature alone can give," answered the Spaniard, lifting a flat pale hand. Overhead a rush of warm wind raised the branches in the tall trees. Glancing upwards I saw, as if painted on the massive, slowly moving storm clouds, a large black hawk stopped still in flight, balancing in mid-air, the world in perpetual rotation beneath its outspread wings. I experienced the sensation that this event had previously occurred to such a degree that I could anticipate every word that Domingo Vallecilla was saying.

"Come, step out of the heat," the words seemed to echo, "and into this shady glade." Vallecilla appeared more frail and limped slightly as he walked before my mare. I allowed him to lead her into the forest coolness. The half-light of the overcast noonday made pale dappled patterns all around. I dismounted, suddenly weary, and sat upon a fallen bough, on the leafy ground. The cool, shaded light served to refresh me. I took a deep breath, and sighed. Vallecilla produced a silver flask, took a sip and passed it on to me. I took a thirsty pull of the cool, slightly tangy drink. The flask itself was wet, dripping water onto my shirt. Vallecilla had previously placed it in the cooling waters of a little stream that ran into the dry river bed.

We spoke of death, and life, and life everlasting. I felt a growing confidence in the thin, gaunt man, who had obviously seen and suffered a great deal in his travels. Vallecilla listened attentively as I searched for words to express my loss, the closeness between my father and myself, and, despite my mistrust, the Spaniard moved me by the sincerity with which he listened.

"You listened well, Brother Domingo." I now spoke of my love for Marie Eugénie and my hopes for our future.

"A listening ear teaches us to hear well the instructions of the Vénérable Master," said Domingo Vallecilla gently.

"I am hardly that," I interjected.

"But more especially that you should listen to the calls and cries of a worthy distressed Brother," continued Vallecilla.

"Thank you for your kindness, Brother." Knowing that my words were somewhat formal, I smiled. Vallecilla possessed a way of incorporating the language of ritual into his common speech. This itself, too, spoke of sincerity and trust in our fraternity of Brothers.

"That is indeed familiar, friend," I said.

"Yes, it is the admonition of the Master to the Entered Apprentice," replied Vallecilla, taking a sip from the flask and passing it to me, I too drank.

"I present you with a new name: it is caution—it teaches you, as you are barely instructed in the rudiments of Masonry, that you should be cautious over all your words and actions, particularly when you are before the enemies of the Craft."

I smiled as I remembered my own initiation. "Brother Benoît Dert was the Master of Les Frères Unis, then he was followed by my father onto the throne of King Solomon, now it is Brother Patrice." Vallecilla reclined against a large boulder, half buried in the leaves.

"From whence came you as an Entered Apprentice Maçon?" he asked rhetorically, his eyes half closed.

"From the Holy Lodge of Saint John, the Almoner, at Jerusalem," I replied immediately.

"Who was he? What recommendations do you bring?"

"His father was King of Cyprus, but he gave up his title to the throne to go to Holy Jerusalem to assist the Knights and pilgrims of the Crusades. I bring recommendations from the Vénérable Master, Surveillants and Brothers of that Vénérable Lodge, who greet you."

"What comest thou hither to do?" asked Domingo.

"To learn to subdue my passions and improve myself in the secret arts and mysteries of ancient Freemasonry."

"You are a Master Maçon then, I presume?"

"I am."

"How shall I know that you are a Maçon?"

"By certain signs and tokens."

"What are the tokens?" Vallecilla opened his eyes and sat straight up. Suddenly he appeared to be wide awake, and I was somewhat startled.

"All right angles, horizontals and perpendiculars," said I slowly.

"And what is a sign?" asked Vallecilla, looking straight into my eyes.

"A certain friendly brotherly grip whereby one Maçon may know another in the dark as in the light." I answered firmly, like a schoolboy who has come well prepared. Vallecilla smiled and leaned back on the boulder again.

"And Euclid's fifth proposition, Book One?"

"The one known as *Pons Asinorum,* the bridge of asses, this neophyte was able to cross it with equilibrium," I laughed. "The angles opposite the two equal sides of an isosceles triangle are equal."

"And?"

"The sum of the areas of the two squares on the legs, a and b, equals the area of the square on the hypotenuse."

The afternoon passed in that pleasant exchange with the evocation of memories and experiences within the Craft. Vallecilla, the older, more versed and greatly experienced, regaled me, with stories that appeared to be more fantastic by far than the tall tales told by Papa and Father Magneval. I felt that Vallecilla was somehow testing me, to see what I knew of the ancient Craft. Indeed I knew very little, but I joined Vallecilla in the repetition of the ritual words as far as I knew them; I had not done much work. I felt at ease now with the older man, we discussed the triangles of Archimedes in the spiral staircase.

When we rose, the sun was already in the western sky. Vallecilla opened his arms to me and took the proscribed step. Then, on cue, we silently advanced towards each other, falling into the steps, while making the precise gestures that enact the ritual for the passing of the substitute for the "lost Word."

"The Word," Vallecilla muttered, placing his ear to my lips.

And the Maçon's Word passed from my lips into a surprisingly long ear that emerged from a mass of greasy grey black curls.

Domingo Vallecilla held me close for an instant, then let me go and laughed, and we separated standing a little awkwardly before each other. Vallecilla laughed again.

"Come, little Brother, it is time," he said. I felt somewhat out of sorts. The change in the mood, the laugh, the difference in the atmosphere left me feeling that perhaps I had gone too far. I walked towards the dry riverbed, the shadows had lengthened, and I noticed that the stream had widened.

"Rain in the mountains," remarked Vallecilla, sniffing the air and wrinkling his bony nose.

"Yes." I looked up into the sky. The large black hawk was still there hanging in its heights, it felt as though time had stopped. As I looked it slipped sideways and with gathering speed it swooped into the topmost branches of a tall tree that grew on the cliff above a bend in the dry river. Time has resumed, I thought. I watched it emerge, flapping its wide wings, a long writhing, squirming snake in its talons. The bird flapped furiously, gaining height, its victim already performing an arabesque of death against the blue-grey late afternoon sky. Domingo Vallecilla mounted his horse and was holding my reins out to me. He too saw the aerial display.

"The natural order of things," he said mildly in a voice reminiscent of the tone of the afternoon's conversation. I said nothing. I felt troubled, vaguely guilty. I glanced at Vallecilla, who smiled with only his thin mouth and turned a long and lumpy cheroot in his yellow fingers.

"These are wild times, young friend. Your father is a great man, and you have been elevated to the Brotherhood, an antique chivalry." We returned in silence and parted at the toll-gate on the Saint Joseph Road. Vallecilla said he felt to say a prayer for the soul of dead Angel Caballero y Calderón and rode towards the Campo Santo at the back of the church. The sky to westward gave the impression of being scorching hot. "Fire in the pot," I said to myself. Just saying that seemed to convey some kind of trouble, in the sense of a freshly discovered omen. I shook my head to dismiss the thought. What had I done? Did I do something wrong with Vallecilla? I wondered, I must tell my father. That man is vile, but surely we are Brothers in the Craft. As I walked the mare towards our house on the square opposite to the grass market, the failing sunlight turned the western sky to lilac, edged with burnished copper. I thought that I could taste it.

I glanced at it again from the upstairs balcony. I was alone, my father was at the Mon Repos estate in Sainte Anne. I wished that he were here. The heat of the day filled the shuttered rooms. The emptiness of the streets, the oppressive silence brought to me a melancholy always lurking at this hour, this led to having too much wine with my solitary dinner.

I awoke before the dawn with a throbbing painful head, and a feeling of confusion. There was a profound stillness about the place, in the house, as I sat up in bed listening and looking around me. The dogs did not bark, nor did cocks crow. Not even the drip of water, filtering through the coral urn into the clay goblet outside my window, made its metronomic plop. There was the feeling of being entirely alone, as though even the clock had stopped. It was then that I realised that there was someone else in the room. In the house! The bedroom door swung open. In the doorway stood a short hooded figure, two other shapes emerged from the darkness. My mouth was dry with fright.

"You are a traitor and a scoundrel," the two voices said in unison. "You shall be outcast."

"Bind him," said the short burly one. I felt transfixed. "Put the hoodwink upon him," said the other.

When I felt the blindfold about my face, I suddenly came to life, but there were other hands that held me, and I was struck upon the forehead and knew little else.

I spent the day in a very small room that held just a chair and a table upon which was a skull and bones, salt, sulphur, an hourglass, and a glass of water. I was told by someone speaking through the door that the coupling of salt and sulphur was an image of ambivalence, of life and death, of light and darkness nourishing each other. There was an inkwell, a quill, a sheet of blank parchment. I was told to make my Will and Testament. I did not. Could this be some ritual, had meeting Vallecilla been a test? "I want to see my father. Send for him!" I shouted. The person outside laughed out loud, and walked away.

On the wall were scrawled the words, *VITRIOLUM, visita interiora terrae.* I thought of the Latin gleaned from Father Magneval. Did it mean, "Visit the centre of the earth?" It made no sense. Hungry, I banged on the door, "Call Master Vincent, I want to see him, now, the Master!" I shouted. There was no one there. Hysteria: a suffocating gradual evolution towards the terrifying advancement of a nightmare. I screamed for help and shouted for my father. Later I heard the Atelier being called to order. That night after the Vénérable Master in a loud voice ordered the Apprentices and Fellows of Craft dismissed, I was put to sit upon a chair in the anteroom that was unbalanced, as if one or two legs were shorter than the others. I heard voices inside the temple say that I had betrayed my Masonic oath. I tried to speak, but was ordered to be silent. It felt like being in a play. I was being tried and judged in absentia. I searched the faces of the Knights who stood around for someone I knew, but in fact I recognised no one.

"Who are these people?" I wondered. "How do they know?" Domingo Vallecilla, that son of a whore, that deceiver. "I will kill, kill him—that he should have done this; he joined us—Angel Caballero died. Angel was buried. He joined me, I was such a fool!—Oh father, forgive me, oh father, forgive me—dear Lord!"

The ritual, when it commenced, I realised was the opposite of that which I had experienced two years before. I was made to reenter the temple shod, walking backwards, wearing my street clothes. My aprons, I saw them burned one after the other in a brazier that someone said contained ketoret, which was the incense offered in the temple in Jerusalem as stated in the Book of Exodus, a mixture of stacte, onycha, galbanum and frankincense, always burnt at the door of the Atelier when a Third Degree was worked for the pacification of the soul of the slain Master Builder. Then Benoît Dert, the Frère Terrible, wearing the mask sardonic, struck me across the face, hard, and turned my right arm around my back and bound it at the wrist and around my neck. This happened so quickly. This was not a ritual. Horror, I tried to get free, I must have screamed very loud. I saw the silver mask bending close to scrutinise me in this agony.

"This sad and solemn scene now before us stirs up recollections with a force and vivid power which we have hitherto un-felt. He who now slumbers in that last long unbroken sleep was our Brother," intoned the black-robed assembly.

The pain in my arm and shoulder became so great that I thought I would go mad, strong arms held me to the floor, I was trying not to choke. It came to me that they were saying the prayers for the dead.

"With him we have walked the pilgrimage of life and kept watch and ward together in its vicissitudes and trials, he is now removed beyond the effect of our praise and censure." The Hierophant stepped forward and turned the extinguished candle wick upon the checkered floor.

"That we loved him our presence here evinces, and we remember him in scenes to which the world was not witness and where the better feelings of humanity were exhibited without disguise."

I choked, I wept, long loud choking sobs coming from my insides. My chest felt ablaze, my shoulder, the pain, no words can describe. I got the other hand away and pushed up the elbow of the bound one to relieve the choking, to breathe. I could hear my howling as I forced my bound right arm up my back so as not to choke. Then I saw the Master bend towards me and loosen the tie. I breathed.

"That he had faults and failures is but to repeat what his mortality demonstrated, that he had a human nature not divine. Over those errors, whatever they might have been, we cast while living the mantle of charity. It should with much more reason enshroud him in death."

"We who have been taught to extend the point of charity even to a foe when fallen, cannot be severe or merciless toward a loved Brother," the assembled recited in unison in sing-song voices.

"The many of his virtues linger in our remembrance," the Hierophant continued, "and they reflect their shiny lustre beyond the portals of the tomb." They began to file past my writhing body as I kicked and squirmed, my arm, twisted up my back and tied around my throat, my breath coming and going in vast gasps. I felt a darkness rising behind my eyes.

I felt my stomach clench, a pain deep within it. I emptied my bowels. "Oh. . . Oh no."

"The earthen vase, which has contained precious odours, will lose none of its fragrance, though the clay be broken and shattered. So be it with our Brother's memory."

"Doe to the book, the candle quenched, now, ring the bell!" intoned the Frère Sacrificier.

"Bind him accordingly and throw him back into the profane world," said Vincent to the brothers Dert.

81

I could see the sky through the little window high in the roof and smell the acrid horse piss and sawdust from the place below.

"Go by Scipio down the Main, he is your father's family, he will take you, and forget all this, boy," Mayotte was telling me. I saw only her eyes, one black and the other blue. "Go down the Main, forget all this shit, boy."

"Healing the dead is a process. To undertake it you must present yourself at death's door and live in his house. Just like Moses did. He lived in the house of Jethro for 40 years, where he married Jethro's daughter Zephora, who was named for an unimaginable aspiration," I told her seriously and looked at old Mayotte, *I love you*, I was thinking. I heard her say "Too much opium in that *tisane* he drink." She was shaking her head, I shook my own as well.

"Rubbish, stupid talk. Gurvand, Gurvand, Gurvand," she muttered, I knew it meant to her "Stubborn! Stubborn! Stubborn!" That evening I was so restless with remorse I could not sleep, although I wanted to so badly. I saw her come and lean over me, her lamp high, so as to not let a shadow fall diagonally across me as she had done when I was a boy. She wanted nothing to cross me. She looked at me, "You healing already—like father, like son. Drink this, here."

"No," I thought I said, "I am going to get married to Marie Eugénie, she will be my eternal star." I drank the bitter cupful and merciful darkness came.

82

Gently closing the door, Mayotte stood on the landing at the top of the stairs, darkly descending into the shadows. From far away she could hear a deep *assator* drum keeping its distance from the quicker, more rhythmic high pitch *léwòz* of a *ka-drum*. Then, the slow toll of the cracked church bell calling for the six o'clock Angelus. All together they made her evening prayer complete. She sat down on the top step and lit her pipe. Muffled voices rose from below.

"He was made to suffer to test his honour, Vincent?"

Vincent Patrice thought long and hard about what he would say to the man whom he considered his friend. He and François de Gurvand shared the most perilous period of their lives in Sainte Lucie. He had been born there. François had come from Grenada with his children. Étienne Morin *fils* had introduced them both to the "Splendour," that fantastic body of knowledge contained in the work of Fabre d'Olivier. The golden triangles of understanding the universe, man, and ultimately, the Great Architect of all creation. They read the writings of the Comte de Gabalis and wondered at the lives and deaths experienced by the mysterious Count of St. Germain, "The Polish Rider," as discussed in the ancient wisdom of the theosophical discourses. They both received, in the true spirit of Brotherly love, despite the social distinction that lay between them, Masonic light in December of 1785 at Lodge Parfait Union in Saint Pierre. After, they laboured together to obtain a Constitution for Les Frères Unis and proceeded with its erection and consecration in Sainte Lucie, in the town of Micoud.

"Yes, François, yes," Vincent finally said.

"My son—Vincent!"

"Yes, my dear François. We live in such times, François. What Adhémar will be called upon to do for the cause of *Ars*

Magna, the Great Work, will demand from him greatness, and you know the rules. The chosen one must die, be cast out, and return to die again, the stone refused then becomes the corner stone."

"Liar, you scoundrel, *un sacre barbare!* Nonsense Vincent! You sent that creature to seduce him, then you maimed my son to weaken me! To get at me, to bind him to your intentions, because I will not support you and that gang of Corsican thieves you have surrounded yourself with. You are a traitor, you commoner, low-born bastard, *restez foutu.* How dare you apply that punishment without a full trial, without conclave and chapter, with only half the Encampment of Knights, people who don't even come to Lodge!"

"François, please, the times are changing, the world we knew has ended. We can create a Grand Lodge for the control of all South America. That revolution over there will sweep the past away. We are old, we need a young man to take the Work, and all that we have done, forward. You know that this is one of many tests that the chosen one will have to face. I am sorry, I beg your forgiveness, but if I had come to you . . ."

"Chosen one? Chosen by whom? Vincent, go away from here, or I will kill you now, here tonight, so help me God!" This last was spoken softly, even gently.

They stood there in the dark for what felt to Mayotte like a long time, then she heard Vincent move away and walk his horse out of the yard.

"That incubus, your Spaniard?" asked François.

"He will die, François, before the night is out," answered Dominic Dert.

"Served your purpose."

"François."

"And the others?"

"Manuel Gual and José María España will be of use to
us, to all of us, François, all of us, remember the Work,
Ars Magna. If they manage to escape La Guaira, we will get
them out and to Victor Hugues in Guadeloupe. Now that
the English are about to take this island, opportunities open.
Julien Fédon has escaped Grenada, he is here with Jean-Pierre
La Vallette."

"You protect him, don't you? He is right here in Trinidad.
He is a murderer of Maçons! As well as the others. And what
of Jean La Valette, Joachim Philippe and Stanislas Besson?"

"This, Trinidad," Dert gestured, "is a resting place for those
who survived in Grenada to fight again. La Valette is to go to
Saint-Domingue, so too Manuel Piar. Julien Fédon will go to
Angostura, Peletan de Molé will arrange this, he imports cattle
from Angostura, Besson can never fight again, but his son
Julien, Fédon's godson, will be initiated and trained. Joachim
Philippe has disappeared, gone to ground, perhaps on his
brother's habitation, Philippine, in the South Naparimas."

For those who survive—François de Gurvand hardly heard
a word he said, these people meant nothing to him. He could
feel the pain that he knew was flaming through that body that
he loved more than his own. His son, his dear, brave son
whom he had fashioned from his own half-forgotten memories
of legends of quests and journeys, tales of ancient broadswords
hung on damp walls in dungeons that were now turning to
dust, in a place across the sea, in a land torn by terrifying strife,
to which they would soon have to return. It was his fault.

"You are a hypocrite, Dominic." Blood pounded in his head.
"Vincent is mad! And you! I may kill him for this. And you.
He will pay for this as sure as there is a God above. And you.

I am finished with this; this Work, and you. I am finished with Les Frères Unis. If that was what you and Vincent and the Corsican scum wanted, you have achieved it."

"François, I . . ."

"Go. Get out, reprobate, go now, go to your master, you dog, and lick his spit."

She could hear the sound of a blade being drawn.

"Yes, Brother Sacrificier, draw it now and die, here, now."

The blade was returned, footsteps retreating, the sounds of a mounted man riding briskly away.

Her master's voice, low, she couldn't catch his words.

6:

1797. Monseigneur Hubertus Magneval,

The Holy Hermandad.

Father Magneval knelt in prayer upon the hard-packed earthen floor of the small, wooden, white-washed church on the Plaza del Marina. So close was it to the mud flats that the waves of the Gulf of Paria would lash its walls on windy March mornings when the tide was high and enormous crabs would join and outnumber the incongruous congregation to hear Mass at both the five and the seven o'clock services.

Solemnly he raised his eyes to the gilded crucifix upon the small altar in genuine supplication, sincere in his Faith, confident in the power of God's power and in His merciful grace. His prayers, directed to the sacred heart of Jesus, appealed for mercy to be shown and swift healing for the young man, Adhémar, the only surviving son of the man he had been sent all the way from Mexico City to spy upon.

He had heard the boy, he knew well his voice, cry out in agony from that cursed place last night. A robust man, he rose from his knees quickly, bowing and making the sign of the cross, his thick fingers conveying a delicate intention.

I must go to him now, he thought. Stepping backwards, he turned and walked from his church across the Plaza del Marina, through the town's small cemetery, its Campo Santo, towards the grass market. On the way he paused to look at the slaughtering of a ewe, by Zenibè, the elderly slave-woman who was the property of the parish. She was in-charge of its flock that grazed on the Holy Field. I must go to him now, he repeated to himself. François, could not have a hand in this, this abomination; I must see him, see the boy, "go to him," he said aloud, walking briskly towards the house across the street from the grass market. Upon arrival he found it shut and barred. He called, loudly. Then, the old mad black witch Mayotte came out to tell him to go away.

At various times, he had acted as teacher, doctor, confessor, and even perhaps friend, to the tall youth with the wide smile and bright countenance. He saw Adhémar de Gurvand grow into a strong young man whom he still thought of as a lad. He came to appreciate him despite the duplicity with which he had entered into the relationship with the remnants of the de Gurvand family.

He valued his relationship with Adhémar's father, François de Gurvand, and recognised in him a man possessed of breeding, of honour, of chivalric *gentillesse*, and a generous temperament. A good man. A deeply religious man, whose faith in the living God was perceived by all. Notwithstanding his ever-watchful eye, his careful analysis of their evening talks and indeed, at times, several days spent in each other's company, he had discovered not very much.

Yet Hubertus Magneval understood that this tall, grave man, this learned, well-educated, sober man possessed a secret. And the nature of that secret and its purpose was his task in life to unravel. Thus, he devoted all his training, all his intuition, to the unmasking of this heretic. For he was in no doubt that heresy it was. What version, which doctrine, whose doctrine he never could decipher because François, erudite and cautious, was well aware of Father Hubertus Magneval's intention.

François de Gurvand knew that Monseigneur Magneval was the apostolic prefect for this colony, as well as the preceptor of the Vatican's most secret society in the New World, the Holy Hermandad. He knew that Father Magneval was the nineteenth to hold that office in Trinidad, and that this secret society had come to this island during the governorship of Don José de Aspe y Zuniga in the early 1600s. The Holy Hermandad became established here because the Inquisition, *Inquisitio Haereticae Pravitatis*, or inquiry on heretical perversity had been discouraged to by Governor Martin de la Hoz y Berrio. François was also aware that Monseigneur Magneval arrived in Trinidad within weeks of his own removal from Sainte Lucie.

The sworn oath of the Holy Hermandad was to "Guard the sovereignty and service of the King and all the rights he ought to have and to guard our bodies and all that we have." The Holy Hermandad, which met in secret conclave, functioned in Trinidad as a militia. At present, it was occupied mostly with espionage. François de Gurvand was mindful that the Holy Hermandad, under the Laws of the Indies, the laws of Trinidad, Spanish law, was judicial in nature, having jurisdiction over crimes including blasphemy, the passing of false money and dissemination of information that could prove inimical to the Crown of Spain. It was vested with the power to have him arrested and deported to Spain.

In spite of his rough manner and disheveled appearance, Hubertus Magneval was a Society of Jesus trained chirurgeon, a doctor of medicine, and a surgeon, as well as being an exponent of the *Corpus Juris Canonici*. Just imagine, a priest with his training, his stature in the church, so far removed from the corridors of ecclesiastical opportunity, dispatched to this backwater of a Spanish colony, to serve as just another parish priest? François de Gurvand, cognizant of all this, was indeed on his guard when it came to Monseigneur Hubertus Magneval.

But, François, too, enjoyed the time spent with this well-read priest. Sometimes in the interminable mid-week of a succession of drowsy afternoons and sultry evenings, their conversations seemed to narrow down to topics deemed in some circles sacrilegious.

Otherwise the conversation could turn to the swiftly changing times, as it did some weeks before the events that altered young Adhémar's life.

The printing press. François set the type himself and printed, page by page, "The Rights of Man" in its entirety. He cut down, trimmed and sewed the printed sheets and bound thirty volumes of this work of Thomas Paine, which posited that popular political revolution is permissible when a government does not safeguard its people, their natural rights, and their national interests. He had these secretly sent to Bogota and later Caracas. It was immediately condemned by the Inquisition in Caracas. The Captaincy General in Caracas deplored the "inevitable introduction of pamphlets from foreign islands and the Old World, in spite of the active vigilance of the magistrates to prevent it. Among these pamphlets is one from neighbouring Trinidad, which contains the most subversive ideas on the independence of the entire continent."

"The Rights of Man," François would say, "contains ideals that are fundamental: human rights originate in Nature, thus, rights cannot be granted via political charter, because that implies that rights are legally revocable and granted as privileges. It is a perversion of terms to say that a charter gives rights," he attempted to explain to Father Magneval. "It operates by a contrary effect—that of taking rights away. Rights are inherent to all the inhabitants of this world; but charters, by annulling those rights in the majority, leave the right, by exclusion, in the hands of a few. They, consequently, are instruments of injustice."

The priest wouldn't or couldn't understand this. "The fact, therefore, must be that the individuals themselves, each in their own personal and sovereign right, enter into a compact with each other to produce a government: and this is the only way governments have a right to arise, and the only principle on which they have a right to exist. Government's sole purpose is safeguarding the family and its inalienable rights; each societal institution that does not benefit the nation is illegitimate—especially the Monarchy, the Nobility, and the Military."

François was fortunate, the priest gleefully informed him, that the Inquisition did not sit in Trinidad, as that blasphemous conventicle to which he and his circle belonged would have long ago ceased to exist. He merely smiled at this.

"In the meantime you have written and printed hundreds of pamphlets, these to find their way to the islands, to Julien Fédon in Grenada, to Victor Hugues wherever he is killing Maçons," said Father Magneval. "They find their way to those on the coast, at Cumana, Güiria, Punta Piedra, Irapa, and inland to Angostura and Maturín, everywhere."

"You know all this, Father Magneval. The governor, Don Chacón, knows what I do here, what we do. He knows that this place, Trinidad, abounds with conspirators and conspiracies, that it is the principal milieu of colonial espionage and the home of the continental liberation movements. But the balance is too delicate: there are too few of you, too many of us. *Us.* He knows that we are here, right here in this Atelier, and have been in contact with Victor Hugues. He understands that if the *sans-culottes* came to Trinidad, if Hugues came, all that he has built would be over. Don Chacón is a royalist but a realist, his loyalty is in the main with the French royalist planters. He will build no defences. Take no aid. He now desires nothing else than for the English to come."

"The Spanish sickness, he has that" answered the priest, passing his hand across his rugged features. "A prisoner of the medieval culture of helplessness, a dreamy melancholy of the hopeless, praying for divine intervention," he said, putting his palms together and rolling his eyes heavenward. "When Admiral Aristizábal offered him troops and guns, the governor obfuscated, then postponed making a decision. The admiral couldn't linger longer, he sailed for Havana."

"That is so," said François. "I understand it was from Havana that Jean François, a former slave of Santo Domingo, who supported the Spaniards in their war against the French republicans, sent the mulatto Colonel Georges Biassou with an offer to bring an army of blacks to defend Trinidad against an attack from Hugues' republicans." François, feeling that Father Magneval was getting the lead in the conversation, and despite his usual reticence to say all he knew, ventured to add, "Alarmed at the very thought, the Don did nothing for a long time, then met Biassou at the home of Santiago de Lezama in San Juan de Acuña, not at his official residence, because Georges Biassou was a republican, a Maçon, and a black. His answer was no. I suppose he feared Jean François, who was a notorious murderer of French colonists in Saint-Domingue.

I understand that Georges Biassou has been allowed to enter Spanish territory and his company of fighters is in Florida at present."

"François, the governor wants an end, he wishes that he could hand the island over to the English. Events frighten him. If the republican fighters take the island for the French Republic, there would be another massacre of royalists, and most likely ourselves as well. We are fortunate that Vincent Patrice has changed sides. And you, my idealistic Brother, where do you stand now that the revolution has turned against the heresy of Freemasonry?"

"I hold as ever to the principles of the Enlightenment, to the purpose of its ideals."

"And what are these?"

"To mobilise the power of reason in order to reform society and advance knowledge. The great *Encyclopédie* contains its ideals. I recommend it to you, my dear Hubertus."

"Francois, François. Do you really actually believe all that?"

"Of course Hubertus, naturally."

"Ha! I don't believe you. You are no republican, Sire de Gurvand."

Their conversation ended in much the manner that it always did. Father Magneval had not learnt very much from François, and came away with the feeling that he had said more than he should have. François was left wondering who, in the Craft, was Magneval's informant.

In the days that followed the ceremonial act that not only humiliated him but also declared him dead, Adhémar de Gurvand existed in a half-light of unspeakable chagrin augmented by throbbing pain in a world circumscribed by an apocalyptic sense of ending, coming over and over to a final stop. His delirium revolved around the memories of that day when he betrayed trust, and on the night when he had been thrown, covered in his own filth, from the Lodge into the street. These incessantly recurring recollections seemed like moveable backdrops in a fantastic stage set, in which he himself appeared in all the roles. It was his own stupid fault, he told himself in the vain hope of escaping the daemon of remorse. He prayed for amnesia.

He was asleep in his room dreaming of chagrin when his father entered. His breathing was shallow and gasping, his bodily frame much reduced. His eyes, sunken deep into their dark-rimmed sockets, shifted quickly from side to side, as if following swiftly swirling landscapes. He awoke with a leap and turned to look at his father. François felt that although his eyes had fallen upon him, he had not seen him for several seconds or not at all. My God, he looks really bad, he thought.

"My dear boy, I'm so glad to see you're looking better."

"Papa, where is Mayotte? I dreamed, I dreamed something, something really. . ."

"Mayotte had to go to Sainte Anne village for me, Adhémar. Jean-Paul has a fever."

Adhémar stared away through the half-open window. His waking was worse than his dreaming. The muscles and sinews of his arm and shoulder, very badly bruised and sprained, were aching; his mind remind tormented. "Father, I'm so sorry," he said again. "I let you down so badly. I beg you, please forgive me. I am so sorry." He looked away, tears running down his face. "I am so, so sorry."

François, sitting at his bedside, the pain of his own losses and the uncertainty of life on this calamitous island threatening to overwhelm him, spoke to him of cause and effect, and the laws of what the Hindu mystics call Karma. He told the young man, with the voice of reassurance, that in his eyes he had not fallen from grace. He was taken in by an unscrupulous man at a time when he was vulnerable, which was very stupid of him. And there was a lesson to be learnt there: at a time when one is emotionally vulnerable, one has to be especially on one's guard.

"Heroes fall from grace, my boy, for one reason or another, but they regain their position and remake themselves," he said briskly, regarding him. To himself he could not help but wonder whether Adhémar had it in him to deal with life's setbacks. Growing up in this stupid place seemed to have made him into a creature of the place, a Creole. A native. Ignorant of the world.

"The opportunity for redemption will present itself, never fear. Life does not let you off so easily. You have been sorely tested by the Vénérable Master, and, having been found wanting you have been punished. Had you fallen into the hands of an enemy you would be dead. Learn that lesson. Do not make a fool of yourself in the future. Remember this: there is no magic word, if you are asked if you have the password your answer is 'No'. Not only does the magic word not exist, we do not know that it does not exist. Admit your ignorance, and you may learn a lot. Know always what you say, never say all that you know. There is serious work to be done, true challenges that will shape the future and influence the lives of people not yet born in countries that do not yet exist. You have been taught a lesson, never forget it."

He never mentioned Vincent or the brothers Dert. He made it plain to his son that in the Craft when a breach of trust occurred, the oath violated, notwithstanding the circumstances, the consequence of that violation would take its course. There was no choice but to redeem himself when the time was right. Not to the Master, for Masters come and then they go. But in his own eyes. And then to the Brotherhood. "Wait and the opportunity for your redemption will present itself. You will not fail."

Adhémar took heart from his father's words, and as the days went by, he became increasingly his former self. The apocalyptic look receded, but the profound chagrin stayed, with a growing sense of self-disgust for his betrayal, which was to become etched forever in his deepest self. Alongside that, however, a firm resolve took form. "I will redeem myself—and Domingo Antonio Vallecilla is a dead man."

Marie Eugénie came to him. She brought him marzipan dipped in granulated sugar, the new process, candied fruit, crème de menthe, and filled the room with flowers. He pressed his face into her bosom and smelled her: the smell of sunshine and Eau de Cologne and vertivert. She accepted what she was told of his bad fall and nursed him with all her love during the following week. She had him moved to her cousin MiMi Gomez' house, which was two-storied, airy and more or less free of the malodorous vapours of the place. She supervised the cook who prepared his meals and fed him, these occasions tender and sensuous.

The nightmares continued, at times astonishingly vivid. They portrayed gaping mouths and rotting hands, faces that fell away to dust upon expression, hearts that burst asunder like cannons bellowing, making monsters in sulfurous fumes, black as tombs, echoing shouts reverberating as claps of thunder on silent Sunday afternoons. A severe palpitation woke him, he was sweating into the already damp sheets. He knew that he knew something. What?

Mayotte thought she saw the shades of death hover about him. She could perceive them with her one black and one blue eye. She clearly discerned the ancient ones, the Obi clothed in primordial fears, coiled, fanged, and winged. She heard the jumbie bird and smelled the dank and worm-filled earth. It rained for nine days straight. She journeyed with him on excursions to and from the nightmares in which he moved. And during that timeless time, she knew that his body was healing fast, but feared for his soul and doubted its capacity to maintain immortality.

"They work a hard magic on him."

She prayed for him, to all her gods and goddesses, to deities so old that they no longer possessed names. She lay awake one hot night on cloying, tepid sheets, smelling her old body, sweat running down her neck, waiting, waiting for it to come. In the darkness, just when sleep was about to cast its dark cloak upon her, she saw it. Death. Listening to its gasping breath, she could just make out a movement about her bed and see, partly in her mind's eye, partly in the darkened room, a form—to her shock a female form, which turned with staring countenance to her.

"My God," she breathed, as she looked into her own face. "My God, it must be a hundred years old."

She saw the trembling mouth, toothless, the yellow eyes, sightless, the shaking, shrinking body, numb with years, the scaled feet, decrepit toes, heard the stamp of a foot, the sound of chains mingling with the rustle of a petticoat. She could taste the flat phlegm of death rattling piteously in a throat that bowed an almost bald head towards her.

The next day, about mid-morning, they found her dead upon the floor of her hut. Suddenly it seemed she was quite old.

François saw Adhémar the following night and told him of Mayotte's death. He could not keep it from him any longer. It was, he said, quite sudden, probably heart failure. This news affected Adhémar deeply and both François and Marie Eugénie did all they could to distract him. Cocoutes was the one who told him the simple truth about the old woman's death.

"When day find she, she looked real dead and real old, Massa Adhémar. Real old. I nebber know a body could look good good one day and next day look like she dead long time."

7:

1797. François de Gurvand,
Les Chambrés.

In the wake of this harrowing experience that so injured his body and almost unhinged his mind, and knowing how much Les Frères Unis and its camaraderie had meant to him, I chanced the opportunity to plant some seeds of a greater truth, one I hoped would form for him a far more profound reality than his Masonic experiences. I knew, as well, that the time had come to relate something of the history of our family, and explain to Adhémar the true reason for our being in the Caribbean and on this island of Trinidad.

Above us, as we sat in the gallery overlooking the now dark and quiet grass market, the clear tropic night was ablaze with stars. I began by pointing, naming the constellations that illuminated the heavens. I was not certain where a story such as this should commence, but eventually found my way by comparing the constellations at this latitude with ours at home in Brittany.

From my earliest youth, I said to him, having exhausted all celestial comparisons, I was aware that we, our family, were not like others who lived in the long valley of Cornouaille. I somehow always knew to be cautious, I said to him, and to never discuss with anyone what transpired in our home, who came to visit my grandparents, and those who stayed on sometimes for months at a time. No one ever told me to be discreet, but I sensed that our difference, as it were, required it.

One spring day, my father, my younger brother, a few trusted henchmen and I started to remove the paving stones and to dig up the floor of the main hall of our old house. The decision to do this was brought about as the result of a visit by a company of riders in the summer of the previous year. I was, at the time of their arrival, then in my early teens, and was helping in the upper meadow together with my brother Alain, when we saw a party of horsemen riding into our valley. They rode in a military manner, in close formation, about an antiquated coach that was drawn by six well-matched greys. That night my grandfather and both my parents spoke in privacy with the three men who came in the coach, the riders quietly assuming positions at the main doors of the house and at other entrances.

Those sentinels were all old, dressed in black and white surcoats of some rich material, and carried heavy, long out of fashion, broadswords. Of the three who were sequestered with my parents, one, the youngest, was treated with great respect, to a point that I felt somewhat excessive. I suppose I found it strange to see my austere, sometimes imposing, grandfather kneel in fidelity before this young person.

I can still recall our visitor's first words, I told Adhémar: "Each people in their turn will light up the world," said he, smiling broadly. He was a prince of the house of Andorra, I was told, and his name was Idelfonso Tiburcio Burgundofara, a name which sounded mysterious and delightful to me, and still does so now. He looked about the room, with a gesture that gathered us all together. I hovered there after my father dismissed the servants and the curious who arrived that morning, and while others, including some of our neighbours, made themselves comfortable, my grandfather placed his large hand on my shoulder and I sank to my knees at his feet.

Prince Idelfonso, in addressing us that night, seemed to me to speak to each person while at the same time no one in particular. He was the object of my utmost attention. I felt that I was experiencing someone unique, although there was nothing particular about him, except perhaps his brow was rather high and round, his fair hair was close cropped, as that of a person in Holy Orders, yet his dress was secular, even fashionable, and his blue eyes tended to bulge a little. I found them bright and filled with light when he looked at me intensely for a moment, and smiled. There was a lightness about him, although he was not frail. His complexion was very fair, but not white, and his hands were long, with well-shaped fingers, but were not soft.

"From today onwards, all of you, our people, members of Les Chambrés, will set a course of events in motion and every person throughout this world will be affected," said Prince Idelfonso solemnly. "I have come from The Upper Room to order the removal of our treasure from the house of Gurvand, so as to place it in readiness for its historic task." He paused, looking for a moment at each one of us. I felt his gaze linger on me a trifle longer than on the others.

The prince, in his address to us, recounted that as the light of learning dimmed, and finally faltered, in western Europe with the collapse of the Roman Empire and the Dark Ages commenced, a small coterie of educated, mostly Gallo-Roman men and women set about laying the foundation of a most unorthodox organisation. This fraternity, for its survival, he said, met in secrecy, when necessary, in a room or chamber placed in an upper storey. As such, it became known amongst its membership simply as "Les Chambrés."

Its actual origins, I told Adhémar, as was told to us that night, dated from the first decades of the ninth century when, at the coronation of Louis the Pious, the crown of France was passed from the hands of Berengar the Wise, Count of Toulouse, in whose charge Louis was put as a boy, to his father Charles, the Emperor, who then placed it upon the head of his son Louis, proclaiming him King of the French. It was Louis the Pious who granted the Charter that brought Les Chambrés into existence, and Berengar the Wise who then became Les Chambrés's first Head. We, the de Gurvand family, were amongst the founders of this very antique society.

The purpose of Les Chambrés, I explained to my son, was to save for coming generations what was left of the wisdom of the ancients that lay abandoned in the ruined repositories of that vanishing world. In much the same manner, wise men at previous end of days had gathered together all that was good and useful so as to save it for the future. The story of the Ark of the biblical Noah is a good example, I told him, which illustrates this idea. Les Chambrés was formed by our forebears, who thought of the creation of an Ark—in this case, the Ark of Memory.

Prince Idelfonso described to us, that evening at Château Beaumanoir, how a rivalry had grown between Les Chambrés and Rome during those centuries when faith grew to supplant science and reason in Europe. How zealous monks and rabid laity destroyed the great libraries and laid waste the academies and placed in infamy all that was considered by them to be heathen or being pagan in origin. Les Chambrés became even more esoteric and changed into what would be called today, a secret society. It searched out the learned, the erudite, they who were called idolaters and heretics, the keepers of the ancient oracles and the masters of the occult sciences, and brought them to safety, so that their work and accumulated knowledge would not be lost to the world. We, I explained to Adhémar, became the refuge of the wizards, a home for the Magi.

Les Chambrés scoured the abandoned ruins and devastated libraries for what was left over from the Classical period, and sent out travellers to distant lands in search of books, ancient scrolls and treatises and procured the expertise of Jewish philosophers, Moslem scholars and translators and Persian antiquarians from the scattered peoples of North Africa and Asia.

The collected works of the Greek classicists came to us before they were rediscovered in Toledo at the start of the twelfth century. Our scholars read *De Anima*, Aristotle's lost book on the soul, long before the theologians. We created new depositories and centres of learning in secret places. The first was in Spain, where centres of Islamic culture, in Toledo and Lisbon, already existed and were flourishing. These were the most civilised environments in the whole of Europe in the twelfth century. Masters of various disciplines worked together to produce a new generation of the truly educated who understood the benefits of a liberal, humane, sensible merging between the various faiths and peoples, a work that would produce a mutual syncretising of knowledge, of cultures and of faiths to benefit all.

Alas, this was not to be, I told my boy, as Prince Idelfonso related to us. With the reconquest of the Iberian Peninsula, all this ended and we were forced to seek survival elsewhere. We saw the Renaissance unfold, we were not taken by surprise. And when the Byzantine Empire fell, we were the beneficiaries of the best of its libraries, long before Còsimo di Giovanni degli Mèdici could lay his hands on them.

From one generation to the next, the fellowship elects its leader, described simply as "the Head," from amongst the descendants of the original fraternity. The leadership passes to the one, man or woman, who commands the greatest respect of his or her cohort, and is an individual often chosen in their early youth. We have never been a *Männerbund*, an all-male fraternity. This person is recognised by having particular qualities, the most significant being that of memory. The Head, together with other selected deputies, is Master of the *Ars Memoriae* and also *Maître du Temps*, who would familiarise himself or herself with the epochs of history, using techniques that those familiar with works such as the *Dialexis* would recognise, and in so doing improve Les Chambrés' archives both new and ancient, and add to it fresh discoveries sourced from the furthest corners of the world. We were the first of the truly secret societies. We have never fallen to the Vatican. They know of our existence, said the Prince, but they have never penetrated us.

The inner circle is where the oral tradition of the Les Chambrés rests, where the Art of Memory is practised and the Mastery of Time from generation to generation is maintained. Les Chambrés, over the centuries, has created centres of learning where the arts and sciences are taught. These have been given many different names. Concealment is our strength and we always hide ourselves under the name of other schools, orders and societies. On that fateful day when I first met Prince Idelfonso, he told us, as we sat together in the upper chamber of the north tower of Château Beaumanoir, that the time was now appropriate to recreate the lock with the distant stars. At the end of the century, he said, there would be a mere two hundred years left to the end of this age. The Equinox of the Gods would commence, and a new order of the ages would be inaugurated.

The prince went on to tell us that a scientific instrument known to mathematicians as a Polyhedron was kept in this house, Château Beaumanoir, here in Brittany, for more than six hundred years. This device expressed a formula that was the key to accessing another infinity, one which would redefine what the common people of the world call "God." This device was now to be removed in preparation for it to be taken to a new location. This was the purpose of the illustrious visitors coming to us at Château Beaumanoir.

I looked up into my grandfather's face that evening. Did this strange prince indeed know more about our house than we did ourselves? Judging from my grandfather's expression, it looked that way. Then, the Head of Les Chambrés arose from his seat and walked towards the eastern end of our hall, where he paused and looked outside the window that opened onto the garden where a large cromlech, weathered and cracked stood. These huge stones, forming a tall table of sorts, had been there from time immemorial, it was said that our earliest forefathers were buried beneath them. Silhouetted it stood, against a night sky that was magnificent with stars. "Observe," he exclaimed, his tone of voice youthful, "the ancient dolmen and the stars combine, to tell us where we shall find the one true stone that fell from heaven's vault which will become the cornerstone of Time." He then ordered all the lights in the room extinguished and as I watched I saw a faint sliver-like shaft of light appear upon the stone flags that brightened to look like an elongated shard of glass. Glancing outside I saw its source. A star, the evening star I was told, was positioned behind the great stone shapes and through a space between them this shaft of starlight beamed and rested, and was already fading. Then, with his cane he struck the old stone floor and declared:

"Commence the excavation here!"

The following day some of our neighbours came, dressed in their best. Again great deference was demonstrated. Meals were served with elaborate formality by the young women, the daughters of our neighbours, since we did not have any girls ourselves. That night all the men met again with my grandfather and father. They were joined by Bonabes, Marquis de Rougé, Baron Charles de la Barquerie, Pierre-Armand Tuffin and others whose names I do not know. They gathered together in the upper room of the north tower of Château Beaumanoir, and remained until morning talking amongst themselves. By the following midday they all departed. The atmosphere in our home changed after these mysterious visits. It became solemn, and a little sad.

The labour of excavating was far more difficult than previously supposed. The stone floor itself was quite worn, cracked in parts and not too difficult to remove. What lay beneath it was a different matter. After much clearing of dirt and rocks, some of huge proportions, a large, very large, perhaps larger than the hall itself, very cleverly constructed dome was partially revealed. It was made entirely of well-dressed stones, each very carefully placed one above the other, just a little forward of the one beneath. It was a great corbelled roof of antique masonry. I could see that it was of superb craftsmanship; a huge barrel that revealed a vast darkness within as we opened it from above.

To create an entrance sufficiently large to admit light took several weeks. A large portion of the external wall of the château was to be removed and cranes erected to hoist the huge blocks of stone out. My father, my grandfather and I entered this space some eight months after the work commenced. With several torches and lamps burning bright and clear, very many candles, some quite large and especially made for this occasion, we entered the room from above, which appeared to arch over in the style of very old Romanesque churches.

I knew very little then of architectural styles. But nevertheless I found the arches, which were supported by what I was told is called fan vaulting, finely proportioned and I admired the beautifully worked patterns cut into the stone of oak leaves and roses, lilies and laurel leaves.

About us, at our feet, surrounded by a decorative iron grating, were eight graves upon which were effigies of knights carved in stone. I was amazed at the existence of this vault or crypt, so huge. Among the graves, according to my elders, were two of our own ancestors. It was, my father whispered, a very holy place. In the distance, towards the end of the nave was a vaulted area that gave the impression of a large apse or semi-dome. At first sight, it appeared completely empty.

That day, no time was spent regarding the ancient graves. The lights were brought and arranged inside the apse at the end of the sepulchre. There stood, what appeared to me to be a plain white marble altar, or perhaps a tomb, comprised, it seemed, of one great stone. We walked around the altar, which was elaborately carved along its edges and inscribed with several groups of initials in an old-fashioned script, edged in gold. Upon this altar was a bouquet of withered flowers, very dry, but still hinting, in their greyness, at the colours that the blossoms once possessed. It was, however, the decorated glass and gold case upon it that caught my attention, as this contained some oddly-shaped objects.

The huge white marble altar was strangely fashioned. Its four upper corners appeared to be shaped like wings or elaborate horns. The vast bulk itself was raised by eight short, thick round columns with gilded capitals about a foot or less above the floor. Behind it, in the floor, there were parallel grooves lined with brass about two inches wide and several deep. They looked like rails emerging from beneath the tomb and running towards the wall behind it. My grandfather bent down to look at them closely, and then the three of us knelt down before the silent stone. My elders were apparently in prayer and in an awestruck state, but I stared about in ignorance and utter curiosity, inhaling ancient odours, imagining the last steps that would have echoed here so very long ago.

To have arrived thus far appeared to have exhausted both my father and grandfather, and to my surprise, we all withdrew through the crypt, up the ladder, and through the opening in the floor of our house above.

I was beside myself with questions. What was this amazing place, this holy place, this chapel or church beneath our house? Who were those knights? Which ones were of our family, and which of the others were great men of renown? Why were they put there? How long ago and why in such a secret place, and what was in the gold case? Who built that place, and when, and why? To my dismay, over the next several days my questions were ignored. It was not until the return of our visitors that I truly understood the reasons and purpose of this place beneath our house, and the role that I, François de Gurvand, from that day forward, would have to play with regard to the things contained in the secret sepulchre.

My grandfather, my father and I returned there some days later. This time the awe-inspiring nature of the place was not as overwhelming, although it did possess the same mysterious atmosphere and a sense of sacredness. With lamps held high, we stood before the graves. Some effigies of the fallen knights were depicted on a smaller scale than others. These lay in stone, carved to depict their dying, looks of agony frozen on stone faces, their postures, their limbs, the twisted mouths gaping, displaying open wounds and amputations. Even the creatures, dogs or great cats, their companions in arms, were displayed in postures of cruel death. "They all died in Prester John's land in Africa," my grandfather whispered.

"Prester John's land in Africa!" I breathed.

Of the two effigies of knights that were life-size, one was quite rigid in his stone coat of mail, his gauntleted hand clutching a huge sword to his chest. As I peered closely, I could see that this one was the older-appearing of the two, and that to my amazement he looked very much like my grandfather.

"Look, Papi, he looks just like you," I whispered.

My grandfather suppressed a chuckle. "That *gisant* is of Torson. He is the one who rode with Godfrey of Bouillon into Jerusalem." His voice echoed softly in the vastness of the space.

My grandfather pointed to an inscription carved upon a book of stone at the figure's feet. It was written in Latin, he translated it for me:

TORSON DE VURFANDUS

BORN 1075. DIED 1141 A.D.

COMPANION IN ARMS OF GODFREY,

ADVOCATUS SANCTI SEPULCHRI

KING OF JERUSALEM.

I looked long at the knight's face, the flickering lights giving motion and colour to the strong features of nose and brow and vast mustaches carved in grey stone.

"Vurfandus," whispered my grandfather, "is the Latin for Gurvand, *gisant* is an ancient word for the recumbent." The other stone-carved, life-size *gisant* was that of Torson's companion in death, who returned with him from the Crusade. The inscription read:

EUDES DE TRÉGUIER

BORN 1064. DIED 1137 A.D.

COMPANION IN ARMS OF GODFREY,

ADVOCATUS SANCTI SEPULCHRI

KING OF JERUSALEM.

Of the two effigies of knights, whose bodies were depicted twisted with the rigour of past agonies, and at whose feet lay the decapitated bodies of the leopards or ferocious dogs that had followed them into battle; one had his left arm thrown back and his right knee raised, his chain mail hauberk, carved in stone, with his helm shattered. The other held a great sword at his side, its hilt in his open right palm, his stone face a mask of pain inside the open visor, the armor on his chest carved in detail, showed the gashes and lacerations of battle. Their inscription read:

LES FRÈRES BONABES ET GEOFFROY

FILS DE LA MAISON ROUGE

COMPANIONS DES ARMES OF GODFREY,

ADVOCATUS SANCTI SEPULCHRI

KING OF JERUSALEM.

MORT AU PAYS DU PRÊTRE JEAN, AFRIQUE, 1109 A.D.

"And who are they, Papa?"

"Our kinsmen, of the Château Rouge," he whispered, "Come, there is work to be done."

The work that he was referring to was the most astounding event of my life. It was to alter my life forever. Arriving at the apse, my father removed the glass and gold case with a display of reverence and carefully placed it in an arched niche in the wall next to the altar. Then, to my surprise, he asked my father and I:

"Come, sons, assist me to remove this altar."

To my even greater surprise, the three of us were able to push this enormous stone all the way to the far wall. The grooves were indeed very precise rails fitted into the floor. Beneath was revealed a very finely made bronze door, with our armorial engraved, de Gurvand: *D'hermine à la bande fuselée azure;* there too was an inscription in Latin, which my grandfather translated:

HERE PUT BY ME

TORSON VURFANDUS IN 1134 A.D.

When I looked up from the bronze door, I saw the flowers disintegrate into a small coat of dust on the altar, occasioned by the motion of the stone.

We raised the trapdoor, finding a square cavity beneath. The paving stones around the opening were removable at three sides, and when we put them aside, and pointed our torches into the hollow, we saw a strange, pointed object, made of polished stone, a golden glass, shining but not reflective like a large jewel, beautiful and strange, precious, it looked to me, of unimaginable value. We erected a hoist and placed ropes under its corners into grooves that we found there, obviously made for that purpose. Using levers and counterweights, we hoisted with some difficulty this stone out of the compartment where it had lain since placed there by Torson, the long-dead crusader.

We had never seen anything like it in our lives. Some five feet tall, and wider than I was able to put my arms around, it shimmered in the torch light and emitted a glow of its own, white, but golden, the biggest diamond in the world, I would have wagered. It was covered with raised, flat, elongated shapes, facets, some square, some triangular, others of a peculiar design. They all came to a many-sided point at the top. The object itself stood perfectly flat on its base. Within it could be glimpsed other rectangular forms and triangular shapes, clearly discernible. It seemed to comprise two aspects, an inner and an outer. It was highly polished, smooth as glass and possessed a sense of being quite artfully finished. The whole thing was very beautiful, like a jewel, original and without flaw. It looked quite new. We carried it on rollers across the echoing floor, and with great care hoisted it up to our main hall, where a well-made wooden chest, clad with iron bands, was constructed to contain it.

Returning, we replaced the floor tiles, the bronze door and the altar to their original positions. My grandfather took the glass and gold box from the niche in the wall and handed it to my father; I peered inside and was able to make out what was in it: several rolls of yellowed parchment, held together with a dark thong, lay at an angle in the case. My grandfather opened it, took the five scrolls out, and handed them to me. They felt cool and somehow slightly damp, like new leather, and they were much heavier than I would have expected.

"Can I open one, Papi?" I whispered to my grandfather. He nodded.

"Yes, but you must be careful. They are very old and certainly most important."

I undid one of the ties and carefully unrolled a parchment, placing it on the tomb-like altar. We all looked at it in the lamplight, and I could see that it was inscribed with a small script, but none of us could read it.

112

The crystal stone, and the parchments excepted, my father and grandfather took great care to make sure that everything was replaced in the manner that we found them. Not even the wax droppings from the candles were left behind to show that we had been there. On our way out, we stopped to look at the fallen knights again, lying grotesquely about, and at the gaunt and rigid figure of Torson, the ancient crusader. It was the last time that I set foot in that mysterious place.

Over the weeks that followed, my elders discovered that the rolled sheets of parchment were written in the Amharic language of the east. Their meaning was revealed to us some months later with the return of the company who visited us previously. This time, we gathered in the hall of Château Beaumanoir as night fell. My father opened the great wooden chest that contained the mysterious object.

Prince Idelfonso explained to us that this crystal stone was a tool of the mathematicians, an instrument, known as a Polyhedron, and that this instrument was contrived by an antediluvian people, a high civilisation that once thrived before the biblical flood, long vanished from the face of the earth, made so as to retain for another time and people their most advanced science. This object was brought, when the last remnant of those people passed away, to the Holy City of Jerusalem. It was once amongst the treasures of King Solomon and rested beneath the Holy of Holies in a vault called the Well of Souls. From there it was carried away to the Land of *Presbyter Johannes* or Prester John, as medieval Europeans called the rulers of the kingdom of Aksum in distant Ethiopia. And it was brought to our house in the eleventh century, during the time of the crusades.

"*Novus Ordo Seclorum,*" said Prince Idelfonso. "A new order of the ages will be inaugurated from what is inscribed hereon."

In my own way I understood what he went on to tell us, which was that this marvel would bring a profound alteration in the manner in which we, humankind, perceive ourselves and the universe of which we are a part. New sciences will be developed from this, engendering an astonishing phase, a start, an original beginning, where there will be no Time as we understand it now, a reality, where only mind and its foster-child, thought, will exist, and we will be our own true image. All creation will be reflected in us, and when we travel into the stars, we will make a name for ourselves in all and everything we see.

The stars! He looked at us, at me! I suspected that the significance of all that he was saying could not be appreciated by the others who sat and stared. But in a strange way, I knew that he knew that I somehow understood of what he spoke because he could see that I could imagine it, see it in my mind.

He addressed me, looking at me with his large luminous eyes. "One day when you, François, have been prepared, you will be initiated into those secrets."

"Me, your Highness?"

"Yes," he smiled, "yes, you will be the one to place this wonder of the world in its right and proper place. The paradise long sought for, and in so doing, inaugurate the new order."

I felt all eyes in the room upon me, and for the first time in my life experienced the bite of fear in the pit of my stomach.

The prince cautioned us that great upheavals would soon come upon this kingdom, France: upheavals that would end the world we knew. That was why this valuable, indeed irreplaceable, scientific tool must be moved away very soon and kept safe, as a great catastrophe was about to take place.

Once again it was in danger of being lost to the world.

"The Polyhedron must be transported to the New World, to the Americas, to an island called *La Trinité*, for this island is 'The Land-in-Waiting,' anticipated by Saint Isidore of Seville," he proclaimed dramatically.

"It is at 10°north latitude, the same latitude as that of the place where it was once kept at a time so distant that it is inconceivable to imagine. It is the paradise long sought.

"For the *Novus Ordo Seclorum,* the new order of the ages would be inaugurated at the end of the second millennium," he emphasized, "at the passing of the age of Pisces that would signal the equinox. The promise that the House of Zion, the Holy City, 'Daughter Zion' Jerusalem, will be remade in the west, was foretold by Abbé Gioacchino da Fiore. Seneca wrote, '. . .when the Ocean Sea will loosen the connection of things, a great continent will emerge. . . then the Island of Thule will no longer be the last land.' This island, *La Trinité,* is beyond Thule, it is Ultima Thule!"

Here the Prince paused, and, taking a silver harp that was placed upon a chair near the one in which my mother sat, sang in a clear and youthful voice:

> *"Now comes the final era of the Sibyl's song;*
> *The great order of the ages is born afresh.*
> *And now justice returns, honoured rules return;*
> *Now a new lineage is sent down from high heaven."*

Our family was to continue being custodians of the Polyhedron, and all arrangements were made for my education to take a different turn and for us to travel and to settle in safety and comfort in the New World, so as to prepare for the next stage when "the great order of the ages would be born afresh."

Dawn was breaking over the eastern hills, as the roosters competed with each other in melancholic choruses. The morning air quite chill, as it is at times in the tropics. My son, I could see, was now asleep. I sincerely hoped that the relating of this story on that starry night had touched him. Naturally not in the same manner as the actual experience affected me, but sufficiently to bring to him an understanding that he was not the same as the others of his age and of this place. At the very least, that was my, if the truth be told, most fervent prayer.

8:

1797. Vincent Patrice,

Le Vénérable Maître.

"Up with the main," I said quietly to the boy, Vargas. *Helveticu*s leaned away from the gentle south-easterly, her sheets creaking in their winches as she picked up the cool light air, the morning's pink turning suddenly to a gilt-edged dragon red in the eastern sky.

Red in the morning, the shepherd's warning, I thought to myself automatically. "Yes, red in the morning."

"What you say, Massa Vincent?" asked Robert, who was at the helm taking me to Chacachacare, an island in the Dragon's Mouth.

"Looks as if rain might come," I answered.

Robert glanced at me from across the deck. He saw my troubled look, I'm sure, contained in a distant stare. "Take up that line in the water, boy," he said sharply to Vargas, the Carib half-caste youth, now in my service.

He looked once more at me, and I could guess his thoughts. His master, he must be thinking, is setting out on a dangerous course, this I knew he knew, and he must be on his guard. The men I would meet at Mr. Carige's island were from the Spanish Main. He knew well that the conversations that would occupy the next few days would be about a revolution to liberate the Spanish colonies of America, would be about what we call the rights of man, of liberty and equality for all, for him, for them. They, whom he knew would always be more equal than he.

"Ah, white people business," Robert murmured to himself, his thoughts already carried away on the light air.

I looked across the placid water towards the pale blue island to which we sailed. It seemed to hover in the distance; enskied, as there was no discernible horizon. The western sky, paler than the sea, was washed a clear, clean blue all the way to Venezuela.

I was to meet Manuel Gual. I must now hear for myself. Gual has failed. España—God only knows where. This was so secondhand. I was in this outpost. The real refinement of ideas far from me. Someone once said, "Sons of liberty. Brothers for freedom. Are we not all rational, gentlemen?" Ironic.

We, I, must remember that the ideals and purpose of this Work is freedom from the altar and the throne, from Europe, in the Americas. That is the end. The means? Whichever. The furtherance of this undertaking was already decided in the highest conclave. I was there. All Entered Apprentices must now be carefully selected. They must be literate, damn it, educated, and be known for their fervent love of freedom and absolute commitment to the cause of South American independence.

The Degrees of Master and Mark Master must now be conferred judiciously, solely on those who actually understand the political implications of the oaths and obligations of those Degrees. This ideology must be seen to provide a different vocabulary. They must grasp the meaning, which gives preponderance to the republican cause in South America. The Work is everything. They must be prepared to die for the revolution.

François. I cannot think about him today.

Port-d'Espagne. A dozen wood fires sending up spirals in the morning air, still, still. On the Laventille hills, I could see the observatory, built by Governor Chacón for the royal astronomer Don Cosme Damián de Churruca y Elorza's observations. François and I had made the same observations that Don Cosme would make the year before he came to Trinidad. I never imagined François as an astronomer or a mathematician, as though trained for the task. We did that together, François wanted to, it was important to him, he was prepared for the experiment, he owned the instruments. We saw eye to eye then.

The shape and position of this island, Trinidad, makes it a place where the four cardinal directions meet. He said. We established the sixty-third meridian of longitude and confirmed that the island was just $10°$ north of the equator. "Perfection," François said. "An island on the square. Possessed of four almost equal sides, each side facing, respectively, east, west, north and south, the entire island on the square. Perfection, paradise found, Vincent. paradise found," were the words used by François. "Why perfection? What do you mean, paradise found?" I asked. He never answered.

I must not think about François today. I wish he would go. Leave.

A flight of ibis suddenly rose from the nearby mangrove, startlingly loud, in their thousands, garish, flamboyantly scarlet.

In the distance another flock appeared like a mile-long bruise in the gentle sky. The receding mangrove coastline that would become Port-d'Espagne proper in just a few years, now blurry in the morning mists, mingled with the wooded foothills to meet the high forested mountains of the Sainte Anne, Maraval and Diego Martin valleys. This island's smell, different from the others to the north, was one of hot molasses and warm rum from the warehouses and distilleries. Out here in the Gulf of Paria those aromas merged with mangrove rot and the mammalian fresh water smells of the monk seal, manatee and whale, dolphin and the deep ocean leather-backed turtle. All islands smell different.

The ideals that would shape the Constitution for the Atelier La Gran Réunion Americana was forged by Francisco de Miranda in London some eight years before its erection and consecration. We gathered in de Miranda's rooms on Grafton Street, Mayfair, in 1790. I had travelled to England on my father's business. To us, de Miranda expressed his conviction that reason and will should be the hammer and the chisel of a relentless creator shaping a future of our own selection. "Thus, we shall repudiate and combat all tyrants and tyrannies," these were his words upon greeting his guests that evening. My God, I was amazed.

I almost spoke aloud. Glancing across to Robert, I saw him impassive. Francisco de Miranda that night appeared in the room into which we were ushered, its ceilings remarkably higher than the ante-room Filled with light, its source impossible to discern, it contained thousand of books. There were large terrestrial and celestial globes, made, I discovered, by the genius of Emery Molyneux. Beautifully crafted brass microscopes, barometers, clocks, sundials, sand and water clocks, magnets, an armillary sphere, huge, an astrarium, shining brass sextants, a spherical astrolabe, an antique torquetum. An orrery, crafted by the Master George Graham, a wonderful mechanical apparatus that demonstrated the relative positions of the planets and moons in the solar system in a heliocentric model. Levels, crucibles, tracing boards and compasses, a trestle table, an ebony mallet, a foundation stone, an altar and two ionic-capped, fluted columns that were inscribed in gold with the letters J and B respectively. He spoke to us of the ordered universe. The treatise of Sir Isaac Newton which proclaims that the purpose of the mechanical and experimental philosophy was to contemplate the works of The Great Architect, to discover causes from their effects and make art and nature subservient to the necessities of life.

Upon the sideboard lay heavy golden collars, chains, aegises and jewelled insignia of knights and princes of ancient orders, some famous, others, we were told, esoteric. There were gauntlets and beautifully illustrated aprons, antiques made from lamb skin and embroidered in gold, displaying ritual objects. There were swords, hallowed in the eyes of the brave, which were raised in the battle of the White Mountain. There were letters patent and the royal charters of orders, some of which were antecedent to the Garter and the Golden Fleece.

Lodge La Gran Réunion Americana, he told us, would be in direct descent of illustrious traditions that, through centuries, were the architects of edifices reflective of mankind's endeavour to find himself in the image of the Great Architect: to enshrine the best ideals, to maintain universal truths. How fortunate I felt to be there.

The wind now quickened, we were swiftly approaching the Bocas del Dragón, a series of straits separating the Gulf of Paria from the Caribbean Sea, an archipelago in miniature, a scattering of small islets, like stepping stones to the southern continent, the Spanish Main, Terra Firma. I took the helm as Robert saw to the foresail. A dangerous passage named by Christopher Columbus in a moment of peril. The First Boca, Boca Monos. The strait between the island of Monos, isle of apes, and Trinidad's north-western peninsula, tricky with crosswinds that could suddenly fail, leaving the sailor to drift with the current on to rocks, from which arose a forest of gigantic growth, so thickly packed. I glanced about, my reverie carrying me away. In the distance I could see scarlet ibis and flamingos, tens of thousands, filling the south-western sky, and ahead, Monos, verdant in the morning sunlight.

The Americans, John Adams, a lawyer, who followed George Washington as President of the United States, Colonel William Smith, and Alexander Hamilton, now the first United States Secretary of the Treasury; my word—these men were there with us. Manuel Gual, a friend of de Miranda's youth, an *hidalgo* from a wealthy Caracas family; his father, Don Mateo, commanded at La Guaira when the English attacked that place in the year 1743. Bernardo O'Higgins, a Chilean, destined for greatness, and I from Castries, Sainte Lucie, were all invited to de Miranda's home.

Francisco de Miranda had recently returned from France. His physical presence, striking. He had been imprisoned by "the Terror", the Committee of Public Safety ordering his arrest in July. He was forty or so, the type of intellectual, I would come to understand, whom revolution turns into a military leader. He had helped to compile the report signed by "the Provincialist" that was sent to the National Assembly. He had stirred up artists and peasants and moved easily from the political clubs and secret societies to command troops in in Belgium and on the Rhine. Political intrigue had caused his imprisonment. He was a follower of Condorcet, skilled in ancient and modern languages, and was able to take with him into gaol the works of Isaac Newton, Jean Desaguliers and Stephen Gray, he told us.

I wrote to my father, whose friend, General Juan de Cajigal y Monserrat, under whom de Miranda served while he was in the Spanish army, recommended me to de Miranda, and I tried my best, in my response to my father's request, to capture the personality of this great man, whom historians would describe as the First Universal Creole:

"Sebastián Francisco de Miranda was born in the city of Caracas, capital of the Captaincy General of Venezuela, on March 28th, 1750," I wrote to my father. "He is the eldest son of the Canary-Spanish Sebastiáen de Miranda y Ravelo and Francisca Antonia Rodriguez y Espinoza. His father came from Las Palmas de Gran Canaria of a merchant family. De Miranda has travelled to North America, to England, to Europe. His education is immense, his manner very imposing. His style courtly, in spite of his coming from a merchant family, his features bold and sensual. For more than half his life, he has proclaimed liberty and equality for South America and travelled through Europe from court to court, visiting those princes not in support of Bourbon Spain. His knowledge of the conduct of war and the organisation of states, of morals and ethics has been derived from the classics. On his travels through Europe he carried with him the collected works of Virgil and Cicero. He has read Racine, Voltaire, Rousseau, and is familiar with the writings of Goethe, with whom he has conversed; he knows men of great power. Father," I wrote in parentheses, "he is a Spanish-American of great consequence—he is possessed of the confidence of his fellow citizens whose political aspirations he can express in English, Spanish, French, Italian and High German. He is aspiring to deliver the Americas, to liberate us. The New World produced its archetypal man in South America.

"He has committed decades of his life to the judicious comprehension of the affairs of states; the origination, advance, and termination of various forms of government; the conditions that bring together and hold together diverse sectors of civil society; and the events through which these societies could be broken down and be consumed by others. I have never met anyone who possesses such capacity to motivate those who surround him, and with such ease. I have found my mentor, my teacher, my master. This man will shape my life."

I was awed by his ideas, at his accomplishments. His collection of rare manuscripts and ciphers. He is an intimate of the Fellows of the last guild of Worshipful Accepted Alchemists at Prague, whose meeting place is in a timbered house next door to the synagogue where the Gollum is kept. His travels have taken him to the Holy Land and to Mesopotamia. He has lived in Russia, a guest of Prince Potemkin. A Lothario, he is reputed to be, and said to have been a lover of Catherine the Great. Last night he taught us to play *lansquenet*, a favourite at that court.

De Miranda told us that he received Masonic Light at the Lodge that meets at Tun Tavern in Philadelphia, Saint John's No. 1 Lodge, in 1783; General Gilbert du Motier, Marquis de Lafayette, was his Principal Recommender. He was passed to the Degree of Fellow-Craft in London in 1785, and raised to the Sublime Degree of Master Maçon in Paris in 1790. He is presently Grand Knight Commander of The Most Worthy Lodge of Rational Knights of Lautaro. Lautaro was chosen in homage to the Araucanian leader who defeated the Spanish Conquistador Pedro Gutiérrez de Valdivia in 1554. He would be, in time, the Grand Master of Lodge La Gran Réunion Americana.

My father provided me with a gentleman's wardrobe: formal suits, overcoats, silk stockings, a wig, slippers, riding boots, rapier, pistols, a black gelding called Captain and a letter of credit drawn on our factor, C. Lloyd Traveline of Berkeley Square.

The oaths sworn that night in London undertook to define the creation of entire peoples, new nations, forms of government and administrations, the application of laws, the governance of judiciary, the constitutions of unborn republics, the political organisation of an entire continent, not meant to evolve through centuries but to appear whole and complete with civic power invested in the people themselves. The republic. To institutionalise it into existence, for me the Great Work, *Ars Magna*, commenced.

Boca de Huevos, the second strait between Monos and Huevos. The island of Huevos in the Dragon's Mouth, named for the ocean-going turtles that lay their eggs there, was golden with poui trees as we sailed past. The boy Vargas asleep in a coil of rope. Robert, his hat turned sideways to shade his face, his hand steady at the helm. I noticed that we were joined by a large school of dolphins that leapt in groups of six or ten in synchronisation with the motion of the boat. Towards the south of us a whale breached the surface of the Gulf that was once named for its species. There were others, a dozen or more, giants, their v-shaped blow indicating their genus. This so reminded me of the Grenadines, when I was a boy in Sainte Lucie and would accompany my father, who was the owner of schooners, to Carriacou and Grenada, then to Barbados, Tobago and as far south as to Trinidad.

In the weeks that followed my arrival in London we were raised as Masters, having been initiated into The Most Worthy Lodge of Rational Knights of Lautaro. We expressed fervent love for the freedom of the Americas and for the cause of independence. At the end of our oaths and obligations, we, the newly raised Master Maçons of this Lodge, stated a special clause, which ended with the phrase with which we were greeted on arrival at Grafton Street: "Thus, I shall repudiate and combat all tyrants and tyrannies." The elevation was on account of the journeys that we were about to undertake. We were to be instructed in a new system of Freemasonry described as Strict Observance, its name derived from the oath it demands, an oath of unswerving, unquestioning obedience to the Ascended Masters. The basic tenet of the Strict Observance was that it proceeded directly from the Knights Templar, who survived the purge of knights in 1307 to 1314 and perpetuated their order in the highlands of Scotland.

At night, we spoke of the ideals of equality and Masonic Harmony, and of striving to perfect the individual whose destiny is to evolve by the aid of reason and science to enlightenment, and be forever freed from fear and doubt. We heard of Karl von Hund, Nicolas Fatio de Duillier, the mathematician, the work of Jean Desaguliers, and of Cagliostro, the Grand Copht who saw Freemasonry as the supreme good for the world.

These orders into which we were initiated introduced higher Degrees than those offered by other Masonic systems. They contained greater and more powerful mysteries. They established a connection between Freemasonry, alchemy, kabalism and hermetic thought, regarded in those days as Rosicrucian.

In the months that followed, I lived in the house of Francisco de Miranda, heard and saw first-hand the Great Work in progress for the emancipation of the continent. I came to know the young American Colonel Samuel Smith, son-in-law of John Adams, whom I described in a letter to my father as a friend of the rights of mankind and the happiness of society. Francisco de Miranda placed in my hands the articles of freedom, the declaration of the Rights of Man and of the Citizen. Francisco thought me, I wrote, "ingenious and intrepid, dedicated to the cause of equality and liberty, committed to the overthrow of the French and Spanish thrones and the dissolution of their empires in the Americas."

"I want you, Vincent, to return to Castries," he told me one night at dinner. "The Charter of Les Frères Unis must be transferred to Trinidad in the event of war there. The revolution in France will reverberate in the islands. Every Maçon there could be killed in the coming conflict. Trinidad will be relatively safe, and will become the staging post for the invasion of the continent. The work of Philippe Roume, such as it was, has succeeded, a population is established, commerce will thrive. There is a basis upon which the Craft can survive and function on the island, which is vital for when the struggle for liberation commences. You must prepare a way." I looked into the eyes of my master and bowed with reverence.

"You will work closely with François de Gurvand. He too is an ally and a man who commands the loyalty of many."

"I believe the English will soon have that island," said Colonel Smith.

"There will be war between England and Spain. You are to place yourself at the disposal of our comrades in Venezuela. The work that Manuel," Francisco glanced at Manuel Gual, "will continue and complete is that which was undertaken by his father Mateo and others. You are to take this, Manuel," he passed his hand over a large pile of gold coins, "with you, and hand it to José María España. Three thousand muskets and three thousand sabers—more later." He regarded me.

"For you, my Brother Vincent, my best wishes."

De Miranda did not smile as he rose.

"Come, Smith, we must prepare for Mr. Pitt." They left the room, arm in arm.

"What gives François de Gurvand the power to command the loyalty of others?" I asked Manuel.

Manuel Gual, who sat across the table from me, shrugged and smiled a boyish, somewhat crooked grin, despite his fifty odd years.

"The habit of command, the tone of fine manners, and the confidence of an aristocrat, and we believe it and accept it."

"What is the most valuable thing he possesses?"

"His bloodline. He and his son, they are the last of his house."

Candle flames burning low in silver candelabra, their reflections in the dark shine of the dining table shimmered as they sparkled in the facets of the cut glass goblets and decanters, to become refracted on the rich mahogany, a spectrum of colour in elongated checkered patterns of light. The wary roses, too, reflected the intimacies of their disarray amongst the shining salt cellars and dishes: amidst the remains of the conversation, an unrolled map of the Antilles, Trinidad, Margarita, Paria, New Grenada—Venezuela. A stack of gold coins, neatly arranged. A letter to José María España embossed with the signet of Francisco de Miranda. That was the last time I saw Manuel Gual.

Boca de Navios. The ship's passage, the strait between Huevos and the island of Chacachacare. We had sailed away from the coast of Trinidad, its blue northern mountains receding eastward like a finger pointing at the now risen sun. The wind quickened. Morning was a bowl of light. The sea rose and fell about us, bright green. Sheets of light and wind and water. The smaller islands now behind, the mountains of Paria on the Venezuelan Mainland dominated the western sky ahead. Los Patos island, named for geese, deserted, a place for pirates and duels. In the distance, the Boca Grande that separates Chacachacare island from the Paria peninsula of Venezuela, where South America begins. The Andes.

The island of Chacachacare, Mr. Carige's island, called El Caracol, the snail, by Columbus. Made famous by Sir Walter Raleigh, its iron pyrite cliffs had fooled him, "All that glisters is not gold; often have you heard that told: Many a man his life hath sold . . ."

Robert took the boat directly into the centre of Coco Bay, wide and placid, where the sharply rising hills reflected themselves.

"Helm's-a-lee, ease that sheet boy, release the throat halyard," Robert said to Vargas sharply. "Down with the main."

The boat tacked over to the wooden jetty that stood out from a sandy pebbly beach. The fore-sail already down, the main fell, clattering on to the wooden decking.

"All right, Vargas, drop the anchor here and she will come about."

I spoke to him in Spanish. The boy smiled and jumped to it.

"Well, you know we will be here for a day or two," I smiled at Robert.

"Yes, yes! Massa Vincent." Robert was arranging for what was going ashore. "I'll look for Pappits and go'n catch some fish."

He stood up. The boat moved silently.

"You fishing too, Massa?"

I actually thought about it for a moment. "Yes. I hope I have the right bait."

The Irishman's dogs were barking on the jetty, setting the digesting pelicans into lazy flight. He arrived on the beach with two muskets and three Negroes armed with machetes. They were followed by a thin, red-skinned man, Geraldine Carige's foreman, a Barbadian freedman called Pappits.

"Ah, Vincent. On the lookout for you since yesterday!"

Geraldine Carige was a large man with a small, balding head, bushy red side whiskers, freckled all over, and of a very fair complexion even after living at this latitude for almost half his life.

"Come, come, come! Leave all that. Quashy will take care of it."

Carrie, as he was called by everyone, had given his name to the island, Chac-chac, meaning cotton in an unknown Amerindian dialect, for his crop, and Carrie a version of his name, Chacachacare, Carige's cotton island. He strode onto the jetty and took my hand, pulling on it to bring the boat in closer.

"We have visitors," he boomed.

"Morning Geraldine. I hope you have fried jacks this morning for breakfast."

"But of course."

The boat rose on a slight swell and I stepped on to the jetty.

"Take care of everything, Master Pappits!" called Carige, for already the boat was being unloaded.

"How sick is he?"

"Sick," said Carige. "He must have been in that boat for more than two weeks."

"Yes? What happened to them?"

"Don't know. He hasn't said a word except something about Guevare y Vasconcelos and the Hermandad. He's hardly making sense. Santiago Mariño, Santiago's son, saved him. Found him drifting. Come. He'll be glad to see you though."

The hacienda Monte de Botella overlooked acres of cotton and tobacco, except for where the island's former giant *ceiba pentandra* forest stood fast. Geraldine Carige had left them standing in copses and in rows or sometimes like solitary sentinels between his cotton fields. The tobacco grown on his habitation was considered to be the best enjoyed anywhere. The island was his. It had been presented to him by His Most Catholic Majesty, Charles III of Spain.

We took the stone steps that rose quickly from the beach, through the forest of manchineel trees, sending flocks of ramier flying, to arrive at the wide wood and stone house that stood on tall square columns made of yellow ballast blocks. A complete arch of finished lime-stone supported two flights of steps leading to a wide grey and white tiled gallery, hung with hammocks and filled with the baggage, paraphernalia and devices of travellers. A young Venezuelan lass, very pretty, was cleaning the firing mechanisms of a pair of pistols at an iron table. There was the smell of breakfast and the voices of women speaking Spanish and French with shrill, lazy accents coming from the back of the house.

"He is here," said Carige, motioning me to the shady side of the gallery. He hadn't noticed that Manuel Gual was standing at the main door.

"Manuel, Manuel . . ." he said, surprised.

"Manuel," I said, taking the thin, dry, hot hand. I looked at him, his skin received its outlines from his bones.

"Vincent."

We embraced with warmth, a Brotherly greeting.

"Vincent, Vasconcellos, that ass, is trying to kill me. He very nearly did. I almost died. The place is in confusion. They have José España . . . Vasconcellos . . ."

"You have to speak slowly, Manuel," I told him. "You're tired, you're sick. You have a very hot fever. You don't look well. Just stop for a while. I am here, we will talk. We will talk. Just come, and lie down."

"I cannot."

A tall, delicately featured, lightly coloured young woman, wearing the costume of the French islands, entered the room. Her name, I learnt, was Henriette Céleste, she was the child of Diego Meany and was reared in his household by his sister, Helena. She carried a tray with mugs of coffee, slices of pawpaw and zaboca, fried carite, crispy salted jacks and fresh bread. She was followed by a beautiful Spanish woman dressed liked a gypsy sojourning in the Caribbean, taller than imaginable and possessed of a languid grace that did not manage to disguise a dramatic temperament. This beautiful woman was Geraldine Carige's wife María de Ortega, daughter of the Marquis Felipe Díaz de Ortega Bustillo y Gonzaga. I kissed her hand.

"This is our gunsmith, Vincent, my granddaughter, María Concepción Mariño, she is my daughter Atanacia's child, she has become our, ah, arms specialist." Geraldine Carige was serious. I regarded the young woman's eagle visage: Scheherazade reassembling Mortimer's hair-triggers. Such an intense countenance, her black eyebrows went straight across her brow with the finality of the underlined, she rose, laying aside the pistols and the firing mechanisms. Wiping her hands on her skirts, she stepped forward to greet me. I bowed before a true American beauty as she curtsied with a girlish charm, her black eyes never leaving my own until the very last moment, even then they contained a hint of, what? A dagger's glancing strike.

"Her brother Santiago Mariño, my grandson." Carige continued, "It was he who found Manuel drifting in the Gran Boca and brought him here." The youngster, tall, sunburnt, red haired. He bowed formally.

"Master."

"None of that here," said Geraldine.

"Not at all," I said and embraced the young man, taller than myself. He must be familiar with the Craft, I thought. "How is your father? When I heard the name mentioned I became confused. Your father . . ?"

"My father, God willing, is well, he will soon be here."

"Caballeros, breakfast is on the terrace."

Santiago Mariño was in his mid-teens, with a lean, hard frame, remarkably fine features and unnerving bright blue eyes. He was a Creole of the island of Margarita whose family was well-connected in Caracas to the older colonial families. These, as his own, had joined the de Tovars, Palacios, Rodriguezes, and Bolívars in support of Alfredo de Leon and Mateo Gual, Manuel's father, a decade earlier in a movement to overthrow Spanish rule in the Americas.

"Santiago, come. Tell me, what has happened?"

We walked, the young man and I, one hand on his shoulder, out to the terrace. The others followed and a moment later, Geraldine's wife brought lemonade and glasses, saying that

Don Manuel had refreshed himself and would be joining us for breakfast.

Santiago leaned on the iron banister, gripping it with both hands. He looked out to the horizon where the high blue mountains of the Andean cordillera met the Caribbean Sea. Directly beneath us, the black sand of the almost circular La Tinta Bay marked a dark crescent shadow around the bright green and placid bay.

The young man spoke rapidly in Spanish, flavoured with the Patois of the Caribbean coast. He described what I already knew. The collapse of the Spanish authority; their loss of credibility in the eyes of a wide range of their subject people; social changes being enforced, such as the inclusion of the Coloureds into the militia.

"Imagine, Master Vincent. Negroes with swords and golden epaulets, and Pardo women wearing mantillas in church. We now have to address them and bow and call them 'Don'." He snorted and wiped his nose with the back of his hand. "Excuse me, Master. The imperial government is in pursuit of popular support. It has stripped away the various taboos of the established order. You can buy your way into society. The Bejarano Negresses are now to be considered whites according to the law."

The young man laughed in his disbelief. The others joined us on the terrace, arranging themselves about a large round iron table.

So many aspects of Spanish royal policy in this period served to antagonise the opinion of the native Spanish Creoles. The Free Coloureds or Pardos, as far as the upper classes were concerned, carried the ignominious origin of slavery and the sinful disgrace of illegitimacy. Santiago argued, speaking loudly, that if these persons were elevated from their inferior status, they would be eligible for public offices, now reserved for whites, among other things, and would be able to occupy them without impediment, mixing on an equal basis with whites and leading persons of great distinction.

"Sitting in the forward pews in the church, Master," he said.

There is a great contradiction here, I thought to myself, these Venezuelans want a republic that's only for the white upper classes.

"Next to your sister," I said. "There is no need to refer to me as 'Master', Santiago, there will be time enough for that later on when you are older."

"Thank you, Señor Vincent. I will be old enough very soon, I will come prepared for what lies ahead of me."

I looked at him, and thought yes, he has it in him. This is confusion, though. It is caused by these conflicts, especially against the background that those most offended by the advancement of the lower classes are the very ones most vociferous and at the forefront of the call for liberty, freedom and equality. Some may not be what they appear to be.

The presence of the African race will define the western world. It was the Spaniards who, after the *reconquista* and the expulsion of the Moors and the Jews, developed the notion of the purity of the blood, *limpieza de sangre*. This they transferred to the colonies in the New World, thus bringing into being an insidious evil. Racial or any other prejudice has no place in Masonry. Outside of the Church, Freemasonry is the only institution now extant where there are none, or hardly any distinctions, all free men may sit as equals, and where roles in the profane world may be indeed reversed, the village cobbler becomes the Master of the Lodge. The Lord of the Manor, the Entered Apprentice. Young Santiago exemplifies the challenge of the age.

"Señor Vincent! The sale of position is odious," he continued, "and the *peninsulares* simply involve themselves in a shameless catering to the one aspect of society, and in fact, reflect the fear and alarm caused by the recent massacre of whites at the hands of the slaves in Santo Domingo."

"I have heard it said," said Carige, "that some of the mulattoes on that island, whose fathers were still alive, made agreements with each other, 'You kill my father and I will kill yours'."

"Señor, it is extremely alarming, the insurrection of the slaves of Coro, they have devastated the countryside. The blacks murdered hundreds of people, the children, the old, they burnt everything," said Santiago.

"And was justice more than swift?" asked Carige. "Were dozens hanged?"

"And the leaders?" I enquired.

"Of those, only José Leonardo Chirinos, a zambo, was taken to Caracas, dragged through the streets, then beheaded," answered Santiago, with disgust.

"His hands were chopped off," he continued, after spitting dexterously over Carige's head where he sat. "His head was placed in an iron cage on a pole more than twenty feet high on the cocoa road, and his hands were placed on the spot on top of a hill where Don José de Tellería was murdered."

"These uprisings, are they spontaneous slave and peon rebellions?" I asked.

"Yes. The more organised rebellion, our rebellion, can now take hold. It will represent a different kind of movement for liberty. The evolution of the continent towards wider forms of justice and integration is possible. But we need the slave uprisings, the popular uprisings, to distract Captain Vasconcelos. The work done by Don Manuel and Don José María España and others will continue, in spite of setbacks. I know that, Master Vincent." So intense was he, this last was delivered to the distant Mainland mountains.

Manuel was now at my side. I took his hot hands in my own. He immediately snatched them away. I said: "Encouraged and supported by Francisco de Miranda, we were guided by our own instincts and fortified by oaths taken, and acted in the solidarity generated by the Brotherhood. Brother Gual's movement was the first to declare independence, categorically proposing a democratic system for the political organisation of the entire continent."

"Manuel," said Carige, "come, sit."

"Thank you, compañero. I will take the hammock."

Tall and gaunt, skin red, burnt by a dozen noonday suns, Manuel Gual's peeling, grey-grizzled head and face stood out from the large starched white shirt that he had borrowed from Geraldine Carige. It was he who issued the provincial ordinances that declared the natural equality of all the inhabitants of the provinces and districts and proclaimed that the greatest accord should exist between whites, Indians, Pardos, Free Coloureds and even the Negroes, all brothers in Jesus Christ and equals before God. He then abolished payment of tribute by the Indians and pronounced slavery ended as contrary to humanity.

"José María España christened it 'the revolution of the people'," shouted Manuel. "Its commanders were instructed to issue orders in the name of the American people. Its objectives: the restoration of liberty to all American people."

His breath came in gasps and he stared about him, already he appeared very old, he started to cough, caught himself, and spat with surpassing aim into a tub of flowering geraniums. He continued hoarsely.

"This movement, inspired by the French Revolution, proposed equality, considered always to have existed, therefore it did not need to be established, but declared. For the same reason liberty was restored to the people."

These notions were still so original, I thought to myself, that even after they had become common usage in the last three or four years, they still managed to evoke alarm and surprise in the minds of the speakers and the hearers after a thousand years of feudalism.

"We surpassed the French, de Miranda, he prophesied we would, Vincent, remember?" rasped Gual. "We want all citizens to live in congruity as brothers before Jesus Christ. Equals before God."

He looked hard at me.

"We surpassed the North Americans because of our readiness to extend natural equality not only to whites but also to Indians and Negroes. We demanded that the punishment of Juan Francisco de Leon be recalled. And even the priest, Father Terrero, spoke out."

He brought the flat of his hand down hard upon the side table, near to which the hammock was hung.

The near noon sounds of the cicadas seemed to harmonise with the sea's nearly silent sigh in the shingle of La Tinta Bay below.

"They, the Inquisition, declared us subversive and heretical, sacrilegious, blasphemous for saying that men were born free and all are equally noble since they are formed from the same dough and are created in the image and likeness of God. The Hermandad network of spies infiltrated us."

His voice, now loud, achieved echo. The household, grown silent. The air still. The gardeners quiet. No breeze stirred as the earth turned carefully towards the new millennium.

"Pédro Carbonell understood. He was a truly noble man. He knew we spoke from the conscience of the primordial world."

Gual's eyes filled suddenly with tears.

"He was the last true Captain General." He again spat into the tub of geraniums. "Guevara y Vasconcelos is the son of a Tenerifeian whore. It was he who ordered the death of the patriots and the confiscation of their ancestral land. Manuel Piar is in Trinidad, you must help him, Vincent."

"I promise. Manuel, come, come. Compose yourself. Have some lemonade," I offered.

Manuel stared at me, took the glass that I offered and drank it in one gulp, then hurled it into the manchineel forest below.

"They hanged them and quartered them and sent their limbs to La Guaira and Macuto. They sent Antonio Duarte de Zaa's wife to gaol! Vincent, she was pregnant! A woman like her, of her quality, family. She, possessed of such dignity. They have sentenced her to eight years in the Casa de Misericordia. Vincent, the others are dead. Dead!"

"I know my friend, I know," I whispered.

"I took the first chance I got. An Irish Brother, Downie, in the gaol made some keys. Not daring to hand them out, he left them where one of the prisoners from Spain, one Juan Piconell, could see them. I do not know by what means he got them in hand, but that night we were breathing free air.

The wife of de la Rosa, the Canary islander, got Piconell on a Danish whaler as a stowaway. The turnkey, a black man from Coro, got me into a fishing boat, an old pirogue with piece of a sail, no oars, a little water, no food. To get away from La Guaira in the night was easy. It was the next nineteen days that was hell. Thank God it rained on some nights. If it was not for Santiago, I would be dead."

He looked about him as someone startled, staring past us.

"And Vasconcelos has sworn to kill me, Vincent. He has dispatched a poisoner, sacred mother of God."

He glanced about him, his thin frame shaking inside the overly large, starched stiff white shirt. His eyes sunken and yellow, his grey stubbled cheeks burnt red and hollow from teeth that had fallen out. A line of spittle was running from the corner of his mouth while his hands made meaningless gestures. The fear of death was upon him. That night, Manuel Gual came near to death from a combination of fear, exhaustion, dehydration, a broken rib perhaps, and certainly a broken heart. I sat at his side, in his delirium he called out loud and stared with sightless eyes, I thinking that this was surely a death watch. As dawn's left hand was in the sky, myself and Robert set sail for Port-d'Espagne to find Father Hubertus Magneval in the hope that the medical knowledge of this priest might save Manuel Gual.

9:

1797. Manuel Gual,

Fate's Hostage.

Father Hubertus Magneval sighed as he sipped his bowl of coffee and rubbed the black grey stubble on his rugged face. He was sitting in his presbytery's small upstairs gallery. The anguish in the voice that he heard the other night, Adhémar de Gurvand's, had horrified him. He too had listened to the young man's screams coming from that house with the three lamps. This was followed by the howling of dogs, and the sounds of someone running through the night. Then silence. The following day he went in search of the lad, but he did not find him. He sought François, who did not receive him.

In angry frustration, he had stood beneath François' window at the back of the house, across the street from the grass market, and called loudly, angrily for him to come out. After several minutes of shouting, which served only to attract the slaves of the house as well as passersby, he gave up, striding away, angrily contemplating throwing stones at the closed windows.

"What the devil is going on?"

The story that Adhémar was thrown after Caballero's funeral filled him with a sense of outrage. He sought the boy. His own knowledge of medicine was considerable, acquired by years of dealing with the various accidents, murder attempts, illnesses, and the multiple mutilations by which people wounded themselves and each other in this godforsaken place.

"To be dismissed by old Mayotte at the door, to have been refused by François, well, there is more to this. Hmm! The work of the Devil," he muttered.

He stared out across the Plaza, fanning himself with a square rattan fan. From the back gallery he could see Símon Agostini's house, the three lamps hanging in the sunlit upstairs gallery.

"They have maimed the boy. My God!" he said out loud.

A large, boisterous flock of parrots now rushed into a tall bushy palmiste palm in the presbytery's garden, from where they regarded him while making a wild raucous racket of squawks, chuckles and hoots. He thought them insolent and mocking and glared at them, then looking about as if to find someone to agree.

"They have done this. To have done this! Why the secrecy? Why would François allow this, not see me, eh? My God, his own child. Inhuman, devilry!" he snorted, coughing, his breath caught in his throat, spilling his coffee onto his cassock.

"Damn it! Damn it!" He pitched the cup of steaming liquid away and stood up.

To his surprise, there was Vincent Patrice in his yard.

"Looks like a thief!" he hissed to himself. "Another one of those"—he searched for the word—"vagrants."

142

"Bonjour Monsieur Patrice!" he shouted. "What you looking for here?"

Vincent looked up. Father Magneval looked quite red in the face, scowling, and evidently angry.

"Good afternoon, Father. If you have the time, I would like a word with you, your help actually."

So angry was he it was hard for him to catch his breath.

"Yes, yes, Monsieur Patrice, forgive my . . . I am . . . upset, yes upset. Come, come up, the side door is open."

Vincent Patrice he knew well. He was the king of contraband. A widower. He attended church. He was kindly, but not to his slaves. He never came to confession nor received the Holy Sacrament. He was one of them. He knew him well, the Master of the Atelier. A Lieutenant of that murderer Hugues.

"Yes Patrice. Do sit, forgive me."

He looked carefully at him. He was unshaven, smelt of the sea and appeared not to have slept for days.

"The lad Adhémar has been hurt. François won't see me and I can't get to see Adhémar. What the hell is going on, eh? I heard him scream. It was the dead of night."

Vincent said nothing.

Not saying, eh, the priest thought to himself. Well it will come out, God willing. In this place everything does. Now let's see, what's this?

"Come. Come Monsieur Patrice, have some coffee. Take some tobacco. Take some rum."

Vincent was glad for the coffee and the rum. He took his own tobacco.

"Thank you, Father. Yes, young Adhémar was thrown I hear. Broke his shoulder? I understand he hurt himself pretty badly. I myself have been," he paused, "abroad."

The priest regarded him keenly. Blaggard, liar, he thought.

Vincent sat and took a long grateful sip of the hot, well-laced drink. Father Magneval looked keenly at him. Something's up here, he thought to himself, scratching his grey hair, sitting back and making an effort to compose himself.

"It is foul weather in us all, good sir, when you are cloudy. What brings you to God's house?" he attempted in his best pastoral manner, despite being still a little out of breath.

"Father, there is a man, a friend, who is ill and is in need of the kind of healing that you can give."

"Yes, son, Is it his body or his eternal soul?"

"It may well be both," said Vincent. "But at this time, I think it more concerns the temporal."

"And what ails him?" inquired Father Magneval.

"A great fever. Sometimes chills followed by delirium." He paused. "He was on a long and dangerous voyage alone. He needs medicine. He needs to feel that he is being really cared for to keep up the will to live. For he must live."

"And where is he now?" asked the priest, with what he hoped would appear as mild curiosity.

"On Mr. Carige's island," answered Vincent. "He is very ill, Father."

"Yes, so you say. You say he is from down the Main. An escapee from . . . from . . ." He waved his coffee cup.

"Yes, he is from La Guaira. He was able to escape some bad business down there and is with the Cariges, but we fear for him. He is a friend, so I thought of you and that's why I've come to you. I can't trust him with Pappits and bush medicine. I . . . I need your help." He looked earnestly at the French priest.

"Yes, I will come." Father Magneval finished his coffee in one swallow. "Ahh," he said, feeling for his pipe in the pocket of his dusty black cassock. "Yes, Vincent, I will go to your friend."

As he left the priest, after making arrangements for them to meet within the hour, he felt surprised at Father Magneval's readiness to help. At the best of times Magneval's behaviour was cantankerous and not very helpful, especially towards him.

He must want to know about Adhémar, he thought to himself. Or he might be curious about Manuel, although I never mentioned his name. In any event, he will come. Manuel needs to be cared for. That swelling on his side is grave. I must see that François receives Magneval. I will speak to Agostini for that. I may have to deal with François' anger, however, first things first.

"Hey," he called to Robert in the street, "prepare to set out again very shortly."

Father Magneval puffed his pipe as he packed his meagre selection of instruments, medicines and cures. In fact many were decoctions of leaves, flowers, fruits, roots and barks of tropical plants. Yes, he would see this one, a nuisance for sure, all the way to the Grand Bocas in the midday sun. But you never know, you never know.

He had received, the night before, a note written in code from a man he never met, a person committed to pass on information. He, this nameless one, was a lay brother of the Hermandad, a part of its society of silence, organised to ensure that valuable information reached the right ears and eyes. Father Magneval was, in this part of the world, its hub.

The note brought to him by an Indian said simply, when decoded, "Two have fallen from the tree. One is safely kept, the other is in danger of—" and there the writer depicted the alchemic symbol for mercury.

"Poison," said Father Magneval. "Someone wants one of those fugitives dead."

❖

"Manuel Gual may soon die."

Standing in the wind-blown gallery was the sad-faced Father Hubertus Magneval.

"What do you mean?" snapped Geraldine Carige, getting to his feet.

"He may soon be dead. There is nothing that I can do."

He regarded the two, while intensifying, as best he might, his woeful appearance.

Vincent was through the bedroom door in an instant. Manuel lay on the bed. Father Magneval's bag was shut.

"How long?" Vincent turned to the priest, his voice loud in the silent house. "How long will he last?" he shouted into the face of the priest.

"He will die when it is the will of God for him to die," said Father Magneval, looking directly into Vincent's staring eyes. "When his time comes, he will die."

"I brought you here to save him!" Vincent shouted even louder at the dishevelled man.

"Stop, Vincent," said Carige. "Come, Father, and tell us."

"Why didn't you call me? How could you see him sink so low without calling us?"

He looked sharply at Magneval.

"What did he tell you?"

"Nothing," said Father Magneval. "Nothing. Nothing at all." And he sat down and looked at his large hands.

Vincent returned to the sick man's side. He brought the candle closer. Manuel was given Extreme Unction, the oil, the salt, the holy water and the crosses. For this to have happened he must have repented or repudiated his oath, turned from the Craft. Confessed all he knew. Everything concerning himself. Them.

"Impossible," hissed Vincent. "Magneval."

Vincent's voice was low.

"Tell me, what did you do? What did he tell you? "

The priest sat impassive, looking towards the eastern sky that was turning to light. Early birds made silly chirping whistles. Vincent's anger appeared to make no impression on him, as he looked upon him with increasing compassion, which only served to anger Vincent even more. Geraldine Carige could see in Vincent the intent to kill this priest. He could sense the rationale formulating in his mind. Magneval knows what Gual has confessed in the fear of death. This was no simple priest. The thought had already occurred to Hubertus Magneval, as he silently observed Vincent.

"Massa Carrie," it was the Barbadian overseer Pappits standing at the door, "there is a sail coming towards La Tinta, from here it look like there are many on board."

"To arms! Mount the swivel-gun and prime it to fire, Mr. Pappits," shouted Carige. "Get it quickly, help him, Santiago, it's in the basement and is heavier than it looks, you will find ball and powder, fuses and its carriage, take it to the platform, Pappits knows."

By this time he was in the front gallery, ringing a large brass bell to summon the gangs of slaves. Already Robert, Vincent's man, was on the door step.

"Massa Vincent, it have a ship coming in fast, you want me to make ready?"

"No, Robert, we will stand by Mr. Carrie. Fetch my case, my brace of pistols, we may have some sport."

Madame Carige and the house servants were already putting up the storm windows, soon the house would be a veritable fortress. In the yard below, Geraldine Carige was handing out muskets to his headmen and directing them to positions above La Tinta Bay.

"What is going on?" It was Manuel, tottering, clinging to the partition in the corridor that led to the bedroom. He was gasping for air. "The commotion, is there a battle?"

"No, Manuel, there is no battle. Just a strange ship in the bay, and Geraldine, as you well know, was taught to be cautious. Come, get back into bed, this is not your day." Father Magneval took the frail Gual around the waist and by the arm and guided him into the room.

"I will sit with you, I too have no place out there."

Soon, by late morning, the drama was resolved. The schooner was indeed laden with passengers, refugees fleeing La Guaira in the aftermath of the uprising. They were making for Guadeloupe, but two of their passengers were to come ashore on Mr. Carige's island so as to make enquiries concerning other patriots who may have made their way there to safety.

"José María España, my God, you are supposed to be dead!"

Manuel Gual was sitting up in bed, the excitement of the morning having improved his colour and spirit.

"Manuel, you look like hell, everyone tells me you are dying, it must be true, look our comrade, Juan Bautista Piconell, our Brother, we are sailing for Guadeloupe to meet Victor Hugues, to regroup, to fight those fuckers another day. Come. You cannot stay here. It is too dangerous. Vasconcelos will kill you," boomed José España. He was short and balding with lively brown eyes, a poised, energetic figure that gave the impression of a duellist.

There was no question about Manuel Gual's joining them; his condition, Father Magneval explained, was touch and go.

"Touch and go, eh?" Vincent regarded him. "When will he be able to travel?"

"That would depend, to where?"

"To Port-d'Espagne, he can't stay here, the Spanish police, Vasconcellos, could arrive at any time, we have to move him. Those who came this morning will sail by mid-day. Juan Piconell may remain in Trinidad for a while. España and the others will sail on to Guadeloupe. We must leave now."

There was no one to whom Hubertus Magneval could relate the events of the previous night, what might have been the last few hours of Manuel Gual's life. "No one," he said aloud to himself.

He sat in the stern of Vincent's sloop; a south-westerly, blowing steadily, carried them swiftly away from the Dragon's Mouth, filling the sails, while creating small whitecaps on the sparkling green water. "No one, no one," he muttered, and glanced across at the mountains of Paria on the Venezuelan coast. He felt the grip of fear in the pit of his stomach. He grasped the gunwale and eased himself to one side. He glanced at Robert, Vincent's slave, impassive at the helm, and at the Spanish boy. The thought, 'he would not do it in front of the boy,' crossed his mind. The sleek craft sped on, lifting ocean spray that sparkled across the decking. He could taste it on his lips.

Manuel Gual lay below, wrapped in a sail. Juan Piconell sat forward with Vincent, his back against the mast, smoking a cheroot. He had been passed to the Second Degree at a secret Lodge while studying law at the University of Madrid, he told Vincent. He was involved in the San Blas Conspiracy, which had plotted to overthrow the Spanish monarchy, and was arrested and sentenced to life imprisonment in Panama. Hubertus Magneval overheard all this. It was easy, surprisingly easy to gain a following in La Guaira, Piconell said. "The place is ripe for revolution, too ripe, Señor Gual is perhaps too open, and spies are everywhere. What we need is to go underground, get out into the countryside, rise up the people, the peons, then the slaves."

Hubertus Magneval turned his back on all that talk of revolution. The previous day he had been surprised by the swollen bruised body that had been revealed to him by Gual himself. He had been badly beaten. A ruptured spleen?

"Look, Father, look," he said, lifting his shirt.

Father Magneval listened to the man's painful breathing. He examined him slowly, with great sympathy. Manuel relaxed visibly as Magneval explained that he might have a broken rib. Not a great problem. His fever, he told him, would pass. He needed him to rest and take a lot of liquids. It was not a ruptured spleen. In any event his agitated state would not help him. He gave him sweetened lime juice to drink and prepared a tisane containing *zornia latifolia,* a mild narcotic that would act as a sedative. Manuel, as a result, slept deeply for several hours, awoke, and slept again.

Over the next day and a half, Vincent and the Carige family, together with Don Santiago Mariño, who had also arrived, fished and swam, dined and slept, while Father Magneval kept watch over Manuel Gual, who drank the fish broth prepared by the women and ate mashed zaboca, lightly salted with bread. Father Magneval made sweetened lime juice, which they both enjoyed. Vincent came, looked in on them, and left again to fish, he said, from the jetty. The house was very still, the sun went down with Mesopotamian splendour. Later Father Magneval encouraged the man to talk, assuming the demeanour of a simple priest. He called him "son" and inquired gently whether he wished to have confession. Gual quietly refused. He was looking better. The sedatives did him good.

"Would you like some broth?"

"Thank you, Father." Magneval smiled. Notwithstanding this man's affiliations, he was at heart a Catholic. With a gentle enthusiasm, Magneval enquired into Gual's life, his adventures, his politics. He coaxed the man to speak with paternal encouragement. Manuel Gual talked about his father, Mateo, his wife, his son, the hacienda that he built and the horses that he bred. The drugs that Magneval placed in his food and drink were taking effect. Gual relaxed and his conversation rambled from one topic to the other. He slept. Still he would not answer Magneval's obliquely put questions about the Craft, its work in the revolutionary movements and to whom he reported. Neither would he discuss his politics, his arrest, his torture or even his escape. "I have nothing to confess, Father," he said.

He was very drowsy as the full moon began to rise above the Gulf of Paria, and appeared to have passed away, so sound was his sleep before the moon's zenith was attained. Hubertus Magneval had seen this before and at midnight, he started to administer the last rites. Manuel Gual awoke and looked at him with passivity. The drugs that Magneval gave him in hope of inducing him to speak, now might serve to ease him on his way. His pulse all but vanished. But he didn't die.

Robert's "Mon Dieu!" startled Father Magneval out of his reflections on the previous night.

"Look, Massa, look! Warships."

To the west, just beyond and to the lee of the island from which they sailed, in the brilliant blue of the late afternoon sky, they could see a quantity of sail, majestic, stately, swiftly entering the Gulf of Paria through the Grand Bocas. It was a large flotilla of battleships. Even at that distance from the flags displayed, they could plainly make out that they were English.

"Well, well, that's it, then. Come Robert, let's make haste. That's the English battle-fleet, the island will fall tonight. Look here, Magneval Manuel Gual's presence is a secret. I will take him to Simon Agostini and you, you will mind him, minister him, cure him. And keep your mouth shut! One word, one! and you are dead! This place has gone to hell, and this is not your business. But he must live—you hear me, live!"

"Of course, yes, Vincent."

'This, this is entirely my affair. This sordid business of yours,' thought Father Magneval as he closed his eyes, assuming an expression of great sadness.

Vincent regarded him, "*Merde.*"

10:

1797. Les Frères Unis & Union Lodge,

A Conclave.

The news of the impending invasion caused many residents to bury all their valuables. Some fled the island, never to return. A few subsequently died. Others, in the panic of the night's rain, couldn't for the life of them remember where the hell they had buried their treasure, thus leaving behind a legacy of legends, gruesome murders, and happy surprises.

The capitulation of the Spanish colony of Trinidad to the English in 1797 was accomplished, *sans valor*, in forty-eight hours. Anticipated, even awaited, by Governor Chacón. When advised by the leading French *colons* on the island, Count Louis-Nicholas de Percin la Roque, former governor of Saint Vincent, Lieutenant-Colonel Count Benjamin de Castelet and some others, that the Loyal Militia should prepare for resistance, Don Chacón screamed: "For the love of the holy mother of God, let the English alone, or we shall be cut to pieces."

An admiral of a visiting Spanish squadron, Don Sebastián de Apodaca, admitted to Manuel Sorzano that the situation was long past critical. In truth, it was at a stage where it was either the republican French, under the murderous Hugues, or the perfidious English. Better the perfidies of the English, he ventured. With hundreds of republicans around, many of them perpetrators of massacres, together with the Free Coloured population with uncertain alliances and the few hundred French *colons,* some of whom were *actually* aristocrats, the handful of royalist Spaniards did not stand a chance. Another massacre like Guadeloupe was in the making. It was clearly a race to the finish.

The English fleet rendezvoused at Carriacou on the morning of February 15th, 1797 and set sail for Trinidad the following day, with the Muhammadan Sharper as the fleet's pilot. Admiral Apodaca and the governor met, sitting at the door of Government House, looking out at the gathering panic in the Plaza. The admiral, thinking out loud, said that he could lift anchor and attempt to flee south by way of the Serpent's Mouth, or he could challenge the superior foe and be destroyed. On the other hand, he could surrender his ships, or he could scuttle them.

In the meantime, the English had established a blockade of the Spanish admiral's squadron in Chaguaramas Bay and had landed some six thousand men.

Rumour, ever rife in Trinidad, said that the governor's natural confusion had been increased by the presence of an Irish lady, recently come from Grenada, one Mademoiselle Lindsey. Besotted, was the word being used. Panic to pandemonium, an easy step. That night in Port-d'Espagne it was mingled with relief.

Hundreds of people filled the streets with loud cries of "to arms, to arms!" Lighted torches, hissing in a perpetual drizzle, brightened excited eyes, while all and everyone rushed to and fro, sowing and reaping even more confusion, selling it as they had bought it. In the meanwhile, the republicans of the town had armed themselves and vanished into the high woods, together with the Loyal Militia. The Spanish forces, too, fled, joining their erstwhile enemies, the republican French, in the uneasy arrangements made by people who find themselves in the same boat.

Crowds, the first ever, surged towards the eastern gate. Overladen carts overturned, and crowded carriages with outriders forced their way towards the Royal Road leading east to the old capital of San José de Oruña.

At 2 a.m., a great glow appeared in the west, and an awful cry arose above the tumult. Apodaca had given the order to set fire to his flotilla. Before dawn, great booming explosions reverberated in the valleys as the gunpowder stores in the Spanish battleships blew up, blazing, illuminating the passing of an empire, marking the beginning of the end of an era when Spain ruled the western world. In such a manner empires pass away, and history holds her breath in anticipation of a repeat performance.

As a sanguine precaution, the governor had sent the archives and the treasury to Don José Mayan, who hid them beneath the floorboards of his home at Valsayn estate. General Sir Ralph Abercromby conveyed to Governor Chacón: "I see, with grief, that sacrifice that you will make of your troops without the least hope of attaining your wishes. Indisputable superiority has made me master of the town and I have you surrounded on the heights and have cut all communication to the resources as is well known, and for forces so unequal, there is no resistance and before giving way to a considerable shedding of blood without the least possibility of being able to resist, I ask you to choose a place where we may talk and that I offer you an honourable surrender which is owed to those good and faithful soldiers who otherwise would be sacrificed needlessly."

On receipt of this most honourable message, the governor met with the Assessor Don Juan Jurado and they agreed to accept the terms.

The Articles of Capitulation, which maintained those of the Cédula of '83, were signed at the colony's ancient capital, San José de Oruña, in the gradually melting ajoupa hacienda of Don Francisco Salazar. He, after the distinguished company had departed, stood weeping on its wooden front step in the pouring rain and addressed his assembled slaves, peons and resident Arawaks, who were all standing bare-headed, with a long explanatory discourse, which he closed by employing the words of our Lord and Saviour "It is finished."

His injuries causing much pain, his arm in a sling, Adhémar, disconsolate as the result of Mayotte's sudden death, left Port-d'Espagne by ox-cart for their coffee estate high on the Ariapita ridge of Mon Repos in the Sainte Anne valley.

It offered a view of the Gulf of Paria and the islands in the Dragon's Mouth; behind these, in the brilliant afternoon sunlight, the distant mountains of the Paria peninsula, shrouded in a dazzling sapphire haze, appeared illusionary.

Mon Repos estate house was surrounded by windy cedars of old growth and set in a copse of tall bois-immortels. It was a cool and comfortable house, raised up some ten feet on yellow ballast brick pillars. There were four high-ceilinged bedrooms, a wide living room, a library, and a deep airy gallery perfect for *petit déjeuner*.

Adhémar, startled by a sudden boom of cannon fire, leapt to his feet. A roar like thunder rolled up Sainte Anne's. The echo, he felt beneath his feet. It rattled teacups in their saucers and caused hearts to race in the de Gurvand household. It set in flight enormous flocks of parrakeets, made indignant gaudy macaws, and disturbed colonies of nesting yellow-tailed birds, as troops of red Alouto monkeys howled along with the estate's dogs in a demented chorus that seemed unable to find closure until he discharged, standing in the gallery, the estate's blunderbuss.

English ships of the line were patrolling the Gulf of Paria, well out of range of Fort San Andrés' five antique pieces of ordinance. Well, then this is it at last, he thought. That night, explosions, louder than the cannon fire, and in the west, flames and smoke rising from what must be Chaguaramas Bay. Worried, fearful, he awaited his father. The English ships of war, by morning, in the Gulf of Paria looked a multitude, and the bustle of smaller craft that were ferrying everything to the shore appeared never-ending. The English occupation of his island had commenced.

Father at last. As they took coffee, he heard of the events. François informed him of the gathering that would be held that day. Later, Símon Agostini, Jean de Boissière, Saint Luce Philippe and Louis-Jean Jobity arrived together. They were followed by Julien Asnières Truxillo, José Mayan, and Auguste Théophile Quiquizola. Then came John Black, James Meany and John Nihell. These last were all members of Union Lodge 601, Irish Brethren who had established themselves in Trinidad some years before, taking advantage of the Catholic clause in the Cédula of 1783.

A stranger also arrived, who was, Adhémar later discovered, Paul William Leonard of Saint John's No. 1 Lodge of

Pennsylvania, the same Atelier at which the famous Francisco de Miranda had been initiated.

They gathered in the library. As the doors closed, he caught his father's eye and smiled and nodded. François knew that Adhémar would see to it that the fields were supervised and the cocoa houses closed in the event of a noon shower, and that *déjeuner* would be served in the long gallery on the eastern side of the house.

The men assembled were all Maçons, plantation owners and merchants, they represented the island's principle agricultural and commercial interest. Those from Les Frères Unis were basically in support of François' stand against Vincent Patrice's attempt to take the membership into the revolutionary conflict rooted in Venezuela, and more or less against his stated long-term intention of elevating the Lodge to an independent Grand Lodge of South America. They all, however, possessed in common the endeavour of the Craft in its present dispensation, which was the dissemination of the ideals of the Enlightenment in the New World, the promotion of science, reason and free thought, inasmuch as the established institutions of the time did not consider freedom of conscience a natural right. None there knew of François' mission to the west, his true reason for being on this island.

François took the role of chairman and ordered the meeting informally. It was plain that conditions would change; the anticipation of these changes was the true object of their meeting. Nihell and Mayan were of the opinion that Spanish law, in the Courts of Judicature, as expressed in the Laws of the Indies, would not be altered and neither would the terms of the Cédula of Population.

"The laws of Spain will give the English ample room to deal with the anarchy of this place. They will simply overlay them with martial law. As for the terms of the Cédula, nothing will change. Except that we will see more English planters. The Cédula's terms are excellent for business," said John Nihell, a jovial, well-educated, Antiguan born Anglo-Irish gentleman.

"And what of the Free Coloureds? Will the English, do you think, allow them to continue owning slaves and inheriting lands?" asked de Boissière. He was the youngest present and more than likely the wealthiest, being the most successful money lender in a colony without a bank. He imported slaves and dealt with the Free Coloured community, which was the largest of its free inhabitants, owning land and slaves. It formed the majority of his clientèle.

"Military rule will take no interest in the vagaries of the cuticle—it's only us colonials who redefine our prejudices with every generation," Nihell said and laughed. "In any event, the blacks are slaves by nature, created to suffer much and to submit to much. I would like the English, however, to deal with the British runaways, the so called 'scape hemps' the poor whites, from Barbados and Antigua, who are thieves and vagabonds . . ."

Louis-Jean Jobity concurred. Slightly built, he was a former Royal Notary recently come from Martinique.

"I see no reason why the coloureds should be affected, they produce almost as much of the wealth as the white Cédulants," added François, handing a bottle of Spanish wine to John Nihell. "This is very good John, try it. In fact, I expect to see one of them, Nicholas Porteras, tomorrow. He is now shipping hogsheads directly from Belleview estate, thirty last week, using the Cipero Creek as a waterway. He is very enterprising; he has built a wharf."

"I expect," said José Mayan, "that the Articles of Capitulation will retain all of what is contained in the Cédula of '83. Don

Chacón was much influenced by his former companion, the mulâtresse Marie-Madeline Beauvais, who is very well off, and the mother of his daughter. He has inserted an important clause in the Capitulation treaty, which has been accepted by the English. It is the twelfth, I have it here, I brought a copy of its text, so that you, Saint Luce, may know. It reads: 'The Free Coloured people, who have been acknowledged as such by the laws of Spain, shall be protected in their liberty, persons and property, like other inhabitants, they taking the oath of allegiance and demeaning themselves as become good and peaceable citizens of His Britannic Majesty'."

"How did you get hold of that?" asked Jobity.

"I penned it," smiled Mayan, "at the governor's request, there was no one else available last night."

"Property meaning land and slaves. Slavery is an inferior economic system that will end, but still, I am pleased to know that. This is of particular significance to us *affranchis*," said Saint Luce Philippe. "Ah, no thank you, Francois, it's a bit early for me. We, as *gens de couleur libres*, are especially vulnerable. The Cédula of Population in its fifth clause and also its final clause is the only guarantee of civic equality with Europeans in Trinidad. They allow for our participation in civil society, and even then . . . but, this clause in the surrender document, if it holds true, will buttress our situation greatly. Thank you, Brother." Philippe was a tall taciturn man, tan complexioned, a *mètif*, with refined features, courtly manners and a deep rumbling voice. He was the leading coloured planter on the island, as well as a medical doctor and a Past Vénérable Master of Les Frères Unis.

José Mayan, who was sitting next to him, placed a hand on Saint Luce's arm and said, "My friend, the English do not want another Grenada in Trinidad. That is why the Marie-

Madeline Beauvais clause, if we may call it that, was agreed to by them. The fact that the Cédula of '83 has been accepted *in toto* makes it, in a way, this island's first constitution. The Free Blacks and Free Coloured people are in the majority amongst the free population, what, seven or eight thousand. Naturally they will be held in suspicion; there are many among them who are rabid, filled with hate and in pursuit of revenge for all sorts of injuries, a quantity already blooded by Victor Hugues in Guadeloupe and by Julien Fédon in Grenada, just year-before-last. Many French royalist refugees are here, living next door to them, the very people who chopped their families to death in Grenada. Suspicion, hatred of the coloureds will last for generations amongst the French Creoles, even after the memory of the circumstances have been forgotten. The English will get rid of some of the murderers, one way or another, the majority will have no problems as long as Trinidad is under military rule, and that may last for another twenty years."

The stone pitcher of sangria made the round. José Mayan, in handing it to Louis-Jean Jobity, who was also a lawyer, remarked quietly to him, "I understand that the governor has taken the beautiful Dorothy Lindsey of Grenada as a wife." Jobity looked astonished as he and the Spanish governor were now on familiar terms.

"What you say?"

"Yes. As the English sail appeared off Peru Lands, he married her. You are surprised?" laughed José Mayan. Continuing the conversation with Saint Luce, "Beyond that, Trinidad is not like the older colonies such as Barbados or Jamaica, which were developed by the English sugar barons. In these colonies the coloured populations are small and un-endowed. In Trinidad, however, the Free Blacks and especially the Free Coloureds are among the founders of the colony, with rights guaranteed in law and with investments in land and labour. Here, the Free Coloureds who came together with the French *colons* are among the patricians. Saint Luce, you are as much a founding father as our host. It is your numbers and your French identity that gives Trinidad its French flavour."

"Thank you, my Brother. Hear that François?"

"Don José, married, you say?" asked Jobity.

"Yes indeed, with Father Magneval officiating and the Spanish admiral as a witness," answered José Mayan with a chuckle. He was a middle-aged Spanish Creole who had read Law at the University of Caracas. "He was paying close attention to her since her arrival from Grenada, she is a widow, well endowed. He knows that all is ended here. I understand that she possesses estates in Ireland, in County Antrim, is that not so, John?"

"Yes. Very true. With luck, the governor might have done well for himself. That is if he escapes the inevitable court marshal," John Black declared with a knowing, corpulent and important air, as he tossed back a glass of rum. He and his partner Edward Barry were the largest importers of slaves on the island.

"I wish the governor well," said François, "but my concern, our concern, is the future, and our place in the scheme of things."

"Ahaa. But, so long as England is at war in Europe, nothing will change in Trinidad, François. This colony is rich," Black continued, looking around him. "Rich and undeveloped, and its greatest asset is the experience and knowledge of the people, white and coloured, who possess the land and the labour, and slavery will not end in our lifetime, my Brothers. There will be no *Société des amis des Noirs* in Trinidad. The English are interested in taxes. I agree with my friends Jobity and José."

He laughed and glanced about him. "Yes, taxes! That will come, notwithstanding what's in the Cédula, José. And when that happens, how you say in the Patois? The profit in the rat's tail is so meagre that the cat might as well take it!"

"Yes, truly, *Bénéfis ki an laché wat, is miyé chat pwand,*" François agreed. "But England is not going to allow a foreign population to dominate the island's wealth for any length of time."

He, too, looked around at the French, Spanish, coloured, Corsican and Irish men in the room. Their agricultural and commercial interests would be at risk, surely the English soldiers would be followed by the interest of the City of London. Such an important territory as this, its large area of virgin soils, its huge unexplored interior, accessible rivers, its anchorage safe from the Atlantic storms.

"What do you suppose, Brother Black?" asked James Meany. He was an Irishman recently working for the former Spanish establishment.

"I have no idea really, what I do know is that the land is worthless without the slaves to work the estates."

"What?! You think the English will free the slaves?" asked Símon Agostini, adjusting his *toupé*.

"No, Símon," said Black. "Saint-Domingue was the biggest producer of sugar in the world, not any more. Then the French republicans freed their slaves to undermine the situation of the royalist planters. When the revolutionary wars are over, the French will re-enslave them—when money appears, high-flown ideals take flight. Right now there is money to be made in sugar, here in Trinidad. The French sugar producers in the islands have been destroyed, their *dépôts* on the Guinée coast taken by the English, perhaps forever. They must now buy

Negroes from us, from me, and you Jean. We must act with vigilance and with severity when it comes to the slaves. They must not rise up. They hate us and we despise them. Remember Grenada. Anyway, if the slaves were freed, you, the foreigners in the English colonies, would be out of the plantation business. You have done the work for the English. At your cost, with the labour that you bought and fed. Large tracts of cleared land would become available cheap: factories, machinery for the taking. The English would not bother with the hurt feelings of a few dozen Frenchmen, and a rabble of coloureds, believe me. They will flood the place with dirt-poor Irish or Scots, or Chinese to work the estates if it serves their purpose. With modern methods, sugar can be produced from different sources. Beets, for instance. Things will change, other crops could be introduced."

"Beets!" exclaimed Símon. "We do not grow that here."

"New technologies, inventions, will come, but the black man is a better worker than three whites," said Black, helping himself to a glass of rum. "But Trinidad will never match Jamaica or Barbados as a sugar colony, or overtake it as a slaughterhouse running with blood, filth, misery and diseases."

"Add some pulp and liquid from the nut of the coco palm to the rum, John," said François. "It's excellent with rum. That's just it, John, slavery is increasingly perceived as cruel and murderous, the English Enlightenment may yet come to express itself with strong feelings of humanity and justice."

"Rubbish!"

"The horrors of that unrighteous traffic," continued François "the misery of the plantation, the corrupting wealth of the sugar barons, all are serving to affect, in fact offend, the sensibilities of tens of thousands of ordinary people in England."

"Nobody listens to them!" shouted Black.

"This is expressed by the Quakers, the Methodists, the Puritans, the do-gooders in the English parliament. The abolitionists could, over time, gain the upper hand in the English parliament," said Francois, handing to Black a glass of rum and coconut water.

"Thank you, François. This is not bad, coconut water, eh. But François, slavery will never end."

"I have heard that the Jamaican planters are alarmed at the gains of the abolitionists, some four hundred thousand signatures from ordinary people sent to the parliament," remarked John Nihell. "They are stocking up on Negroes. Public pressure could end it."

"No. Never!" shouted Black. "Listen to what I am telling you. Over night the price of sugar has risen, the highest for more than twenty years. The French islands produce little or no sugar since the revolution and the wars in Saint-Domingue. Trinidad and the other British-held islands are now too lucrative for them to simply bring slavery to an end because of petitioners. The demand for sugar in Europe is great, money is to be made."

"The English will retain the slave economies as long as they are profitable and look to support what the insurgents are up to in Venezuela," said José Mayan. "It's in their interest that Spain suffers, that Spanish rule ends, and that new markets are opened up for them. For the manufacturers who own the mills, the wharves, the mines, they all sit in the parliament, they own the banks, humanity and justice be damned, that will not be their concern."

Auguste Quiquizola, a diminutive man with small features and neat gestures, had been silent for most of the discussion, but as the conversation moved away from commerce and politics and began to concern itself with the future workings of the Craft, he became more involved.

"Do you believe," he asked, "that the English will countenance this Atelier to continue its existence under its French constitution? England is at war with France, you forget the Directorate in Paris and what they did to us?" He looked about. *"Mnm baton ke bat chien nwa-la, pé bat chien blan-la.* As the Patois people say, 'the same stick that beats the black dog can beat the white dog'." He laughed ruefully.

This was a contentious issue. The Grand Orient de France no longer existed in France, and Les Frères Unis was chartered to no Grand Lodge, as *émigré* members found refuge in the Caribbean, the United States of America and Scotland.

"Our Brother Vincent has been in contact with Seth Driggs of the Grand Lodge of Pennsylvania," said François. "Francisco de Miranda, with whom he is closely linked, is well connected there. Remember, Pennsylvania is de Miranda's Lodge. We may have to treat with Pennsylvania, as the English, at war with France, will not countenance a secret assembly of Frenchmen in their newly acquired colony. Auguste is right."

"They are now at peace with the United States," said Quiquizola, "so Pennsylvania could be the answer. But remember, Vincent and Francisco de Miranda are linked, and de Miranda has a close association with the Americans. De Miranda has participated in fraternal meetings and dined in Harmony with George Washington at a number of Masonic gatherings. I understand that we do not have much of a choice at the moment. But the time may soon come to be on the level with the Grand Lodge of Scotland, notwithstanding our ritual differences, because at the end of the day, this will be an English colony, if they hold it."

"The Craft is in disarray in Venezuela. The senior masters have either fled or are dead," said Saint Luce. "Some have come to Trinidad, they live quietly in the Naparimas, while others have gone north to the United States. If the English have it in mind to destabilise the Spanish crown, they will allow us to continue to exist; Brother Vincent will be their cat's paw."

"We should welcome the Venezuelans here. Some political Brothers would join Hugues in Guadeloupe," snorted John Black, pouring some rum into his glass. "The English may not countenance a French republican movement in Trinidad, but," he looked at François, "they may encourage a Masonic-inspired republican subversion of the Spanish crown in Venezuela. This would suit Brother Vincent indeed."

Black was constrained by no particular desire to see *The Rights of Man* promulgated, or subject peoples, be they black, Indian, or Irish for that matter, freed or otherwise. He privately believed that his compatriots, his Brothers in the Craft, were hypocritical in their fine talk of equality and freedom for all men, while they, themselves, possessed slaves. How can freedom be built on slavery? He knew that all men were created unfree and unequal. If education and opportunity were given to all, it would be folly to think that every man would become an Isaac Newton. In his world dogs ate dogs, and the devil took the hindmost.

"The revolutions in France, in Saint-Domingue, in North America, and what is taking place here in South America will change the fabric of history, John," said François. "The uprising of the slaves in Saint-Domingue, if successful, will contribute to the end of feudalism in Europe. Freedom and equality means more to the blacks than to any of the *sans culottes* in Paris."

John Black chuckled, money will talk, he thought, but held his peace as he drained his glass. "Aha."

"And what of Vincent's idea of an independent Grand Lodge of South America?" asked Quiquizola. "*Sé bouch kabwit ki ka wand kabwit.*"

"Well," said John Black, "that is true, the goat does betray itself by its voice. From where I sit, Patrice's intentions are plain. Francisco de Miranda is a bellwether of sorts, he is exalted in the eyes of the exalted, in England and in the United States. Am I not correct?"

"Yes," said François, "if de Miranda gains the support of the English prime minister, the English government, the bankers, if his revolution is successful, if it overthrows the Spanish Crown in South America, a Grand Lodge of the Americas, that is South America, will have concentrated significant power in the hands of those who control the new states. Remember that de Miranda has already founded The Most Worthy Lodge of Rational Knights of Lautaro. The first step has been taken by the English, they are here, the next step will be to take them there." François rose and pointed to the blue mountains of the Paria peninsula, Venezuela. "Trinidad will be the staging post for trade with an English-controlled South America. As John has suggested, all this has nothing to do with slavery, plantations or sugar. It only has to do with trade, English manufactured goods, trade with a vast new market. Masonry, its idealism, all men being created equal—brotherly love, relief, truth, will serve the cause of ambitious men. As you said, José, they all sit in the House of Lords, they own the banks."

"So Brother Vincent would take Les Frères Unis into an association with The Most Worthy Lodge of Rational Knights of Lautaro, bring with him the secret rituals of the Rose Croix Degree which they do not possess, and be a king-maker, if you pardon the expression, all in the service of the bankers of the City of London!" laughed Jean de Boissière. His father was at present a member of *Le Conseil des Cinq-Cents,* the lower house of the legislature of France, the greatly feared Directory.

"Yes," said François. "That would make Vincent a very powerful man indeed."

"After the generals, of course. Always remember they have the guns. And you, François, what is your interest?" asked Quiquizola. "Why are we here?"

"Chat chaudé pè dufe, gasçon. We are here to maintain the purpose of the Great Work, Auguste, and to further our own interest," said François. "I personally cannot follow Vincent. What he seeks is beyond me. He desires to be a power, yes, a great power, in the new republics. In the world. With the Catholic Church's influence, if not broken, certainly substantially reduced, the organisation that he has in mind, a Grand Lodge of the Americas that he would erect, would seek to replace the Church as the moral authority. A different eschatology, a redefinition of the four last things: death, judgement, heaven, and hell, could emerge."

"A theocracy!" exclaimed John Black. "The *hidalgos* would never allow it! They merely desire to replace the Spanish bureaucracy with their own home-grown aristocracy of bastards, nearly all of whom are black or whatever. They already own the land and the slaves, they crave independence for themselves! They will turn their backs on Freemasonry as the French republicans have, and put them to rot in gaol."

"That's not as far-fetched as some may believe, Señor Black," remarked Julien Truxillo. "The lust for power is appetising, it grows, spreads. What is taken away, the trappings, the regalia, the pomp and ceremony of the vice-regency and the Church, would be replaced by what the Craft possesses: high-flown orders, new titles, different uniforms, an even more elaborate display of deference, a hierarchy, hidden mysterious rites that purport to maintain the secrets of the ancients. The new regime, the military, would want a tool such as this to control the minds, the imagination of the ordinary people. There will be no democracy, the masses will continue to be illiterate and primitive and too tired to think. These people will create oligarchies, powerful and enduring." He looked about him.

"That is a corruption," said de Boissière.

"That is *the* corruption," said François.

"Have some rum, Brother Truxillo," said Black.

"My countrymen will become enormously wealthy," chuckled Símon Agostini. "If banks existed in that godforsaken wilderness, they would laugh as they made their deposits. Ah well." He removed his *toupé* and wiped his dome with an embroidered white kerchief.

"Yes," said Nihell, who listened silently. "Paul Pietri has transported gold ingots to La Guaira. Your countrymen would finance the revolution so as to make their way into the new economic order." He raised his hands. "Don't ask."

"My spies told your spies," smiled Símon Agostini, "that Joseph Susini was able to purchase an arsenal from that scoundrel Enrique." Replacing his *toupé* back-to-front, he smiled broadly.

"Yes, that is where the money to finance the new revolution on the Main is coming from, the Corsican investors, our Brethren," said Jean de Boissière. "I must say, it is not a bad investment, there is a fortune to made in this war."

"Jean, we as Maçons support the movements to liberate the colonies, it is the ideal of the Great Work. There are, however, fundamental moral issues here," said Quiquizola.

De Boissière merely smiled and said nothing.

"The military rule that will be established here in Trinidad will be harsh," said François. "There is a lieutenant colonel in their headquarters' command, Picton, I believe his name to be. I'll wager that's the fellow who will be in control after the squadron has sailed."

"Is he a Maçon, François?" asked Black.

"I have no idea."

"Captain Thomas Mallet, the civil engineer, is," said Paul William Leonard, who had been recently installed as Master of Union Lodge. "Your Brother Maingot, the surveyor, will soon make his acquaintance, I am sure." He glanced around the room, his attention directed particularly at his Irish Brothers. "The English will try to divide us, us here, as you know," he said. "We must hold together, even as we must expect the order of things to change."

His eyes rested on John Black, an Irish Brother but also fervently independent, he and others like John Shine and Paul Gloster had made money under the Spanish administration. "We," he looked at François, "and all the others must support the English in the implementation of law and order, *corpus juris civilis.*"

"Brother Vincent certainly will. They have no idea what Trinidad is really like," said de Boissière.

"Yes, but we do," said Jobity. "Our information network must be kept secure."

"Business will have to go on," continued Leonard, whose ships sailed regularly between New York and the Caribbean.

"I believe our greatest danger is the slaves," said Símon Agostini.

"You mean as in Saint-Domingue, Símon?" asked José Mayan.

"No, no, they will take them from us and give them to their own people." Agostini looked about him.

"I take Símon's point," said François.

"Yes," said Black, rising from his seat. "They control the high seas, they control the traffic of slaves, the supply. That reminds me, Símon, I have bought you a fine Negro girl, young, well developed. What . . ?" he remarked, amused by his friend's evident embarrassment.

"The question now is," asked Saint Luce, "how are you, François, going to deal with Vincent after what he has done to your son? And the extent to which he has caused a schism in this Lodge. I have heard of your intention to resign, to leave. I caution against it, as it will weaken *us*." He gestured, indicating all who sat in that room.

"I will remain true to the Craft, my Brother," answered François. "The assault on my son was an attack on me, disguised as justice, meted out for an indiscretion with the supposed intention of creating greater devotion and loyalty. It is a lesson that my son will learn. What I have understood is where the enemy is, and I will tile accordingly. Have no fear."

"I admire your forbearance, your lack of malice, or even vengeful spite. You are *l'homme providentiel*. We all support you," said de Boissière, "you know that."

"Yes Jean, thank you, and I thank you all. Let us, however, keep the whole picture in view and not be distracted. There is much at stake, the world begins afresh in this hemisphere, what we do here on this island will shape events for decades, centuries, perhaps. We will support Vincent in his petition to be chartered under the Grand Lodge of Pennsylvania, but I caution against his broader schemes," said François.

"So mote it be," they all answered.

"In the meanwhile the Atelier is a magnet for the Corsicans," said Quiquizola, "No offence, my Brother."

"None taken, my Brother," said Símon Agostini, "none taken, *si van pa vanté ou oaka wè bonda poul.* Ah, well."

The gathering was invited to lunch by Adhémar announcing that *ragouts* and *entremets* would be served in the gallery.

François rose as Simon Giuseppi and Cipriano Cipriani joined them. "Cipriano, Simon, are just in time for *déjeuner,* welcome!"

"John," said François, taking John Black aside as they walked towards the gallery, "my son will soon marry Marie Eugénie, the daughter of Pierre-Louis Roget. I would like to set them up in the town." He regarded him fraternally. "There is an old Spanish hacienda on the Calle Santa Ana, I believe you have an interest in it."

"I certainly do François, I live there . . . Oh I see, well let's talk about it."

Adhémar and Marie Eugénie were married, a magnificent affair held in Santa Cruz that was managed entirely by her mother and Father Magneval. In silent and mutual understanding no further discussions concerning the Craft were pursued between Adhémar's father and himself. François continued to be a Maçon, declining office, but contributing to the Work of the Atelier. His activities as a pamphleteer and as an *agent provocateur* came to an end as a result of the governor's actions and the new administration's way of dealing with the Venezuelan patriots. Vincent, suspicious of François' equanimous manner, but mindful of his competence with *d'épée*, maintained a cautious distance.

Adhémar, now a married man, left Masonry behind him. Increasingly influenced by his father-in-law, and soon to be a father himself, he became ambitious, taking a responsible interest in the affairs of the family's estates. With the encouragement of John Black, he purchased town properties. He spoke often of the opportunities presented in trade, something that was, of course, out of the question for François. Out of an abundance of caution, François refrained from dissuading him from these ventures, as he was concerned that any attempt to turn him away from them would merely serve to harden his resolve. He would speak to Adhémar from time to time concerning their undertaking, that which had brought them to the west, but as time passed he saw plainly that the visions evoked in Adhémar's imagination by the telling of the accounts of past times, of Château Beaumanoir, of Les Chambrés, became increasingly like stories told, something from his childhood, and that his son humoured him by participating in them as though they were playing an old and familiar game. As for François, he could only bide his time, waiting for the summons that he knew, one day, would arrive.

11:

1797. Lieutenant Colonel Thomas Picton,

The English Colony.

Lieutenant Colonel Thomas Picton was appointed governor of Trinidad by Sir Ralph Abercromby, his commander-in-chief, and was given the following mandate: "I have placed you in a trying and delicate position—nor, to give you any chance of overcoming the difficulties which are opposed to you, can I leave you a strong garrison; but I shall give you ample powers. Execute Spanish laws as well as you can; do justice according to your conscience, and that is all that can be expected of you. His Majesty's government will be minutely informed of your situation, and will no doubt make all due allowances."

On the fourth day of the capitulation, Brother Don Juan José Martiniano Mayan was invited to take up the important post of Teniente by Sir Ralph Abercromby. This post long seen by the older Spanish inhabitants as honorary, was in fact a lieutenant governorship.

As Teniente he became privy to important despatches and decisions. It was plain that the English government did intended to retain the colony's Spanish Courts of Judicature with its entire legal system, which favored the debtor, and that resident Spaniards were to be enlisted in their functioning. At this news, the French planters, and especially the *gens de couleur libres* breathed a sigh of relief.

The lieutenant colonel, now Governor Picton, needed an interpreter of Spanish laws, the Laws of the Indies, which were on the whole incomprehensible to him, mostly because of his ignorance of Spanish, his impatience and his prejudices; to him it was all popish rigmarole. Notwithstanding, in Don José Mayan he recognised a person whose calm and studied manner and obvious knowledge of the Law made him someone in whom his confidence could be placed: he could do business with this Spaniard, albeit while holding his nose.

Acting together, and with the unanimity of the other members of the Illustrious Cabildo, the island's governing body, a council of advice was created. This included, amongst others, John Shine, Paul Gloster and Brother John Black. They gathered together in a dilapidated building on the Calle de Santa Ana, and inaugurated the new administration by ordering that two slaves be hanged that very same afternoon for the alleged incitement of other slaves on an estate owned by one M. Henri la Bastide. Their owner was never compensated, despite Don José Mayan's advice.

Governor Picton gave all non-English colonists four days to swear allegiance to the British Crown or leave the island. He then banished several dozen republican French and Free Coloured fighters, sympathisers of Victor Hugues, Johnny Crapauds, he called them, as well as a number of Spaniards suspected of plotting a reconquest of the island. In all, several hundred French republicans left for down the Main, vowing revenge and promising to return to retake the island, some said for Spain, some others said for the French Republic. All their names were supplied by Saint Hilaire Bégorrat. The French royalist element, who considered themselves an upper class, were delighted. Already Bégorrat's head-man and sometime *chantwell,* Gros Jean was composing denigrating songs about Don Chacón, in which he was portrayed as having straw for guts.

> *Governeur boudin paill*
> *I pas bai bataille*
> *Soldats anglais entwez*
> *Pwend toute la Twinté.*

As the new English governor assumed control, he came to understand that this island of *la Twinté,* in spite of its appearance of being paradisal, was a dangerous place. Bodies of the dead and dying, all sorts of people, appeared on the streets every morning, at times in startling quantities, as revenge was taken on informers and others who were seen as collaborators of the various contending factions. Old scores were settled and domestic quarrels ended in decapitation. Duels, an everyday affair, were made at times spectacular by the dramas with which they were accompanied. Poison and poisoners appeared, to vanish, to appear again, to strike, causing horrific and expensive deaths to slaves and to livestock. People were obsessed with the paranoia of being buried alive, by accident or by design, for revenge or as a lesson to others, then to be disinterred and sold off as *zombis.* I, Littais L'Eau, have certain knowledge of this.

The black people were possessed, in all their varieties, of an astonishing attractiveness and liveliness. This, the new governor discovered to his delight. It was related that as he was sitting, digesting, in his own rummy vapour in the heat of noon the German Jäger sentry, with an ill-concealed smirk, announced that "a lady" was without, demanding an audience. His first instinct was to strike the man. But he held his hand, perhaps because of the smirk. It was his first encounter with a person with no last name: Rosette, just Rosette. She was as tall and as vulgar as he, and as loud and as violent. She was of no discernible racial content or background. In appearance she was large and yellow with exaggerated features, with a head of hair like copper wire, her manner was forward and avaricious. Upon entering the bedroom that passed as his office, she lifted her garments and showed him her huge posterior. He took her there, with his pantaloons about his jackboots, the German sentries howling with laughter in the corridor. She came away, that very day, with the concession for laundering everything.

The Negroes, slave or free, all speaking French and Patois along with their native dialects, reinvented religion. This was the first step towards their creation of an alternative reality. The blacks invested profound intellectual energy in the creation of complicated theologies, pondering upon these, and paying elaborate attention to the precepts developed. This metaphysical acuity espoused a deep spirituality that expressed itself with creative spontaneity. On the surface, all of this appeared to be amusing to us, even ridiculous, but this spirituality was in fact subversive. All this found its way into the daily life of the governor. She gave him a talisman, a fetish, concocted by herself. "Wear this thing next to your skin, it will save you."

"From what?"

"Me."

This invented world allowed the blacks to move, to act in the ordinary roles that we created for them by day, but, at night, or in the privacy of their own company, they became what their alternative reality had made them. Emperors, presidents, daemons, shape-changers. Picton glimpsed that sometimes while in her company. Thus, the island possessed a majority whose lives moved on two different levels of reality, a public one for us Europeans, and a hidden, private one for them. He commanded that she be followed, he discovered that she was a Queen and ruled a domain almost as large as the town and was the sponsor of a society known as *Les Cochons Sans Poils*, the pigs without hair, a society of assassins who terrified people into paying for protection, from them. He hired them. She became his director of espionage. He gave her the concession to mine limestone from the Laventille hills. His words to her were: "Accept this bagatelle, my darling. The profits of it will enable you to buy trinkets, etc, etc . . ." She soon became Mrs. Rosette Smith.

Because of the fear that Europeans were haunted with, the slaves were brutalised, Picton came to understand this. Beaten, maimed, branded with red hot irons, roasted alive, made useless in spite of their escalating prices. The governor and Rosette did well in this enterprise.

"The governor has adapted to the environment," said François, as he and I, Littais L'Eau, walked on the Mole. The late afternoon sunlight was sparkling upon the choppy Gulf, as a stiff southerly brought the fresh water smells of the Caroni swamp towards us. "He has acquired a mistress. She is an astonishingly common person, one Rosette. A real *mabuya*, as they call her in the town. He has put her in charge of all corruption. The place will never look back."

I laughed. "So true."

"This island seems to produce a hallucinogenic effect on everyone," I told him. "The usually bovine Hessian troopers, here since the capitulation, have suddenly turned violent, haven't you noticed, disorderly and given to drink and rapine. They were ordered to be confined to the new barracks next to Fort San Andrés."

I, Littais L'Eau, have noticed that even the long resident Europeans and educated *gens de couleur libres* all appear to move within their own bizarre dramas, only eccentrically connected to each other and to the real world and its events. The savagery, the cruelty to the slaves occasions this. It alters one.

"What I have noticed," François remarked, "is that the popular customs, the folkways of other islands, are introduced and taken for granted and soon acquire a prescriptive right to exist, appearing as having always existed here."

"It is a society in formation," I answered.

"But lawlessness, Littais, is the norm. Everybody a law unto themselves. Everybody with their own laws; Spanish law, French law, Republican law, Catholic law, English law, for every season, a law. There has never been a colony with so many lawyers."

"Indeed, my friend. It will be Christmas soon and there will be martial law, the governor will declare it. All able-bodied free men would be made to report to him, under arms, for two months. A general state of emergency, which would give him the opportunity to arrest anyone."

"He, to his disgust, has become popular," laughed François.

On the first day of March John Nihell, our Irish Brother, who is an unprofessional West Indian gentleman of the old school with no legal training, accepted the position of the colony's first Chief Judge and Auditor, in and over the whole island, from the hands of Governor Picton. A Monsieur *Rosbif et pommes de terre,* the Creoles called him, the first of many.

John Nihell was given a splendid cap and gown, but was told that he must procure his own wig, which he did. Between himself and Brother Mayan the Craft was well represented in the new government, and, as a consequence, could influence affairs.

I received Captain Mallet, the Crown surveyor, as Frère Servant, at Les Frères Unis in due form and ceremonial style as a Vénérable Past-Master of Old Cumberland No. 12 Lodge and as a member of the governor's headquarter's staff. He was invited to the Atelier by Brother Joseph Maingot de Surgères, the surveyor. Vincent, as Vénérable Master, and François as immediate Past-Master, were his hosts and sat on either side of him at Harmony; they acted out the role of genial hosts, spoke to each other politely and assured the Captain of the Lodge's support for the new English administration. The following day they were summoned into the presence of Governor Picton, who got straight to the point, as François related.

"Gentlemen," he said, sitting at a desk, as they entered what was once Governor Chacón's bedroom overlooking the Plaza del Marina, and which was now, it would appear, Picton's office. "Gentlemen, I know that your society of Freemasons is the source of all subversion in this place. I warn you now, from this moment onwards, to cease all activities of a revolutionary or subversive nature. No more intrigue. I am in control of this island, not you. You handle your differences well, I see. Be quiet, no need to explain!

"You are not expelled from the colony or executed out of hand for treason, as yet, because your membership, as it presently stands, collectively represents almost all of the planter and merchant interests in Trinidad. I intend that this island remain prosperous and that is where you lot come in. Your society, Lodge whatever, as I understand it, is some sort of noble, royalist democrat Jacobin salad, a Chamber of Commerce of sedition, and, in the eyes of many, of heresy. Apart from that, I intend to make use of your network when needed. I expect your cooperation, if you hesitate, I will hang you both to start with, and set an example.

"Yours is a French Lodge, I hear, I don't like Frenchies, slippery lot, spies and traitors, buying and selling each other, what! Now cut your cards very straight, or I will have the lot of you executed for treason. You see that gallows out there, the wind will pass beneath your feet, quick sharp. I hear that you invite darkies into your company, dangerous business, I warn you! British merchants and planters will come when this war is won, you will all be replaced. Now get to hell out and stick to your mumbo jumbo and leave the politics to me. I know that you, Patrice, are the agent for Francisco de Miranda. I know him, saw him at Gibraltar, he is a poser, an adventurer, an opportunist, and a dammed bounder, just your sort. And Mister de Gurvand, the Sergeant at Arms has picked up your printing press, you will not need it. And Mister Patrice, take my advice, disband your spies, you have been infiltrated. Now go, get out!"

Governor Picton was a plain man for all to see. Laws, the law of the Indies and English military law, were to be obeyed; these were enforced and demonstrated publicly with full force. Under the aegis of both systems, the powers of the governor were vast in this heterogeneous landscape with its bizarre collection of foreigners. The fact that he was outnumbered was not lost on him. He could hardly tell the difference between them and couldn't care less. He did not possess unlimited manpower. The Germans in his Hessian ranks were already becoming undisciplined—one man receiving one thousand lashes. He was dead by the two hundredth, but received the remainder of the punishment all the same. He was collected by the Provost Sergeant and carried away in a seaman's canvas bag. The next day, handwritten posters appeared that spoke of humanity and justice. Governor Picton ordered all the posters collected and sent to François de Gurvand's house.

The following morning, well-printed notices appeared all over the place: the Spanish custom of church altars being a place of sanctuary was abolished. The people of the town witnessed, just the day before, an extraordinarily tall gallows constructed from indestructible purple heart wood, erected by government-owned slaves in front of the little wooden white-washed church in the shuddering heat of noon. One hour later, three Spaniards, all men, and a free Negro girl were hanged in the presence of a large cheering crowd. Governor Picton ordered five Martiniquan blacks hanged the following morning to an ear-shattering caterwauling of a large mob of women. Then, three coloured men, two English Creoles, and a Spaniard. A Negro slave was hanged at twelve noon, his death throes, disconcertingly loud, were accompanied by the tolling bells rung for the Angelus. In the town's principal square, directly in front of the church, a large crowd gathered to cheer.

Two weeks later, he executed fourteen men, English and Germans, from his garrison, all hanged in one afternoon. He then paraded the battalion through the town and introduced the custom of trooping the colour once a week in front of his residence on the Plaza del Marina. He erected a very tall flagpole, beneath which he stood alone to take the salute.

There were regular *autos-da-fé* now, public burning, whipping and mutilation of ears and noses, and several brandings a week with red-hot irons. This tended to take place at nightfall, as it was believed to be more effective then; the people could see the iron's red heat when it was placed against a cheek or a breast. Governor Picton appeared to enjoy passing these un-English sentences that were all executed in public, with crowds looking on, looking at him watching, moving from window to window and directing and encouraging the operations from the upstairs of Government House on the north-western corner of the Calle de Santa Ana, recently renamed Charlotte Street by the English for the Prussian-born wife of "George the Turd," as the King of England was referred to by the locals.

Medieval tortures sanctioned under Spanish Law became common practice. The wheel, the rack and the spike or *picong* were used when "the question" was applied in the supine heat of the day. He introduced the first treadmill in the Caribbean, a huge contraption kept in a vacant lot next to the Royal Gaol on the Calle de San José, now known as George Street. It survived there for decades after its use was abolished by the eventual emancipation of its most regular occupants.

Like Don Chacón, his greatest threat was from within. Unlike Chacón, Governor Colonel Picton tended to act in anticipation of events. He put his regular troops in garrison at a barrack that he built opposite to the Mole that led to Fort San Andrés, knowing full well their vulnerability to tropical diseases and their addiction to rum and whores, and proceeded to create an irregular unit policed by English sergeants.

This unit was comprised of former slaves, master-less men, and freemen of several nationalities and of all colours. This was the other thing about the governor: he could not tell, unless a person was as black as pitch, if they were mulatto, mestizo, quadroon or zambo. He named them Picton's Rangers. He provided them with uniforms, a hodgepodge of army and navy kit, forced their enormous feet into English army-issue boots, armed them with truncheons, bayonets and muskets, enforced upon them British infantry drill, kept them on a firing range that he improvised in the Dry River in the blazing sun without a drink of anything, gave them a badge of his own design, a six-pointed star that he told them was the star of Saint David, the patron saint of Wales, from whence he came and hence magical, drilled them fourteen hours a day, kept them on permanent duty, flogged the entire unit regularly for infractions mostly invented, sent them in pursuit of runaway slaves, who had sought to maroon themselves in the island's unexplored interior, and then paraded them with their captives in tow, in chains through the town to the accompaniment of the pipes and drums of the 42nd Royal Highland Regiment of Foot band (the Regiment was actually on its way to India) to the obvious delight of the citizenry and the growing pride of this, his private army. The people of the town loved it, loved it so much that they parodied it, and him, at their carnival!

In the meanwhile, he increased around him the council of rascals, adding mostly ruffians, while steadily enlarging the circle of informers who were well paid, but tended to vanish when he concluded that they knew too much. After considerable prompting, he named the new members of the Illustrious Cabildo; it was explained to him by Don José Mayan that the Cabildo was a Spanish form of Legislative Council, and as such necessary so as to implement Spanish Law: They would not hold another meeting for five years.

François described to me, Littais L'Eau, another amusing interview with Colonel Picton some months later, when he was summoned to the governor's office late one night: "I understand that your son will soon marry. You have done very well for yourself here, while not becoming overextended. What! Good. Sit there, take some whisky, there, come on man, relax. I am not going to have you hanged." He laughed, in spite of himself. "I know, I know. But good order and subordination is my aim."

"Thank you Sir, yes, I have avoided . . . ah, debt," said François, taking a chair in the middle of the room next to a table that held a variety of liquors. Rosette, florid and enormous, was asleep or unconscious, lying in a heap of soiled linen in the governor's massive bed. The governor handed him a full glass of whisky.

"You speak English well. Your land holdings are modest, Mr. de Gurvand. Your activities could be considered seditious by my government. Hold, don't explain. I understand that you spent some time on the island of Grenada, then Saint Lucia."

"Yes, Sir."

"I intend to strengthen my irregulars by bringing in Colonel Drualt's Guadeloupe Rangers. They have been fighting Hugues' forces in the mountains of Saint Lucia. I am thinking of merging them with my own people here. I would like you to take command of these men, you understand the lingo and know how to take charge of Negroes. I would give you the rank of Captain and team you up with another Frenchman, Gaudin de Soter, who will have responsibility for the entire unit and be answerable to me."

The governor's knowledge of his affairs and his demand did not take him by surprise. Yes, his son would marry. Yes, there were some small but successful ventures, his plantations were doing well. The greatest risk had been coming here to Trinidad from Grenada, prompted by the exhaustion of the soil, the attacks by the ants and the devastation of the hurricanes. And frankly, his gravest misgiving had come to pass: the English conquest of this island, Trinidad, but then they had also taken Grenada. The first question was: would England hold this island? Already on the Mainland there were forces building to retake it.

"Aided by you. You clown!" growled the governor.

Picton regarded him for a spell. There's something more there, he thought. Walking to the window, he said, speaking over his shoulder, that he was urged by his French advisors, his Syndic Procurator, Saint Hilaire Bégorrat in particular and some others recently arrived from Saint-Domingue, Saint Lucia, Grenada, and other French territories, islands that experienced violent uprisings or were recently devastated at the prompting of Victor Hugues, that he should bring his attention to bear on the Free Coloureds as well as the African practitioners of tribal magic and animism, the witch doctors, shamans, the Obeah-men and women. The poisoners.

"I have seen myself, Rosette in a state, drunk on rum, crazy as a lune, jumping about, with Bégorrat, that old goat, joining in." He laughed aloud and glanced at her, she was still fast asleep. Or pretending to be. "What do you know of this?"

"Your Excellency, the Free People of Colour, the family men, the ambitious, have invested heavily in this colony, Sir. Every family has a story, a myth of their origins that they imagine to be unique. They should be treated differently."

"Rubbish, they are all the bloody same, all black, can't tell them apart."

"With respect, Sir, that is not the case. The Free People of Colour have their grievances, strong feelings of injustice, personal animosities, jealousies that I dare say would be difficult for the newly arrived to understand, if I may say so, Sir. But they have invested a lot in the future, they are counting on the law, English law, to maintain their position, that is on the articles in the Spanish Cédula of '83, accepted by the English in the surrender document, remaining unchanged.

"Now, there are others, Free Blacks and Coloureds from the French islands, veterans who are vengeful and dangerous, who have killed Europeans, white people, as we call those from the temperate zones, and will do so again, here. These must be dealt with, rigorously.

"This place is not like Barbados, Sir, it will develop differently. Free People of Colour with wealth, slaves and education will make this place different. They see themselves as French. In Trinidad, they are the majority, outnumbering the whites five-to-one, and together with the small European French population, who can't return to France because of the revolution, they dominate the culture. Trinidad has acquired a French identity from them, that identity will last for generations."

"Yes. Rubbish, but I understand, it's a French thing, go on."

"Your Excellency, the Free People of Colour should be encouraged to do well. I would advise against allowing them to grant manumission to coloured, mixed race slaves in their possession. In Grenada this tipped the balance towards an uprising in '95."

"Yes, I see that. Go on."

"Their concerns have mostly to do with inheritance, the right to practise their religion, and their professions, and, the holding of commissions in the militia, there aren't many of those yet, but there will be. Actually, all they really want is to be respected and to have lighter complexions."

He smiled. The governor did not. Rosette was farting like a forest donkey.

"In this colony, Sir," François continued, "the majority of slaves, for the moment, are in the town. They are domestics, trades-men, some are dangerous, but most enjoy the comparative laxity and opportunities that the town's life offers; they are rented out, some save money so as to purchase their freedom. All this should be safeguarded, and then there will not be any trouble from that quarter.

"The slaves on the estates are a different matter; in a different world. As the ones brought in from the French islands die out their replacements are African born imports, some are primitives and must be cowed. Fortunately, most of the estates are far apart. The proprietors, their owners, know how to keep discipline, which must of necessity be harsh. However, the *Code Noir* must be applied fairly. The slaves know about this law. A great many planters are very cruel."

"Cruel, what d'you mean?"

"Men who are afraid to lose their investment work their slaves to death, slavery generates wealth, the price of sugar is high since the fall of Hispaniola, your Excellency. In the Naparimas where the estates adjoin one another, an uprising there will spread quickly. I have heard rumours . . ."

"Yes, so have I. I will deal with that, with them, go on man. Go on!"

"I have been told that recently on many estates the torture of the blacks is on the increase. Some are burnt, roasted alive, others crippled, to keep them in terror. There are great crimes taking place, which will become known abroad, in London, Sir. In response to these excesses on the estates, the African born Obeah-men assemble a body of Negroes, many fresh from Africa, to draw a little blood from all present. This they mix in a bowl with gunpowder and some graveyard dirt. A match is put to it, and the fetish or blood oath is administered. By this they solemnly pledge themselves to inviolable secrecy and to wage perpetual war against their enemies, us."

"What rot, I'll declare martial law and hang the lot."

"That would be very expensive, Your Excellency. This ceremony is referred to as 'Taking the Swear,' and is a most powerful ritual. After the explosion, and as the smoke clears, dirt from a freshly opened grave is mixed with blood and put into the mouths of those assembled. If guilty of a falsehood, the false one's belly will swell and he will expire. It's quite a spectacle, your Excellency, the fire blazing, drums beating loudly, frantically, people excited. The slave society has created a new religion."

"Religion, eh? Sounds more like the sort of thing that my mother-in-law and her relatives get up to in Llanrhaeadr-yng-Nghinmeirch. North Wales. Been there? No. I expect to have several of these magicians executed, burnt at the stake in the main square, next to the gallows. That's what. What you say, eh, Rosette?" More loud snoring from there, accompanied by farting.

"I would caution vigilance, Sir, the planters have experience, they will deal with individuals on the estates. The government should act only within the law."

"Humbug!"

Beyond all that, François was curious: how long was slavery going to last? Vast profits were being made in England from the West Indian colonies, as a result of the revolution in Hispaniola. But, from what he understood, there was a strong movement in England, led by a committee for the abolition of the slave trade, to end the trade on the grounds of justice and humanity.

"If I may say, your Excellency, in the United States, I understand, there are some states that have outlawed the importation of slaves, Rhode Island was the first. Now the Slave Trade Act of 1794 has been passed. This prohibits ships destined to transport slaves to any foreign country, from entering or outfitting in American ports . . ."

"No fear, Mr. de Gurvand. Some in London talk of making this colony a model for the abolitionists, but, I understand that this is a commercial colony. We will keep all that we have conquered, slaves, plantations, factories, you lot, hard at work. We will win the war against France. We took Martinique, St. Lucia and Guadeloupe in '94. We dealt with Hugues and his brigands in Grenada and St. Vincent, now we are here! And will open up the South Americas. No fear. You will make your fortune. England will not relinquish this island or any island in the Caribbean Sea. I speak for myself, I will take it to them, those who have it in mind to invade me here from the Main. I know where they are. As for your concerns with regard to the slave trade, it will last another one hundred years, too much profit in it. Let Paris free their blacks and see what happens, France suffers. Your fellows in Paris, they have no vision of the world. All their wars will be continental. And they will lose them in the end. Mark my words. They will re-enslave the slaves. Finish your whisky. Yes, knock it back, good man. I will not detain you. Go now, we will speak again. Good night, Mr. de Gurvand. Good man, that's right, close the door . . . Rosette! Rosette!"

12:

1797. José Maria España,
A Patriot's Death.

José Maria España sailed for Guadeloupe from La Tinta Bay on Chacachacare, there he met Victor Hugues. They were soon joined by Juan Piconell and those others who managed to escape the executioners of La Guaira. Very quickly, they realised that the man who was once aggrandised by the South American patriots as a hero of all revolutions and the doyen of the republican movement, a fellow Maçon, a philanthropist, was now an unapproachable despot. Hugues, assuming the role of demagogue, ruled the island by appealing to the popular demands of the ex-slaves and the perpetual petulance of the coloured class, whose ridiculous claims for satisfaction he accommodated, making sure to collect a commission for all transactions.

He was now engrossed in the business of enriching himself. All revenues of this rich and formerly prosperous colony passed through his hands. His power was immense, his personality, megalomaniacal; he was the master of his own island kingdom and wanted to hear none but himself speak, and took neither time nor patience to listen to what he called the carping pointlessness of philosophical discourses.

"I have no use for Masonic jargon. There is no place for that here. The revolution has been accomplished. I warn you, now, do not engage in that form of discussion with the people around me. Do not seek out those who have survived the purge of traitors. I will consider that treasonable. You will be guillotined!"

His outburst, particularly as it was accompanied by a crescendo of resounding slaps upon the table at which they were dining, sent bottles tumbling over, and freshly fried fish and fritters flying. This shocked and frightened the already confused España.

"I have read the letters addressed to you that came from Trinidad. Colonel Picton is manipulating events in Güiria and in other places on the Main; well, you are better off there, where you can do his work for him."

After this, Hugues stormed from the room. This signalled an end, as far as the Venezuelans were concerned, to their hoped-for support from their erstwhile hero's sanctuary. They became aware that they were being followed, and after the death of two of their number, who were garrotted, Sicilian style, they made plans to leave the island. They were not prevented, in fact they were facilitated. Juan Piconell left for Florida that very night.

Upon returning to Trinidad, José Maria España found Manuel Gual living in the town-house of the Corsican planter Símon Agostini, which also housed the Atelier Les Frères Unis. He was recovering from his ordeal and appeared better, but did not leave the building, not even to go to the rum shop. He was visited regularly by the local priest, a Father

Magneval, with whom he appeared to have a surprisingly familiar relationship. España noticed that there was a guard post, manned by English soldiers, within sight of the building on the Rue des Trois Chandelles, and its surveillance was open and indeed known to all. It was now altogether a different environment. Under English rule, or more specifically, under Governor Picton's rule, everyone was more discreet. Vincent Patrice and the brothers Dert, to España's surprise, appeared to report to the governor.

The afternoon's shower over, a cool southerly brought the rankness of the mangrove into the room to mingle with the aroma of the governor's dinner on the boil, and with the rich breath emanating from hogsheads of rum recently received in payment of favours.

"Señor España, it is my intention to take advantage of the confusion that is at present taking place in the Spanish provinces on the Main." Governor Picton, speaking very loudly, was standing in the full dress uniform of a British colonial governor, at a window in Government House, overlooking the Plaza del Marina. "I will offer protection to those who are prepared to rise up against the Spanish authorities, and offer free trade, yes, to the people of Caracas. I will distribute pamphlets and manuscripts up and down the coast, I will incite the people to visualise the successful achievement of independence. Free trade with England. The world is full of the discontented. Seduce them with the first maxims of revolution. That's the ticket. I expect you to help me. I will give you gold, muskets, men, some trained, some willing to commit themselves, others, well, we could turn events in the direction that you and your compatriots have in mind. England is at war with Spain, a Spanish empire rotted at its core, with an imbecilic religion. Superstitious rubbish. Spain is now at the end of its life."

Below, on the Plaza, the southerly breeze was causing the bodies of Jean Ricard, a Free Mulatto, and another, Hugh Gallagher, whom he had sentenced to be hanged from the newly erected gallows for larceny of livestock that morning, to sway and bump into each other. His gaze, however, was directed at the quiet western sky, which had assumed a delicate blue that tinged quickly to pink and then suddenly to a powerful magenta with rays of gold, illuminating his epaulets and backlighting the pale purple mountains of the Paria peninsula.

José España's head was pounding. He was affronted to hear his religion and native land spoken of in such a manner; anger brought him to his feet. This governor was no different from Victor Hugues. Vincent's raised hand and his look of alarm caused him to pause and regain his seat.

"We are at your service, Excellency," said Vincent. "The Spanish authorities are bewildered and overstretched, the people are ripe for an uprising, oppression has pauperised a generation, all that is needed is . . . "

"Enough. What you say, España? Let the man speak, Patrice, for God's sake!"

But with hardly any English, José España, now beside himself, was just able to bow, and hope that his expression conveyed compliance to what he thought Vincent said to the governor.

"Sí, Señor, Your Excellency, we are appreciating all helping hands that, that *como se llama* . . .".

"Excellent, excellent, Patrice, tell him we will supply him with what he requires. Hey, Patrice, have you heard that the people at Caracas and the governor of the province have offered a bounty of twenty thousand silver dollars for my head, eh, what you think about that, eh?"

"I think you should offer two dollars for his."

"Excellent idea. I'll have a thousand pamphlets printed. Excellent, excellent, good man. Now be off with you both. I expect Mr. Maingot, the surveyor. He is to draw up some plans for me. I will expect you to call on me Monday week, Patrice."

José Maria España left for Güiria by the month's end. He travelled aboard the sloop *Barbara*, a vessel converted by Governor Picton into a sloop-of-war to raid the coast, to transport arms and to propagandise the villages on the Caribbean coast with leaflets printed by Picton's people on François' press now with much greater effect. José España's brother Manuel was the ship's pilot. Once more disappointed, José's return to his hacienda was haunted by misfortune. News came to him within weeks that his brother was arrested by the Captain General of Caracas. Vasconcelos was alerted by Don Miguel Herrera, the governor of Margarita, who was ever watchful for news from the islands, and in particular Trinidad, where numerous spies posing as religious penitents were in his pay. Manuel was found with a cache of arms and a large supply of gunpowder together with documents that gave the names of people with whom Governor Picton was in contact. He, together with others, was executed with medieval tortures.

José María España, no doubt acting without the caution that he may have previously employed, set about raising a militia for the purpose of starting the final revolt. He was especially angry having heard the rumour that Manuel was manipulated by Picton to draw the Spanish authorities into an action that was sure to anger the people and cause rebellion, and in so doing further destabilise the area. José decided to arm the slaves on his hacienda and to train them in anticipation of the uprising that was now imminent. He was betrayed.

Some months after the conclave at Mon Repos, Geraldine Carige handed a number of letters to Vincent Patrice. They were brought over from the Spanish Main by Santiago Mareño Sr. and were from Brothers in Isla Margarita. One of them was from the Premier Surveillant of Lodge Excelsior 651, Juan Gonzales Ibarra. In it, Ibarra described the execution of José María España, an act that had horrified the country.

"The time has come to tell of torments new . . . The entire province is in mourning," he wrote. "The book of fate was wrong by several years. The houses are closed and all doors barred. Every window in the city of Caracas is hung with black crêpe; the anguished voices of mothers and daughters who mourn proscribe an already reluctant dawn. The melancholic tolling of bells from every church has gone on for days, and there is a disconsolate, in truth fearful, silence of people in the streets, this tells of an uncommon and appalling event. The market is empty.

"José Maria España's wife has been jailed for life. She is being proclaimed a heroine by the common people. When the soldiers came to her she held pistols in both hands. Her belt, with a sabre, displayed a copper plaque on which was written 'Long live liberty.' They said to her 'You are pregnant' and told her that she should not appear in public in the absence of her husband. She replied that 'to birth a child she did not need her husband.' She is fearless. They asked her how many people she knew in La Guaira who were involved in the insurrection. She told them 'Even the women.' I am assured that she is not in want in her incarceration as the gentlemen of Caracas have helped her with all her needs.

"On the morning of the crime, small groups of people gathered silently. Like a crowd left behind, they were like strangers to the place and gazed around. A column of children, on the way to church with their professor, appeared in a state of stop, as though painted on the rain. In the main square, ironclad soldiers stood still, some distressed, others affecting boredom. Just then, a confused coterie of hooded, barefoot friars emerged from the misty drizzle, mumbling imperfectly the Latin prayers for the condemned that they could barely understand.

"Soldiers, marching in step and armed with pikes, exited the gaol in close formation, anxiously glancing at the still and noiseless crowd that quietly grew and converged and drew near to where I and an Irish Brother stood in the shelter of a doorway; it was drizzling from before the beginning of the world. The friars, joined by those of the Order of Monks of the Adoration, carried wine and water and alms bowls and cried in funereal tones, 'Perform generous acts for the soul of a man they are about to execute.' In a slow moving cart he came, wrapped in a blanket. The cart, pulled by the emaciated white mule once the possession of the Archbishop of Caracas during the Vice-Regency of Don Cristobal Felix de Mendoza y la Hoz, was followed by several priests who spoke to José María España alternately. He appeared to listen intensely, nodding and looking up into the low-hanging clouds or perhaps he was looking at the windows, at the ones who were there to see how he would manage the act that marked the end of his life.

"This was José María España, now a man in his forties, I would guess, haggard, badly bruised, being hauled to his execution. Even in this desperate condition he must be admired for his courageous demeanour and his upstanding and graceful figure. The harsh voice of the town-crier, loud against the melancholy that pervaded everything, strode ahead of the cart, ringing a big brass bell and proclaiming the sentence. As José María España reached the foot of the scaffold, the pigeons took flight and vanished into the rising anguish. Handed from the cart, he appeared to falter, but surrounded by the priests who could be heard admonishing him against the sin of pride and cautioning him as to the imminence of judgement, he resumed his posture, squared his shoulders, and lifted his chin. He stood, barefoot with bound hands, among the party of officials, whose wet great-coats shimmered black in the perpetual drizzle, deepening the sense of tragedy with their carrion-bird-like appearance. As the people pressed around, their silence caused alarm in the hearts of those mandated to organise his execution, and he was swiftly moved towards the scaffold and pushed up its steps to stand out for a long moment alone next to the gibbet. This was when assembled sobs, wailing cries and heart-wrenching entreaties began to rise above the rattle of weapons, the doleful murmur of those who prayed, the chant of the clergy, the tolling of the iron bells, the rain, the stamping of the horses, and the choruses of angels weeping for the devastated souls of this lost and hopeless people, who silently sanction the murder of their hero sons.

"José María España turned to face those about him and those who were gathered in the wet square below the scaffold that reflected in its rain-washed stones the memories of nightmares destined to reappear whenever it rained the tears of mothers. With eyes that looked them all in their eyes, he said, 'My ashes will be honoured in this very spot by my country.' He was then hanged by the neck until he was nearly dead, was emasculated, disembowelled, and beheaded, then chopped into four pieces; these to be dispatched posthaste to various distant parts of the country as an urgent reminder to would-be insurgents and conspirators of the consequences of disturbing the King's peace. The simple people were then innocent and not accustomed to perceiving public death. They found it impossible to leave so as to resume ordinariness and for a long time waited for a different ending to commence, until the increasing downpour made them invisible to each other.

"In this manner did the New World form her political characteristics. I tell you this that it may make you sad."

13:

1797–1803. Domingo Antonio Vallecilla,

The Poisoner.

Having instigated de Gurvand's betrayal of his Masonic oaths and successfully evaded Vincent Patrice and the brothers Dert & Dert, Domingo Vallecilla, with the aid of the intrepid Enrique, the dealer in this, that, and the other, was able to assume invisibility. First, he stayed in the bowels of Enrique's emporium on the Calle de Santa Ana, avoiding the live cargo that passed through on their way to hell. He then appeared to have vanished. In fact he was disguised as a Warahoon woman, after being painted red with roucou, and was put aboard a corial that was paddled by real Warahoons westward towards the estuary of the Mucurapo River into which they disappeared before the sun arose.

In the weeks and months that followed, Domingo Vallecilla was hidden by them in the heights above the Bellevue valley in Maraval, first from the local militia who were fleeing in the wake of the collapsing Spanish establishment, then from the pursuing English, and later from the black republicans who were escaping the execution squads despatched by Governor Picton.

Because of his reptilian physiognomy, he was seen as a curiosity by the savages, becoming a favourite with the children. His original purpose never far from his mind, he made discreet enquiries concerning the whereabouts of Manuel Gual. Enrique had warned him to be cautious. Gual, he told him, was in the custody of the Maçons who were controlled by the English governor, who was possessed by a hanging daemon, so unless he wanted to have his neck "popped," as the English say, his advice to him was to stay well-hidden.

This advice he took seriously, and when the tribe, towards the middle of that year, commenced its migration to their rainy season habitation high up in the Northern Range above the mosquito belt, he was pleased to be allowed to follow them. Nudity appealed to him, voyeurism came naturally and had its charms; the climate was salubrious, the only thing he could not get accustomed to was the food; he hated lizard.

Father Hubertus Magneval, during this time, became increasingly and uncharacteristically humble. His craggy features grey with his unshaven beard, his cassock often filthy, he polished off this affectation with a convincing pretence of encroaching dementia, a silly forgetfulness of names, and an artful habit of vagueness and feebleness. He actually "forgot" to say Holy Mass. All this was concocted so as to deflect the attention of the governor from his ongoing intrigues. Picton actually threw him out of his office window. Father Magneval had attempted to bless him, after pronouncing a benediction in perfect Latin, when it appeared that that was to be followed by some form of laying on of hands.

Vincent, Magneval knew, was as deadly an undertaking as the governor, and was in truth, one that was more imminent.

"Magneval, the governor threw you out the window, eh?"

". . . . . . ? "

"Serves you right, but I can see right through your antics, your pseudo-decrepit pose. You want to be suddenly old and simple, to hoodwink him, to deceive Manuel into revealing something, anything, and to spy on everybody. Take care, one word from me and the wind will pass beneath your feet, as you hang from yonder gallows."

He is becoming very similar to the governor, thought Father Magneval. In truth, he, Vincent, John Black and that swinish Saint Hilaire Bégorrat are all adopting the governor's manner of speaking.

"Vincent, my son, tomorrow is the feast of the Sacred Heart of Mary . . . its roots are in the Marian apostolate of St. John Eudes."

"Hubertus Magneval, you have become so obvious, anyone can see that you are just pretending to be, all of a sudden, a simpleton."

"Vincent, old age and this climate have taken their toll. I know that I am not myself, but I beg of you kindness and patience, these are horrible horrible times. The Governor Picton, yes, he pushed me through the window, I could have been killed, but praise the good God, I lived, I have lived through terrible times. Vincent, tomorrow is the feast of the Sacred Heart of Mary, Manuel will attend Holy Mass . . . this to be followed by a special procession in which . . ."

"Look here, Magneval, Manuel Gual is in danger of his life, there are people who will kill him if they see him on the street, and God will not help him."

"Do you believe in God, Vincent?"

"No, I believe in good. Your religion is a melancholy affair where crucified life is venerated and sorrow is promoted together with ill-defined regret, based on the notion of being the victims of a mythological crime which took place at a time antecedent to all understanding, which resulted in the propagation of perpetual guilt that can only be alleviated by the likes of you. No, Manuel Gual will stay where he is, now be off with you, go to the confessional, make yourself useful, mind people's business."

Father Magneval left Vincent's store on the Rue de la Place and walked slowly towards the grass market. He was overtaken by a grunting, shackled column of branded slaves as he passed into the Plaza del Marina. Vincent, who followed him out, stood at the door and watched him as he went, tripping over his feet, down the muddy, filth-filled street. Manuel crossed his mind anxiously. I must get him away from this priest, who has served his purpose. Manuel is well enough now. Picton appears distracted by the arrival of this Colonel Fullarton, who has come to investigate him. With another one on the way, that's English politics. Picton has overstepped his mark. The English, I hope, are creating an army to invade South America. I must get Manuel back to La Guaira, he has to take up where José España left off, if he has it in him, is able, but that's another thing. Picton too has served our purpose. He has kept the Spanish authorities occupied with the threat of an imminent uprising, so as to prevent an organised attempt by them to recapture this island. He is damn smart, beneath all that bluster. His irregulars stormed that fort in Güiria, destroyed it and killed dozens of the French fighters who were expelled from here just last year. He sent the others scampering into the high woods, where they are sure to be picked up by the cannibals, put into cages, strung up into the trees and fattened up. They would have staged a rebellion there for the single purpose of transporting it to Trinidad, and then welcomed Victor Hugues who would have taken the place from the English and introduced the guillotine. Picton thinks that we are waiting for the uprising to start. Does he know that we are waiting for Francisco de Miranda?

Now, I must get Manuel out of here, to somewhere safe, perhaps San José de Oruña, and from there to Maracas Bay and then to somewhere on the Mainland. Picton controls the waterfront, the Bocas, he controls every damn thing. Everybody is working for him, even old Señor Mariño, he has made him his harbour master, the old crook is delighted, this legitimises his contraband business. The entire Gulf of Paria is patrolled, spies like termites flying on a rainy day. He promised to allow the use of the parcel of land, Don Chacón's redoubt, just overlooking the Dry River, at the eastern end of Calle de San Louis, that he has renamed Queen Street, to erect a new temple for Les Frères Unis. I must see that he signs the deed, his days may be short here. Mount Moriah I will name it. Does he know that we are waiting for Francisco de Miranda?

The tribe, with Domingo Antonio Vallecilla in tow, had arrived at the petroglyph, an enormous boulder embedded high up in the southern flank of El Cerro del Aripo. It carried on its mildewed surface deeply engraved messages, which were the memories of an extinct people's experience of when the world had last ended. It told how these fortunate survivors of that cataclysm had managed to survive only at this altitude on account of the dramatic increase of the sea level that had occurred when the Andean ice caps suddenly melted, as the result of the meteors colliding with the earth, causing this island to be sundered from the rest of the world. They left this account that no one was now able to read.

Manuel Gual was subsequently ensconced at the dilapidated hacienda of Don José Ramón Muxica y de Basanta, Trinidad's last Spanish royal treasurer, in San José de Oruña, the colony's ancient capital. Don José was currently in Spain liquidating his family's fortune, having come to the conclusion that his interest would be better served in British Trinidad. Knowledge of Manuel Gual's presence at the hacienda filtered from the atrium of the crumbling ajoupa mansion that was situated directly opposite to the capital's daub and wattle church, and trickled down the steep hill in the shouted gossip of the *blanchisseuses* to the river bank, where an impromptu market had taken root on the very spot at present occupied by the overflow of the old cemetery. From there, as news, it was carried by canoe, up the Caroni River to the tribal *encomienda* at Arima, where the unfortunate remnant of the Taíno tribe existed in travail. As a fragment of general information that was already confused with other stories concerning buried treasure, it spread into the network of villages beyond the heights of Guanapo, reaching as far west as Tacarigua, and eastward to Toco. This buried treasure story came about as the result of the elaborate secrecy that was enacted on the part of the Maçons surrounding Gual's removal from the Atelier on the Rue des Trois Chandelles in Port-d'Espagne, thus instantly arousing the suspicious imagination of the ever-watchful.

From Arima it travelled as a rumour told over campfires up and through the Cumuto forest, then across the footpaths that crisscrossed the ridges of the island's Northern Range. It developed a sense of drama that was aided by premonitions of the return of the effigy of Yúcahu Maórocoti, the deity of cassava. These held that the deity had not merely returned, but was reincarnated and had manifested himself as a marvellous quartz of amber and purple that possessed its own light source, and that Yúcahu Maórocoti had come to redeem the tribes, despite their lack of piety and the inauspicious presence of the aliens who had ruined their ancestral hunting grounds, desecrated their burial sites by the construction of missions and *encomiendas*, and were persistently denigrating the custom of ceremonially ingesting one's enemies, while preaching to them the very same thing, exhorting them to: "Do this in commemoration of me."

Domingo Vallecilla would not have picked up the rumour at all if it were not for the parrot that accompanied the constant retelling of the story. This parrot, Macomer, whose name was appropriate to his inclinations, belonged to Floriencia Matarol, the Catalonian cook who was emotionally attached to Manuel Gual and accompanied him to his hide-out in the old colonial capital.

Escaping, so as to explore his new environment, Macomer was soon seduced by some juveniles high up in a mango zabrico tree, where he found himself stuck in *la gli* and was taken away by a party of tribal people loosely affiliated with the Warahoons, with whom Domingo Vallecilla was sojourning. Immediately upon entering the misty encampment high in the low-hanging clouds that encircled the petroglyph, and upon sighting Domingo Vallecilla, despite his nudity and absurd costuming, Macomer immediately shouted "Manuel Gual, Manuel Gual," chuckled, rolled his tongue in the style of Catalan market women and asked for a cigar, proffering his right claw with an insinuating tilt of his head that contained a knowing expression in his one-thousand-year-old-eyes.

Domingo Vallecilla decamped the very same night and five days later was once more with Enrique, who provided him with a change of clothes and a competent description of Floriencia Matarol, the Catalonian cook and owner of the parrot who, Enrique felt, was sure to accompany Manuel Gual wherever he was taken. Enrique also supplied him with an introduction to a poisoner by the name of Zinga who lived in the slave quarters of the La Fantasie Estate in Sainte Anne. Next came a frightful afternoon with the old black man who displayed several snakes in his hat that appeared during the interview, giving him the atmosphere of an Egyptian pharaoh, after having bought several capsules made from bee's wax containing opium and some others concealing finely ground glass from the Obeah-man, Vallecilla came away with an urgent attack of diarrhea.

Devoid of any inclination to either dilly or dally, he resumed nudity, arranged to be painted red by the Carib boy with the obsidian knife, and started immediately for the heights of Aripo, making sure to carry his western clothes in a tightly woven *macoute* that was slung across his forehead and hung down his back as seen done by the Warahoons.

Dressed as a poor penitent, he entered San José de Oruña and made directly for the little thatched roofed church at the top of the hill that had been built in the decade before the visit of Sir Walter Raleigh in 1595, and immediately sought absolution. His litany of sins, some invented, many true, alarmed the young Capuchin Father Francisco Antonio Santaella to such a degree that Domingo Vallecilla's penance was in no way dissimilar to the legendary labours of Hercules. Satisfied with these, his obligations, as they would allow him to be under the watchful care of Father Francisco Antonio Santaella, the impetuous Domingo Vallecilla became a pillar of the church, in a manner of speaking.

In the weeks and months that followed the commencement of his penances, some of these medieval—and of the type to be conducted in public—he gathered about him a circle of pathetic supplicants. And because he had memorised the legend of *The Very Sorrowful Romance,* a morbid tale of those who had been reluctantly converted and who had taken revenge for that imposition, resulting in the martyrdom of several Capuchin missionaries at the nearby Arena savanna and the subsequent death by suicide of these tribal people. He retold this in dramatic renderings at times embellished with angelic visitations, becoming immensely popular with the post-menopausal women of the parish. All this was made especially poignant as the very Capuchin missionaries martyred were interred beneath the floor boards of the church, where their bodies were found unviolated by decay, emitting the aroma of freshly baked cassava pone one hundred and seventeen years later.

Amongst these pathetic supplicants was Floriencia Matarol, who perceived in Vallecilla a certain vulnerability, discernible in his naturally weak chin, shifty yellow eyes, plaintive voice and vague resemblance to a dwarf turtle to which she had formed an unnatural attachment during a period spent with the Sisters of Perpetual Sorrow in their convent in La Vall de Gallinera, where the now deceased Duke of Gandia had brought from Majorca one hundred and fifty families to repopulate the valley after the *reconquista* in 1609. Her family was one of these.

Their subsequent familiarity was of the purest conception, as they discovered astonishing similarities in the manner in which they both conducted their devotions and in their mutual affliction of sleeplessness. Domingo Vallecilla suggested prayer, vigil, and mortification of the flesh. In these they both avidly participated, sharing tracts, hand-written copies of devotional prayers directed to Saints Merozanes, Aristaces and Gregory I, the Illuminator, to grant wisdom, and to Saint Tdeus, the Apostle, for immunity from the sin of carnal knowledge. They compared knee callouses, brought about by constant and impulsive devotion, and on one rainy evening she allowed him to glimpse, for the briefest moment, the cause of her self-inflicted mortification.

St Paul speaks of joy in suffering in Colossians, he reminded her, when he said, "I rejoice in my sufferings for your sake." She obtained blissful rest, and dreamed dreams of unspeakable ecstasy after accepting a tisane comprising decoctions of cerasse, chamomile and cannabis. Now convinced of his knowledge of botanicals, a knowledge that in modesty he tried his best to diminish, she was pleased to accept from him several dozen somewhat larger pellets of the same preparation for Don Manuel who was plagued by the daemons of the night, and, as such, needed much stronger medication. Later, the suffering of this poor man's passing was heard throughout the parish as minute slivers of glass sliced through his intestines, producing agony so potent that it disorganised his opium dreams, inducing nightmares beyond the imagination of Durante degli Alighieri, commonly known as Dante.

Manuel Gual's funeral was attended by the entire San José de Oruña parish, who overheard his anguished cries on the moonless night of his final agony, even though not one of them had ever laid eyes on him, with most of them standing in the rain outside the church's closed doors. They were all astounded by the appearance of the full complement of the Atelier Les Frères Unis in ceremonial attire, resplendent with hoods, capes, sashes, collars, jewels and insignia, green and gold gauntlets, lambskin aprons decorated with esoteric symbols expressed in Renaissance-inspired metaphor and allegory, wearing the white gloves of the innocent, while bearing naked blades. The ritual for a Lodge of Sorrow was conducted at the grave-side by the ancient Past-Master, Chevalier de l'Orient, Thomas Maturín de Gannes de la Chancellerie, to the horror of Father Francisco Antonio Santaella, who, being unacquainted with rites of excommunication, hurled curses at the Maçons in an incomprehensible Andalusian dialect, to the amazement of the Warahoons who noticed that some words and phrases curiously resembled endearments in their own language.

Domingo Vallecilla, resuming nudity, painted bright red, decorated with a gorgeous head dress of parrot feathers, the remnants of the insouciant Macomer, whose last words had been "Fuck the British," faded into the cemetery's surrounding underbrush to vanish from history.

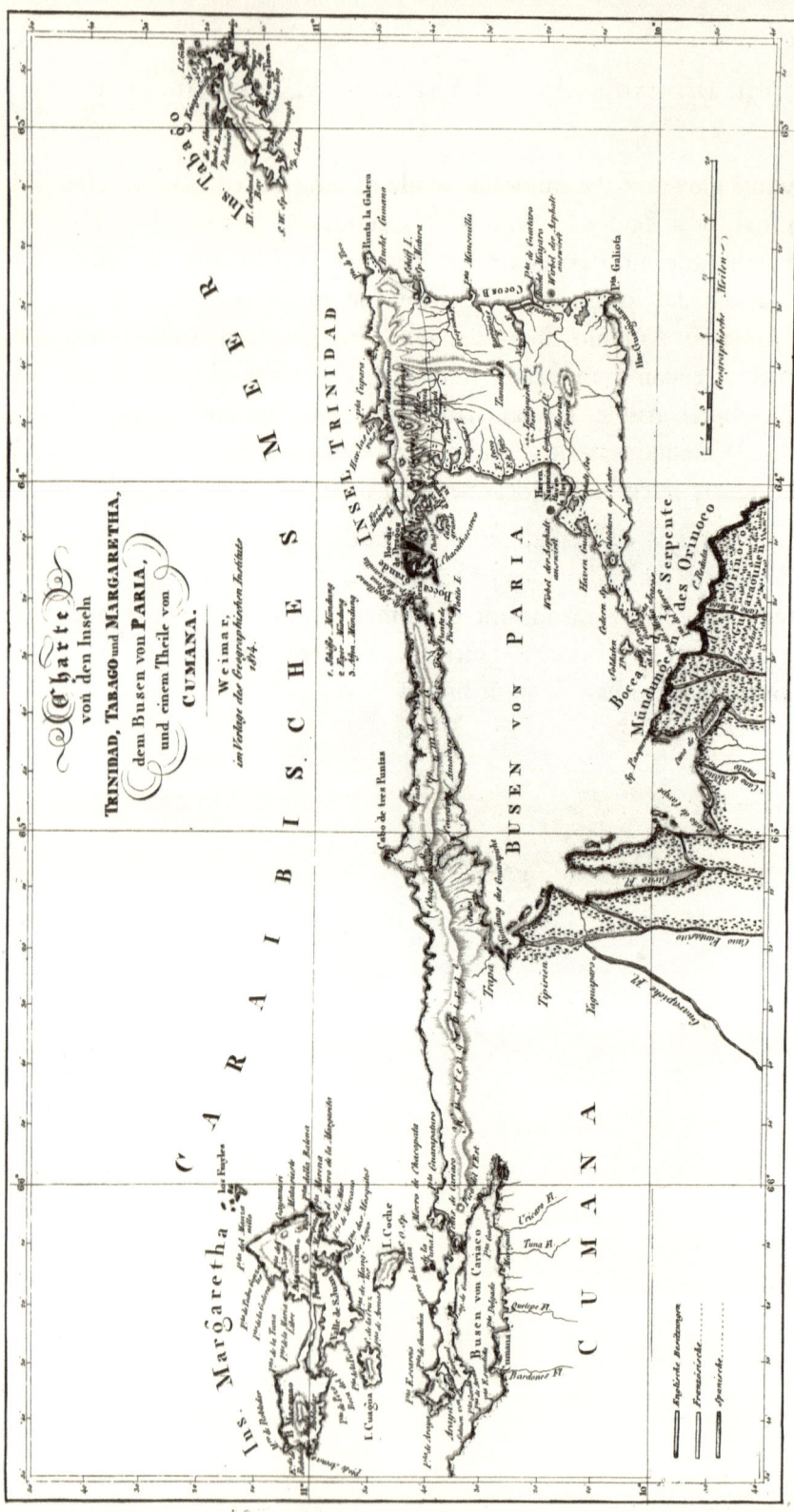

Map by the *Weimar Geografisches Institut, 1814*

BOOK TWO

14:

1804 –1808. Francisco de Miranda,

Maître de Guerre.

Riding on the winds of chance, Sebastián Francisco de Miranda Ravelo y Rodríguez de Espinoza, attired as a lieutenant general of the imperial Russian general staff, stood on the foredeck of the *Leander* and contemplated the mud flats exposed by the receding tide.

Black into grey slimy streaks of muddy sand burbled up the hot breath of the mangrove's rot, held hostage gigantic Amazonian driftwood, exposed marooned flotsam, entertained diverse crustaceans, comatose algae, evaporating Portuguese men-of-war, tufts of sullen metallic green seaweed, and was pockmarked, beneath the hammer of noon, with innumerable holes of various sizes from which millions of crabs sought cautious egress and eager ingress in a frenzy for survival beneath the watchful shadows of swift, low-flying egrets. He did not feel the anvil heat. Beyond the fringe of stalking, oyster-bearing mangrove lay Port-d'Espagne, discernible from this distance by slim columns of wood smoke.

He thought that he was either too early, or too late. The moon, doing her duty, caused the sea to rise, bringing with it the exhilarating odour of incalculable distances. In a dreamscape silence, disturbed only by the clunk of the oars in the rollocks and the grunts of the blacker-than-the-night oarsmen, he sat in his own splendour, moving in the time and space of the traveller who was still connected to his point of departure.

His ship, the *Leander*, named for the beauty who swam the Hellespont to meet a lover, turned at anchor, putting the schooner *Trimmer* into eclipse. Further in the roadstead, the Royal Navy's *HMS Express* and *HMS Lilly* stood by, fully rigged, their companies on deck.

The *Leander's* boat unable to venture further, Francisco de Miranda was lifted from his seat by the giant, evil-smelling coxswain and deposited on a turfette, where he was immediately ambushed by hordes of *phlebotominae* and *aedes aegypti*.

Rescued by a deputation of nine with drawn blades, headed by the Vénérable Maître Vincent Patrice, he was conducted to the residence of Frère Símon Agostini for refreshment, and then escorted upstairs where he was received by me, Littais L'Eau, in my capacity of Frère Servant with due and ceremonial form in the dingy light of the sparsely furnished anteroom. I relieved him of his martial cloak, plumed, gold-trimmed lieutenant general's hat and ebony stick with its gold death's head knob and assisted him with his apron, sash, collar and golden chain of Vénérable Grand Maître of La Gran Réunion Americana, founded by himself, handed him his white, kidskin, monogrammed gloves and his green and gold gauntlets, after adjusting the black Moroccan leather gold-bound scabbard that displayed the diamond-studded hilt of the ceremonial sword that was presented to him by Her Imperial Majesty, the Empress Catherine, soon to be called Great, of all the Russias.

With practised grace, he turned to receive the attentions of Frère Expert Tuileur, who with breathless haste passed him through the mandatory "testing" of visitors, putting to him, while smiling apologetically for impudences imagined only by himself, a miscellany of disconnected questions drawn from the rituals of the seven Degrees worked by this Atelier, which he answered in clear, perfect, unaccented French.

This act of Tuileur was assisted by Dominic Dert, the Frère Sacrificier who also, acting as Frère Deuxième Surveillant, invited him to sit in the *salle des pas perdus,* a tiny dull-green alcove that contained just a small straight chair whose cushion was stuffed with human hair, and a miniature deal table upon which rested the skull of Louis-Philippe René Nicolas Estribaud, the first Vénérable Maître of Les Frères Unis, which was extricated from a pile of others after the massacre of Maçons on the island of Sainte Lucie several years previously.

Alone for the first time, he took it in his hand, held it and regarded, face to face, the grim reminder, with the flickering flame of the single candle playing life and death tricks of light and shade upon it. He might have been reminded of the words of the Persian poet " . . . the first morning of creation wrote what the last dawn of reckoning shall read."

Interrupted in his reverie by the nine who formed a *voûte d'acier,* he passed beneath their arch of glinting blades to the main door of the Atelier, which opened before him. There, he was met by the Vénérable Maître with the three mallets of the principal officer-bearers on a red, velvet cushion. These were presented to him; he accepted them with a courtly bow after placing his hands for a moment upon them. Following behind the standard-bearer, sword-bearer, bearer of the Volume of the Sacred Law, both Surveillants and twelve Brethren, together with selected Entered Apprentices, all dressed in black frock coats, knee breeches, white stockings, black shoes with silver buckles, carrying the three mallets, the keys of the Atelier and of the fund chest, and passing beneath another arch of steel, this time comprised of eighteen blades, he entered the temple last, the assembled company singing lustily, *The Most Excellent Master's Song,* and stood before the altar and saluted the Vénérable Maître, who rose in response. He was then conducted to the east by the Director of Ceremonies, where he was invited by the Vénérable Maître to occupy the throne of King Solomon, placed upon an elevated dais beneath a canopy of sky blue, decorated with golden stars thereon. For this momentous occasion, the Atelier was draped in crimson silk.

His first words were, "Assist me, Brethren, to open this Lodge."

In his war diary that night, sitting in the lamp-lit attic of Símon Agostini's town house, he wrote: "We have decided to immediately send to Trinidad all the armament, uniforms and everything else that is ready, so that there will be no delay in our operations on the continent, in case war is declared against France, the probability of which is imminent."

In the weeks that followed he made the acquaintance of Brigadier General Sir Thomas Hislop, the colony's second governor who replaced the indomitable Lieutenant Colonel Thomas Picton after a furious scandal involving a post-pubescent girl of indeterminable racial background, her lover, stolen money, the *coquin* Saint Hilaire Bégorrat, Valot, the gaoler, his Negro henchman, Porto Rico, the inevitable torture in the garret of the old Spanish gaol opposite to the market on the Calle de San José, called by the French, Rue de la Place, which would be named George Street for mad King George III.

All of the above was further complicated with the arrival in the colony of a person by the name of Fullarton, a commissioner representing the English parliament's interest in the governance of the island; this precipitated the island's first commission of enquiry, the first of hundreds that were concluded inconclusively, and eventually ignored. Picton's situation worsened when the London papers published shocking accounts of the torture of slaves in Trinidad, thus instigating virulent anti-slavery protest. This was followed by the eventual recall of Lieutenant Colonel Picton to England, his disgrace, his half pay, his rehabilitation and subsequent death, which was heroic, at the battle of Waterloo that decided the fate of the world. Picton, from his appointment as governor of this unruly colony, was seduced by its hallucinating lifestyle, becoming the victim of indiscretions caused by distraction in the midst of the aforementioned.

Francisco de Miranda was born to be a celebrity. His first public act upon arriving in Trinidad was to issue an address to the general public in Spanish, French, and English. It called upon all Spaniards and French Creoles to join him in the liberation of his native land. He concluded with: "The gulf that Columbus first discovered, and honoured with his presence, will now witness the illustrious actions of your gallant efforts."

Having associated with the most powerful, the most celebrated persons in Europe and the United States of America, which included the Prime Minister of the United Kingdom, The Right Hon. William Pitt; Catherine of Russia; Francis II, last Holy Roman Emperor; Napoleon Bonaparte, Emperor of the French; the first President of the newly created United States of America, George Washington, with whom he dined in Masonic Harmony, having just left President Thomas Jefferson, whose acquaintance he made during his Paris days at the Lodge of Nine Muses, after he won their support in Paris, London, Washington and St. Petersburg, where he was commissioned lieutenant general of the imperial Russian general staff, presented with six thousand pounds by the British Prime Minister, William Pitt the Younger, ships of war by the New York business community, several of whom were members of the Lodge at which he had received Masonic Light for the very first time, he now stood poised to be immortalised.

He found support in Admiral Alexander Forrester Inglis Cochrane, commander of the Leeward Islands station, who supplied the English squadron, which were stationed at Barbados, to escort his arrival in Port-d'Espagne. He now proceeded to make the acquaintance of the town's notables, seeking their support, guidance and discretion in his sacred undertaking, which was to establish an Inca empire of the South Americas that would be administered within a Masonic Constitution, similar to the one created by his Masonic Brothers in Washington that brought the United States into official existence.

His undertaking was greeted with alarm by some who feared the possibility of an exaggerated war so soon after the depredations that were so recently endured, spilling across the narrow straits of the Serpent's and the Dragon's Mouths. Others looked forward to war on the Spanish Main as a way to make easy money; many saw it as an adventure that they would be loath to pass up, just in case someone said two decades hence, "Hang yourself, there was a great battle for the liberation of the Americas—and you were not there," while a dedicated few perceived the magnitude of these reality-changing events and understood that this was how the world was altered in the past and that the time was now, and there was only ever one moment to strike iron.

One of his first actions was to journey to the island's ancient capital, San José de Oruña, so as to acquire for his voluminous records the death certificate of Don Manuel Gual, his comrade in arms, Brother and friend of his youth. He carried with him the last correspondence received from Gual, which read; "My friend, I would not write to you if it were possible to see you." And went on, " . . . the American people only desire one person—come and save us . . . I only have one passion in life and that is to see this dream become reality, the only honour I desire is to be your subordinate. I am proud to have been outlawed by the Spanish government as the author of the planned revolution of Caracas in 1797 . . . You will be, if not the principal, then the agent of your country to give effect to that wonderful liberty that only needs to be begun." Oh this dear man, he almost sobbed. "The revolution failed because of my absence from Caracas as the government discovered my plan through the indiscretion of a stupid person . . ." He had read it so many times, but always . . .

To his horror, upon arrival at the little daub and wattle, thatch-covered church at the top of the hill, beneath which the Arena martyrs slept while emitting the odour of freshly baked cassava pone, he was informed by the pious women who tended the altar that there was no grave to be visited, and by the blushing boy sexton that there was no death certificate to be seen. Father Francisco Antonio Santaella, he was informed, in his rage that very day of Señor Gual's interment, personally exhumed the body of Manuel Gual from the consecrated ground in which it was laid because he, Manuel Gual, had died impenitent and was buried with a funeral service that was heretical, apostate, agnostic and pagan, and he, Father Francisco Antonio Santaella, personally threw the exhumed body of Señor Gual into the Caroni river.

Francisco de Miranda's ensuing rage, it was told, caused the church bell to ring in alarm of its own accord and the little organ in the choir loft to groan softly to itself. He turned visibly greyer as thunder rolled out of context in a perfectly innocent sky. He went in search of the priest who had performed an act so dastardly that could only be dealt with by instant death, swift and unequivocal. Father Francisco Antonio Santaella was never heard of again.

This crisis marked his future with an X. Everything was dated before or after. John Black and the Irish Brethren of Union Lodge received him and honoured him. John Black wrote to him—"Dear General, Christmas times *con nosotros* are times of feasting and merriment. Esther and I would be delighted if you would honour us . . ." He received a letter from John Adams, the American lawyer, statesman, diplomat and political theorist. A leading champion of independence in 1776, the second president of the United States, who thought him "an Achilles, hurt by some personal injury, real or imaginary." He was touched to tears, how did he know already?

His dejection in the mud flats at Port-d'Espagne came about as a result of his failure at Puerto Cabello, six months, eleven days and sixteen hours earlier.

He had sailed from New York. The awesome mantle of destiny, like armor plate bestowed by the proximity of the great, hung about him. The rumour of his potential eminence, sensed even by the senseless, differentiated him. Jefferson's Masonic handshake still pressed in fraternal solidarity into his imagination, the grip of Brotherly Love, Relief and Truth, a faithful promise in an unfaithful world, made him feel invincible.

It took no more than a round of cannon fire, the town of Puerto Cabello in plain view, to disperse his little fleet, two schooners, the *Bee* and the *Bacchus*, and he in his beloved *Leander*, a swift corvette, thank God, of two-hundred-and-ten tons that was armed with eighteen guns.

That encounter with the Spanish Royal Navy was an unqualified disaster. Had he landed his contingent, the world would now be a different place. Glory, he so wanted all this to be over, this war that must be won, quickly, so he could become one with them, Washington, Jefferson, Adams, Smith, even the Negro Toussaint-Louverture, all fellow Maçons: "We hold these truths to be self-evident, that all men are created equal, that they are endowed by their Creator with certain unalienable Rights, that among these are Life, Liberty and the pursuit of Happiness."

That dreadful night, on a gently rolling sea, where upon the mottled surface of an enormous yellow peregrine moon, which seemed to occupy the entire horizon as it trembled on the edge of a silvery sky that marked the precipice of a glorious day, there appeared the ink-black silhouettes of the *Ceres* and the *Argos*, Spanish ships of the line. Their rapid fire and dexterous maneuvers shattered the ocean's serenity, and the fore-day morning promise of the purity of glory.

How he read of and wept for the fate of the sixty men whom he abandoned in his flight. Forty put in chains to rot. Ten shot by firing squad, then beheaded, their heads neatly packaged in iron cages and sent to hang over his America's city gates. He made for Bonaire and then Barbados. Cochrane was there. He was not abandoned by the English. His spirits soared. Governor Hislop, by far a more refined person than his predecessor, welcomed him, and gave him the freedom of the town of Port-d'Espagne.

He wrote letters, kept in uniform, shoes shiny, danced at the ball held at Government House with a superb French matron, a widow, with fireflies sewn into the lace of her gown. He took her for a stroll, she lit up the walkway, he flirted, he wanted to see how bright her ethereal lights could glow. They illuminated the governor's love seat. He worked hard, he recruited, they came to see him. He was sunburnt from the voyage, his hair white, his eyes a warrior's.

He met the Maçons. François de Gurvand, courtly, inscrutable, self-effacing. Vincent Patrice, the Maître now. Between them the fissures of ideological incompatibilities—of no interest to him. His obeisances to the elderly Chevaliers, Símon de Gannes de la Chancellerie, Henri-Dieudonné de Jacques de la Bastide, Michel du Pont du Vivier de Gourville, all Past-Masters of Les Frères Unis, old royalists, their world ended, were appreciated, admired, minuted. He met the henchmen, the bothers Dert. The Corsican Brethren, the bankers, eager, greedy, optimistic, with cash in hand and an eye to the future. Outside a voice sang:

Ma Leideo sans de gleau

Dit fey dans Ma Leideo . . .

He sailed to Chacachacare in the company of a flotilla of bedecked small craft, darting ahead like dolphin, others wallowing in the *Leander's* wake. He stepped ashore booted and spurred, his uniform resplendent, on Carige's jetty, his elegance not conspicuous, nor inconsistent with the howling red monkeys, the flocks of migratory Orinoco parrots, the somnolent iguanas, the visiting troupials, the indifferent pelicans, the rusticities of the environment, if only because of the beauty that greeted him with aristocratic charm, the Old World's grace that he so cherished, adored, desired, glorified. She, María Rosa Carige y Ortega, and her daughter, María Atanacia, her husband, Don Santiago Mariño de Acuña, their handsome son, Santiago, made speechless, his sister, the beautiful María Concepción. Disdain and hauteur, smoldering in her shining eyes, were instantly recognisable as being a part of his world, as was Geraldine Carige, husband of María Rosa Carige y Ortega, son of William Carige, Laird of Kilfenora. The real world. He did not perspire. He did not even feel the heat of the day.

They listened, bewildered, as he explained to them the familial intricacies of the Inca imperial dynasty. How a Masonic theocracy might replace Catholicism as a method for national identity formation. He spoke of the retention of aristocratic values, once the vile Bourbons were retired to an appendix of history. He was in a hurry, he said, to meet with Admiral Cochrane, a man with whom he could go into a war, he told them.

"There," he pointed at the sails entering the Grand Bocas, "there is Cochrane now!"

He rose to his feet, a telescope appearing as if by magic in his hand, to expand to more than two feet in length, its shining brass catching the afternoon light to reflect into the hazel eyes of María Concepción for the briefest moment.

He could make out the ships of the line, identify them. "There, *HMS Lilly*, twenty guns, *HMS Express*, twelve guns. There, *HMS Attentive*, fourteen guns, *HMS Prevast*, eighteen guns! Sixty-four guns, my dear Geraldine."

And before Carige could answer, he exclaimed, "Look, look, there the gunboats *Bulldog* and *Mastif*, they carry mortars,

Carige." His spreading hands could hardly describe the size of shot, he slapped his thigh, and turned about to face Santiago, whose excited eyes could barely contain him.

The impression left upon Santiago and his sister María Concepción would become embedded and be recounted in their families for centuries. They had met the Precursor. His proclamations were issued, he now commanded five or six hundred men under arms in Port-d'Espagne. The English were with him, he forgot his distrust, his inhibitions and his frustration in his dealings with them. The President of the United States of America wished him good luck . . .

"You see, there is Cochrane."

That Amerigo Vespucci gave his name to the New World. That Vespucci had walked the Caribbean shore of La Vela de Coro, that shore, there, now made invisible by an early rainy season storm that was presently delaying his landing. This was of enormous consequence to him as he stood on the *Leander's* plunging deck with sheets of wind-driven rain arriving, wave after wave, blown seaward by powerful westerlies that took his breath away and put into disorder his thoughts. The significance of his landing place had just occurred to him. The conquest of America commences now, where Amerigo Vespucci and Alonso de Ojeda had walked in 1499. The bombardment of the fortress's defences commenced as the clouds lifted, August 3rd, 1806. He was thinking of the opening statement for his war diary. His men swept ashore. The sea boomed on a high, vast curve of sand. The sun came out. He came ashore. Behind him, on the horizon to the lee of the harbour, he could see the seven English sail, fine ships of the line. He accepted the salt on his lips as a sacrament, *Do this in commemoration of me.* Up ahead on the low hill he could see the crumpled outline of the fortress San Pedro, its guns in disarray. The captaincy general of Venezuela, his to have.

The flag, of his design, first flown at Jacmel, Haiti, re-sewn by the beautiful Señorita María Concepción Mariño y de Carige, the gunsmith who handed it to him with her eyes lowered, modest, with hands that trembled, just a little, that glistened with sweat, just a little, as the sun set gloriously on the wooden jetty at Chacachacare that evening in the soft air as he left to meet Cochrane in Port-d'Espagne. The memory indelible, as when a man sees something wonderful, and both believes and disbelieves at once. Now it floated in a rain-washed sky above the fort named for Saint Peter. *Upon this rock I will build my church, and the gates of hell shall not prevail against it.* All events, names, places were possessed of significance. It was that time of his life. "Your destiny is to create in your land a place where primary colours are not distorted," Johann Wolfgang von Goethe said to him. Yellow, Blue, Red. Now to Coro across a rolling deserted landscape, thunderheads black as nightmares, booming, ceaseless rolling thunder, the artillery of the gods, Coro, deserted, not a cat in the streets. They hung the tricolour from a church's steeple.

Later he wondered what became of the Spanish royal standard. Nobody came. He regarded the well-washed air that teemed with flying ants. Ten days later he sailed from the port where America was given its name. There was no popular uprising. After the violent suppressions which followed the aborted Gual and España attempt to alter history, and the end of the pamphleteering of Governor Picton and François de Gurvand, the population on the Caribbean coast did not have the inspiration or heart for it. He dined with Les Frères Unis, at Harmony the Brothers *fêted* him. The Vénérable Maître, instructed me, Littais L'Eau, as Frère Servant, to be of service to him.

15:

1804 –1808. Vincent Patrice,

Courage and Patience.

Damn it! Now it becomes a joke. Fault. That's a corpse that no one wants to be related to. He, de Miranda went there, to Coro, hoisted into a windstorm of glory, howling mostly in his own imagining. He was in a hurry. Do it quick, then write to Washington, to Pitt, to Russia, hold a parade, move into the palace of the viceroys.

Now, they say I should have warned him, that we should have stirred up the people more effectively. That the partisans were deprived of the mechanisms for subversion, of hope of revenge, sedition administered as flyers, pamphlets, rumours, dreams of acquiring what was not worked for, the right to sleep in other people's beds, with their daughters, their wives, their sons, their dogs, their donkeys. We did not remind them recently of the yoke of Spain, of their medieval travail, the weight of immemorial suffering.

We had, we did. François did. Picton did. Up until the other day. Damn it! Cochrane left him. De Miranda sailed for Aruba. "Shall I take it?" he wrote to Cochrane. That was outside Cochrane's remit. Napoleon's forces were on it in small numbers. Cochrane's instructions were to go, go to Trinidad. Then they limped into the harbour here. Damp flags, limp, the red has run into the yellow and all into the blue.

The common people, the slaves, the inevitable Negroes, the republicans, the idle coloureds, the poor whites are *fêteing* him and his freedom fighters. When I saw them disembarking, their heads bowed, defeated, ashamed, I felt for them. But the crowd cheered. There was food and rum and women to go around; in these islands that is all that matters.

A party of English officers on the quay side opposite to the Mole that leads to Fort San Andrés, where a slave auction was just concluding, laughed out loud when he came ashore. Mocking him. He looked good, though. Smart. He was freshly shaven, his uniform impeccable, his diamond-studded sword worn high on the hip, Russian style. His boots gleamed, his spurs jingled. His hair, white as snow. A black groom held the stallion's head, a guardsman the stirrup. The Englishmen's laughter became audibly forced. Someone shouted, "Spit in the air, and it will fall on your nose." Was that meant for him or for the English? Who the hell knows, this Trinidad is decorated with such ambiguities. A society that delights in the unintelligible, in every kind of confusion and obscurity. A black woman said, *"Eh bien, c'est gai."* Another, *"Eille le gros, on voit ta graine!"* I have news today that Geraldine Carige has died, I must write to Doña Antanacia and María Concepción.

Undeterred. "There is an army being trained in Ireland," said de Miranda. We were at Harmony, Les Frères Unis' festive board, meagre these days. Littais L'Eau, the Frère Servant, has become his batman. Good. The Corsican Brethren, who now sit together at the bottom of the column, no longer fawn and favour him, their former clinging ways subsiding in the face of diminishing returns. "Do you know how many money has gone in the spout?" asked old Pietri, his Mediterranean accent thick with rum. "He is to come back the leader of a new state. No?"

"Not yet." I answered.

"Stay? For what?" I said to de Miranda that very night. "There is nothing here. Yes the people hailed you as a hero who fought for freedom, but in this place that could change tomorrow. Tomorrow those same people could be hailing a Grenadian adventurer, a rebellious slave or an English pirate. Go to London," I told him, "there are men in Caracas, now, who will take up the cause. Young men infused with idealism. Patriotism is refocused. And there is money, these young men have money, family money."

He still speaks of Manuel in the present tense, as though he were alive.

He hid the dunning letters coming from London. But his debts were in the newspapers coming from London, exposed by his creditors. He owes money to tradesmen, to booksellers, to antique dealers. He does not feel ashamed, "Everyone always owes these people," he said, he cares nothing for the tortuosities of the common mind. White Hall still believes in him. The Right Honourable Nicholas Vansittart has written to him.

"Turnbull presses me very much by his last communication to come to England. . . There is an army being trained in Ireland, under Moore. The English parliament has accepted the idea that South America is ready for an invasion. Pitt will want to see me."

"Return to London," I repeated to him some days later, when we were awaiting Sir Thomas Hislop's pleasure in the old unpainted plantation house owned by Edward Barry, on

Belmont Hill, which serves as Hislop's official residence. He was pacing the sitting room, or what passed for it in the leaky, drafty, dilapidated house, which contained in all its rooms, the foetid smell of unwashed house slaves. That night the house was buffeted by a strong north-easterly that blew out the candles and brought in a misty, invisible drizzle covering every piece of furniture with a layer of damp that turns to mould, which turns to rot.

"Return to London," said the governor over dinner. "The army in Ireland was in preparation even before Colonel Picton left Trinidad. My brother tells me that Arthur Wellesley will take it."

"He is in Denmark at present, I hear," said he.

"He is to go to Ireland in January. Where he will take command of nine thousand infantry, my brother tells me," the governor added.

"Nine thousand infantry. Sir, I must meet my commitments to my men here, in Trinidad. This means that the *Leander* must be sold."

"John Littlepage, I believe may be the man. I, myself, am disposed to enter into this cause. I know the country, General. As you know I was there, in Demerara, Berbice on the Essequibo."

"You took them from the Dutch," de Miranda said, taking from his coat pocket a pamphlet that I recognised at once, it was one of Picton's. He read it out: "Good fortune is offered to the inhabitants of the Spanish Main: complete and entire liberty for all your commercial activity; suppression of duties both incoming and outgoing; permission to cultivate whatever is desired and sell the fruits thereof; election of the government of their desire, under the protection of the British armed forces."

"It is not difficult to excite rebellion in the Spanish provinces of Cumana and Caracas, whose effect and example will encourage the whole continent to revolt."

"It is not difficult, General," said Governor Hislop. "Not difficult, I will make myself, how shall I say . . ."

"The Spanish are entrenched in ways that we can hardly imagine," I interrupted. "It is, very difficult."

Then the true purpose of the meeting: "My dear sir, it saddens me to report, Mr. Pitt, the Prime Minister, has passed away."

He took it well. He sat in silence for a while, placing one silver napkin-ring upon the other on the governor's thick, white tablecloth, making a little tower. He must have some deep place within that rock-hard frame to take things like the death of his only pillar of support in a bastard's world, a hell of a place. To face defeat, ignore disgrace, derision, that few men can out-stare; risk failure from which there is no reprieve: he takes it all well. He rose from the table and wandered out into the rainy, dimly lit front gallery, walking softly so as not to disturb the sleeping sentry.

He sailed for London in October of 1807, to discover that Pitt had left no documentary evidence or record of having dealings with him with regard to an expedition of a military nature. But there was an army in waiting in Ireland to invade South America.

Tonight, as the Atelier emptied, I was able to detain Brother Agostini. I have not received any communication from the Premier Surveillant of Lodge Excelsior, Juan Gonzales Ibarra, in almost a year.

It was a noisy meeting. It would appear that Frère Charles Hugon has been accused of exchanging Masonic secrets for two dollars and six bottles of porter. He is reported to have uttered injurious allegations against the Craft, stating that curiosity alone prompted him to become a Maçon. A Monsieur Louis de Montrichard is the other party involved. The matter is to be called to the tribunal, his sentence, if he is found guilty, cannot be less than that of de Gurvand's.

All this has excited Frère Pierre Lange, popularly referred to as *L'ange de diable,* who slapped Frère D'Abadie hard across the face as we sat at Harmony. This absurd squabble actually taking place as the Atelier dined at the festive board, over the head of the seated freshly installed Premier Surveillant, Frère Verteuil *fils.* Blades were drawn. There will be a duel, in Point Fortin, I suppose. Good. Not even those regular bloodlettings have eased the social tensions. Panic, as contagious as cholera, is the epidemic raging amongst these planters. This colony's economy is doomed. The abolition of the slave trade, unthinkable just a few years ago, has meant the closure of the bottomless pit that has spewed the endless stream of miserable blacks sold out of Africa by their rapacious rulers. This, of course, means ruin for the overstretched. And sheer greed has made them all overstretched. When the London trading houses begin to fail, a disgraceful portion of history will come to a close. Their world has ended. I have received the news that the great soul Cagliostro has died. The world is now a smaller, shabbier place.

"Símon, walk with me."

Símon Agostini, sly, snobbish, avuncular, loyal to François de Gurvand, is a font of trivia. Information flows to him ongoingly from eavesdroppers, spies, informers, his network of filial allegiances, fellow Corsicans and their multitude of relations on

Terra Firma. We all suffered loss of property and in some cases, loved ones in the catastrophe of the conflagration that destroyed almost the entire town earlier this year. Agostini in particular: his town residence, which was the first home of the Atelier, his store-room and warehouse continued to be a smoking ruin that was only finally quenched by the onset of an early rainy season. That calamity will set back the colony decades.

Agostini could not have wanted for a better audience than myself. First he spoke of the money that he lost in virtually all his most recent transactions, not to mention investments, loans and Powers of Attorney that he extended to his multitude of cousins, Giuseppi, being the most villainous it would appear.

The new temple at Mount Moriah had been erected. He admires the appurtenances. The Corsican craftsmen have done wonders with depictions of the Tracing Boards for all the work executed in the twenty-five Degrees of the Rite of Perfection on the temple's walls. Then, we discussed our new Pennsylvanian Constitution. Then, Holy Royal Arch, this Chapter was constituted in 1804. He appeared to be in doubt. We will keep our own workings, I assured him, our cherished Symbolic Voyages in all Degrees, no fear.

"De Miranda," Simon said, tilting his *toupé* forward, "after scrutinising the emptiness that lay before him, decided to re-embark, eh? I do not blame him. Venezuela is a wilderness beyond imagining. It would have been out of the question for him to venture into the interior with a small band of mostly foreign mercenaries. He has left the printing press with me."

Printing press. That was news. From North America, well, now there were two printing presses on this godforsaken island that possesses a population of two or three thousand, with all but half illiterate.

"The hangman has burned a portrait of him. Do you know?"

"No."

"Yes, in the main plaza in Caracas. His pamphlets, by the hundreds, burned, and his proclamation for the independence of the Americas, burned. The Bishop of Mérida has declared him 'atheist' and 'heretic'. They fear him. Has his luck left him?"

"No. He makes his own good fortune. He has the support of the English and those in Washington. But he will need the support of Venezuelans of substance. Now, what of that young fellow, Bolívar? I understand that he was passed and raised in Cádiz?"

"Bolívar was initiated into the Scottish Rite, Vénérable, in 1806. He was raised to the sublime Degree of Master Maçon in the Scottish Mother of St. Alexander of Scotland in Paris. He is now in Charleston, South Carolina, Vincent. I have this from Isaac de Costa's son, Abraham, Jacob Pinto's brother-in-law."

Now, that is of interest. The founders of the Scottish Rite, the so-called eleven gentlemen of Charleston, of which de Costa was foremost, brought into being the Mother Supreme Council at Charleston in 1801. They work thirty-three Degrees. So now Bolívar is there. That American Supreme Council, if Bolívar and the partisans who are reorganising themselves become successful, will, through him, them, the Americans, attempt to assume jurisdiction over South America, if only by virtue of the attractive "higher" Degrees they offer, which outstrip ours at Les Frères Unis, or what de Miranda has cobbled together in La Gran Réunion Americana. If Bolívar takes up the mantle of revolution, these American Scottish Rite practitioners of Charleston, with money to invest, would be in a very fortunate place. I must inform de Miranda at once. I wonder if Bolívar has the courage, the charisma, the luck?

"La Candeur Lodge in Charleston, Bolívar has dined there, Vincent. He has met with Alexander de Grasse Tilly, the son of the French admiral, the most famously connected of all the gentlemanly eleven. De Grasse is named to become the Grand Commander of the West Indian islands, perhaps South America. Vincent, the Southern States are the future for us. Not so? We should be seeking close friendship with the people who are most like us, planters, not the Northerners in Pennsylvania. No? We have a similar economy, the slaves, when the English cut them off from us so as to get our land, we will have to find a place to go. The South, Carolina, will be a good connection. No?"

"No, Símon, our future is with the South Americans, over there, four or five miles away, which the English will help us to win, through Francisco de Miranda and the new young patriots. Our connection with the Grand Lodge of Pennsylvania is a convenience for the moment, to stop the English colonial governors from perceiving us, Frenchmen, all together in Les Frères Unis, a French Lodge, as republicans in support of France, with whom they are at war. Not with Washington, yet. But Símon, tell me about Bolívar, have you met him, do you know him, what sort of man is he?"

"I have never met him. His people are well-established in Caracas. Very old family, connected to Diego de Losada, the founder of the city. They were there when de Berrio was looking for El Dorado, and Raleigh was looking for him here in San José de Oruña. People say his father is descended in a questionable way."

"What do you mean, questionable?"

"Oh many generations before, they say, a name appeared on the Bolívar family tree, a Señorita Josefa Marín de Návaez. She was the offspring of the important Don Francisco Marín de Návaez, but the mother's name, which, we are assured, is most illustrious, cannot be mentioned because Josefa's birth, it is one of those mysteries of nature."

"I see. I understand, with the aristocracy all and sundry must be accounted for, please go on, what about it, why do you mention it at all?"

"Well, Vénérable, if the young Bolívar has the blood of the native American in his veins, which is what is implied, he will be of significance to the population in general, more so than de Miranda, I believe."

"Yes, I see what you mean, Símon. But how do you know that Señorita Josefa's mother has Indian blood?"

"Because it is a very small society. If the mother of Josefa was a Spaniard, an *hidalgo*, an aristocrat, everyone would know of her indiscretion, it would have been a scandal, but if she was a mixed race person, the daughter for instance, of an eminent man and an Indian, or even a mixed Negro woman, few would know, it would be of little consequence. It is not uncommon for a person such as Don Francisco Marín de Návaez to have a half-breed mistress and for a daughter, the child of the liaison, to be reared as a lady, educated in the convent and brought up in his household, and for her to marry into a family of quality, such as the Bolívars. It is the life in the colonies. She may have been an heiress, bringing silver, gold or copper mines into the Bolívar family from her Indian heritage, or her father's, for all we know. The seventeenth century is a dark age in the history of the colonies. But his Indian blood, resurrected at the right moment, could serve a revolution's purpose."

"Quite so Símon, quite so, but go on, what sort of man is he?"

"A serious man. Don Simón José Antonio de la Santísima Trinidad Bolívar y Palacios Ponte y Blanco. A high-strung man. He was orphaned in his youth, his mother's people, the Palacios y Sojo y Gil family, are as grand as his father's, very refined. He and his brother Juan Vincente and his two sisters inherited one of the continent's greatest fortunes. They were well brought up by relatives. I have all this from my cousin Alfonso Giuseppi, he married Doña Antonia de Salas, do you know him?"

"No, no, can't say I do."

"I see. Ah well. His daughter is the celebrated beauty Señorita María Scholastica Trinidad de los Angeles of San Juan de Aricagua estate, such a virtuoso. No?"

"No."

"Ah well. Caracas copper, as it is known throughout the world, don't you know it is the cornerstone of the wealth of the Bolívar family, as well as sugar plantations?"

"No."

"He was well-educated from his early youth. Tutored by Andrés Bello, almost his contemporary, and of course, Antonio Negrete. And later by Simón Rodríguez, who was his private instructor and mentor. Rodríguez, as you know, was forced to abandon the country. He came here in '96 with his brother Alfonso, who is a Maçon."

"I had no idea."

"Rodríguez was accused of conspiracy at the time of Don Manuel Gual and José España. Bolívar entered the military academy in Valles de Aragua as a cadet, when he was fourteen years of age. His father was once the Colonel-Director there. He is a serious young man, not as playful as many of his generation. He married in 1802, but his bride passed away the following year, too sad, too sad. She was of the well known Rodríguez del Toro of Madrid, don't you know?"

"No."

"Ah well. My cousin Don Antonio Juan Prieto de Posada and his wife Doña Josefa will travel to Caracas in the *petite carême* and will bring more news for us. But my Brother, tell me, what do you make of the good father Dom Magneval, he has so many curious visitors. Spies?"

"So it would appear, Símon, so it would appear:—
Whence things have their origin,
Thence also their destruction happens,
According to necessity;
For they give to each other justice and recompense
For their injustice
In conformity with the ordinance of Time."

"What does that conjure, Vénérable Master? It seems a charm."

"No, it is a verse by Anaximander the mathematician, it crossed my mind as you mentioned Magneval. But come let us return to your house, where I may press you for a nightcap."

After leaving Símon I returned to my lodgings on the Rue Sainte Anne and sat in contemplation. Colombia was being born even as Agostini and I spoke. The degenerate Bourbons in Spain fear the parvenu Napoleon; the presence of such vigor sends them into the confusion of abdication. The news from Europe is full of Manuel de Godoy as Prime Minister of

Spain, he is the real master of the House of Bourbon, he sleeps in their beds.

The British naval victory at Trafalgar in '05 has changed everything: France and Spain are no longer powers on the high seas. I have lost track of the times that Spain has changed sides between England and France in the last two or three years, it hardly matters now. Charles IV gave way to his son, Ferdinand. King Charles understood that the Crown Prince Ferdinand appealed to Napoleon to aid in the ousting of Manuel de Godoy, whom he, Charles, rushed to support. Imagine, Godoy, his wife's lover. He did this to preserve the life of Godoy, the Prince of the Peace, who became a prisoner of the French. Then the populace rose at Aranjuez. Charles' abdication took place in March of this year, the next day his son slipped into his place as King. Ferdinand, they say, is mistrusted by Napoleon, who has one hundred thousand soldiers in Spain.

Ferdinand now has been forced to abdicate as of the 6th of May, 1808, but because his imbecilic father relinquished his rights to the Spanish crown on the 5th of May, the day prior, in favour of Emperor Napoleon, Ferdinand has effectively given the throne to Napoleon. What idiots.

Napoleon has put his brother Joseph on the Spanish throne. What is it they have with thrones? The Spanish people have not accepted that, with the exception of some of the nobility seeking their own interest. Uprisings are taking place in the cities and towns all over the country. Provincial juntas are being established, that is significant, that is revolutionary, since the central government has acknowledged Joseph. But the news of the success of Spanish arms at the Battle of Bailén has proven to the people that they can resist Napoleon, for the moment. The Council of Castile has opened negotiations with the provincial juntas for the establishment of a Supreme Central Junta, in support of Ferdinand. A revolution has now commenced, in Spain just as the English are preparing the army in Ireland for the Venezuelan expedition. Choices.

News of all this has, of course, come to Caracas. De Miranda is publishing a journal from London that he has called *El Colombiano*, which he makes sure is on every ship leaving English ports to cross the Atlantic bound for the Indies, and in which he makes the point that the Spanish Bourbons have allied themselves to the executioners of Louis XVI. Venezuelans, royalists, now understand that the Spanish people have risen up against the shameful abdication of their Kings, those Kings who have handed over the crown to such a common person as Napoleon's brother Joseph. This family, as everyone knows, is related to the Ciprianis, now residing in Trinidad, Güiria and Tucupita, for Heaven's sake. Cipriano Cipriani is in Tucupita living in a hut with an Indian woman, and is drunk on *cacapoule* rum every day. His son is bankrupt in Trinidad and lives a hand to mouth existence in a ruin of a house on the Rue Sainte Anne, receiving charity from the Lodge's Almoner. For these Spanish Creoles this person can never be a King.

De Miranda, a master of propaganda, is finally getting the people in Caracas to believe that the English, despite being all heretics, plus their accumulation sins, have been of help in the struggles in Spain against Napoleon, by landing troops on the Spanish peninsula. This will deprive de Miranda of military aid for his conquest of the Americas. Another grave disappointment. That army that he was counting on, which was being built up in Ireland, is now for Spain. The English War Office asked Sir Arthur Wellesley to give him the news. He took it badly. He bellowed at Wellesley as they walked on the Strand, Wellesley tried to escape by walking ahead. When he cooled, Wellesley offered to take him to Spain with the army, he refused. He said that he did not want to interfere with Spain. Ridiculous. Thomas Picton is with Wellesley. He is now a major general. De Miranda could have been there, it would have served a good purpose, particularly in the eyes of the Creoles in Caracas.

As the news that juntas were to be formed in Spain, in support of Ferdinand and against Napoleon's brother Joseph, reached Caracas, the Cabildo there followed suit. But the situation is different over there, in Caracas, they have included a representative of the farmers, one for the merchants, and one for the ordinary people, which includes the pardos, the mestizos, the Free Blacks, the peasants, the Indians. Naturally, the Cabildo in Caracas views the junta as a subversive grouping, and quite rightly, as it is mostly comprised of Creoles who own extensive properties in this province, being in the main from families that have been here in the New World for two hundred or more years. They want to take the continent for themselves. Now, that is what de Miranda has been wishing for. Lucky, lucky man. As one door closes . . .

The following morning the letter from Juan Gonzales Ibarra comes to hand. Incoherent. Badly written. He must have written this in a coach. What he says is that April 19th, 1808, must be forever remembered in the history of the world because it marks the starting date of the South American revolution. Ibarra writes that there are a great many differences separating the several revolutionary groups. And of course being colonials, they are falling out over race, "indiscreet murmurings of equality". I can just imagine: who is black, who is zambo, who is Indian; whose mother's great-grandmother came into Caracas on the back of a donkey cart in the year that Vasco de Balboa discovered the Pacific Ocean...

Now this is important. Ibarra closes his letter saying that Simón Bolívar has suggested to the supreme junta that he be sent to London to establish a relationship with the English government and to seek aid, or at least neutrality. Bolívar understands that the English do not want to appear to be helping the colonies of Spain to revolt, while the Spaniards are helping the English to fight Napoleon on the peninsula. Simón Bolívar, it would appear, has received permission from the junta, with the proviso that he meet his own expenses, as there is no money in the treasury. He is to be accompanied by Don Luis López Méndez, in whom they have confidence as well as his friend and teacher, Andrés Bello. Bolívar is to be granted the rank of lieutenant colonel. Francisco de Miranda must hear of this.

Now. I have heard that Don Santiago Mariño de Acuña has died. I must write to them, I must see to his son Santiago. Yes, Santiago Mariño comes of age, he will be an asset, no, he will become a jewel to the Craft. The Atelier must go into deep mourning for three months. I will give crêpe to the membership, to be worn publicly.

16:

1810–1812. Francisco de Miranda,
The Precursor.

Because of his youth, his natural hauteur, his inborn self-assuredness, his inherited wealth, his New World panther instincts, the originality of his dreams and his previous experience of foreign travel, he was indifferent to the icy rain, the rolling fog, the darkness at noon, the grey averted faces, the incomprehensible language, the icy beds, the unpalatable food, the remoteness of the women, the undrinkable liquor; his arrival in the capital city of London held for him few surprises and contained neither disappointment nor alarm.

Along with his two companions, he came too late to the same conclusion. There would be no assistance from England in their attempt to liberate the New World. The English required the complicity of Spain in this historic war against a personality of such epochal magnitude as Napoleon Bonaparte, whose mere existence appeared to mount an inexorable challenge to their wished-for achievement and maintenance of world hegemony where their shopkeepers would become Peers of the Realm.

Simón Bolívar recognised in Richard Wellesley, First Marquis Wellesley, instantly upon meeting, a kindred character. Like himself, he existed in a landscape of heraldic glamour, enjoyed similar epicurean taste, and appreciated enigmatic women, well-bred horses, war, honour, and death with glory. They both had attended the coronation of the Emperor Napoleon.

As Foreign Secretary, Wellesley explained that His Majesty's government was opposed to any innovation in the American provinces. And England, now perceiving Spain as "her natural friend and ally," intended to prohibit all forms of trade, particularly of arms, in the Caribbean Sea, so as to leave the insurgent rebels in all of Spain's New World provinces defenceless.

Simón Bolívar, Luis López Méndez and Andrés de Jesús María y José Bello were to be spared the duplicity, the fickleness and the inherently perfidious nature of English foreign policy experienced by me.

They were shown, by Wellesley, the well-laid plans that were complete and ready to be expedited in support of the liberating troops I had raised on the island of Trinidad as well as the logistics of the army of Ireland, so long held in waiting for an English invasion of the South American continent. This would cripple Spain and contain her in her medieval geography. The hindrance to the execution of this plan to attack Spanish America was the spontaneous uprising of the Spanish citizenry, occasioned by the shameful abdications of their kings and the ascension to the most Catholic throne in Europe of Napoleon's brother, Joseph, a despicable upstart. Instead of sending this well-trained and more-than-adequately equipped army into South America, England seized the opportunity to defeat Napoleon in a divided Spain. The English army was placed under the command of Richard's brother, Arthur, to make the final lunge for the Napoleonic jugular. And the plan to invade South America now was to be indefinitely postponed. All undertakings, promises, oaths sworn and fraternal covenants discussed and agreed with me by the previous government were forgotten.

As Grand Master of the Grand Lodge of Ireland, the second most senior Grand Lodge of Freemasons in the world, Richard Wellesley entertained the young Americans in the Lodges and Guild Halls of the City of London, where he introduced them to significant interest, and, in so doing, facilitated the foundation for future investment and trade and opened opportunities for like-minded young men to seek their fortunes in commerce, and others, with glory, in the continental wars to be occasioned by the spontaneous coming into existence of the largest quantity of new nations ever witnessed in this world.

Naturally their most life-altering occasion occurred when they arrived at Grafton Street and were received by me, Francisco de Miranda, in my vaulted library, which contained, at this stage more than six thousand volumes, some of venerable age, crammed into gorgeous antique shelving. The scientific apparatus that filled the room appeared to them, I am sure, to anticipate the unknowable and to speak of unimaginable epochs. The lives of all of us, as South Americans, were now to be merged, crossed and mingled in a matrix that would forge the crucible from which republics would be poured into and out of and across a continent, changing the course of human development for a millennium.

Some flames burn brighter than others. As a distinguished Spanish writer and critic prophesied some time after this historic meeting: "The former Captaincy General of Caracas, now the Republic of Venezuela, has the glory of having given Spanish America its best man of arms and its best man of letters: Simón Bolívar and Andrés Bello." But others in that company must also be remembered and exalted by history. As Bolívar was to say to me, the *true* liberator of Colombia was López Méndez, who provided "the effective assistance . . . from London by pledging his own responsibility and that of the still insecure government of Venezuela"—to the extent that this Creole was imprisoned in London for debt as a result of personally guaranteeing credits granted to Colombia.

As for myself, called the precursor by some, I commenced this crusade for Liberty on July 24th, 1783, on the day that Bolívar was born. I told him that. The arrival of these three signalled for me, the recommencement and refocussing of my fabulous vision of a revolutionised and unified republic, stretching from the Gulf of Mexico to Tierra del Fuego.

Sitting in the same room, bathed in the diffused crepuscular light emitted from a source unknown to them, where Gual, Adams, Patrice, O'Higgins and men who would be presidents of the United States of America have met, at this same mahogany table, to discuss the future of the world before they were born, these young lions must have felt their impalpable presence, I am sure. They said they were honoured to sit at my feet. They saw me as their imposing compatriot, a fabled man, a great revolutionary who had been preparing the pathway to freedom for more than half his life and whose very presence, it was believed by the three, would ensure certain victory. I could not conceal the emotion that manifested like rolling thunder in my breast by the presence of those who were here to seek me out so as to complete my destiny.

Andrés Bello and Luis López Méndez were to remain in London; the former to sharpen his prolific mind in my library, and the latter to cement contacts with financiers and political lobbyists and to recruit the ones who must be more than

246

audacious, but also dauntless, intrepid and prepared to chance their lives in the creation of the New World's new world.

Simón Bolívar and I sailed from the Port of London for the Caribbean with November's driving wind chasing iron-black thunderheads above the Atlantic's icy rollers.

"A Colombian continent!" I shouted. "A canal across the isthmus linking the two oceans, where a capital city for the southern hemisphere may be established. I proposed this to the English government in '90. A gold and marble Corinthian capital straddling the Atlantic and the Pacific Oceans. We need vast ideas to stimulate the torpid minds of these Creoles, Simón. An emperor in the west, with the blood of the continent running in his veins."

I was bellowing now above the wind, my legs spread wide, hands gripping the quarterdeck's slanting rail. Beside me, Bolívar, shorter, frailer, with chattering teeth, his hair standing up straight from the edge of his skull having elevated his expression, nodded at my every word.

"Brass monkey weather, eh, Bolívar."

"What the hell is that?"

"When it's cold enough to freeze the balls off a brass monkey!"

Bolívar, ignoring the frivolity, said at the top of his voice, "Public morality to be altered by the introduction of energised political institutions. We cannot wait for them to evolve." The wind, streaming through the vibrating shrouds, tore away his words.

"We must be daring in this America," I said, laughing out loud, "where everything is new, where few things even have names. The republics that we will create must have a leading role in the evolution of science and commerce. We must take the lead in the new political dispensation of the world. We must not be like the tribes of Africa or become as the Negroes in the Caribbean. We must be at the fore of development of the human condition."

Bolívar nodded and found his voice, which was high pitched, but strong and resonant in the gale of wind. "To declare ourselves independent not knowing what will become of our children would be specious, would breed a macabre future with calamitous consequences."

"True," I answered, steadying myself as the ship dropped into the bosom of a giant wave.

"To imagine freedom without achieving genuine sovereignty, which can only be of the soul, live in the soul, would mean as much as the loose talk in the saloon bars of Maracaibo," continued Bolívar. I could see by his complexion that he felt the contents of his stomach rising as the ship rose from the trench of that enormous roller. "Where now men talk of these very things, forgetting that the ground beneath their feet belongs to people that they will never meet."

His eyes closed tight, his ears, by this time, I was sure had been made numb by the icy wind. "Where the ideas that they express are not their own, possessing no originality of thought."

"You're looking a little green, comrade, have no fear, she handles well both by and large." I meant the ship—she handled well, both into the wind, and with the wind. "A clipper, she's a clipper," I shouted.

"Yes. Please don't talk about it, *Maestro*. In Venezuela, where all things are imported, even religion, institutions need to be reinvented. Even our style of venerating crosses the sea, becoming something else by the time it is unpacked, stored in the suffocation of idleness, in the mindless warehouses of the uninitiated, to be disseminated to the barefoot priests who have no place for it in their consciousness and perform it as a charade without even understanding the meaning of that word."

He involuntarily reopened his eyes as the ship shuddered, pitched and sank again, leaving his stomach in his mouth. He gasped and swallowed nothing. "Then the night falls quickly, and in the dark they fumble to reproduce more of the same." He gasped and swallowed again.

"Indeed, Símon. Indeed. How could they understand the need to save the very language that they dream in?" I shouted, thrilled by the speed, the sounds with which the wind tore past, through us, as he shifted his frame to accommodate the rolling motion forward.

"By the creation of a new vocabulary that escapes servility, invent new vowel sounds that allow new thought to electrify the fibres of the brain," shouted Bolívar, holding fast to the slippery rail, and shaking his head so as to fling away the rain, the sea spray, the nausea. "So that unthought-of ideas might bloom in the sleepless vigilance of originality," he managed, dreading, I could see the inevitable descent into the abyss which would be followed by an incalculable ascent. The thought: *this fucking thing is never, ever, going to end*, must have crossed his mind.

"I have seen, *Maestro*," shouted Simón, his eyes, wide with horror, regarding the declination of the ship's bow sideways as it fell down and away, "young women from the best families of Caracas at the meetings where republican ideals are discussed, without reservation or inhibition, modesty forgotten, perspiration streaming down their bodies, how they forgot decorum, forgot themselves, in the heat of debate, shouting louder than the cockfight aficionados." He shook his head again and breathed in deeply the cold wet air. "They go, not to demand retribution, but to promise their unborn sons, their adolescent brothers, their lazy husbands to the revolution, and swear that they would, like the ladies, the Duchesses and the Queen of France herself, ride bare-breasted before the charging cavalry in the crusades against the Moors. They dream of a virgin America, and come from everywhere, from the dogfight districts, from the swamps, from villages so isolated that crabs come walking into church just in time for Sunday lunch."

"Well done, mi amigo, keep your eyes on the horizon. The world still believes in justice, spirituality and liberty, but has lost the faith needed to achieve these ideals. That is why they are dejected and live in fear and desperation. But this is a new age, Simón, the women of the New World are prepared to make the revolution for their daughters, they know that they are alone against everything."

"I made a vow," shouted Bolívar, clutching his soaked coat to his throat. His face, in fact, had acquired a greenish tint. "On Monte Sacro in the cold, gold dawn light of Rome, it was as though I experienced my destiny that night. I have no fear in my heart. I do not seek God's mercy or blessing. I know that I will die in this revolution. I will not be an old man in the lands that we will take." He shook his head and looked into the unrelenting wind tearing past us.

This wind, now becoming more tempestuous than our idealistic discourses, drove us below decks where our conversations continued beyond the Tropic of Cancer and even through the still and stagnant suffocation of the Sargasso Sea, in whose clear, midnight-blue, indeterminable depths we saw on nights so black that the universe found a mirror image of itself there, the enchanted eyes and glimpsed, in the phosphorescent glow, the sensuous forms of the mythological sea people who inhabit this suboceanic jungle.

I, Littais L'Eau, Frère Servant, received them at the bottom of the carriageway at the very front gate of Mount Moriah. Their ship had paused at La Tinta Bay, Chacachacare, en route to Barbados just long enough to lower a boat with them on board and land them and their belongings on the black sand beach. Taking the cliffside track with unsteady sealegs in the lingering dusk, they found the great house at Monte de Botella deserted, the bay empty and night fallen. Pappits, the old watchman, discovered them asleep on the grey and white marble tiles in the windy, leaf-strewn gallery and brought them and their baggage, which he rescued from La Tinta's black sand, to me.

Having informed the Vénérable Master, I arranged for the two to be accommodated at the house of Frère Tuileur and, the following evening, received General Francisco de Miranda and Colonel Simón Bolívar as fraternal Brothers in due and ceremonial form, according to and in recognition of their individual Masonic rank and attainments, in keeping with ancient custom as maintained at Les Frères Unis, where, after a regular meeting held in our new temple, I personally attended them at the festive board.

Vincent Patrice, as Vénérable Master, could hardly contain his excitement, as his emotional state vacillated between a profound humility in the presence of a person, de Miranda, whom he regarded as Olympian, and a deeply felt and apparent, at least to those who knew him well, rapaciousness, as he welcomed these distinguished and fateful guests. Their appearance signalled the resurrection of all his ambitions and his hopes for continental power. They, as travellers, could hardly have found a more enthusiastic listener. He called together Frères Paul Pietri, Felix Giuseppi, Miguel Peña, Alvarada Azque and Joseph Susini for them to meet the ones who would be remembered for all time as the financiers of the Liberators of the New World.

Toasted with champagne, they were assured of the loyalty of this Atelier, where several Frères, including myself, were already volunteering for active service in the cause, now about to be made flesh. The visitors, anxious to get away, left for Venezuela by different routes the following day, December 22nd. I, Littais L'Eau, Frère Servant, left Trinidad for Venezuela in the company of Frère Francisco de Miranda. Our departure, much in the same manner as their arrival, was to be kept shrouded in the deepest secrecy, as the English governor, General Hislop, would do everything in his power to detain them in Trinidad so as to prevent their support of the junta in Caracas that was beginning to show signs of becoming independent of Spain, in as much as strong alliances were now being forged between these two erstwhile implacable foes.

News of the arrival of the Precursor, as he was increasingly known, however, preceded us, for as John Black's ballahoo schooner, the *Crispin Wayne*, came within sight of the walls of La Guaira, the gateway to Caracas, there were small craft already tacking dizzily out to sea to greet us. Ashore, the people came to see the man promised, by destiny, to take them into a different future in this new century. They brought a white mule, festooned and caparisoned, for him to ride upon and a handsome, frisky burro called Nicodemus for me and, with a band of trumpeters in the midst of a swelling crowd, we rode towards the central plaza, where the mayor gave a patriotic speech in three languages, first in Castilian Spanish, then in an algebra of Caribbean Patois, and finally in imperfect French, so as to accommodate the revolutionary partisans who had been expelled from Trinidad some ten years previously, with the arrival of the English, during the tyranny of the infamous Governor Thomas Picton; these stayed on in La Guaira in hope of the Precursor's return to the continent. Amongst them I could recognise several Corsicans, presently non-financial members of Les Frères Unis. This was when a beautiful woman with golden eyes made her appearance, the crowd parting for her. She was escorted by a retinue of desperate-appearing men, all with a terrible resemblance, and she came to him, imploring him to make haste to impregnate her so that they might commence a race of giants who would rule the hemisphere in a dynasty that would last one thousand generations.

That very night, after we attended two dozen patriotic fiestas, applauded a thousand fandango dancers, attempted an extemporaneous castanet solo, admired innumerable babies, attended three dinners held in his honour, listened to seven patriotic speeches of welcome, drank thirty-five patriotic toasts, inspected the revolutionary guard, the fortifications, the barracks, the cisterns, the cockpits, the cocks, the bull ring, the bulls, the fireworks that I did not have the strength to admire kept me wide awake, causing me to bear witness to the night sounds of the creation of giants, plainly audible through the paper-thin walls of the Hotel Esmeralda. By the following morning, there was a line of hopefuls stretching from the door of the Hotel Esmeralda all the way to the confessional box of the cathedral church of San Jerez de la Frontera, which was comprised of women of all ages, stages and conditions who were inspired by a rumour that the Precursor possessed the power to create living saints in the wombs of women who were pure of sins, venial, mortal, original, or commonplace.

We were afforded a means of escape provided by a lapsed Brother of Les Frères Unis, one Pedro Gianetti, and ascended, by donkey, the tortuous mountainway that led to the city of Caracas, where we were given lodging in the house of Colonel Simón Bolívar. The news of his brother's death put the household into mourning and, in a profound manner, altered his domestic affairs and future relationships. Juan Vicente Bolívar's son Fernando would, over time, become less of a nephew to him and more like the son never born to him.

Thus, the Precursor, in spite of previous disappointments and heart-wrenching disillusionments, was persuaded that the revolution was finally triumphing in his country. People of all shades and classes became united in a display of enthusiasm and nationalistic fervour, previously unknown and sadly forgotten when the normal course of history muddled events that were commenced beneath the aegis of such magnanimous and epoch-shaping circumstances. People are shallow, ungrateful and easily distracted by trivia.

The *jéfes* of the junta in Caracas displayed little enthusiasm for de Miranda, and he understood why. They, he explained to us all, were obliged to adopt that attitude because if they came out in support of him and the revolution, the English government, who, they were hoping, would send support, would withhold it in their wish not to anger the Spanish government in Spain at that time. And, besides which, there are those who perpetuate the propaganda that he is an agent of the English, not to mention the petty jealousies of fastidious colonials who created intrigues and resented him because of his reputation as an international conspirator, possessed of natural elegance, learning and worldly ways. Then, there were the

Caraqueños, the snobs who would never forget his commercial origins, the vulgarity of his father, who had been sued by them fifty years before so as to disallow him from appearing in public in a military uniform and carrying a baton, and who had ridiculed him because he sought, but could never find, an aristocratic origin which, because of his love and admiration for his son, he would want him to have so as to decorate his inevitable immortality.

Nonetheless, de Miranda presided over the first anniversary of the Patriotic Society's celebration of the 19th of April revolution, where his exotic uniform, his superior manners, his easy grasp of command, his domineering voice, his penetrating gaze, enthralled and entertained the society and the crowd of common people that filled the auditorium. He moved and inspired them with the ardent manner in which he addressed them, reminding them of the courage of their race, the sacrifices of their fathers, evoking the ghosts of dead heroes, calling on them to rise from their seats in respect of these fallen ones, so to allow their ghosts to find places amongst them. This moved the crowd to emotional depths that only the superstitious and those morbidly addicted to religion can imagine and experience.

He won them over with his personality, in which they recognised the fabled heroes of their childhood stories, told at their mothers' knee, of the return of the conqueror, the promised redeemer, the expected one who would die for them to achieve liberty. They recognised him. They knew that they were right all along. They knew that he would come. To his surprise he saw and recognised, by his red mop of hair, the youthful Santiago Mariño, standing with a group of young Cornets at the auditorium's door.

Colonel Simón Bolívar stepped forward and took the podium in the wave of rising ebullience, which he orchestrated to crescendo by declaring that the revolution should be republican and democratic. Speaking from the heart and speaking for the young people in the name of optimism, hope and the ideals of liberty and opportunity for all, he challenged the Congress to declare independence. He exhorted them to fearlessly lay the foundation, the cornerstone of South American liberty. He cautioned them, that if they hesitated, even for a day, they would be lost. He reminded them that their doubts are but the sad consequences of their ancient fetters. He told them what they already knew—that the time for discussion had passed. He closed by saying, his voice rising, even to the echo: "If we hesitate, we are lost. I propose that a committee representing this body convey these sentiments to the sovereign Congress." The crowded room rose to its feet and the masses in the plaza roared their approval, having heard not a word. Later, when Don Simón Bolívar stepped outside, he was hoisted upon the shoulders of young men and carried forward, into the future. We, de Miranda and I, Littais L'Eau, Frère Servant, stood on the balcony and watched this preamble to history take shape. For it was they, the Venezuelan youths, the boys and girls of yesterday, the men and women of today, who decided to give constitutional form to the revolution.

Within days, the Congress, summoned by the patriotic junta, was installed, and on July 5th, 1811, seven of the ten provinces of the Captaincy General of Venezuela declared their independence. I went with de Miranda, the Precursor of all this, on the 14th of July to see for ourselves the proclamations, the first in South America, posted on the stone walls of the city of Caracas. We went, incognito, in the early morning, the night watchmen's lanterns still alight, and mingled with the silent crowd unnoticed; then, in silence we slipped away. He said nothing as we walked along the quiet cobbled streets, the damp red rooftop tiles just tinged with the cool morning's gold, the air filled with the aroma of coffee and *arepas*, fresh and hot from the oven. Above us, a woman's voice, a rich high contralto, rose to soar in the solar air above the city's spires.

> *Bailen los sin camisas*
> *y viva el són,*
> *bailen los sin camisas*
> *y viva el son del cañón.*
> *Yo que soy un sin camisa*
> *un baile tengo que dar*
> *y en lugar de guitarras,*
> *cañones sonaran.*
> *Si alguno quiere saber*
> *por que estoy descamisado,*
> *porque con los tributos*
> *el rey me ha desnudado.*
> *Bailen los sin camisas . . .*

That day the national flag, his flag, the one that he designed with the colours that Wolfgang von Goethe applauded, that was handed to him by the beautiful María Concepción that evening on the jetty at Chacachacare, was hoisted in the main square of Caracas by the sons of José María España, who, in so doing, fulfilled their father's prophecy concerning his memory, which he foretold to many of those who were gathered there now, whereby he, José María España, would be remembered on this very spot where he died that rainy misty morning. I watched the flag of liberty fly in the brilliant blue sky and I wept.

Vicente Salias wrote, sitting on the patio of the house where we now live: "Glory to the Brave People. Joined by knots which heaven fashioned, the whole of America exists as a nation." It was to become the national anthem. He was the founder and the leader of the patriotic society of Caracas; himself and Don Simón Bolívar and all the others came that evening to celebrate with Francisco de Miranda. I, Littais L'Eau, Frère Servant, served them at table, where they enjoyed a meal of roast suckling pig, piping hot arepas, blood sausage with rice, sweet potatoes with melted cheese, a mushroom sauce and lettuce, cucumber and tomato salad, with several bottles of Bodegas Hidalgo La Gitana Jerez Cortado as an aperitif, and some excellent grenache, Palacio de Bornos Rueda Superior, with the main course.

"Never issue an order unless you're sure it's going to be carried out," he told Colonel Simón Bolívar. "That is the one mistake that a man invested with authority and power must never make, not even once in his lifetime. Never issue an order that you are not sure will be carried out, to the letter."

And that is precisely why he failed at the fortress of Puerto Cabello.

The new government was haunted by miscalculations, missteps and unimaginable blunders. Perhaps the worst, the most calamitous, was the issuance of paper money. Said Don Simón Bolívar: "In the eyes of most people, this new money is a direct violation of property rights. They feel that they are being deprived of objects of intrinsic value in exchange for others of problematical worth. The paper money has aroused discontent amongst an otherwise indifferent people of the interior and they call upon the commandant of the Spanish troops to come and free them from a currency which they regard as a horror greater than slavery."

Captain Juan Domingo de Monteverde's arrival from Puerto Rico distracted all debate. The one crucial ally that aided him and the royalist cause was the social dissatisfaction of the common people with the new rulers. Monteverde, with a detachment of Royal Marines, arrived to reinforce royalist forces stationed in the fortress at Coro. He received orders from the governor of Coro to march into the interior of the country with a small force of fifteen hundred and fifty men to aid the town of Siquisique, which sent Father Andrés Torellas with news that it intended to defect from the new republic. This he undertook with Spaniards and residents of Coro, a surgeon, ten thousand cartridges, a howitzer, and ten hundredweights of food. As he neared the hamlet of Barquisimeto, an Indian by the name of Juan de los Vargas, impressed by the display and organisation of Monteverde's military force, went over to him together with a large number of patriots.

Monteverde, I can assure you, was in no position to mount a successful military campaign. The scarcity of resources held by the royalists was well known. Spain, fighting the Peninsular War against the Napoleonic forces in order to regain control over its own territory, and having spent the previous decade fighting mostly as an ally of France, found itself hard-pressed to deal with an insurgency. There were no resources in the New World. Nonetheless, the Royal Arms of Spain displayed caused many to defect the republican cause.

Monteverde's march across the countryside, his bugle calls at dawn, his colour parties, parades, drills and maneuvers of ragged but ever increasing forces were sufficient to cause desertions from the ranks of the inexperienced republican leaders. Just the roll of his drums scattered the patriots without a shot being fired. Fear in the ranks, men with quaking knees and shaking hands, icy sweat pouring, bellies turning into liquid, causing their contents to go running down the inside of their trousers' legs.

Monteverde's appearance was a jolt of reality. A greater jolt was felt at four in the afternoon on Holy Thursday of March 26th, 1812, when the country experienced the calamity of an earthquake that appeared not to know where, when or how to end—a catastrophe that took the lives of more than ten thousand souls in the city of Caracas alone.

I was just recuperating from the languor of a too-long siesta in the courtyard garden of Don Simón Bolívar's family home, when I heard a noise of what sounded to me like a battalion of iron-wheeled field artillery moving at a pace along the town's cobbled streets. Starting to my feet, I stumbled and was immediately thrown to the ground which heaved up beneath my body like a wave that I could see crossing the yard, lifting the tiles and tumbling over the big pots with the begonias and causing the patio to rise up, pillars, roof and all, in a grotesque and sickening manner.

From all about me came the quaking sounds of everything shaking, falling, rolling over, crashing and being smashed and crushed. I saw the eastern wall move towards me, the small upstairs balcony with its iron railing and pots of camellias coming apart, falling. I ran, crawled, stumbled and rolled towards the fountain and threw myself in as an unrecognisable part of the building came crashing down upon it.

I could hear the screams of the house servants above the noise of the clattering fall of roof tiles, everything being thrown down, torn apart, raised up and dashed to the ground. From a distance came the noise of what sounded like huge waves pounding, pounding and the voices and screams of thousands. The earth moved afresh, this time with a greater agitation, a vibrating that cracked the walls of the fountain and brought the decorative pediment down on me, causing a fracture of my right collarbone and a terrible gash on my left leg just below the knee.

Around me I could see the garden wall collapsing, large stones falling, coming down, furniture, things, tumbling out of rooms that no longer held any dimensional integrity, and yet the earth still moved more, shuddering, groaning, emitting unimaginable sounds, unearthly sounds that came from deep within its very interior, and still everything continued to crash, to lurch, shake and tumble. The already fallen pillars rolled and smashed against those already destroyed, as household objects dropped from the upper stories to crash onto all and everything. Then it stopped, to shudder again and again. All around I could hear screams, cries and shouts, the hysterical barking of dogs maddened by terror that filled the air, the neigh of horses trapped in stables, and prayers too, as people appealed to the God Most High for mercy please, please, please. Then it shook and quaked again, this renewed shock was like a blow, an explosion from below that brought down everything that was left standing, and yet it continued shaking and the earth groaning deep inside as if engaged in an agony of its own.

I was buried beneath the rubble of the house, which, fortunately, had been built much more than one hundred years before, and whose upper floors were constructed of wattle and mud, plastered over with lime, held together with animal and human hair and contained no masonry, just a large frame of timbers that mercifully and miraculously missed me. Barely able to breathe, in pain and bleeding, and not able to get out from under the debris, I remained where I was through the very cold night, and experienced the terror of five or more shocks, which altered the nature of my incarceration and allowed me to crawl from it as morning came up sickly. My first thoughts were for Francisco de Miranda and our host Don Simón Bolívar and his household. Silence all about. From what once was the hall I could see a light, lamp light, and hear the voices of men. They found me, I was told, on the former patio, unconscious, lying in the wreckage of the begonias.

This was the kiss of death to the already half dead. The earthquake destroyed more than half of the country, its most populous half, which was held by the patriots. Seven churches in the city of Caracas collapsed, killing most of the people within them who were attending Holy Thursday devotions. Despair filled the hearts of the officers when the news came to us that the main army barracks, where several divisions were confined, was destroyed with almost one hundred per cent fatalities.

I could see plainly, through my own distress the heartfelt and desperate sorrow that Colonel Bolívar tried to hide as he busied himself in his ancestral library that was miraculously spared. General de Miranda joined the survivors at the barracks in a desperate attempt to deal with the tragedy of thousands of corpses of soldiers and others that must be burnt so as to prevent disease. The catastrophe continued to worsen as thousands of people lay trapped beneath the fallen city and thousands more with terrible injuries could not be attended to and in awful, indescribable conditions, died in agony all over the place, their bodies to be discovered months and in some cases, years later. Indeed, large parts of the city remained in rubble, which covered the bones of the fallen, for more than fifty years.

It was on the morning after the disaster, Good Friday, that I witnessed the sickening scene of a monk ringing an enormous brass bell, leading a procession of hysterical supplicants dressed in black, who wore medieval pointed hoods that covered their faces and long black capes from which their bare feet appeared, flagellating themselves and others, carrying the decomposing corpses and body parts of the previous day's victims and bearing banners, reliquaries full of bones from other forgotten tragedies, and statues, some shattered, limbless and headless, calling for the end of the republic as the earthquake was a sign of heavenly punishment inasmuch as it occurred on Holy Thursday, mostly destroying the patriotic cities, while the royalist cities had been spared.

This infuriated Colonel Bolívar and he rushed from his work and stood upon the collapsed wall of his mansion and railed against the crowd, demanding their dispersal and condemning the monk for engaging in superstition, encouraging pessimism and hopelessness, of being fallacious. Later that day, still incensed but also frustrated and feeling that all was lost, he, together with several others, with myself limping behind, went to the city's centre, to the ruined church of San Jacinto, and, scrambling up into the ruins, he shouted his deeply felt impeachments against those whom he perceived as traitors to the republic, and ended his diatribe by saying: "If nature is against us, we will fight her, too, and make her do what we want."

Bolívar's remarks were made much of by the ones who were in waiting to make the patriotic cause seem illegitimate in some metaphysical manner and, in so doing, destroy the fledgling republic. These comments of his, which made him conspicuous, were taken as profane and blasphemous and typical of Freemasonic thought, a godless discourse, typical of the vain, the treasonous, the sacrilegious and of the profane minority that was taking the country to hell and certainly, to the gallows.

I was fortunate to receive the consolation of Rosaria, a pardo girl belonging to the household of Don Simón, during my convalescence. She had formed an attachment to me some nights before the earthquake. The weeks that followed were punctuated by alarming shocks, inducing *coitus interruptus,* most disconcerting, particularly at my age, which further destroyed the house and brought down more buildings in the city, or what was left of them.

Monteverde's advance was now joined by thousands who were waiting to see who was on the winning side. The deaths of the soldiers at the barracks in the city were now severely felt, as division after division deserted to the royalists. It was then that the members of the congress, seeing defeat facing them, along with the merciless retribution and revenge that was certain to follow, allowed General de Miranda to take full command of the republic's remaining forces. Even then, there were those who sought to hedge their bets and hide their thoughts in a perspiring jungle of evasions, obfuscations and prevarications.

Still in pain, I waited on de Miranda as he ate his Spartan meals of sardines, rice and baked beans in the makeshift accommodation that he constructed for himself out of the ruins of the Bolívar mansion. There, he received the news of the revolt of the Negroes in Barlovento, which was spreading murderously across the region as slaves rose up to incinerate their owners in their haciendas very near to Caracas.

Monteverde's acts of retribution, reprisal and revenge, perpetrated against the general population, and in particular those patriotic to the republican cause, sympathetic towards or merely supportive of persons viewed by them as their patrons, overlords or masters, inculcated a wave of fear, suspicion and betrayals mingled with revulsion, mass hysteria and the recourse to primitive local superstitions. This was manifested particularly in the aftermath of the earthquake, and was demonstrated in a collapse of the common will to function, work, exist or dream dreams outside of those that depicted chaos and the mayhem of the nightmare's nest, decorated with the skulls of long-dead poets and other devotees of the great goddess.

All this served to create fissures in the ranks of the patriotic, as, with each passing day, the future became more obscure. "What must not be, cannot be," was whispered into the ears of the most ardent by their most beloved and trusted, their children, old parents and the women who shared their most vulnerable moments expressed with desperation in their eyes a terror beyond words. This, I was able to perceive myself, as I became increasingly familiar with the manners and behaviour of this inbred colonial Creole-society.

However, in command of the remnant hope and tapping into his wellspring of epochal vision, de Miranda was serene in his confidence of the ultimate destiny of this imperiled continent, now impelled by the momentum of millenial changes already in progress. The General's actions combined the surety of purpose with the finality of an arrow that has already achieved the target.

He embarked upon a dictatorship that, in my opinion, was dumped upon him by the terrified congress without an army to support him and impotent against the indeterminable intrigues that sought to undo his every action. The handful who stood in support trembled visibly, and sweated on chilly mornings into their brand-new gold-braided uniforms, glancing self-consciously at their gilded epaulets while stumbling over their newly acquired rank, ignorant of military etiquette, procedure and law. After all, they had all been farmers or city slickers just the day before yesterday.

I, Littais L'Eau, Frère Servant, having assumed the position of majordomo of Don Simón's household, administering over all domestic affairs, became compelled to deal with the servants who sniggered behind the pantry door or in the washrooms of the rebuilt mansion at the awkwardness displayed by the newly hatched officers. I condemned and chastised them and had cause to inflict corporal punishment on two maids and one serving man. Discipline, like all virtues, must begin in the home.

Colonel Simón Bolívar's first taste of battle at Valencia left him breathless. He retired to his ancestral sugar plantation, San Mateo, seeking to find a place within his immortal soul where he could be reconciled with his conscience as the dispenser of death. This was understandable, bearing in mind his upbringing, but it may have put off the General, as he was heard to remark that Colonel Bolívar was a dangerous young man. Notwithstanding, the General, when the time came, placed ultimate confidence in Colonel Bolívar and put him in command of the most significant fortification under the control of the patriotic forces, Puerto Cabello. His last words to the Colonel were: "Never issue an order unless you're sure it's going to be carried out. That is the one mistake that a man invested with authority and power must never make, not even once in his lifetime. Never issue an order that you are not sure will be carried out to the letter."

They parted on the square with a fraternal—perhaps even paternal—embrace. The General was sitting at his desk, re-reading the Colonel's last dispatch, when the news of the fall of the fortress Puerto Cabello came to him. " . . .your wise policies were just beginning to restore order in Caracas and discipline in the army, when the Spanish prisoners in the fortress of Puerto Cabello seized control of it. A traitor has led a revolt of the garrison and he is now able to control the city. Colonel Bolívar tried desperately and valiantly to retake control of the castle." The fatal words were, "*Arriving on the scene as news of the uproar was heard,* he put himself to the fore, but it was too late. This did not halt his endeavours as he persevered against all odds, even when he was deserted by his fellow officers."

I stood at his side, still holding the tray that held the letter in the position from which the notice was taken, that declaration of finality.

"This is a mortal wound to the heart of Venezuela," he said, rising and walking to the window that overlooked the reposeful gardens of La Victoria. He, too, was defeated before Puerto Cabello. "He arrived on the scene. . . he was not *in situ,* he gave the command over to another, to another person, he was not in Puerto Cabello. The last thing that I said to him was not to issue an order that he was not sure would be carried out."

Before the end of the day, he received the catastrophic news of the slave revolt that now overflowed from Barlovento into Guatenas and Guatire and was about to enter Caracas, as large numbers of fleeing refugees from the countryside streamed into the city, pursued by an advance guard of murderous, machete-wielding bands of field slaves seeking revenge for centuries of agony, debasement, subjugation and ignominy.

We entered this maelstrom of confusion, panic and fear that brought thousands of city dwellers onto the streets and into the ruined, roofless churches where masses were being sung in an invisible drizzle upon broken altars, amongst fallen cloisters, decapitated statuary and over the debris that still held captive the decaying bodies of the recent dead, the clouds of incense mingling with the stench of death. I saw the expression of his despair as he hid his face in his martial cloak, afraid of being recognised. All around, fires that were burning the bodies still being taken from the earthquake's wreckage blazed into the night, throwing spectral forms and figures upon destroyed lives. It was a city in terror with no hope for salvation.

We left that night for San Mateo, after making an assessment of the remnant of his forces and consulting members of the junta who we could find in the chaos, to meet with Monteverde to beg for help to stop the rampaging slave uprising that was beyond de Miranda's capacity. He did not command the firepower, nor did he have it in him to face the blacks. Caracas must be saved from them, otherwise all slaves would rise and Venezuela would become a black republic, like Haiti. He would return, he said to me privately, as he always did. He pleaded for a treaty that would seek to respect the persons and the property of the patriots, a treaty that would grant passports to those who would leave and the release of all prisoners. The capitulation was complete, it was the moment of surrender. The republic had failed. He would have preferred to resign as the commander-in-chief, however, there was no one to replace him. He did not want to surrender. The violations of the treaty commenced within hours of its signing with the massacre of children; a chaplain loudly exhorting the Spanish soldiers who were leaving for San Carlos to "spare nobody above the age of seven."

He handed me the pathetic letter from Colonel Bolívar which began: "General, my spirits are so depressed that I do not feel that I have the courage to command a single soldier. My vanity forced me to believe that my desire to succeed and my burning zeal for my country would serve to replace the talents which I lack as a commander . . ." I could not bear to read more, but stood before him waiting for instructions.

"Pack."

I did. We were to sail for New Granada. He was counting on aid from his fraternal Brothers in the United States or from the English. Already, rumours abounded that he had sold out the republic. The anger in the patriotic army when the news of the surrender reached the common soldiers, the people in the street, was astounding. They knew that revenge was on the way. The displays of hostility, the promise of violence to his person, to my own, became alarming. To him, to me.

The news that Captain Hayes of the eighteen-gun sloop-of-war, *HMS Sapphire,* was anchored at La Guaira, waiting for him, lifted his spirits. They had remembered him.

So had the one with the golden eyes. As our lonely caravan topped the rise above the port, she stood in the town's plaza, a solitary figure, just as solitary as the English sloop-of-war that swung upon its anchor chain in the wide glassy expanse of La Guaira's harbour.

"The ship, *Maestro?*"

"No."

"The ship's boat is at the quay side."

"No."

The heavy hand upon the door startled me to wakeful alert. I slept on the floor with my boots on.

"*Maestro,*" I called at the bedroom door, "*Maestro.*"

"It's too damn early."

I could not bring myself to say what I knew. The heavy hand sounded again.

"Tell them they will have to wait, I will be with them shortly."

He understood.

To my amazement, in the torchlight in the open doorway stood Colonel Bolívar and some others. Our eyes did not meet. I held open the door and they entered. I stood at the open door, the early morning wind bringing the smell of the sea, the salt of the nets, the sounds of the fishermen making ready their boats.

He entered the room, lit only by the candle that the woman with the golden eyes behind him held high. He was attired in the full ceremonial dress uniform of an imperial Russian general staff officer. They involuntarily stood to attention. He handed his diamond-studded sword to Colonel Bolívar with a small, I thought ironic, inclination of his head, turned and walked to the door; they followed after him. I, Littais L'Eau, Frère Servant, came behind them.

17:

1811–1813. François de Gurvand,

From the Gates of Aksum.

Motion, turning. A warm south-easterly. The smell of tar. Here, the harbour fort swinging away to starboard, there a flambeau, burning a smoky yellow, haloed in a misty drizzle. Beyond, the dark southern horizon of the Gulf of Paria, ringed blue-black grey.

The snap and creek of sail and sheet, the swaying masts above me, the deck rose to roll and wallow, to move again, to rise once more beneath my feet: the wind across my face, the hum of taut rigging, the sound of water splashing, all the effects of the quickening breeze that I felt and heard as the ship heeled to settle on the tack that would leave the town abeam, taking her towards the Boca Grande, the Caribbean Sea and onwards into the open ocean where ever-rushing trade-winds gave birth to long, low Atlantic rollers that would carry us, me and my son, ever forward and towards a very different future.

I stood at the *Entreprenant's* gunwale, one hand grasping her damp shrouds. For a moment all was lit by the quick flash

271

of a brief sunset that brightened at its closing to gold. I had received the summons.

To myself: *Wope se woka asem Nyamea, kakyere inframa.* A West African phrase meaning, I was told, "You want to talk to God, tell it to the wind." I must want to talk to God, I supposed, that's why I was standing here listening to the wind. Already the handful of lights that marked the town of Port-d'Espagne had disappeared from sight, the island's northern mountains swiftly becoming indistinguishable from the darkening sky against an onrush of huge clouds, erasing a somewhat shallow past. Above, there were no stars in sight.

At first Adhémar was not at all inclined to embark upon this voyage to France. He refused, outright, pointing to the time-consuming journeys that would ensue, keeping us abroad for two, possibly three years, perhaps even more, in a Europe convulsed by war. Having taken a responsible interest in the affairs of the family's estates, and with the encouragement of John Black, he now owned town properties and spoke increasingly of the opportunities presented in trade, which to me were unthinkable. He resisted the idea of leaving Trinidad, leaving his wife, his family life, his crops, and his circle of friends. Over the last few years, I, concerned that any attempt to turn him away from these preoccupations would merely serve to harden his resolve, would speak to him but occasionally, on the subject that was responsible for us being here, in the New World. As time passed, I saw plainly that the visions evoked in my recounting of past times, of Château Beaumanoir, of Les Chambrés, became increasingly to him as legends, tall tales from his childhood days. He humoured me by participating in their retelling, as though we played an old, familiar game. But, upon receiving the long expected summons, I insisted, in fact demanded, and he complied.

At six a.m. I could see Grenada. The breeze, fresh and fine from the north-east, brought with it the island's vegetal smell mixed with wood smoke. I was to join the captain at his invitation to take coffee. By 10 a.m., in brilliant sunshine, Point Salines was abeam, twenty-odd miles distant.

The *Entreprenant*, an elegant, full-rigged ship known for her good performance before the wind and her ability to sail relatively close to it, was our swift ship: she was now averaging fifteen knots, raising before her vast schools of silvery flying fish, flashing in the morning light, to vanish, to rise again, in the wine dark sea.

At midnight, according to my reckoning, our position was 14° 55" north latitude and 62° 30" west longitude, seventy-five miles due west from Castries. The following day all land was out of sight. By my chronometer the ship tacked at precisely five p.m. Martinique bore east thirty-five miles. At eight that night, Captain Ambrose Vigo ordered another tack, Fort Royal Bay, Martinique, bore east twenty miles off. During all of that night, we made short tacks to windward between Dominica and Martinique, and steered from the Caribbean Sea into the open Atlantic Ocean.

I felt I was retracing my steps on the very route travelled so many years before. The tiny lights on these islands, on which I spent most of my life, were being swiftly swallowed by the Atlantic night. I recalled to mind their rugged shapes, mountainous but cultivatable, fertile, lightly populated, in a sense idyllic, still in the age of innocence. My father, my wife and a son, all these lay buried on one of those now swiftly receding. Ahead the open sea and beyond that, France, from whence I had journeyed as a lad. I nailed my colours to the mast, one could say that in truth, there could be no change of course for me now.

By dawn of the next day we were crossing a sparkling green Atlantic beneath a brilliant sky at our tremendous best. That day we did three hundred and thirty knots to noon, and it was not yet a full day, and we only commenced to run heavily the evening before. That day we spoke of Adèle, now married to Pierre Joachim Frontin, a Mayaro planter with whom she was very much in love. He was a person who came from the simple folk, not at all a suitable match for my gentle Adèle, but things were often done differently in the New World. We spoke of her that day, in a manner which occurred to me later, as I dozed in my bunk, as if we, I, had said farewell. This saddened me.

The velocity of the wind increased. Captain Vigo ordered the main royal, the fore and mizzen top gallant sails taken in so as to preserve his shrouds and yards. My son and I passed a pleasant morning beneath the shadows of the sails, looking at the sailors high above, at work in the rigging, while enjoying her motion and the fresh, bracing sea air. The captain informed us that we were attaining top speeds of seventeen knots for most of the day.

There is great beauty and a marvellous fascination in the experience of a ship such as the *Entreprenant* under sail, driven to her greatest speeds by the pounding force of the wind, amidst the power of the water. Towards mid-day, a cold and chilling breeze arose to drive the foaming, white-capped waves before us. We thrilled to see her bow breaking free to rise out above them, like some great creature of the deep, alive with the energy of the wind that throbbed through the entire ship, filling her every inch of canvas.

By late afternoon, the sea emitted a different smell and became fearsome in appearance; it appeared almost black, with towering, breaking crests, an endless avalanche of water crashing down, sending a salty spray into our eyes, making it difficult to stay above decks. An even brisker wind brought a heavy shower of huge raindrops that shone like molten silver in the last moments of sunlight. Rolling waves kept the decks awash, rushing from rail to rail and exploding against the capstan; translucent green and white foam in the lingering light. Stays, guys and halyards taut, vibrated and hummed.

I became fearful of what the night might bring. In the distance we could see the horizon nearer and filled with a stupefying dark blue-black mass, a body of clouds so dark, so dense, that at this distance it appeared to possess solidity made shockingly grotesque by the flashes of lightning that illuminated its interior, revealing spectral forms, instantly vanishing. Forked lightning, sudden, ominous, stalked us with bony, ghostlike fingers across a dangerous, ever closing-in horizon, to be followed by claps of thunder. Within a very short time, the huge driving waves and gusts of rain-filled, icy wind changed the ocean into a churning cauldron. Bolts of lightning electrified the howling sky, the world, as the torrents descended and the ship was hurtled from side to side, and from bow to stern.

The captain ordered safety lines set to facilitate the working of the ship and sent his men aloft once more. Sail after sail was furled against the powerful wind, driving rain and the terrifying sea. The ship groaned as every timber, beam and board took the strain of the wind and wrenching waves. We, as well as the other passengers, were afraid, in truth, terror-stricken. We could hardly stand or sit or even lie safely, but were forced to strap ourselves into our bunks. The huge seas and massive gusts of the tempest lasted through the day and into a red and furious morn to continue for the next four days.

This gave way by week's end to the first calm evening, purified by the brimstone of the whirlwind, as we found egress from the storm to behold a glorious blue and sunlit sky where the sun was setting with tropical drama.

We were all so grateful for the sunshine, warm and bright, which lifted our spirits and dried our sodden clothes and surroundings, and we lifted our hearts and minds in gratitude to the Virgin of Perpetual Help and to the Creator and gave to Him our humble thanks.

The fresh steady breeze that followed the storm was salubrious and that night, with our moon-rakers and sky-sails billowing high above us at the very tip-top of the main-royal-mast, we resumed a north-north-easterly course. The sky erupted with an amazing display of falling and fixed stars, showers of meteors and a vast display of the Milky Way, said to have originated from the breast of the great goddess Hera. It was a delight to hear the men sing shanties, some high above in the rigging, others upon the decks. Some danced to the sounds of accordion, flute and guitar. One tall, ferocious-appearing Jamaican Negro played a banjo as the night progressed and the universe reeled overhead, he sang:

> *As I was a . . .walk . ing down Paradise . . .*
> *Street . . .O . . .Blow, Blow, the man down . . .*
> *A saucy young . . . Bobby I hap . . .pened to . . .Meet*
> *I know you're a Black . . . baller by the cut of*
> *your hair—*
> *. . .O . . .Blow, Blow, Blow the man down . . .*

I had, some years before, taken time to tell Adhémar of the coming of Prince Idelfonso of Les Chambrés to Château Beaumanoir and of the discovery of the great vaulted room that lay beneath it, of the tombs of our ancestors and of the recovery of the fabulous object. Now, as my heir and its future custodian, perhaps last custodian, he had to learn of our family's enduring commitment to the doom or the destiny of this world, as envisioned by Les Chambrés.

As the festive hour drew to a close, I invited him to join me for a turn upon the *Entreprenant's* deck. I began, on that first night of calm weather, to relate to him the remainder of the amazing history that has served to alter our family's fate. I commenced with the almost half-remembered account of how a succession of teachers, holy men perhaps, as they were presently thought to have been, had come over the sea to our shores. This, even prior to the Roman conquest of what became known as Gaul. These holy men brought with them a unique understanding of the nature and purpose of existence.

Strange, indeed bizarre tales were told of these teachers, myths portrayed them as having supernatural powers, particularly their ability to perform divination and foretell the future. It was told that they cast spells and turned people into animals or stones, or caused crops to be blighted.

These myths were put about principally by the primitive people who came out of the north to work in our fields or in the mines. They could not understand the culture, the sciences or the arts of our teachers, so naturally, as it was with all simple people, they believed that these were magical.

I told Adhémar that night of the legends that were passed down over the centuries as recounted by my elders to me, such as: "These men predicted the future by observing the flight and

277

calls of birds and by the sacrifice of holy animals: all orders of society were in their power, and in deciding important matters they would sacrifice a human victim, and by observing the way his limbs convulsed as he fell and the gushing of his blood, they were able to read the future." What rot.

In truth, the foretelling of the future was at times based on their use of homing pigeons. This, naturally, was a secret at the time, as it allowed the teachers to be in touch with each other across vast areas: from here, at home, to the islands in the narrow sea, to Britain, Ireland and, some say, in relays across Northern Africa to the great oracle centres and thence to Greece, to Delphi, or Samothrace. News of wars, migrations of peoples, calamities, epidemics, changes in the weather, were received, and could be told as predictions and forecasted as omens and portents. Information could be transmitted over thousands of miles in a matter of weeks, and, in many instances in hours. Common sense often did the rest.

Their knowledge and use of astronomy, mechanics and hydraulics caused amazement and reinforced the simple folks' belief in their supernatural powers. For example, to make "prophecies" of an eclipse, or even the sight of a mill-wheel powered by a stream, used to grind wheat, was seen as miraculous by some. What looked like a small hill could rise up on marble pillars to reveal a beautifully appointed room inside it, and then be lowered to become a hill again, covered in grass, perhaps with even a cow standing on it. This, surely, would have been perceived as the work of the devil by an audience that did not understand the secrets of hydraulics. Myriad stories were told of the "hollow hills."

They erected lighthouses upon the high cliffs and on rocky islands, equipped with massive mirrors and lenses that could cast a beam of light from a bonfire across unimaginable distances of night and, in the day, show reflections of ships beyond the diameter of the horizon in their shimmering surfaces. They gave the fisher-folk the tool that made them into travellers, traders, and explorers. It was a little iron needle that sought perpetually to point north. They called it a compass.

We experienced peace, found comfort and benefited from these teachings. Our lands prospered.

My grandfather once related that in the year of our Lord 1057, following in the tradition of the others who came amongst us from olden times, there appeared a wise teacher, Pol Aurélien, as he was called. The last of his kind, as it would turn out. He was not concerned with entertaining erudite discourses on the nature of the divine, nor with the introduction of the newest inventions. He was, he told them, a draughtsman. Although he possessed neither compass nor square, he was, he said, a designer of men. He explained to them that he was in search of brave men, ferocious men, strong in their convictions, stubborn men, to prepare them to undertake a great journey, and be a part of a fabulous quest, the outcome of which would not just make them rich, but cause them to be remembered, as the heroes of legends were, even to the end of time.

The sage expounded to Torson de Gurvand and to his wide-eyed companions that this quest would reveal a treasure of great significance, greater even than what had been looted from the city of Rome by the Gothic kings of long ago. He spoke to them while sitting in the open fields, and while walking along the high precipices of jagged rock, the sea breaking bright and green, with the ever-constant wind pouring in upon them from across the unimaginable Atlantic Ocean.

Using the old megalithic circles and standing stones, he demonstrated the passing of the seasons; the summer equinox and the winter solstice. He described to them the earth itself, its shape and the nature of its rotation around the sun; the moon, and its phases. The architecture of the universe. The imagination of young Torson, I told Adhémar, must have been revolving around these marvels, as on dark, clear, cold nights Pol Aurélien demonstrated the precession of the equinoxes, the arrangement of the fixed stars, and the Houses of the Zodiac, bringing to life the wonders of the night sky with the telling of ancient myths, as the cosmos wheeled above and about in its never-ending display.

During the time that this great teacher stayed with our people, those who could dream the dreams of other worlds, who could feel the celestial energies and yes, listen to the harmony of the spheres, felt in their hearts inspired to go with this wonderful man of knowledge, who possessed in his kind, magnificent eyes the accumulated wisdom of the ages.

In the year 1094, those who could afford it—and even some of those who could not—set out with Pol Aurélien. It was said that a great crusade was preached at Clermont in the Auvergne to free the Holy Land from Moslem domination, to liberate the Holy Land, and rescue the Christenfolk who dwelt there. Torson de Gurvand, his friends and relatives, joined Pol Aurélien in this adventure.

Torson and the company traversed the realms and passed into the great cities; Orléans, Clermont, Grenoble, then over the Alps to Turin and to Verona. Their fellowship was held together by the bonds of kinship and camaraderie and entertained with epitaphs, epistolary tales, praise-poems and songs, while Pol Aurélien taught them how to chart their passage by the sighting of the stars.

They travelled on into Croatia, to Zara and through the Balkans to take ship from the island of Corfu to join Pol Aurélien's colleague Abbot Peter of Maillezais, and the

Frankish princes on the holy crusade. Old, but hardly frail Pol Aurélien was then, as they rode into Constantinople to meet the Emperor Alexius I Comnenus. He was summoned and joined the councils of the great.

Their little band of knights stood beneath the royal banners in the magnificent ships that took the host across the Bosphorus and into Asia. They knelt in prayerful gratitude, asking that God's deeds be done through themselves and the Franks and that they be victorious over all the Moslems. Too old to charge the infidel, Pol Aurélien cautioned those who accompanied him and others now of their company, not to kill and slay for its own sake, but to take care as there were Christians there, people whose churches were of long standing, and that there were Jews and other "People of the Book," as they were described in the Koran, who were not their enemy and who would be of great good use to them when the wars were won and peace filled the land. He spoke this message to the leaders and the princes who, in turn, advised their knights commanders. This, however, did not halt the massacres and rapine, and did not stem the veritable avalanche of destruction that the crusading armies unleashed, destroying the lives of the very people they had come to liberate.

The crusader armies laid siege to the cities of the coast and fought ferocious battles against a brave and valiant enemy. Great deeds were accomplished, and the hearts of men and knights were lifted to great heights of valour and filled with the purpose of this wonderful undertaking.

Torson de Gurvand, as the story is told in the chronicles recorded by Baldric of Dol, the abbot of Bourgueil, and the other knights of Brittany, fought beneath the banner of our lords. They were in the fore of the Frankish armies on the 15th of July, 1099, when the breach was stormed by Duke Godfrey of Bouillon and Tancred of Hauteville, and scorched by the fires that leapt against the awful skies. They were covered in glory and in the blood of friend and foe as they rampaged through the sacred city in a maelstrom of revenge, in a massive spasm of violent destruction that shook the ancient walls and caused the ghosts of other massacres, both sacred and profane, to flee the fiery storm.

The crusading armies poured into the vast, walled enclaves of Holy City like a torrent filling some bottomless cauldron: Bohemond of Taranto, Fulk of Anjou, Raymond of Toulouse, the Knights of Flanders, the Belgians, the French princes, German dukes in command of Teutonic ironclads, the Brethren of the Sword, chivalric orders, the army of England led by the brother of King William, knights from Tuscany and Savoy, Saxon bowmen, Nordic ax-men, lancers and halberdiers, wild berserkers from the Balkans and Christians from the Asiatic kingdoms who were press-ganged by the emperor's own commanders to serve in his legions.

Entire towns and communities were on the move, travelling with this conquering horde, and they now swelled into the city: women and children, some abandoned, others widowed or orphaned, thousands of the helpless and the hopeless, monks and priests of various orders, domineering Cistercians, the Brothers of Saint Bernard, Peter the Hermit and the Bishop of Augsburg. Amongst all these were the Brethren of the Cross, the companions of the nascent Order of the Temple, and the Hospitalisers of Saint John who sought to bring comfort.

Amongst those great hosts, I explained to Adhémar, rode some with their own purpose, who, taking advantage of the conquest of the Holy Land, were there to keep a long and distant appointment, to seal a pact and remake a date with destiny, to re-forge a lock, broken for more than two thousand years.

Torson de Gurvand and the small band of knights from Brittany, as it is related in the histories, the followers of Pol Aurélien, the companions-in-arms from our own rock-strewn land, were amongst those. The Knights of Brittany or the Knights of Aurélien, as they were called by some, found sanctuary and a degree of comfort in that turmoil by making contact with those who would aid their purpose. It took the Frankish princes several months to settle the factious disputes and to contain the wholesale slaughter of the population in the countryside and, at times, the pitched battles which were fought amongst the crusaders themselves. Pol Aurélien, their teacher and leader, father and physician, made arrangements for them, their squires and sergeants-at-arms, wagons and baggage-animals, palfreys and battle chargers, to leave the Holy City.

They travelled southward for several days on the main road from Jerusalem to Hebron, eventually coming to a monastery hidden in the folds of the Jehoshaphat Valley, the "Valley of Blessing", of which it is written, "I will gather together all nations, and will bring them down into the valley of Jehoshaphat: and I will plead with them there for my people, and for my inheritance Israel, whom they have scattered among the nations." There, they proceeded to refit themselves, re-equip, remount and reorganise the company for a very different journey.

Under the protection of Abu Abi Al' lazeraa the Sage, they crossed the sandy wastes and the steaming swamps of Sinaï, to take ship to the Land of Prester John. Pol Aurélien confessed to those longest with him that he, as both Christian priest and the last arch-druid of his order, was obsessed with one final quest: to return to the western kingdoms, bearing with him the most unique treasure of the Hebrews, the great Ark of the Covenant. This treasure, this miracle, this wonder of the Old

Testament, would unite the endeavour of all Christendom and join them in brotherhood with the Moslems and the Jews. He was, he told them, obliged to find an army of brave men— they themselves—to journey to the Holy Land, together with the hosts of the Frankish princes and, with God's blessing, after the land was pacified, to travel to the domain of the N'egus that lay to the south, well beyond the iron walls of Old Dongola into the High Mesa, and, by careful observation of the heavens, arrive at a latitude determined by the immersion of the star Aldebaran into the disk of the third moon of Jupiter. Thereupon, at 10° north of the equator, in a wild land known as Sheger, in the Kingdom of Aksum, would be discovered the greatest treasure of the world.

Guided by an ancient chart found in the tome *Periplus of the Erythraean Sea*, Pol Aurélien and his followers sailed into the Mare Rubrum, past the eucalyptus forest and the mountain of Opel, rounded the Horn of Africa, and sailed into the Erythraean Sea, on whose shores great, hairy, manlike creatures hurled precious rubies and emeralds the size of apples in wild chases on beaches at each other, and where no human had set foot since the voyages of the great Queen Hatshepsut. They beheld the mountains of fire rising from the sea and saw the land of Punt, whence holy frankincense was taken to the pharaohs of old. They saw savage dwarves, armed with poisoned arrows, riding on strange striped beasts, and heard the wailing screams, the sounds made by the Sirens, as they called them to their watery death in the depths of the great ocean. They sailed south along cliffs of iron rising vertically from the waves, pouring rivers of orange rust, streaming in cataracts and waterfalls into the boiling foam. They came upon vast forests of gigantic trees, all of the same height and girth, as though some great hand at the beginning of time once reached out and cast their seeds upon the land. They beheld herds of wild beasts, fleeing from walls of fire racing across savannahs ringed by snow-capped mountains so high and so distant that they had the appearance of floating high above the plains and to possess no foundation.

At last, they came to Rhapta, the last marketplace of Azania, a massive, walled port, presided over by a lighthouse in the shape of a standing giant with one huge eye in the middle of its forehead from which shone a beam of light at night, and between his spread legs they sailed into the harbour that was guarded by this lost brother of the Cyclops. From this city, set in a forest of date palms, whose populace was the most graceful, elegant and hospitable people encountered, they journeyed inland after saying farewell to its king and queen and to their beautiful daughters who all were named for the eternal stars.

Their journey now took them into a wild countryside of great forests, followed by a bolder-strewn landscape, then into grasslands inhabited by herds of animals that their eyes had never seen, nor their ears ever heard. Rising steadily, the air grew cold and thin, and grey mists blended into the low, fast-fleeing clouds. They came across crevices, creases in the folds of the earth, so deep that their recesses never caught the light of day. They saw pythons of unknowable length, behemoths vast enough to shake the earth, causing it to tremble. They slew or drove away giant cats, and befriended a race of shy and very gifted people of remarkably small stature, who worked with gold and made coats of mail of extremely fine but very strong rings of a black metal. They came upon a wild and warlike tribe that Pol Aurélien frightened and dispersed by displays of pyrotechnic wonders that exploded like claps of thunder, showering iridescent clouds of falling sparks upon them. They discovered the bones of giant men whose skulls were so large that they could be used as bathtubs.

One morning, the night's mists still lingering, they awoke with the emissaries of the Bahr N'egus standing silently amongst them, extremely tall, thin, with elongated skulls, slanted eyes, high cheekbones, hooked noses, protruding teeth, and remarkably long necks. The N'egus were clothed in long, loose, white linen gowns, which contrasted with the colour of their ebony skin. Their hair was artfully arranged in three high combs, surrounded by curling locks that fell to their shoulders. With them they carried long rods of ivory, and indicated that the travellers should follow them into the Mountains of the Moon, where they had a king who lived beneath these mountains.

This journey lasted for many weeks and they travelled at a great speed. The N'egus strode ahead, covering distances at times so quickly as to appear magical, causing them to spur their own weary mounts ever forward to keep up and indeed to catch up with their swiftly striding guides. They entered finally the Kingdom of Aksum and came upon a vast, deserted metropolis set into high cliffs and walked their tired beasts towards it. After many days of rest and bathing in sulfurous waters, eating well and drinking the sweet rich wine of the N'egus, they were taken to meet their king, the Negusä nägäst, Mara Takla Sembrouthes, called Prester John in the west, who, though old in years, displayed a vigour and an energy that belied his age. He was in the company of lovely women, in whose black hair pins of gold trembled, and in whose ears were embedded diamonds. They all possessed aquiline features and long, slender limbs. Their ebony bodies, hardly covered, looked like the ancient frescos of Nubia come to life. The king and his ministers gave the impression of being always filled with mirth, and their rooms rang with laughter.

They welcomed the travellers with great good hospitality and explained in an archaic Greek dialect, which Pol Aurélien understood and spoke, that he was long expected, and he, an arch-druid of the ancient rings of stone from the lands beyond the Hyperborean, was long ago foretold.

With youthful laughter in their voices, excited by the presence of the visitors, King Mara Takla Sembrouthes, his empress consort, the Itege, the ministers and the gorgeous courtesans, showed them treasures that no Goth or Frank, Gaul, Celt or Roman had ever beheld. There were rooms and storehouses filled with golden objects and statuary made of ivory, carved in likeness of the gods and goddesses of old, and gems beyond description. There were precious vessels, chests and sarcophagi, spheres of solid silver and gold. There were crystal skulls, inset with diamond and lapis lazuli eyes that looked as though alive. There were golden trees covered with precious stones that leafed and budded and bore fruit as you watched. Animated birds made of silver and gold flew about, uttering metallic squeaks and whistles. They saw fantastic devices for measuring the time of day and sheets of glass through which objects increased their size, metal bars that attracted other metals, and some of the company had to be pried loose from them, so powerfully did their magic hold. There were other spheres made of some translucent material, in which objects and even people at a great distance could be viewed. There were wands and magic staffs that could restore health to the sick and even return the dead to this world.

There was the pillar at which the King of the Jews was scourged, a crown of thorns, a wreath of thorny acanthus, a prickly fragrant plant that symbolised the need for the groom to be patient with his bride. Kept in a wondrously crafted reliquary were the Teraphim, which were the oracular jawbones of Adam and those of Abraham. The Urim ve Tumim, which was once worn by the patriarch Aaron. The humerus of Ruth. The mask and tripod of Apollo and the winged slippers of Perseus, and his crane-skin bag in which the serpents still writhed as they grew out of Medusa's hideous severed head. An unhatched egg of Leda's in a nest of swan feathers. The bones of Orestes and Theseus. There was, amongst these treasures, in a place set apart, a great golden pyramidion, a capstone that was at one time the zenith of an ancient obelisk now long stolen. This was covered with inscriptions, inlaid in gold and decorated with what appeared to be an eye. An Encolpion that carried within it a fragment of the holy swaddling cloth, the great gold and emerald scepter of the Qara-Khitai Khanate. Amongst these wonders there was an exceptional object of multifaceted crystal, clear and clean-cut, strangely out of place because of its unique appearance, it was a Polyhedron of antique make. And there it was, the Golden Ark of the Hebrews, as well as the Tabernacle, the vase of manna, the Altar of Incense, and the veil of the *sanctum sanctorum* of the Temple of Jerusalem.

"The Golden Ark of the Hebrews," said Pol Aurélien, "has been my quest, my goal. I, we have come to thee, oh King, to fulfil an oath that I made upon my entering this ministry and that is to bring it to the emperor as an offering, a symbol that all the Peoples of the Book, the Jews, the Christians and the Moslems, could share. This holy object will become the unifying emblem, as the common root from which our faiths have sprung. I beg of you, oh King, give us this Ark, so it may save the world."

"Forget this golden trinket, this Ark," said King Mara Takla Sembrouthes. "It is but an overrated piece of jewelry, a trophy from a time that has passed, it is no longer possessed of power, it no longer kills by discharging electric shocks more powerful than the fish called the thunderer of the Nile."

"It would be viewed as a mere curiosity and probably be stolen right away. The cherubim are of solid gold," said a beautiful one with an emerald on her brow.

"It would cause naught but strife," said the Nigiste Negest, the regal Queen of Kings.

"No one would believe it is real, its powers have faded. Look," said the King, placing his hand upon it. "But this," the King patted the shining, multifaceted glass-like thing, "this is a machine that could alter the understanding of what mankind calls the course of time. We know it as 'The Gates of Aksum' because it unlocks the forever lasting."

Aware that their hosts were by nature light-hearted, Pol Aurélien pursued his argument that the Sacred Ark, powerless or not, would be of enormous significance as a unifying symbol for the Peoples of the Book. It was, he argued, commonly held in great reverence by Moslems, Jews and Christians. It symbolised the power of the universe on earth. "It has demonstrated God's will over man's intention before, while unifying His chosen people. It could do that again," Pol Aurélien said. The king and his court laughed uproariously.

"It will stop the mayhem and the destruction. It will bring a focus to the minds of man in this generation, as it did in days of yore," repeated Pol Aurélien. The lovely ladies of the court tittered and the high priest could hardly keep his composure.

"You do not understand the reverence in which this is held!" cried Pol Aurélien. The king smiled good-naturedly as the others tried to contain themselves. "For more than a thousand years, my order has waited for this!" Pol Aurélien waved his rod towards the splendid, golden, awesome artifact. "It will bring these fractious people together, unify them and, in so doing, the process of creating a new view of religion will be at hand. From this,"—he almost dared to lay his hand upon the golden cherubs' wings—"we will teach again the ancient truths, bind the people into believing in the just God, demonstrate to them their place in the order of creation, create a new conception for the divine plan." He stopped. The N'egus were speaking amongst themselves. The king whispered to the high priest, the minister to the king, the king to the beautiful one with the diamonds in her ear.

"Holy Hermit," said the king, "in ancient times, this golden Holy Ark was brought to us by a band of Lemba nomads. It had been removed, in ancient times, from the Temple in Jerusalem, where it was kept in the Holy of Holies by the Hebrew prophet Jeremiah. He had harkened unto the words of God before the invasion of Israel by the Babylonians. As commanded, Jeremiah took this Holy Ark, and another known as the Ark of War, together with the fragments of the two tablets of the Law, along with other objects and trophies that were stored in the Holy of Holies, namely the rod of Aaron, the robes, shoes, and the mitres of Moses, the vase of manna, together with the Tabernacle and the Altar of Incense, away, beyond the Jordan river, and concealed them in a cave on Mount Nebo, at Syagha. There, Jeremiah built a shrine that was guarded by the Hebrew forebears of the nomadic Lemba people, who are presently the natives of Great Zimbabwe, and labour there, even now, in the gold mines of King Solomon. During the wars that followed the captivity of the Jews, these guardians, realising that this Holy Ark, together with the other relics of the Hebrew kings, could become lost, took them from Syagha to a sheltered valley named Senna in the Yemen desert. After generations they brought these relics to us for safekeeping. The Holy Ark of the Covenant was paid for by us with its weight in gold.

"The Lemba people, to whom we are related by our common Hebrew ancestors, then made a small replica of the Holy Ark out of the gold with which we paid them, calling it the *ngoma lungundu* or 'voice of God,' as a memento, and took it away with them, together with the Ark of War which was carved in wood by the Patriarch Moses. These events occurred towards the end of the fifth century before the birth of the Holy One, the Fisher-King Messiah who is known to the world as the Christ, that is to say, the anointed.

"You have come to us, as it was expected that a great one would come from the west. We,"—he gestured at his court, now grown uncharacteristically sombre—"sent to the west our emissaries, to Byzantium and to Rome, to make our existence known to the world for the first time, knowing that a wise one would come. We will soon pass away. These here are the last of our kind. These daughters will bear no children. After us there will be some who will appear like us and who may act like us, but the way of the world is powerful, and all that you see here will be dispersed. Some things will be destroyed in ignorance, while others will be hidden away until their time of use comes. These halls will be deserted, and only the lions and the lizards will know and see the domes and courtyards, the empty palaces of Aksum, where we gloried. This trinket that you have come so far to retrieve is now obsolete. The aeon of its usefulness is long past, as it was of the age when the great clock of the cosmos chimed in the house of the Aries-Ram three thousand years ago. Few souls are left on the earth today whose destiny is linked to the Great Ark of the Covenant of the Hebrews.

"The Egyptian and the Hebrew priest kings have passed away. It will soon be time to commence the process that will re-recreate the notion of Time. As you know, my friend, there was an age when we, both your order and my own, maintained on this earth both terrestrial and celestial time; when the movement of the stars in their stations and the disposition of the earth upon her axis were preserved in harmony with the morning star, Sirius, *Canis Major*. The heliacal ascent of the star Sirius, as the fixed companion of her father Ra, our own star, defined for us Time, and marked the seasons on earth. These two suns are fixed and have chimed in unison since the creation of this universe, forming a vast inter-stellar system that spans the void of space, one living entity, intelligent and conscious.

"For us on earth, the great cosmic year is marked at twenty six thousand five hundred years by the precession of the equinoxes. This brings a new constellation of star worlds into our view, on the vast wheel of the zodiac, every two thousand, three hundred years. This change of constellation is marked in the dominant religions with the legendary death and rebirth of the archetype of the new zodiacal sign, signalling an advancement of the human condition. But then the lock, the understanding of these phenomena, was lost as the ones with the knowledge of the laws of the planetary systems became extinct. Science vanished and the Age of Faith commenced. Celestial time stopped, as the great temples, which were truly observatories of the stars, were left to decay and the old gods died, because the wise ones passed away and no one believed in their existence anymore."

The hall was still and the children looked fearfully at the king. The beautiful ones bowed their elegant heads and looked at their finely made hands lying in their laps.

"This water age of Pisces that we entered more than a thousand years ago," continued King Mara Takla Sembrouthes, "ruled by its archetype, the cosmic Fisher-King Messiah, with his Virgin

Mother, is one where the power of water has washed away all guilt, and, when brought to steam by heat, will drive great engines in deep-ocean going ships. Water will conquer water. The seas of the world will be mastered by adventurous men. Towards the end of that equinox, the Virgin Mother, none greater in the universe, will work wonders in the heavens and in the hearts of mankind, and her daughters on earth will be freed from the domination of men. It will be a time of great advancement but it will be a time when many things, great and good, will pass away forever.

"The symbols of the Fisher-King Messiah, wounded in his sacred heel, will be replaced by that of the Aquarian, whose interconnected network of energy fields will encompass the entire world. Terrible wars will pass over the lands, whole peoples will become extinct. Yet, the energy fields of the Aquarian will rise to dominate, not only this earth, but also other worlds. The suns, ours and those of the Sirius system, like young lions, will be harnessed for their power.

"Our star, called Sun, and his daughter Sirius, must once again chime in consonance across the vastness of space, rising in heliacal splendour. This," said the king, placing his hand upon the gleaming crystal, "holds, as one of its many mysteries, the mathematical equation that will achieve that advancement for humankind on earth, which is to be as one with The Name of God.

"To bring about this celestial achievement, this crystal stone, which is a compendium of knowledge, must be employed so as to access the mathematics of an infinity which exists beyond the infinity of the one we now know. It is the infinity of infinities." The king again pointed to, and placed his hand upon, the crystal stone. "This stone is the gateway to the forever lasting, it is what the Greek polymaths called a Polyhedron, which is a geometric solid of multiple dimensions. It must be taken from this hall in Aksum, where it has rested from the days of our ancestor, Prince Menelik, who brought it with him from the Well of Souls, the vault beneath the Holy of Holies, in the temple built by our venerated forefather, King Solomon, in Jerusalem. It must now be removed and carried to the lands beyond the Middle Sea, so that when the time is proper, it may be taken to the new, as yet unknown land in the furthest west, and a New Order will be initiated for all humankind. It must be placed at the same latitude as our halls, that is, at $10°$ north of the equator, in that hemisphere across the sea. This will signal the commencement of a mutation of the human species. A new man will be created. A different vision of the universe will be experienced by the future man. This is the destiny of humankind. This is the key that unlocks Time itself."

Pol Aurélien and his knightly companions were astounded by these the king's words, and their astonishment increased with what he subsequently demonstrated to them. They saw in an illuminated globe the passages of the stars, the incredible sweep of the universe, the portals of Time through which the genius of the human race transcends from one level of creation to another, striving to attain the divine and the unknowable, ineffable All, as It, in turn, proceeds to become everything created, in a never-ending wheel, spinning in and out of consciously knowing and forgetting utterly, to finally enter a great gate of the forever lasting.

Torson de Gurvand, the eight knight-companions and Pol Aurélien drank deeply from the golden cup of the king and that night, they entered into the sleep of Siloam, lying in ten stone coffins. There, they experienced the cycles of man's evolution, the universal truths of life's progress and an understanding of immortality, the forever lasting.

Their souls left their bodies to wander freely in other realms. They came to accept that the crystal-stone contained the key to access an alternate reality, one beyond imagining. Upon awakening from the sleep of Siloam, the wise Pol Aurélien was confirmed in his obligation to take the Polyhedron away with him, to be held in safekeeping, until the time when mankind would be prepared for the knowledge that it unlocks.

When the company departed Aksum with the Polyhedron, the journey from the high plateau took a different route. The Polyhedron, placed in a reinforced wagon, was drawn by a team of four mules. They were accompanied by the warrior priest of the N'egus and by numerous wild tribesmen. They travelled across a barren landscape, passing colossal monuments and great figures carved out of the towering rocks in narrow divides through which the light of day hardly penetrated. They came upon churches, chiseled from one massive monolith, embedded in the earth, and immensely tall obelisks and steles.

There was the nature of giants about the land, for everything appeared to be on a scale well beyond human proportions. They saw the ancient remains of Israelite temples, built upon much older Nubian sanctuaries. They saw the caves in which holy hermits dwell, their hair, toe and fingernails grown to great length. They came upon Coptic monasteries, perched on mountaintops. To gain access, the visitor would have to be hauled in a basket up the rock's face. They heard the lions of Judah roaring in the wasteland, and beheld landscapes known to the patriarchs of biblical times.

They were told that they were now at the place where Moses once tended the flocks of Jethro and saw, in the distance far below, the silver thread of the river Nile.

Their journey was blessed until then, but when they descended by a winding, perilous road to the sandy wastes of the ancient Christian kingdom of Nobatia with its burning plain, and prepared to cross this desert and to take ship to the Gulf of Suez, their fate changed. Out of the desert haze arose a horde of wild-riding, marauding horsemen who descended upon them with banners and battle-flags, swinging scimitars and hurling javelins into their midst. Their companions, the highland warriors, fought mightily, but, as they saw it was to no avail, they fled on their swift ponies. The priestly warriors and the knights of Pol Aurélien fought on, accounting for a great number of the enemy's dead.

In the annals of our family's history it is related how Torson de Gurvand saw the head of Pol Aurélien taken from his shoulders by a giant scimitar swung by an enormous man. His long beard and hair streaming, Pol Aurélien's eyes turned to him, his mouth uttering a silent scream. He saw Guibert of Dol fall, the lances raising him clear from his saddle, and with both his arms amputated, his reins still in his teeth. The swordsmen overwhelmed the brothers Guillaume and Bohemond, sons of the House of Rougé, his kinsmen, and cut them into ribbons. He saw his squire, Alain, fall, their banner in his bloody hands, the iron hooves of the enemy stamping his young body into the sand.

The annals tell how Torson de Gurvand experienced the sharp pains of sword and javelin and a great crushing blow, and saw blood in his eyes. How he heard his own shout fill and echo within his shattered helm. He saw the crouched and charging figure and felt the tearing away of himself, but did not feel the impact of the ground upon his body, nor the scimitar that ripped into his chest, nor the blood or the flies; he was unaware of the heat of the day, the cold of night and the hyenas that ate into his shoulder.

He did remember the hum of bees, it is related, and the pain of being pried out of his armour plate, the chain-mail embedded in his putrid flesh. He did remember the yellow glow of a fire seen from the inside of a white tent, and the smell of food. He recounted, upon his return to Brittany, the half-remembrance of delirium, a confusion of dreams, and Pol Aurélien's head, separated from his body, speaking with great difficulty a message that he could not recall. He became aware of the noise of a vast encampment, of dogs barking, the sounds of horses, the cries of children, and, with indescribable pain in his head, he opened his eyes and tried to see about him. He saw or thought he saw a vision of angels. He heard melodious voices and felt great agony throughout his body as he tried to turn so as to see about him. His consciousness came only to blend into wild dreams, in which he fought the charging horsemen and saw in vivid colour the landscape of the highland plateau, the great gates of Aksum, where the laughter of the old black King echoed in his empty halls. The crystal Polyhedron set amongst the stars, the high cliffs of Brittany, the sea, the blue sky with white seabirds, far . . . The way back from the abyss was long and full of pain.

The wild-riding horsemen were on their way to make war on the Frankish kings in Jerusalem, when they encountered, much to their astonishment, the knights of Aurélien. Appalled at their presence in what they considered to be their holy land, they administered retributive justice upon the imprudence of these notorious infidels. Discovering nothing more than an ancient, pagan artefact, they stripped the knights of their armour and weapons and appropriated their water and possessions, what little that was left after their long journey, and rode away shrieking victory toward the Holy City in pursuit of astounding destinies.

The tribe of Banu Kanz, who were Rabi'ah Arabs, encountered the conquering horde riding wildly westward, their blood-lust triumphantly amplified, and proceeded to retrace their wake. As the sun achieved the meridian, before them lay a rocky defile, strewn with corpses. Already the great black birds of the desert were descending in a vast spiral to feast upon these dead. But because the sons of the Banu Kanz are compelled to bury the dead, they went amongst the corpses so as to perform their bounden duty. Towards the close of day they came upon two Frankish knights and discovered that there was still a breath of life in them. Torson de Gurvand and his kinsman, Eudes de Tréguier, were taken to their camp and there, nursed back to life.

After many months they could sit upon a horse, and with the assistance of Sheikh Talal ibn Kanz ad-Dawla Nasir, they returned to the place of the massacre. "There was nothing there except the Polyhedron," I told my son Adhémar. "Already the desert sand was claiming it for its own. The Polyhedron would have been lost in the blowing sand, if it were not for the Banu Kanz. It was viewed as a curiosity, an old relic. They hoisted it upon a sledge and hauled it back to the encampment. It was not until the following year that they, Torson de Gurvand and Eudes de Tréguier and their strange stone companion, found their way to the Gulf of Suez, then over land to Gaza and eventually by a coastal dhow, all the way to Jisr az-Zarqa and thence, at considerable expense, across the Mediterranean Sea, through the Pillars of Hercules, into the great Atlantic Ocean and, finally, to the shores of Camaret-sur-Mer, in Brittany."

The sun was rising when Adhémar and I returned to our cabins. We spent that final night above deck as the *Entreprenant* sailed through a vast phosphorescent sea full of dark lights that caught the stars and celestial orbs in the domain of the decans, as they played their timeless game with time, upon the distant horizon. Our conversation remembered those significant events of my boyhood concerning the secret place beneath our home in Brittany. How the great adventure undertaken by our forebears became the history and fate of our family. He, I could see, now grasped the meaning of this grave responsibility, in truth duty, that was placed upon us. And that all this would come to him. The telling, the retelling of our people's history and of our place in Les Chambrés' plan was now made plain. I hoped that it would rekindle in him the wonderment of his youth. 'Epic', was the word he used, it appeared to me that perhaps it was unreal to him in a way that I could not imagine. The task to be undertaken was grave. A doomsday task.

As I lay upon the bunk, the words of the Prophet came to me—"Praise the name of thy Lord The Most High, Who hath created and balanced all things."

18:

1812–1813. Adhémar de Gurvand,

Château Beaumanoir.

The clatter of the anchor chains woke me. At once I knew we were here. My reluctance, in truth disinclination, to accompany my father on this fateful quest had left me as the weeks went by, particularly after his recounting of the experiences of our crusader forebears, and especially as life at sea became eventful and exhilarating. I looked forward to the commencement of an adventure. Standing on the dew-covered deck in the dawn light, I recognised her from the originality of the air I breathed, the icy wind that passed my forehead, the aromas of a million hearths drifting out from the low distant hills. In the darkness, stretched a wide, wide expanse of a boulder-strewn, sandy beach, then the massive thousand year-old stone walls of Saint Malo, the island fortress city, and France.

Sea legs sent me wobbling along steeply ascending, empty, cobbled streets, made shiny by a cold, misty drizzle. Smoky torchlight threw our wavering shadows to disappear into pitch-black corners. We passed beneath an ancient arch, its huge stones damp with age-old drudgery. A fountain dripped, topped by an unknown commemoration. The cobblestones echoed unseen footsteps.

The shadowed upper floors of tall, red-bricked, black timber-framed medieval buildings bent towards each other, engaged in age-old conspiracies whispered through lumpy, glazed, hard, unreflecting double-mullioned windows with leaded diamond amber panes. The chimneys. So many.

A passage made opalescent by unseen lamp light. Penumbra, becoming blacker than the surrounding dark, opened. Great old doors, iron-studded, bolted, barred, a dragon's face, ghostly, fierce, sinking its teeth into an iron ring. The silence amplified the rain water's rattle in the drain pipes. The unfamiliar smells of very old things, of a very old place, tasted in the throat. From whence I came, everything was new, and I could taste the difference. Grey-black, slanting, soft-edged moon shadows across a stone wall, a small slit for a window high up to the right contained a yellow light. The cold emptiness was possessed of its own presences. A hooded figure drifted towards us, his tattered coat's odour of mildew, of dirt, of damp brushing past my father. I heard him mutter, "Take care Gurvand, the shadow of the Gnomon of Anaximander marks those who disembark." To which my father whispered, "Theon of Smyrna knows the shadow closes, to fall upon us all." The first contact with Les Chambrés. Through the gloom of the narrowest passage, water falling from high above, my father and I entered one of these places, and, after a short wait in a warm, well-lit room brimming with delicious aromas, a pleasant, pretty woman with a rosy complexion, an abundance of black hair and coal black eyes, in the colourful costume of the Bretagne, invited us to supper.

That night my father gravely said to me, "Adhémar, my dear son, you will now transcend the years of your age."

He left to meet with a man, a Monsieur de Tanzac, a tall, lean man of indeterminable station with the magenta nose, my father would say later, of a tippler, with whom he spoke until the early morning. Our second contact with Les Chambrés. I dreamed of Marie Eugénie and home.

Dressed for the climate with hat and scarf, greatcoat and leather gloves. Then the countryside. Seen from our rented four-in-hand, rattling past vast, undulating fields, distances as never seen before, flocks of sheep, their coats so thick, so woolly, so different from ours in Trinidad. Startlingly vivid variations in the colouring of unfamiliar trees, from red, to maroon, to orange, to sepia, to yellow, and others stubbornly green. I liked the green ones and admired their tenacity. Stay green, I said. I meant it for myself.

Dinan. A misty drizzle. A crowded hilltop market, rows of multi-coloured timber-framed houses, boisterous, ruddy people dressed in smock-frocks, worsted stockings and great boots. Bells. Flower sellers, lace sellers, letter writers. Red, white and blue rosettes, cockades, carnivalesque drums, the Imperial Guard. Emboldened by the upheavals of the world, now upside down, faces come up close to stare at our sunburnt faces, to smell the salt of travel on our breath, to catch the glint of faraway places in our eyes and to look to see if these were the enemies of the people, the promise of instant retribution.

The smell of leek soup, of hot pastries, of black mussels cooked in wine. Calls and shouts of cartermen, of pie men, of public commentators handing out pamphlets, of fishwives, of famished prostitutes, so thin, of procurers and touts, of music, a violin, coming from above. Bells. An enormous, red-faced woman selling herrings spiced with vinegar and chives. Musketeers. Journeymen. Corpulent businessmen, stylish gentlemen in citron jackets and striped satin, the rosy cheeks of pretty girls and women, of people, people all about, but no blacks. Blondes, brunettes, redheads. Leave the habit of the ubiquitous slave presence, no one to ignore; white people doing things that blacks do, did; coming silently to take the night soil from the bedroom, handling the piss pot, serving supper, being quick and thoughtful, anticipating willingly all needs, so unlike the slaves in Trinidad. Whites being poor, being ridiculous in an unfamiliar manner. Gabbling in vernacular. They are not white, my father said, they are French, people are only white in the Antilles, in Trinidad, in the New World.

The livestock, bigger, fatter than in the tropics, majestic horned cattle, horses taller, finer and nobler in attitude.

Vive l'Empereur! A Corsican, Bonaparte is a relative of old Cipriano Cipriani who is in business with Símon Agostini, someone said this to me before we sailed from Trinidad. The world is truly upside down. The graves of the revolutionary dead, so many. The starving eyes, how white these people are. And poor. Why are they like that? Peasants, I was told by my father, are always like that. But they are white. Yes, but they are not like us. It is only in the New World that all Europeans acquire a status foreign to them here.

Along the Lamballe Road. A great encampment, an army maneuvers across fields where a low mist mingles with the smoke of cannon fire, the earth shudders and a rumble more like thunder than thunder, felt in the chest. Then Saint Brieuc, the returning nobility to dilapidated châteaux. The first stop we made outside of Dinan was such a one.

Getting dark. We drive through a wind-blown wooded countryside and through large, grey, stone gateposts and along a rutted, windy lane. My hands are cold. My breath freezes before my eyes. Le Château de Bonnefontaine's desolated park. Before us, an impressive building, round towers with pointed roofs seen through a whirlwind of leaves. The fountain full of leaves, naked trees full of crows. Everything is black and white. So windy. Massacred, headless garden statuary. The *porte-cochère*, imposing. Marble steps, cracked, showing where something grave and heavy had been dragged down and across them. Tall, lichen-covered pseudo-funereal urns on a broken balustrade. Wood smoke. Chickens in the wide, marble-flagged hallway. Meeting the Baron Hurault Gulard de Montferan in his almost bare drawing room, everything broken, torn, shattered. Gilded rococo frames, gaping, empty, vacant, their former occupants departed. The smell of rot. My father and Monsieur de Tanzac, quite polite, careful, on guard. This, the third contact with Les Chambrés. The baron is a rugged unshaven man, more like a farmer or perhaps a soldier.

The password ventured: "Is this the upper floor?" uttered casually by my father in conversation as he stood before a shattered, fractured mirror, its million and one facets reflecting the altered state of circumstances, of all and nothing. The response casually dropped almost an hour later as the Baron showed us what remained of his wine cellar.

"Château Tonquedec, I believe, has an upper chamber."

My father: "I believe that our family is distantly connected to the Penthièvre family, but that was long ago, in another time."

"Dismantled by order of Duke Jean, in 1395," remarked Baron de Montferan.

"Yes," said my father, "it passed into the hands of Goyon de La Moussaye in the mid-16th century."

"An erudite Catholic, Abbé Goyon de La Moussaye," said the Baron.

"Protestant," remarked my father.

"True, I stand corrected, Monsieur de Gurvand."

"Not at all, Monsieur, but tell me, do you know of the name Rougé? It comes from the Latin *rubiacus* and means the red place?"

"But of course, the Lords of Rougé, they have associations with your people's relatives, the House of Penthièvre, and Château Tonquedec, I do believe, not so?"

"Named, I understand, because of the high iron-composition of the ground."

"In the ground, I believe would be the best response."

"Yes, thank you very much."

"You are well informed, François de Gurvand. As a matter of interest, do you know the motto of the House of Rougé?"

"Yes, naturally," replied my father. "It is *Deo Meisque—Pour Dieu et les miens.* For God and my family."

"Good. Come then, Theon of Smyrna, as you called yourself at Saint Malo. We shall see what is in store for us, dinner is always a surprise at Château de Bonnefontaine." I noticed that our baggage was being unloaded.

"Château Beaumanoir," said Baron de Montferan, "no longer exists, my friend. I am sorry, very sorry to say this to you. It was razed to the ground. First the fire, then the dismantling commenced, stone by stone, in 1791. It was to be treated as a stone quarry by the revolutionaries. But the peasants, the people, would not let it happen, they stopped it. At Pontrieux the people rallied to their lords. That spread through the countryside. The peasants rose up and made war upon the *sans-culottes*, the republic." The shock received by my father at this news was plain to see by all who sat at the Baron's table. He rose like a person without sight and walked towards the window. Both the Baron and I came to his side. I felt my heart with my hand, it was throbbing in my chest. My father's face seemed of stone. "My cousin Alain. We have not heard, I wrote, but because of the situation, I thought, perhaps he . . . What has happened to them, Monsieur, I . . ."

"Your cousins, their wives and the children were saved by Jean Cottereau and Pierre Guillemot. You will meet these brave men, perhaps. Les Chouans, they fight for Brittany. They were the ones who stood over the ruins of your house and kept the marauders, the robbers, the criminals, at bay. Why? Because they knew that something sacred, something precious to Brittany, was kept there from antiquity."

"Where are Alain and Pierre?"

"They are in the Bas-Poitou, safe. Perhaps you may meet them?"

"I heard that Joseph-Geneviève de Puisaye raised a force against the criminals, but, I did not, I had no . . ."

"No, not that one. The son of your father's old comrade, Charles Armand Tuffin de la Rouërie, was the one who rallied the countryside, François. It was he who saved the ancient treasure of your house."

"Tuffin, I thought he was in America. I thought . . ."

"But," said the Baron, "the secret, *le bijou*, was saved, removed long before the savages could destroy it. It was taken away even as many châteaux were looted and the countryside burned. The smell of death, burning title deeds, filled the air. You don't know how it was. We knew that a time was at hand when many old and venerable things would pass away, so my friend, having faith in your father, who is no longer with us, in you, François, and in you, Adhémar, we took the real treasure of the house de Gurvand and hid it in the ruins of Tonquedec. Ah—*les crêpes salés*, please my friends, come to table, do put your minds at rest, enjoy our favourite Muscadet, we find it in the Pays de la Loire. It is made from the Melon de Bourgogne grape. Now we toast, yes, François, Les Chambrés! And a return to the future."

My father's grief at the loss of our home hung about him, a mantle of disbelief that he wished he could throw into the fire. A tragedy with no horizon that he will never navigate, nor bear to hear of, or to speak of. His heart, tight inside him. This moved him to cry out loud in the bed that night. I had never seen him weep. No, he would never see the ruins. No, never. Beaumanoir, the beautiful house, would remain a memory dedicated to the proclamation of eternity.

The following morning we awoke to a brilliant dawn, my father bereft of all decisiveness. Château de Tonquedec was vast, a huge ruined fortress on the Côte d'Armor, which, I understood, in the Breton is *Aodoù-an-Arvo*. Walls high and massive, vast sloping glacis, sprouting tufts of grass between large slabs of stone. It sprawled on a wide hilltop plane, frowning, its grey and stony white ramparts and towers rigid with old grievance above a boulder-strewn landscape that rolled to cliffs which dropped into the Atlantic Ocean. A late autumn morning, windy, cold, and bright.

White seabirds above moved slowly across the sky, so blue. I could not express to my father what it meant for me to be in France. Standing on a grassy swath within the walls, a lone piper, a *binioù*, caused a melancholy that afflicted us all. He piped for Prince Idelfonso Tiburcio Burgundofara. From a ruined donjon came forward a party of elderly men, capes and hoods in grey and red. My father dropped to his knees upon the grass. The baron and I followed.

We, then, were raised by kind hands, kisses followed, above a great banner was unfurled, *azure, falcon volente gules,* soon lost from view in the solar blaze of noon. We descended a spiral stair, entered through a shattered wall. The smell of cool damp, a distant sound of water running over stones. We walked wordlessly down, along a brightly illuminated passage to a large circular room. In the middle of it, a circular shape, a well. About the well, standing, straddling it, was a three-legged structure that I recognised. It was a Lewis hoist attached to a crane, a ritual object once seen at Les Frères Unis. Two men worked at its ropes, pulleys creaked, the men strained, the Polyhedron emerged, wet, glistening in the light of a dozen torches. My father, the Prince and I stood together, apart from the others, before it, as it hung suspended and turned, glistening, and lowered its multifaceted pointed end towards us as if to say . . . what?

Prince Idelfonso, tall, pale, grey-haired, a little stooped, almost transparent in the torch light, standing in an aura of spiritual glamour. He appeared to have skirted all macabre destinies, steering an undisclosed course. Alone. He avoided, it appeared to me, crossroads, ominous eclipses, inauspicious choices, the prognostications of unpropitious oracles. The depredations of the revolution. He has his own luck, the luck of timelessness. His eyes, blue, protruded from under a round forehead, delicate, he looked a prince, to me, in truth.

We sat in a circle about this crystal stone, this Polyhedron that, because of its uniqueness, seemed to occupy its own space and place, separate from all else about it, and to possess an originality that spoke of the fulfilment of the most ancient predictions. It made no hum or murmur—had it done, I for one would not have been surprised. Had it spoken Greek or posed an impenetrable query so as to test our own veracity, wit or daring, no one there would have been amazed, dumbfounded, made speechless. It looked brand-new, complete, perfect, sharp-edged, a glass-like object covered with geometric shapes and facets in very low relief; in the torch light I could see, or almost see, other shapes inside that seemed to be brighter than the ones on the outside.

He, my father, persuaded by Prince Idelfonso, decided to return to Château Beaumanoir.

"Sire de Gurvand, ride with me. Together we will see the land that you left when last we met, you so young, it was long ago. The emperor's peace allows it. We will travel as merchants or mendicant pilgrims, or as two old friends who are showing a young man the hills and forest, the standing stones of the land of his forefathers. I think you may have forgotten what our twilights can do. Come, ride with me. Do not be afraid to face the scattered heaps of devastated memories. Do not abandon them, as banished to the Limbo of the Fathers, the *limbus patrum* of childhood fantasies. Come ride with me please. *Fallaces sunt rerum species.*"

"True," answered my father, "the appearances of things can be deceptive." The Polyhedron returned to its watery bed. We, together with Baron Hurault de Montferan and a party of nine, set out across the fields to follow the winding trails and forested paths of this beautiful land, Brittany. It was so old.

"Yes," said Prince Idelfonso, as we walked our mounts into the unfolding countryside, "it is old. It may be one of the oldest inhabited places in Europe. The stand of stones at *La Trinité-sur-Mer*, the *Mané-Kerioned*, the Pixies' mound or *Grotte de Grionnec* at Karnac, no one knows who built them, magic, perhaps giants."

The landscape was bewildering. I could barely place myself within it. I stood astounded at the side of these massive stones, some as large as houses, piled clumsily like children's toys upon each other. For an instant I could imagine the giant's hand that jokingly placed them one atop the other, the gigantic thumb and fingers, a massive face bending down, all reflected in some brilliant eye, a head the size of a village bending close. These stones seemed alive, asleep, yet to be moving with prehistoric, time-consuming motion, not perceptible to us— perhaps in tandem with some other universe. The vastness and the solitude of the landscape absorbed the very wind itself that lost its way to hide in the folds of glens and rocky rills. The empty nothingness gave, to me, a new meaning to the idea of beyond, expressing the solitude of eternity.

Into Cornouaille, the land towards the north-western extremity of the valley, into Bro-Gernev, we travelled, riding easily so as to save our mounts. Camping beneath the stars. I could see how my father rode on alone, moving in a sadness that contained the remaining residue of last memories, which perhaps he had not treated with the care that he might have, if he'd known. Now he sought to preserve them, to reflect them in the tears that he wanted no one to see.

He said to me that evening, as we sat beneath a monumental cromlech: "Our people are of the category, as they say: '*Cuius est solum, eius est usque ad coelum et ad infernos*'—or, to translate this loosely: for whoever owns the soil, it is theirs all the way up to heaven and down to hell.

"We are *primus inter pares,* never having been made noble by any law or king, but are, by ancient custom, *noblesse immemorial,* springing from one of the earliest families of Brittany on record. Our allegiance in times gone past was to the counts of Porhoët and the House of Rohan, to whom we are related by blood and heritage. We have been in this place from antiquity. In Cornouaille, the land towards the north-western extremity of the valley, Bro-Gernev, the wooded mountain sides, the valley

310

floor, the river running there, the standing stones, beneath whose shadows are our bones, the very sky above, has been ours from the beginning of time, or so it felt to me. There the ancestors built a beautiful house called Beaumanoir."

The domain of Beaumanoir. A vast, early autumn sky, so blue. Cold westerly winds. The long, long, low stone boundary wall of the domain undulating across great distances, over fields to the horizon. Lichen-covered stonework leaning against the weather, against time. We rode alongside it. Prince Idelfonso, with whom I rode, pointed out to me the chestnut trees providing shade along the avenues of horn-beam hedges, the venerable lindens, the flying rowans emerging from the rocky cliffs, the giant plane trees, the fine stands of thousand year old oaks in the open fields, sentinels that shelter massive stones.

"Come," my father called out to us, "this way."

We turned our horses through an opening in the long, low stone wall and followed a path down and around and through a copse of large oak trees; sunlight filtered green, a wild flower garden, they explained to me, comprising camellias and magnolias. Cool and shaded, birdsong, a startled creature scuttling. A rutted way cut through a grass-covered forest floor, a fawn, transfixed, caught in the solitude of its startled stare. Across a shining stream that flowed into two wide ponds, exotic tropical ferns, more camellias and rhododendrons. Moss, sparkling, covering boulders, fallen tree trunks.

"There," said my father, standing in his stirrups and pointing, "there, the chestnut tree of the Duchess Anne of Brittany, our last Duchess. She would sit there, the trees crowding for her into a shade, there under that tree."

We emerged from this forest. A wide expanse of lawn, going on, rolled downhill towards a large turreted châteaux that was surrounded by a circle of tall rowans.

Beaumanoir, no more. The fallen walls exposed the decency of past domesticity. The intimacy of charming rooms, the intricacy of corridors, halved. Tall Gothic windows, stained glass, one miraculously still perfect, the western sun illuminating a biblical scene, throwing a kaleidoscope of medieval red and blue, yellow, green light across a room-less space, walls, tapestry ripped, charred, floorings burnt, decapitated stories, purposeless doors, timber, massive beams burnt, stone-littered, stones huge, some of prehistoric proportion, rusting armor from another time, an armory, rusting, fallen chimneys, kitchen utensils, entire rooms still intact, burnt-out wings, two perfect towers, another gaping open, gutted, dark, inside a looted library, fireplaces, the family's armorial fallen from the ceiling, from above the main door, still on the stable gate, the gardens, perfect, as if maintained.

"It was a big castle, Papa. I didn't know that it was a castle."

"Parts of it, the oldest parts, where you see the really large stones. There, that is old; the entire place was built in granite, taken from our quarries, down there by the river, where those big oaks stand. It withstood the Salian Franks in the fifth century. First built of oak, then of stone built about it, enlarged, but first it was just this tower, a single tower more than twenty-four feet in width, five floors. See the entrance, ten feet up, topped with crenellations, surrounded by ditches. The original tower became the central part of the house, the window of the chapel, there, above it. These timbers are oak, four feet thick, twenty long. These beams, see the carved portions, they were in the main hall, up there. This is the donjon, called the keep, a citadel in small, motte and bailey, a little castle, built on this hill in the forth century. We, our people, fought off the Viking long ships in the year 874; the trophies of those battles still hung upon our walls. The south-east tower was destroyed in the religious wars of the 1580s. There are four superimposed halls. The lowest hall is on the right of the entry, and the upper-hall is arranged in the roof that gives access to the covered wall-walk, look there."

I stood at his side and tried to see his memories.

"There were originally four corner towers, but one was taken down, I forget why. Then a lower-walled enclosure that was eventually roofed. The house grew with every generation and became a fortified hall. It was a farm house, really, from the first. Then it became a fortified manor house, a beaumanoir, a beautiful home. These trees are rowans, you know, they are very old. They were planted for our good fortune."

"The language and culture of *Breizh*, Brittany," my father was saying, "is very particular, actually original. Outside of Galicia in Spain there is no other quite like it on the European continent."

"I read that Brittany was called Armorica in times long past. That sounded to me so like America. Does it mean the same thing, Papa?"

"No, not at all," he answered. "The Romans in the first century were very keen on maps. They might have enquired of someone what this area was called, and the shepherd or the fisherman would have looked at the Roman surveyor with some puzzlement and said 'Armorica,' which in his tongue meant 'coastal area'. And the Roman wrote that down on the map that he was making and went off."

Prince Idelfonso, who joined us at the campfire, where we had pitched our tents beneath the walls of Beaumanoir, sat upon a stone and continued the story. "With the establishment of Romano-British settlements originating mainly from Wales, the peninsula's transformation into Brittany, named again by the Roman map-makers, occurred. In the manuscript, 'The Dream of Macsen Wledig,' a personage known as Conan Meriadoc is said to have been the one who transferred a population here from Britannia."

"I believe that history was first written in the book 'The Life of Saint Gurthiern'," said my father, as he added a broken bough to the fire. "We have a copy—there was once a copy, I should say, in manuscript." I glanced at him in the red and orange glow; he appeared to carry the burden of his every word a little easier now. "That old manuscript traced the antecedents of Gurthiern all the way back to our mythical ancestral figure, Beli Mawr, and there our story, our family's story, becomes myth." He glanced at me and smiled. "Beyond that point no one knows."

"I have it on good authority," said the Prince, "that he was the son of Outham Senis, called the Old, he being another son, Kenan, who is said to have been the founder of Brittany. Over the ages the Armorican British colony grew, and formed a number of little kingdoms."

"One of which were your people, the princes of Gurvand, who ruled in days of yore," said Baron de Montferan.

"We were once princes, father?" I asked in wonder.

"*Are* princes, my boy. You are of a princely house," said Prince Idelfonso.

"Truly," said my father, "on this very land where we sit this night. All the lands were later unified in the 840s under Prince Nominoe known as Tad ar Vro, 'father of the country'."

"At the assembly at Ingelheim am Rhein," added the Prince.

"Yes. That, too, is told in the Welsh tale known as 'The Dream of Macsen Wledig'," said my father. "The manuscript that's gone."

"A pity, my friend, your family's library was a treasure," said Prince Idelfonso. "It was at that very assembly at Ingelheim in May of 831, when the Emperor Louis the Pious appointed Nominoe, the Breton prince, to rule over all the Bretons as your first duke that the Charter of Les Chambrés was granted, by Louis, to the founders of our Order, who were there present. It was at Abbaye Saint-Sauveur de Redon that we held our first conclave in 846. Then, it was a simple place, merely a piece of land on a bleak hill, overlooking the confluence of the rivers Oust and the Vilaine, in the midst of a very dark wood, where the holy man, Conwoïon, founded a little wooden church that he built from thousand year old oak trees felled from a sacred grove that he dedicated to the Holy Saviour," said Prince Idelfonso, as he carefully placed to one side a rowan wand that he had whittled.

"Les Chambrés came into being because by the ninth century the old classical world was all but ended. Knowledge of most things had virtually trickled away even before the first half of the first millennium was past," he said, passing around cups of mulled wine, poured from a stone jar that he had placed close to the fire.

"It became the Dark Ages, following the collapse of the Roman Empire in the west," he continued. "So much science, art and technology was being forgotten—history, lost. The light of learning disappeared in the west. Superstition was once more gaining ground, as villas burnt and libraries were destroyed by the barbarians. The Franks. The academies of learning, be they under the trees in these forests, or in the marble temples of Greece and Rome, were turned into churches where faith was inculcated instead of the sciences and the pursuit of new knowledge.

"By the Old World I mean not just the classical world of ancient Rome, but our world, the world of the Celtic people as well. Both these worlds were founded in different ways upon remnants left over from another time. Remnants of a more ancient civilisation that were preserved by the Egyptians who, themselves, were its inheritors, along with the wise men who lived in the highest mountains of the distant east and down and along the Indus river valley. Their wisdom derived from cultures that antedated the great flood. Those cultures were destroyed by a hail of giant meteors that fell upon the earth. These meteors, thought of by the common people as dragons, when they fell into the seas, generated huge waves that flooded the land, causing to vanish the cities and entire peoples, bringing about an ending of the world. Just a small number of people survived. Their stories are told in many epics, in many ways, in many lands. The survivors of this cataclysm who lived along the Nile, in the Euphrates valley and in the high mountains of the east, recommenced what we call civilisation, ten or more thousand years ago."

As he spoke, what came to my mind was my father's recounting of the ancient legends of our people and the journey made to the Holy Land and beyond, and the discovery of the Polyhedron, by the teacher, Pol Aurélien.

"But how did the teacher, the last old wise one to come to Brittany, Pol Aurélien, how did he know of the existence of Prester John's land and of the kingdom of Aksum?" I asked.

"The Lombard Prince Landulf V of Benevento's eldest son, Dauferius, became pope in 1086," said the Prince. "He styled himself Pope Victor III. An unremarkable figure by all accounts. In the first year of his pontificate he was visited by a secret emissary claiming to be from the kingdom of Aksum or Prester John's land, which we know now to be Ethiopia, who travelled first to the court of the Byzantine Emperor Alexius I Comnenus at Constantinople in the company of the Patriarch of India, from whence they came to Rome. They spoke to the pope of a great Christian empire in Africa that was ruled by a wise monarch known by all as Prester John, who was of Solomonic origin in direct descent of Prince Menelik of Aksum, the first ruler of Ethiopia.

"Presbyter Johannes, Christian patriarch and king, the emissary told Pope Victor, was a most righteous ruler and a virtuous man. He presided over a high mountain empire, where his halls were filled with riches and fabulous treasures, and the scions of the tribe of Judah disported about his royal throne. It is there that the patriarchs of the Saint Thomas Christians resided, the successors of Saint Thomas the Apostle. The treasuries of this kingdom, the pope was informed, contained great marvels: the winged sandals of Perseus, Urim ve Tumim, worn by the Patriarch Aaron, the brother of Moses, the first High Priest of the Hebrews, the fabled Ark of the Covenant, and other great wonders of the ancient world.

"The details of the news of the secret visit of Prester John's ambassadors to Pope Victor, who in the profane world was a prince of the Lombards, naturally found its way into the courts of the hereditary rulers, the monarchs of Europe and, eventually, to Brittany. No one knows when, or in what manner, did the venerable Pol Aurélien come by this knowledge, but in the year 1087 another letter from Prester John, written to the Emperor Alexius, arrived in the eastern empire. It caused a fresh furor of interest. The letter gave an assurance to his fellow emperor that the Ark of the Covenant was safely kept by the descendants of the twenty sons of the Levites who had conducted his ancestor,

Prince Menelik, into the Holy of Holies. The imagination of European rulers was greatly moved by this correspondence, which was translated into numerous languages. It circulated in ever more embellished forms in manuscripts that purported to provide the route to this far off and mysterious land. This, over time, reached the hands of the learned in all countries.

"Pope Urban II, the successor of Pope Victor III, preached a crusade, a military expedition to be mounted by the princes of the west to regain the holy places taken in the Moslem conquest of the Levant, in which the Holy City of Jerusalem was captured. News of the crusade was heard by the nobility as, not just a call to arms in which salvation could be gained and the Holy City relieved, but as an opportunity to pursue personal ambitions and other endeavours. Such a one was the venerable Pol Aurélien and his entourage of the knights from Brittany, of which your ancestor and my own were leading figures," said Prince Idelfonso.

"Indeed," said my father, "as a lad I descended with my father and my grandfather into the chamber beneath this house, where I saw the effigies of Torson de Gurvand and his comrades in arms, some fallen in the Holy Land, and others, like himself, who lived to return, and who brought with them the Polyhedron to Brittany. We hoisted it up and packed it in an iron-bound crate. It was kept in the main hall, just inside the door, in plain view. My grandfather thought up this idea. 'If,' he said, 'you have a secret, the best place to keep it is in the open.'"

"Is the Polyhedron, then, that we saw taken from the well at Château de Tonquedec, the same as the famous 'stone that the builder refused, which has become the headstone of the corner' as mentioned in the gospel of Saint Matthew?" asked the Baron, helping himself from the jar that rested on a stone near to the fire that was blazing bright, warming us, as the night air grew chill.

"No, my friend. The Polyhedron that you saw is older than the gospels," said Prince Idelfonso. "It may have more to do with another allusion of his when he speaks of 'things hidden since the foundation of the world,' which you will find in his *Gospel, 13:35*, I think. Moses, who was an educated Egyptian, gave to the Hebrews the epitome of the mathematics of that day, which was the knowledge of *an* infinity: Pi, the universal constant, 3.14159 . . ." The prince waved his finger in a sideways figure eight.

"The *lemniscatus*," said my father. "Symbol of infinity."

"They built it into the Temple, it was demonstrated in the Holy of Holies. It is broadly hinted at in the *First Book of Kings*, Chapter 6, Verse 20. Six and two equals eight, which is the symbol for infinity. Its measurements are given in *First Kings*, twenty cubits by twenty cubits by twenty cubits. It formed a perfect empty cube. The Holy of Holies was also a Polyhedron, a geometric device. The first number, three, declares it three dimensional, while .14159. . . is what it is all about: infinity expressed, or demonstrated in the third dimension. One of the symbolic properties of the *lemniscatus* is termed 'squarability'. This construction represents the squaring of the circle."

"Were not Giovanni Cassini, and before him Jacob Bernoulli, preoccupied with the challenges presented by the *lemniscatus*?" inquired my father, in a somewhat rhetorical manner.

"Yes, they were. The *lemniscatus* matches the apparent orbit of the planets around the sun, as observed from the earth. With regard to Moses," he continued, smiling, it would appear that they shared some arcane joke, "who 'was learned in all the wisdom of Egypt,' as is stated in *Acts 7:22*, Egyptian culture was dominated by the pyramids, which demonstrated Pi. Pi is twenty-two over seven. And again in the prayer; 'Hear, O Israel, the Lord is our God, the Lord is One,' as declared in the *Book of Deuteronomy 6:4–9*, if the numbers are added and reduced to one number, that number is One. The Bible reveals, as it conceals. Infinity, Pi, was a religious secret, a state secret, which became the state religion in Israel. In the Hebrew language, infinity is the *Ein Sof*, the Endless One, that is, *she-en lo tiklah*, which means the Infinite. Thus, the empty Holy of Holies indeed 'housed' The Name of God, which is infinite no-thingness. For the Hebrews, this concept was expressed in the Tetragrammaton, the four-letter name of the One Infinite God. *Yod Hay Vav Hay*. I Am that I Am. Or will be, ongoing; Or, as we say, Jehovah. Our Lord."

"So, the great pyramids too, 'housed' fantastic achievements, the sciences of the time," said the Baron. "Amazing, I heard that they were tombs."

"No, they are geometric solids, vast Polyhedrons. We find in the pyramids the exact calculation of the solar year and the radius and weight of the earth, the distance from the earth to the sun, the true north, the law of the precession of the equinoxes, the figure of the degree of longitude and the universal constant Pi, amongst other geometric and mathematical wonders. The pyramids, as huge polyhedrons, were not the tombs of the kings, nor were they intended to register the passage of time and the movements of the heavenly bodies, which they did, naturally. They were built to restart, or, if you will, recreate Time," said the Prince.

"The number of degrees in a circle is 360," my father said. "The origin of the system of degrees in a circle is a mystery.

So, too, is what is called sexagesimal mathematics. It gives us 60 seconds one minute, 60 minutes one hour; it measures time, angles, and geographic coordinates. These are all remnants of an antediluvian science that was preserved by the ancient Sumerian and Egyptian scientists. This Polyhedron, like the Holy of Holies and the pyramids, contains the secrets of the achievements of an older human race."

My father smiled. Seeing my surprise, and no doubt the keen interest in my expression, he continued: "The Hebrews, with the scientific knowledge given to them by Moses, were able to set in motion the altering, an awakening, of human consciousness and, in so doing, arrive at a profound appreciation of the fundamental nature of reality and of existence. So primary was this idea that it came to demonstrate civilisation's greatest advancement, monotheism, the belief in one God. Now, mind you, they were not alone."

"This meant Almighty God for the peoples of the Middle East, and all of the western world?" asked Baron de Montferan. My father nodded.

"Amazing."

"Indeed," said my father, "the author of the *Book of Revelations*, John of Patmos, knew that mathematics would one day, as it did in the past, alter our understanding of God, of Time and of reality, and, eventually the uniqueness of absolute infinity—as in the nature of God. That is why he depicted the 'Christ' as the Alpha and the Omega, the beginning and the end, all happening at that same Time, which means that the Lord Jesus existed from eternity and will exist eternally. Infinity is another way to think of The Name of God. So, although faith replaced science, a scientific guarantee was put into place for the erudite."

"Quite so. This is the Judeo-Christian or Abrahamic understanding," said the Prince. "Now all that will be forever changed. We now are entering an era in the history of knowledge where the possibilities for other or parallel infinities will come into being. This waking consciousness that you describe, which was arrived at over three thousand years ago, will be replaced by a higher state. Reality and existence as we know it will appear as being asleep. The epoch of mankind's true awakening is at hand. The sciences that will be unveiled by the Polyhedron will demonstrate the symbiosis that has existed between our solar system and that of the star system, Sirius, revealing an actual universal intelligence. To mark these and other revelations, Les Chambrés will establish a new Jerusalem, a new *axis mundi*, with the Polyhedron as the supreme incident of the epoch, its navel, its Omphalos. And for the simple people, a new understanding of God will be revealed, and for some, the status of the superlative man will be achieved, a biological mutation that will demonstrate an exaltation of the human species not seen since the great civilisations that antedated the meteor storms of fifteen thousand years ago. The new man will be audacious and intrepid. But, to some others, he will appear abominable."

I felt this was all outside of my understanding. "Will the world come to an end, again?" I asked.

"In a manner of speaking, yes," answered Prince Idelfonso.

I felt afraid and looked at my father, who appeared grave and unbearably sad from across the dying fire.

"You mean to say that God, as we know him, is arithmetic, and arithmetic will give us another God, in the stars?" asked the Baron incredulously, stretching out nearer to the fire.

"You may be right, baron, but the Church, the world, will not simply accept all that," my father said. "Remember, the mathematicians—Copernicus, Tycho Brahe, Galileo Galilei. They were persecuted for their work. Giordano Bruno was killed by the Roman Inquisition, burned at the stake, because they saw in his endeavour one that would liberate man from the fear of death and the 'gods'. Mathematicians, physicists and astronomers pay a price for venturing into the unorthodox."

"Giordano Bruno's ideas were born in the teachings of Les Chambrés," said the Prince. "He was a Master of the Art of Memory. His interpretations, particularly as a mathematician, of the divine were very different from the Vatican's. He lived before his time. He was meant to die. The Polyhedron holds the key to a future, a future beyond mankind's comprehension. It is the next phase of the relationship between man and what he calls God."

My father appeared quite moved as he said, "Sire, François Rabelais wrote: 'Science without conscience is the ruin of the soul.' By this he meant, science without superior consciousness. The significance that profound scientific innovations have on humanity may be perceived in history. These create realities that can become increasingly alarming. Pi, that is to say infinity, describing fundamental principles of the universe, brought about monotheism some three thousand years ago. This, over time, saw the gradual end of polytheism and, with it, goddess worship in the west and the rise of the material world, which collapsed with the fall of Rome, thus ushering in the calamity of the Dark Ages. The advances of science alter our perception of the physical world, and I dare say make us masters of it. But they also alter our ideas. This could have devastating results."

"What do you mean?" asked the Baron.

"Well, science impacts, for better or for worse, on mankind far more so than the despot or the soldier. Galileo's understanding that all knowledge is derived from sensory experience created social upheavals that reduced the power of the Vatican and produced the advent of natural philosophy in the 1600s, which led to radical gains in science and industry. And Sir Isaac Newton's advances in physics laid the ground for the eighteenth-century Enlightenment, of which Freemasonry is but a parlour-game, but which gave rise to notions of nationalism and, ultimately, of revolution." My father sighed.

"It will alter what we call consciousness, my friend," said the Prince, with a compassionate smile. "The Berlin Academy has offered a prize for the best essay on whether the metaphysical sciences are susceptible of such evidence as the mathematical. But we inhabit a changing world. A rejuvenation of the human condition, a mutation is at hand, we will live in a world of great mystery abounding in the astonishing."

"This, the Polyhedron, then is a double-edged sword?" asked Baron de Montferan.

"Yes it is. And it may inadvertently cut society off from its traditional moorings of faith and morals of the Judeo-Christian culture, with who knows what repercussions," answered my father. "Giordano Bruno and many others knew this. So did the Vatican. Imagine, if from one infinity came Almighty God, can you imagine what would come from an infinity of infinities?"

"A soldier I am," said the Baron, yawning, "and steadfast to you, Sire, and to the House of Gurvand. All else, I must say, is beyond my comprehension."

The fire burned low. The baron, perhaps bored, was now asleep. The Prince had disappeared; my father and I sat for a while beneath the fallen walls. He appeared to be lost in his own thoughts. I felt, for the first time, that there was about him a sense of doubt, a dubious subtle fear. I retired, to fall asleep and dream of vast iron spheres wheeling, flying through a star-sprinkled space, producing a harmony beyond description. The following day, the company departed the ruins of Beaumanoir and rode for Château de Tonquedec and the Polyhedron.

19:

1813. Monseigneur Hubertus Magneval,
The Trap.

We must now, as they say, take up the handkerchief of history by another corner. He has arrived. Praise God. I have waited, starving, in this godforsaken place, or I should say monk-abandoned place, for five weeks. From the battlements of the tallest tower of Landévennec Abbey, a Benedictine monastery in Brittany that was built in the fifth century, I can see them riding up the valley below me. The monks left here in 1793, it will now be picked over stone by stone by the wretched villagers.

"Your Eminence." He is tall, finely-made and past middle-aged with the patina of pedigree and the Papacy. I kneel to kiss Cardinal Pallavicino's ruby ring. He possesses the fastidious hands of a well-bred woman of a certain vintage. He does not raise me, I scramble up. Am I framed in an ambuscade? No. His retinue is unpacking. Food, I hope.

"Come, Hubertus."

We enter the chapel and descend into the crypt of the founder, Abbot Winwaloe, the son of Fracan, a prince of Dumnonia.

"Your Eminence . . ."

"It will wait, my Lord Bishop Magneval, first we shall dine."

"Thanks be to God."

"And wash? In there."

I have only the clothes that I have lived in for the past several months. Pfui!

To my amazement, the crypt contains a secret door, which swings open at his touch. We enter a warm, well-appointed chamber, large, vaulted with Gallo-Roman arches; a fire-place, beds; a table, laid for three. Rugs. Medieval tapestries, vast quantities of bones, shelves, with rows of skulls. Labelled. It's an ossuary.

He sits on one of the two armchairs that face the hearth and points to the other, while reclining backward, his long, booted legs reaching almost to the fire irons.

The door opens and another Eminence, Cardinal Pacca, appears, as resplendent in black, gold and crimson as the other. I rise to drop to my knees to kiss the ruby on another ethereal hand, much aware of my own miserable appearance. I am immediately assisted to my feet, and assured that I need not kneel. I am aware of little or nothing, if the truth be known. I try to arrange my physiognomy in such a manner that I hope will convey a natural propriety and grace that I have surely forgotten, after having lived in Trinidad for what seems like an indeterminable number of lifetimes. All I do know is that de Gurvand has made contact with some sort of clandestine society, that they have visited the ruins of an ancient fortress and that they . . . Ah, the servants, the food arrives.

"Please sit. Let us pray."

Mussel soup. Galettes, veal pie, roasted leg of lamb, olives, loaves of bread, fried leeks. Apples, large and red. I have not seen a meal like this for years. Mulled wine.

"Lord Bishop," Cardinal Pallavicino begins formally, "your mission, *sui iuris,* to the island of Trinidad, which was of a secret nature, where you acted as Ecclesiastical Superior *nullius diœceseos,* a Bishop without a diocese but with diocesan jurisdiction falling directly under the dominion of his Holiness, in which you demonstrated outstanding perspicuity and discretion, is perceived by us as having met its main goals. This," he spreads his extraordinarily long arms wide, "endeavour of yours, Monsignor, with particular regard to François de Gurvand, is greatly appreciated by the secret Council of the Consistory Court."

"Now pray tell us, Hubertus, what you know," smiles Cardinal Pacca.

I bow. "Your Eminences, François de Gurvand is here, in Brittany with his son Adhémar. He has made contact with a number of persons, aristocrats, who are able to command a following. These are very disciplined; they act in a military manner. Some of the company are treated with great respect, de Gurvand as well. They were all together at the fortress, Château de Tonquedec. He, they, are spied upon by an agent of the government, of Napoleon, a bag-pipe player, he pipes for them and serves them. A factotum of sorts. He reports to the police in Saint-Brieuc. Recently they visited the ruined Château Beaumanoir, the seat of the de Gurvand family in the vale of Cornouaille. Then, returning, they retrieved an object of some sort from Château de Tonquedec and are presently seeking a passage to the west with their cargo."

"You say retrieved something, what sort of thing?" demands Cardinal Pallavicino. I am surprised to see surprise on a face long accustomed to languid reticence. Alarm too. Laconic calm evaporating. Mmmm . . .

"What did you see?"

"Something large wrapped in canvas, it was carried away in a farm-dray, the dray was packed with equipment, travelling gear, bags, boxes, I don't know. It was pulled by four horses. It was escorted by a score or more of armed men," I say, my heart racing.

"And you say it was heavily guarded, Hubertus?"

"Yes, very, I counted twenty, thirty riders, some riding before, others following. They even sent others ahead. François de Gurvand and his son rode beside the dray, together with an older man, the one who is treated with great respect. And there is another who appears to be in charge of the contingent of armed guards."

"The stone, then, is on the move at last. Château de Tonquedec, an obscure a place as any, I suppose," says Cardinal Pacca. "Well done, old friend, well done."

"Excellent. My Lord Bishop, excellent! You have been abroad for a long time, allow me to put things into perspective. God's Church is in danger of being —" Cardinal Pallavicino seems at a loss for words.

"Checkmated," says Cardinal Pacca. "Wine, my Lord Bishop? As you are aware, the bull of excommunication against the Emperor Napoleon was prepared in 1806, to be published in the expected event of his annexation of the Papal States." He rises and moves towards the fire, which blazes up at his approach, illuminating the rows of grinning skulls, and picks up a decanter.

"When the French entered Rome in 1808," continues Cardinal Pallavicino, "and formally abolished the temporal power of the Pope Pius VII, annexing the Papal States in June of the following year, and the change of government took place, the bull was promulgated. On the 6th of July, the Quirinal Palace was attacked by French forces and His Holiness was arrested and taken from Rome into France and thence to Savona. Cardinal Pacca was among those who accompanied His Holiness. The emperor, as king, has captured the bishop, that is to say the pope, incarcerating him in Savona. We are, just now, most vulnerable. We are forced to negotiate with the emperor in the hope of arriving at an agreement, an arrangement, another concordat. Hopefully."

"The emperor has remarked, 'Skilful conquerors have not got entangled with priests. They can both contain them and use them'," says the other, seating himself. "In the meantime, there are plans to take advantage of this lapse, this absence of His Holiness from the Vatican. The papacy is vulnerable, it flounders now in a period of slow decline as the inroads of education, the advances of science, and the resurgence of occultism, the work of the satanists, the adversary, the Freemasons, leave the Church with a dangerously reduced support in the influential classes of western Europe. Its revenue is diminished."

I regard Pacca closely in the table's candlelight, a small man with a large, clean-shaved head, red skull cap, a face like old parchment stretched tightly across gargoyle features, bushy eyebrows, sharp penetrating eyes, wise, old as Rome. In another life, he could have been at the side of Tiberius, or Tiberius himself.

"I understand," I venture to say, "that according to some, the Curia as a court is now much discredited. And the internal affairs, its finances, are in much disorder."

"This has been the case since my great-great-grandfather was pope in the sixteenth century. What is your point, Monsignor?" Cardinal Pallavicino, testily, looking sharply at me, I, apologetic, speechless. Cowed.

Cardinal Pacca, with a well-practised conciliatory smile, his voice and left hand just a little raised, says, "This sadly is the case." I notice that the other has sat up straight. "We have lost the Papal States of the Church, which are now annexed to France. These are renamed the départements of Tibre and Trasimène. Avignon also has been lost to France. And our previous Holy Father, Pius VI, died a prisoner of the Paris Directory."

And the monk Luigi Chiaramonti became Pius VII in 1800, crowned with a papier-mâché papal tiara, the French having seized the crown jewels of the Vatican along with Pius VI, I think to myself, murmuring something unintelligible to the remnant of the leeks.

"The emperor has institutionalised the metric system, first thought of by the Dutchman, Símon Stevin, and then taken up by the Jacobins," adds Pallavicino, changing the subject. He has hardly touched his veal pie, just tasted some leeks, and barely sipped the wine. "Charles the Great created the *pied du roi,* the king's foot, as the unit of measure, which has remained unchanged for a thousand years. What we know, have known for a millennium as measure, is to be replaced by the decimal system based on the kilogram and the metre."

"This metric system," Cardinal Pacca rejoins, "it is said is 'for all people for all time' and is to be central to the reforms of the emperor. The unit of length, the metre, is to be based on the dimensions of the earth, and the unit of mass, the kilogram, will be based on the mass of water having a volume of one litre or one thousandth of a cubic metre."

"This is yet another departure from the measure of the world that we know!" says Cardinal Pallavicino.

"You are quite right, Eminence," says Cardinal Pacca, walking over to a sideboard. "Cognac?—New ideas alter certainty as defined by the biblical understanding of creation. New ideas have produced the framework for the so-called Enlightenment. These ideas will engender a host of scientific discoveries and will bring forth an industrial age that will lead to a different understanding of man's role, his subserviency to the eternal, as interpreted by us. All this will undermine the Church of Christ in this era of confusion."

"It will be only a matter of time until the idea takes hold that there are no longer any absolutes of good or of evil, of knowledge or of value, this will be readily accepted as common knowledge," I say. I have to remember then the conversations with François de Gurvand. I see with a glance the suspicion in Pallavicino's look. Pacca looks at him, and, almost imperceptibly, nods. Mostly with his eyelids.

"Monsignor Magneval," Pallavicino addresses me, "we know what the object is that de Gurvand has come to get. In taking the surrender of the island of Malta in 1798 from Ferdinand von Hompesch, the Grand Master of the Order of Malta, Napoleon Bonaparte, was informed of a marvel, a stone said to have come from the stars, fallen from heaven, containing the mathematical secrets of the universe. A Polyhedron, a geometric solid of some sort, as *we* know it to be." His thin voice, dry. He places his fingertips at the base of his Florentine chin, and enjoys a sad little smile.

"Then, Bonaparte confessed that he knew not of such a thing," he continues, "and was told by the Grand Master as they parted that it is only the true initiate who knows that he does not know. This candour naturally appealed to Bonaparte's vanity. The information sparked his imagination. Presently pure science has become his preoccupation, when he is not thinking about war. He has honoured Alessandro Volta, the physicist. Volta went to Paris and demonstrated his theories of electric current. Gaspard Monge, the mathematician, has explained to him his theory of descriptive geometry, which is a method of representing three-dimensional objects on a two-dimensional plane. He has also introduced him to kabalistic ideas, to numerology as forms of proto physics. Lagrange and Legendre discussed with him the equations involved in the calculus of variations. In 1806 Napoleon, now emperor, caused a grand convocation of all the notable Jews of the world to be called."

"They came because he had offered Jerusalem to them in 1799. This has prompted the Austrian Chancellor Metternich to say publicly that he fears that the Jews will believe Napoleon to be their promised Messiah," says Cardinal Pacca. "Out of those who came, he then summoned a Grand Sanhedrin, as he chose to name this miscellany of wanderers, peddlers, tinkers, financiers and charlatans who met in Paris at his behest." Pacca pauses, savouring a sip of cognac. "What he desires to know concerns the rumour that he has heard, which is about the stone that fell from the heavens, that came into the hands of the ancient biblical Hebrews and was taken away from them at a distant epoch of time. He seeks that stone now. He has come to believe that it is a compendium of archaic scientific thought. The emperor understands the impact that significant scientific innovations have had on the human condition in the past. Gaspard Monge *is* his friend.

"Some maintain that the stone's existence is a myth. We of the Vatican, however, know that it does exist and became aware of its survival when it departed the Holy Land in the twelfth century. The emperor is convinced that only the Jewish kabalists possess the knowledge to unlock the stone's secrets. Now he has promised them fiscal access to Europe in exchange for this knowledge, if he finds the stone or if it is brought to him."

"Metternich may be right. What he seeks," says Cardinal Pallavicino, "could be in truth a key to put him, Napoleon Bonaparte, in a position where he believes that he could be proclaimed the expected Messiah of a new dispensation. He failed in Russia. He has been reversed on the Peninsula. He needs a miracle, something to dazzle the *poilus*. Raise a new army. As yet, he has no clear notion of the Polyhedron's potentiality or even its whereabouts."

"But he will learn quickly, as we just did," continues the other. "He has married a Hapsburg archduchess, he would make their son *Romanorum Rex*, King of the Romans, an ancient title of that house. This title is claimed by German kings who would be emperors and it also has a profound religious aspect and is dependent on a coronation performed by a pope. With the blood of the Hapsburgs in his veins, the child would rule the Europe that his father has conquered, after Bonaparte has been proclaimed Messiah, as high priest and emperor."

"The Church as we know it could become irrelevant, politically subservient to the new imperium," says Pallavicino. "Once the mystery is gone, a vacuum forms. The churches will stand empty, no young men will receive the calling, they will become politicians, and those remaining will fall into unspeakable iniquity, as the priests of the temples of old did. It is the fate of religions as they wither."

These views, this desperate pessimism and obvious fear, come as a great surprise to me, and it must be registering on my face. Turning to me, Cardinal Pacca says gently: "Monsignor,

Hubertus, old colleague and friend, the emperor must not put his hands on this ancient wicked thing."

The other leans towards me, the room seems to have become smaller, darker, all light now concentrated on us three, and says, "We must now discuss another aspect of this difficult situation. We know that you have had a special undertaking, a *missio sui iuris* under the auspices of our ancient brotherhood, the Holy Hermandad, where you assumed the role of apostolic prefect and preceptor of that sacred society, which involved the close surveillance of a key personage of our oldest and most tenacious enemy, Les Chambrés. We know that you have no idea of the name and nature of this society, but you have, on our instructions, for the last several years paid close attention to one of its most important members, a Monsieur François de Gurvand, who poses as a Freemason, and to his activities on the island of Trinidad and on the company that he has kept."

I say, wonderingly, the enormity of all this dawning, "Is it, then, that François de Gurvand is not a Freemason?"

"François de Gurvand," says Cardinal Pallavicino, "is the scion of one of the oldest houses in Europe, a heretic house that has defied and fought Holy Mother Church for much more than a thousand years."

The other continues, "The secret order of which he is a leading member, Les Chambrés, possesses a doctrine, hateful and sacrilegious. It is of the same root as the Gnostics, the Bogomils, the Manicheans, the Albigensians. Yes, he hides in Freemasonry, even pretending to be a republican—for them a cover is vital."

"I knew that!" I say, "I knew he was no republican!"

The other raises his hand for silence and Pacca continues.

"Incapable of controlling the destiny of mankind, as we have done for seventeen hundred years, these occult orders can only act through the secret societies, which are contrived to appear in contention, opposing each other, but they are all connected, and have one purpose: to bring us down. It is in concealment that they have grown strong. For that reason the members of Les Chambrés always hide themselves in or under the name of another group."

"Les Chambrés understands," says Cardinal Pallavicino, "that to exploit their secret—for they are the keepers of this device, this, this, stone this geometric solid, this Polyhedron—for it to achieve its full potential, they have had to wait for the technical advances and the social changes to emerge and, most importantly, for the absolutely correct place to be discovered on the face of the earth where this stone must be positioned."

"Recent history has provided all of these," murmurs Pacca. "Go on, old friend, say what else you know, what else you saw."

"I know that de Gurvand possesses a telescope and an erudite library and that he received, even during the most desperate times of the revolution, the Terror, much correspondence from France," I tell them. "These documents, my informers tell me, were covered with mathematical formulae. But, I saw them, Eminence: Vincent Patrice, who is another Freemason, and de Gurvand, as they made astronomical observations of the stars from a hilltop overlooking the town of Port-d'Espagne over several months. That was long before the Spanish astronomers came to the island in 1792 to perform the very same observations that they did."

"Go on, Hubertus."

"Well, these observations were made from a place that the Freemasons have since called Mount Moriah, and where now stands a Masonic temple. But, I must tell you this, I witnessed myself a great division, a serious rift, emerge between them, de Gurvand and Patrice. Patrice, at present, is the Master of Freemasonry on the island, he has allied himself to the revolutionaries on the Spanish Mainland. The other, de Gurvand, does not support this, actually, and notwithstanding insults to his honour, he has held himself in check, for years and has now made his way to France, to Brittany. These men have, I assure you, very separate goals."

"Most fascinating, Hubertus," says Cardinal Pacca. "The events of history often lead to islands. What were the findings of the Spanish astronomers? Do you know?"

"Why yes, your Eminence, it became public knowledge. The island of Trinidad is almost a square, you could draw a perfect square within its land mass. Also it lies just at 10° north of the equator, with the sixty-third parallel running through the main town."

"It would be more truthful to say that islands are often made use of," says Cardinal Pacca grimly. "But it is written in *Second Chronicles 3:1*, 'Then Solomon began to build the house of the Lord at Jerusalem on Mount Moriah.' Could the Freemasons be seeking to establish a new Jerusalem on this island of Trinidad?"

"No, no," I say. "The name Mount Moriah here is Freemasonry jargon. They are devoted to the cult of King Solomon. They, the Freemasons in Trinidad, seek power in the new lands, in the Americas. They know nothing of de Gurvand's true endeavour, which, I now understand, involves the stone that fell from heaven and its positioning on the face of the earth."

"It did not fall from heaven. It would Les Chambrés' intention to build an Académie of science on the island

337

of Trinidad. A Lyceum, a university, not a temple. My God," breathes Pacca. "This island, then, is perfect for the establishment of the *Umbilicus Telluris,* the Omphalos, the navel of the world, the *axis mundi,* a point of connection as told in heathen myth and in legend, between heaven and earth, from whence the greatest revelation in the history of science, a new understanding of the mathematics of eternity, would be promulgated, for the purpose of the intention of Les Chambrés: which is to put an end to the Age of Faith, and to create for themselves a new kingdom in the western world. This is not compatible with God's law."

"It fulfils a dream held in the hearts of western man, of islands, star-scattered like diamonds on the cape of night, Utopia," I say.

"Well expressed, Hubertus. Man is a future creature," says Pallavicino, "but one who is moving in God's time, and the coming of Utopia is not under the control of mankind, but is determined by God's will. In this millennium's tradition, these Utopiae are created by Almighty God and are not to be made by his creatures. This thinking produces ideals that are always quite beyond the lifetimes of God's creatures and are located in heaven, or at the end of days, when, at God's discretion, the second coming will commence. With the new thinking introduced by Les Chambrés, all this will change. Mankind will attempt to use science in order to manipulate its own destiny, moving in the dramas of an alternative truth."

"This Omphalos, then, would become a landmark that witnesses the world's ending as well as its beginning. Mathematics has always been a powerful, even seen as a divine, force in the world from the most ancient times," says Cardinal Pallavicino.

Pacca continues, "This is why we have always been wary of the mathematicians. 'God is the integers; all else is the work of man' is a point of view held by all atheists from Archimedes to Euclid to Pythagoras to René Descartes. Only One God, as the Jews, Christians and the Moslems have understood God and disseminated that understanding, can be accepted. If this is disproved, the foundation of the universe as we have known it will be destroyed. Once this is known by the common man the idea of the sacred, the ineffable will end. The time of relativistic thought will commence, morality will be reinvented to suit circumstance."

"The Islamic world will rise up against such a threat," it occurs to me.

"The creation of a metropolis, a capital for the western hemisphere, on an island; the creation of an island city state where the earth's magnetic fields meet, at the mouth of one of the great river systems, that is the intention of Les Chambrés," says Cardinal Pacca softly. "We cannot allow that, any more than we can allow the emperor to get his hands on the treasure of Les Chambrés, for he will use it for the same reason. A synthesis of numbers, mysticism, imperial posturing and fiction, will be the result."

"We are faced with two great difficulties: on the one hand the ambitions of the emperor, and on the other the intention of a powerful secret order. One that will no doubt outlast him."

"Or us."

"De Gurvand must be stopped."

"And relieved of it."

"At all costs."

❖

The Breton countryside. Receiving the Atlantic wind. Perpetual drizzle and the cold rolling fog of February, it's a baleful prospect. We are bound for an ambush.

Brother Klagenhuber. He rides ahead of a retinue of two dozen-and-a-half Suisse guardsmen disguised as monks. I follow on an elderly mule leading a baggage train. We are meant to appear as returning clergy. Pilgrims.

Brother Bonifazius Klagenhuber, a Styrian, is close to seven foot and is possessed of enormous hands, feet and jaws with invisible hair and eyebrows, and a self-inflicted tonsure. He wears a cilice and appears the type given to mortification of the flesh, which literally means putting the flesh to death with the use of a medieval device worn in some private area. Corporal mortification, not my cup of tea, as the English would say.

And then there are a score of others, these are Tyrolians, Brothers of the Crown of Thorns, young, sullen and really should be on the farms. We have set out to meet François de Gurvand and whoever rides with him to take possession of the stone, at all costs.

Suddenly a rider, high to the left coming hard, a tiny silhouette against the flat grey sky flickering through and vanishing into a long avenue of tall plane trees. To emerge again closer. Klagenhuber shouting. A party of horsemen appear, black against grey moving parallel. The Tyrolians, Brothers of the Crown of Thorns, are now crossbowmen. The retinue of Suisse guardsmen draw muskets and fire. A rider falls. The party of horsemen wheel to the right to disappear into the fold of a field. Hooves reverberate. A huge flock of birds rises to soar and vanish into the thunderheads. The rider is joined by two others. The musketeers fire. A rider goes flying from his collapsed mount. Whack, thud. Neck broken. The mounted party appears, suddenly in our midst, a sword flashes before me, the mule, startled, leaves me in mid-air, I hold my head, roll and draw up my knees against the stamping hooves. A fight ensues about me, grunts and howls of pain, blood splashes across my face. The Tyrolian Brethren release their bolts, twang, thud, more groans, followed by yowling. The clash of steel on steel. The light fading. A command, shouted above the rest. The riders depart. Four are dead, two dying, another is running, twang, thud. The Tyrolians raise a shout. Klagenhuber is furious, he wanted him alive.

Klagenhuber is convinced that this was a test of strength. Ride. Black night falls, and rain and thunder with lightning. We ride for the Loudéac road. We know it by the clatter of the hooves on its metalled surface and the rows of Lombardy poplars. Ride! I am falling behind.

Klagenhuber is bellowing in a Styrian dialect. I come upon a swirling melee of men and horses who battle around a dray. The rain has recommenced, with wind in gusts. And lightning. The scene, hardly lit by the smoking torchlight from the dray, is illuminated for a phantasmagoric second by a bolt of lightning which is instantly followed by a resounding clap of thunder. Klagenhuber and the body of mounted Swiss guardsmen in phalanx are forcing a passage through a line of horsemen. Swords and axes. The sounds of battle, steel and iron, the cry and scream of man and horse. I am shaking, my teeth chattering. Soaked. Cold. Off the mule, I stumble forward to a tree and try to climb up into it and fail. Another flickering flash of lightning reveals the phalanx no nearer to the dray, but in the last moment I see two men at the dray's front. They must want to lead it away. Damn it, that's it. I jump to my feet, my knees are weak but I stumble forward. To where? It's dark all round except for shadowy forms in the vague glow, red, yellow, of the torches hissing in the rain. I run to where

I think I saw them. The fight is now close to me, I can see the straining, rain-streaked, blood-soaked faces of men on foot, horses rearing, kicking. A mass of sword-swinging, swearing, screaming men and Klagenhuber head and shoulders above them, the rain streaming in solid shafts, a long sword held in both hands, his habit torn from his upper body to reveal chain mail. Another flash of lightning, a multiple strobe that illuminates three fighters in a desperate moment about him, before his swinging blade, a rider charges to his left, a thunder clap rolling like a cannonade, another flash of light, this time striking a silver-blue streak that explodes into the midst of the fighters, the horse rears, striding forward on its hind legs, the rider standing straight in the stirrups. Its forelegs coming down, the strobe of blinding light blinks out, another follows and Klagenhuber is down. An axe is raised. The smell of burning brimstone. The battle rages, moving on and down the road. A groaning, moaning sound, a chorus, the Tyrolians are singing their swan song?

The Suisse guardsmen all about me, they too are trying to take the wagon, their sergeant's booming voice, the huge horses neighing, rearing in their traces, the dray rolls forward and then slides down the muddy incline where the road falls away into a ditch. I grab hold and swing myself up and into the seat and reach for the reins, the whip. "Gedde up!" The team lurches forward, scrambling in the mud to gain the roadway. Fighters all around, the Suisse guardsmen understand, the dray sways to the left, some heave at the wheels. I stand and lash out at the team, at the fighters, the horses strain, the dray is sliding backwards, I lash and lash their flanks, they scramble on and up and gain ground and move forward, the fight is before me, around me. Lightning. A stronger wind whips the downpour into a maelstrom. There is François de Gurvand wielding a broadsword! The Tyrolians all about him, shouting a battlecry.

In the orange torchlight I see two fall to his sword, another is running away. His son and another are at his side and back, they move forward into the struggling mass, hacking, slashing. They are now fighting for their lives. François' party is joined by two others. Two axe-wielding guardsmen strain to reach them on the right.

"François, look, there!" I shout with all my might.

The rain is blinding. The team has caught itself, they move forward onto the road, I lash them hard. They slither. A fighter climbs up on to the seat as the team gains ground and takes off. I fight him off with the loaded butt end of the whip, his face appears in the half-light of the flaming torch, it is Adhémar de Gurvand. Surprise in both our faces. I am hurled from the dray and fall heavily, painfully, very painfully, before me a man, I try to rise but I drop to my knees and grovel, a blow rips through and through, blackness.

I come to myself, I am not dead. I know that because I am lying in my own shit, soaked in blood and the rain is pelting down. About me are heaped the bodies of the dead and wounded. The sword stroke that has taken off my right ear and cheek and cleaved into my shoulder will kill me for sure. They think that I am dead already. The dawn is rising pale. I can see men moving about. Torches. Horses staggering. I can hear the groans, the cries, the prayers. I pray "Dear God, take me sooner than later: *Corpum meum tibi offero domine prompte et sincere,*" and try to rise—no good. There is no pain, there is just a dull ache in my chest and arm and shoulder. But the blood is pouring. There is pain in my hip. Broken.

"Here, here I am alive. Over here!" I shout, or think I shout. Two are coming over.

"Adhémar," I call, "Adhémar!" A bit louder, I see him turn and look about. "Here!" They come forward.

"Adhémar, my dear boy, it is I, Father Magneval, help, I bear a terrible wound." Adhémar kneels at my side and rolls away a body that has held me pinned. "Father Magneval, is that you? What in hell . . . Father Magneval! . . . Here, over here, Eurispoe, come! Quickly!"

"Your father, I saw him, where is he? Adhémar, tell me, I saw him. There. Where is he, I must tell . . ."

"Father . . . father is dead, over there. Oh, oh, this is hell, come, come quickly, over here." Some others come, they take me up, oh, this is painful, all is going down without . . . *sans viaticum.* "Adhémar, my dear, dear son, forgive me." I see that a cloud, a darkness gathers. My God. My Lord, take me to your everlasting peace. Forgive me . . . please, I have served with my whole self, in love of thee, in love of thee. "Adhémar, listen, the piper is a spy . . . the pi . . ."

"Father . . . what? Which piper?"

"He is gone, Adhémar, leave him. You must come. We must ride."

"My father . . ?"

"We must leave them, we have no choice, we must go, now."

20:

1813. Adhémar de Gurvand,

The Binioù.

"Adhémar! Stay awake."

I ride together with Baron Hurault at the head of our battered, bedraggled party of wounded, exhausted men. I am aching all over. The dray with the Polyhedron wrapped in canvas in our midst. People on the road-side stare. A battle, they say, a battle. Of the forty-four who set out, there are now sixteen. My father is dead. Prince Idelfonso has vanished.

"Prince Idelfonso?"

"He rode to Plestin-les-Grèves as the fight commenced. He cannot risk injury or death. He alone knows the mystery of this thing."

Plestin-les-Grèves. At the end of the earth; Cape Finisterre is our destination. Then a ship. Then to Trinidad. My God, what a fight. Father. My God. What am I to do? He is dead in that field with no one. Nobody to bury him. No one. Oh Papa, Papa. I am so weary. My teeth, I have lost teeth, there, and my arm has not stopped bleeding. The rain has stopped, but the sky's all wrong. No telling the time. It could be

morning or afternoon. Monotone slate grey. Later come sooner.
An invisible sun. Somewhere the sun is shining. Up there. In
Trinidad. Eugénie. I want to go home.

"Adhémar! Stay awake. You are nodding off."

We ride until we can go no more and stop on the bank
of a swift running river, exhausted. A fire. Hot wine. Sleep.
Everything wheels and tumbles. Dreams. Thank God I
have forgotten them. But their taste remains. This thing, this
damn thing.

"I don't want it, Hurault, I want to go home."

I have slept for ten hours. The men are cooking. Some
are standing watch. The sun is somewhere far away. In the
remote distance. I can see the evidence of its existence in the
livid gash of red and purple, orange and black, on the edge
of the world. Perhaps even further. Enormous lichen-covered
stones, standing, leaning. Black. Invisibly breathing. Wet. An
icy wind. I reach in myself for a great pain, sorrow, to remind
me of father's death. To grieve. There is only fear. My God.
What am I to do? Panic.

"Adhémar, there is only duty. If you leave this, you would
have abandoned, left behind, six hundred years of your family's
history. They have kept this, this thing, for this purpose.
Your father, François, gave his life for it. You, almost yours.
All those men, out there, dead. They were not strangers to
me, Adhémar!"

He can say no more. I know. Neither can I.

I am not hungry. But when the plates of steaming stew are
handed round, I find that I am.

"Rest, we will leave well before dawn."

Dreaming of this huge man. His sword swinging round,
whirling, whirling round. The lightning. I didn't see it happen.

346

I saw it in my dream. It was as how he described the old Druid's death in Prester John's Land. I see it coming to me, Papa's head. His face, his mouth saying "Adhémar". I am awake, lightning. Am I awake? I can still see him. The huge man. After the Baron rode him down and they killed him, battered him, chopped him with axes. The others started to run off, run away. Except for the monks. They sang their dirge and shouted something incomprehensible till the last one was hacked to death. And Father Magneval. Father Magneval! On the wagon, trying to drive it away. And Papa. Dead. What's this? . . . Who's there?

"Who's there!" My shout is weak. "Hold there! Stop that man!" A man has hitched the team to the dray. "Hold there!" My shouts have set men running, some to the road. The man is under those trees. To my feet, my sword. I run, two others are running. The man dives into the river. Another goes after him and another. They haul him in.

"Coade, Coade? Is that you?"

Baron Hurault has him by the collar at the fire. He can feel the heat.

"Coade, it is you! Damn it! What are you doing here, why are you trying to steal my wagon?"

"Who is he?"

"He is the notary at Moncontour, he is a lay member of the Order. He pipes, he is a bag pipe player, a *binioù* . . ."

"Hurault, he is the piper! He is a spy! Father Magneval, those were his last words."

We stare at this face, this plump, balding, gulping, wet, shining face. Eyes wild. Hurault slaps him hard across it several times with his gloved hand. Blood appears. The man starts to cry. A long thin dagger with a death's head and cross bones as a hilt appears in Hurault's hand. He slices off a piece of the man's ear, and pushes it into his mouth, and with a gloved finger forces it down the man's throat.

"Talk!"

The man chokes. Blood, everywhere.

"Talk!"

Hurault takes hold of his nose.

"Talk!"

The man, Coade, talks. He is an informer, a spy. Yes, he is in the pay of the secret police. Yes, since he was a boy. Long entangled story: a priest, buggery, sordid. Blackmail. Hurault takes the role of confessor. "Yes my son." The man weeps. He tells of reporting the visit of the Prince and his party, us, to Château de Tonquedec.

"To whom?" mildly.

"To Sire de Pontrieux at Dinan."

He saw the Polyhedron taken from the well. He had seen the man who followed them, followed us, to the Château. The man hidden in a tree. The man saw him spying. The man vanished. The man was Father Magneval. Father Magneval followed us to France! He followed us everywhere. And he was there at the battle with them. My God.

"So you have spied on us, for the, emperor?"

Hurault puts it to him in a mild tone, almost conversational. The man nods and is about to say something when Hurault cuffs him several times in the head. And then the knife, off comes an ear! My God. Into the mouth, down, down. The man gulps, retches, Hurault cuffs him hard, two three times.

"Swallow it!" He swallows. "Talk! Who else?"

Hurault passes the knife across the man's neck, lightly. Blood. It must sting, he screams, and tries to break away. No chance. More blows.

"Talk!"

The man, Coade, babbles and cries, weeps. I am appalled. My stomach clenches. One of our riders, Eurispoe seeks to draw me away.

"This goes badly, come away my Lord. Step away."

"NO! No."

I take in deep breaths of the cold air.

"Take away his trousers, let's see what he has there that so fascinated the priests."

His trousers are ripped away.

Hurault grabs him by the scrotum, by everything, the knife.

"Talk, who else?"

He kicks, cries and writhes. They hold him fast. Some men are laughing.

Hurault. "Shut up!"

They stop.

The knife is at his belly button, it sinks in. Blood. Coade screams. "The Provost, the Provost, I tell the Provost everything, everything, everything."

He is weeping now hysterically. His hands make meaningless movements. Blood is everywhere. Hurault slaps him hard several times across the face.

"Stop. Talk. What Provost, from where? His name."

Through his tears he answers. Something. Not enough. More slaps.

"Talk up!"

"The Provost-Marshal at Saint-Brieuc," he screams. "Monsieur Dupuis, Fernand Dupuis. And another, Mazzacorati, an Italian police inspector. Please, please, am I going to die?"

"Yes!"

"Please, do not kill me, my daughter is little, we have no one, please do not kill me, Sire, please . . ."

More slaps.

"Did you tell the Inspector of the visit to Château de Tonquedec and the route of this journey?"

"Yes Sire, yes. Please do not kill me. There's no one . . ."

"Kill him."

It's done.

I think I lost consciousness, darkness. I feel ashamed as I wake.

"No worry, every man here has faced death. You did well in the battle, you saved that thing, and that is what really counts, the only thing that counts," remarks Hurault as we sit by the fire waiting for the men to make ready for the day's march. I fall asleep, to dream nightmares.

Morning. Feeling like a future ghost. We are on the road. The weather is becoming fine and cold. A bitter wind slices through everything. Thank God it has stopped raining. They killed that man, slit his throat, and then threw his body into the river. My father was the apogee, the summit of my life. All roads led to, or from him. I am now a frightened man, travelling with strangers who, as I have seen, are capable of anything, including murder. That poor man. That battle. My God. Eugénie. Oh my love, my love. I want to go home.

A rider on the crest of a distant hummock. The company halts and is on guard. The rider raises a banner and waves it. It is a signal. Baron Hurault rides with another to meet the rider. We wait. Muskets are primed. Three take up position on the dray. They are expecting an attack. Hurault returns, we are being pursued by a detachment of imperial cavalry, who are at present on the wrong road which will take them to Belle-Isle-en-Terre and they will have to cross country to meet up with us. Our destination is Plestin-les-Grèves, where a ship awaits us, but we must make haste.

We too cross country, a labyrinth of lanes and tracks. We are bypassing Saint Michel-en-Grève. The sea. I see a vast seascape, washed clean. Blue. We ride along tremendous cliffs. Below, clear icy green bashes itself against jagged black to become white foam that rises in a fine mist, which is tinged to pale pastels of pink and a greenish yellow by a cold, distant, indifferent sun.

Plestin-les-Grèves is an obscure place, an almost deserted hamlet built at an indeterminable period inside a sprawling ruined citadel on a hilltop overlooking a wide bay. There is no ship in sight. Really massive stones, boulders, lie about. The baron is not dismayed. We put up at 'Le Bateau Travail', a dilapidated inn. The baron is in charge. Hot water, hot wine and food. Soft beds. An anxious night and day passes. Another. Prince Idelfonso appears, kind, soft spoken, gracious; we must make ready immediately. The ship will approach the bay below at half past five when the tide is at its highest. We must be at sea with the cargo to meet it as it must sail with the receding tide and, hopefully, take advantage of the evening's land breeze.

We set out. The dray with the Polyhedron, still wrapped in canvas, is taken down to a sandy knoll at the seaside. A sledge is brought for it that will be dragged to a waiting, careened longboat, and the Polyhedron will be put aboard. We wait for the tide. It rises. The men drag the sledge and its cargo across the wide expanse of hard sand to the waiting longboat and, with some effort, get it into the careened boat, making it secure. In the meantime the tide is coming in.

Cries of seabirds circling above. We are all standing in foamy water, sand melting beneath our bare feet, cold, sunny. The longboat is being manhandled by its gunwales to set it upright and afloat, when from across the bay's vast curve, where a milky sun is attempting to set, we see riders. We must right the boat. It must not be filled with water as it lies upon its side. The effort is redoubled. In the meanwhile some others, led by the Baron, set out to meet the riders and take to their mounts to halt them, to give those who are righting the boat the chance to push it out, to get it afloat.

Prince Idelfonso and I stand in the clear seawater that is now swirling around our calves. A steady breeze picks up from the direction of a sandy knoll. We watch the fight, the Baron has divided his small troop into two columns who ride straight at the oncoming riders, at a distance hard to gauge from where we stand. His troop separates, to the left and to the right, this throws the others into some disarray. Then, both columns wheel and charge into the flanks of the oncoming riders. The manoeuvre has caused sufficient confusion to slow the advance. From this distance all is a melee of whirling horses, sand, foam, water and the glints and the flash of steel in the evening sunlight. But our force is quickly overwhelmed by the greater numbers of the heavy cavalry.

Several riders break away from the skirmish, perhaps to draw the others, but this fails and they rejoin the fight. I can see three, four riderless horses. Five, now six. More. My heart is thumping violently, my mouth, dry, I am shaking feverishly in

352

every limb, what was a deep anxiety now become fear. Prince Idelfonso, at my side, calm. A page dressed in livery, his, has brought one mount to the water's edge. The attempt to slow the cavalry further is failing. Has failed. The longboat is afloat. The baron and one other are riding full tilt towards us. He is being overtaken. He falls to a heavy, sabre-wielding hussar.

We enter the longboat, the oars, there are but three, one is floating away. Leave it. We make to sea. No ship in sight. The open sea is the only option. The hussars ride into the waves, an officer rises in his saddle, stands in his stirrups, levels a pistol, and fires. The bullet takes the Prince in the middle of his forehead and he falls to the bottom of the longboat with the cry of an eagle.

21:

1813–1814. Vincent Patrice,

The Immortal Forty-five.

At that particular convocation, I believe it was in September of 1809, they stood to order before me, the Vénérable Master of Les Frères Unis, for the first time as Entered Apprentices. He, Santiago Mariño, visibly shaken. I could see the impact made upon him by the lecture in the Cloistered Place in his altered demeanour. Humbled. The Frère Sacrificier's words had shifted his consciousness, the spectre he regarded when the hood-wink was removed had appalled him. He would now have a different relationship with death. Good.

Jean Baptiste Bideau, attentive. Dedicated to republican ideals; he, I accepted into the Atelier for that reason. Loyalty. A dark-skinned mulatto, of middle age, from a well-off family of shipmasters in Sainte Lucie. He was amongst those recruited by Victor Hugues and routed in Chaguaramas Bay by Captain Skinner, just before the English conquest. Bideau, educated, upright in bearing, everything about him spoke of a good upbringing. At the interview he said to me that all the people of the Americas were linked to a common destiny, and what they needed were the mechanisms by which they could submit themselves to honest, enthusiastic, visionary leadership of the type that would guide them towards the creation of democratic and republican institutions. I hope that he will be to Santiago a trusted lieutenant. Time will tell what he has gained from the initiation. That was four years ago.

Santiago Mariño, Jean Baptiste Bideau, Julien Besson, Francisco Bermudez and Juan de la Cova are all conspirators. They look and act like conspirators.

"Go and conspire somewhere else," I said seriously to them. The others were long gone from the Harmony of the Festive Board to carouse in the port with the immature Colombian prostitutes who, as a result of the war on the Mainland, were now arriving by the pirogue-load. These now sat with their heads together, the candle almost guttered, drinking the last of the rum, the smoke from their cheroots like a rain-cloud hovering above their heads.

"No politics in the Lodge, get out, go!" I stood on the gallery and saw them enter the darkness just before passing over the Dry River bridge to Calle St. Louis, these days called Queen Street, their seditious voices to carry over and above the sleeping town. The English authorities, because of their new relationship with Spain, made it plain. "We will shut you down if plots are hatched under this roof." Times certainly have not changed.

Magneval has vanished. What in hell? The presbytery is deserted. The priest from San Juan de Aricagua, a Spaniard by the name of Diaz, Father Manuel Diaz, has come.

Santiago received his education in Port-d'Espagne at a school for Irish boys founded by his grandfather, Geraldine Carige, and maintained by Union Lodge. The school, of a good enough standard, was comprised of twenty-one boys, almost all from Irish families. They were instructed by "professors" imported from England, except for the one who taught Castilian grammar—he was a Spaniard. The youth Santiago was taught French, English, Spanish, arithmetic, literature, the foil, the sabre and the classics. Later on, he studied land surveying and physics. He grew to be tall, over six feet, well built and agile, with the red hair and eyes of an intense blue that I remember him by from when I first saw him. He joined the Trinidad militia, where he received Governor Picton's commission and held the rank of cornet. When he came to us he was well-liked, very popular in the Atelier and with the coloured men in the ranks of the militia.

They, his family, lived, when not at their plantation on Chacachacare, in a large, two-storied house on the corner of Pembroke Street opposite to Brunswick Square. One of the few in the town, which, rebuilt after the fire, was possessed of an architectural style; it looked Spanish. On receiving the news of his father's death in Margarita, Santiago felt himself no longer obligated to abstain from events on the Mainland and as an ardent republican, together with his fellow conspirators, got himself across the Gulf of Paria to the swampy hamlet of Punta Piedra on the Main and went in search of the war. They fell in with Colonel Manuel Villapol who marched into Guayana. Santiago fought there. Later, in command of a detachment of infantry attached to the patriotic colours at Güiria against superior royalist forces, he held his position, preventing a rout and defending the flag of the new republic. He was, I heard, at Valencia under de Miranda in 1811. Two Spanish assaults on the city by Captain Domingo de Monteverde were repulsed by the patriotic forces that were entrenched in the city, and Monteverde was compelled to fall back to San Mateo. I heard that he acquired a reputation for recklessness. There, on the field, Santiago was promoted to the rank of lieutenant colonel.

"Massa." It was my boatman Robert. He startled me, I must have been dozing at my desk. The lamp burned low, my watch said half-past eleven. "Massa, Massa Santiago send to say come by he, he home. Master, you 'wake?"

María Concepción met me at the door. "Master Vincent, come, he sent for you. He is exhausted. He, Jean Bideau and Francisco Bermudez, and some others, were able to get out of Güiria."

He lay abed, fast asleep in the master bedroom, baggage strewn about, arms, muskets, swords, bayonets, ammunition, lots of ammunition. Bideau snored in an armchair in the corner. Fernando Gomez de Zaa, she said, had brought Santiago and Bermudez to Yaguaraparo, to the hacienda of Don Augustín Galdona, where they took refuge. From there they fought their way to Güiria. Bideau, she told me in a whisper, had not left his side since he had rescued them in Güiria, taken them off the jetty in a rowboat with the Spanish troops firing salvoes at them, to get them aboard the gaff-rigged schooner *Botón de Rosa*, of which he was in command.

Bideau sailed for Chacachacare, but the house, with iridescent iguanas scurrying in the leaf-strewn terrace, was in disrepair, and there was no food, so there was no choice but to risk getting caught by the Trinidad harbour police, which mercifully did not happen, and here they were. The colony's new governor, Sir Ralph Woodford, unlike Governor Picton or even Hislop, enforced little control of the harbour.

"How many?"

"Six: Bermudez, Isava, Besson, Gomez, Bideau, and Santiago. We, I, cannot keep them here, Master Vincent, by morning the whole town will know that they are here, there will be a mob of recruits; the English will come."

"And there will be a riot." He was awake. "Master Vincent, I am glad you have come."

He was even taller. He took my hand in fraternal greeting and bowed, his hand was calloused and bony.

"Santiago," I said, "you have been conspiring again I see. Now we leave quietly, awaken your compatriots. María, I seem to remember a wagon in the stable . . ."

"Yes, Master Vincent, I have already brought it to the back door, it is covered, I await your directions."

Bravo, what a sensible child. With the help of Robert and the house-slaves we were able to load them all, together with their accoutrements, onto the wagon and set out as quietly as a wagon drawn by two sleepy, unwilling mules could possibly be at two in the morning, around the Square, down Frederick Street and up Queen Street towards Mount Moriah and Les Frères Unis, where I installed them in the undercroft, the very place where they once heard the lecture in the Solitary Room.

I arrived at Sir Ralph's residence before five o'clock. The sentry was fast asleep. I rapped loudly on his box.

"Inform the governor that I am here."

Woodford was a very difficult man. It took an hour to convince him that if these men were arrested there would be a riot. More than a riot, an uprising, one that would require military intervention on a scale that he did neither command nor wish for, particularly now, at the start of his administration. It would be better if they left, immediately. I was glad to have arrived ahead of the alguacil major, who rode into the yard in

358

a great clatter of mud and drizzle as the governor and I were taking breakfast.

Following his instructions, I got these foreign subversives out of Port-d'Espagne and on Chacachacare island by the following night. It was a very rainy October, so they had to make do. I supplied them with food. María Concepción took up residence at Monte de Botella and, by the following week, the old house was much the same as when Manuel Gual and I were last there, what? Fourteen years ago. It cost Santiago and his family five hundred gold escudos, at sixteen reales per escudo, to give the governor ease of mind.

In the weeks and months that followed they came to him from all over the coast: the remnants of armed bands, some who had fought with Gual and España, individuals, some sick, others wounded, all exhausted by the extremes of surviving in the primeval environment of the impenetrably high forest, the unimaginable expanses of water, the silence, the darkness, so complete that you forgot to breathe, the unrelenting rain, quicksand and mud of the Orinoco delta; hunted by the cannibals, haunted by the invisible presence of gigantic boa constrictors, stalked by jaguars, ambushed by crocodiles and ambuscaded by the royalists who never abandoned their hot pursuit.

Some went mad, jabbering stories of having seen men, trunks walking without a head, that stalked the night . . . carrying their severed heads, holding them out before them, like a lantern, by the hair. Leaping from their hammocks to run screaming into the mangrove, pursued by the daemons of their frightful nightmares. They came to hide in the mountains on the north-western peninsula, others to slip into Port-d'Espagne and to disappear into the extended Venezuelan families who ranged in racial mixture from blond to black to Arawak, with a few to stay with Santiago at Monte de Botella. Those closest to him were Antonio José de Sucre, Manuel Piar, Jean-Baptiste Bideau and Francisco Azcue, along with Julien Besson and Antonio Carige, his cousin, and two or three others who went to the war with him and survived the arduous rescue from Güiria. Sucre had served with de Miranda as a youthful member of his staff, his baptism of fire was at Valencia and at Arugua.

Sucre, fleeing the inevitable reprisals, brought the news of de Miranda's change of fortune to Trinidad himself. He came to his relative Diego María Solis in Port-d'Espagne. They told Santiago of the cruel, sad and humiliating depravations being carried out in Venezuela and the ill-treatment, the debasement that was inflicted on de Miranda and the other patriotic men. All this made Santiago angry, he vowed that he would take revenge for this, this disgrace. He could not bear to hear anything about the fate that had befallen de Miranda, whom he regarded as a hero, a patriot and the first great American, the Precursor of the revolution whom he loved like a parent. A fire was blazing in the belly of this man, Santiago Mariño.

More news came. As Piar related, they were fishing off the rocks at Aremada, Chacachacare's eastern extremity, the first quarter moon high, their campfire almost burnt out, the rum done and a chilly wind coming up from the north-east, when suddenly, there was Bermudez holding a young man by the neck, who appeared in a poor state.

"We have a priest," he said.

"Let's cook him. I am fed up with fish," said Manuel Piar.

"Seriously," said Bermudez, "look."

"Where did you find him?"

"The tide brought him in, he was in a pirogue that ran aground on Bolo Rock, look, there, he swam in."

"Who are you, boy?"

"Look, his priest's outfit, beads, a prayer-book . . . a letter."

"Who are you, boy? Give me the letter."

Juan Domingo Valenilla, as it turned out, was from Maturín. He carried a letter addressed to Manuel Valdez, Governor Woodford's secretary. He was quite open; he was a seminarian and a patriot. Manuel Valdez was a spy and worked for de Miranda. His news was that Bolívar had left for Curaçao and was now, perhaps, in Cartagena, where, he believed, the junta would take an offensive stand. Valenilla's last instructions from de Miranda were to get the news to Valdez, failing that, to get a message to him, telling him that his allegiance was now to be transferred to Colonel Santiago Mariño and to me, Vincent Patrice, the Maçon.

He was also instructed to tell the patriots in Trinidad that they must avoid the notoriously perfidious Saint Hilaire Bégorrat, who was an agent for the English, reporting directly to London with a view to protecting particular French royalist interest in Trinidad, families who were betraying the patriots to curry favour with the English to secure a position for themselves in English Trinidad and whose loyalty, if any existed at all, was only to the Vatican, inasmuch as they no longer had a king, and that the patriots on Chacachacare could have been infiltrated by a spy who was reporting directly to Bégorrat.

For Santiago, there was the not unexpected news that the Spanish government now occupied all the Mariño properties and was confiscating the slaves on the plantations and the

Indians in the *encomiendas* to the Crown. He was now in the same position as Bolívar and de Miranda.

The letter also contained for me, and for Santiago and the other patriots, the startling details of de Miranda's capture and fall from position. That he was betrayed by Bolívar at the instigation of traitors to both the royalist and the republican causes, with whom Bolívar sought refuge as the calamities of the last days of the First Republic arranged themselves. These traitors, de Miranda was informed, urged Bolívar to save himself, if only to fight another day, by turning de Miranda in to the royalists and to Monteverde, in exchange for a passport. Bolívar agreed. His acceptance I was disappointed in, but it did not surprise me.

Further, the First Republic's entire treasury was in the house of the republic's last director-general of finances. He showed the gold to Bolívar. This man's view was that de Miranda was finished and should be captured and sent to Spain. Bolívar accepted that. The shame of losing the fortress at Puerto Cabello was still with him and he was obsessed with the idea of redeeming himself. And there was money, gold.

It was de Miranda's view and Santiago should know it, he wrote, that it was the goal of the traitors in Caracas to divide the patriots and to weaken their resolve by creating suspicion. "Support Colonel Simón Bolívar," de Miranda advised, "because he has chosen to sacrifice me to save himself for the Great Work, the republic, and for America, a hard choice that he is punishing himself for already. I have already forgiven him, and await him here in La Guaira. When he comes, I will be ready. History will judge him. My servant, Littais L'Eau, will follow him to Curaçao."

De Miranda has fallen. He is in the hands of the Spaniards. His days, what are left of them, will be spent in the deepest

Spanish dungeon where he will die in his own filth. A great depression has overtaken me, a desperation that I have not known for years, notwithstanding the vicissitudes of this lunatic island, in truth since the failure of Victor Hugues and his betrayal, should I say the betrayal of the French revolution. That is the end of that. De Miranda's luck has run out. History will forget him. What will become of me, of all this?

That news has made me understand that my future, the future of the Great Work, as I would have it, as de Miranda inspired us to achieve it, me, Manuel Gual, O'Higgins, the Americans, the others, in London so long ago, has come to nothing. The future as I want it to be cannot be tied to Bolívar, that dog of a traitor, who is in with the American Maçons of Charlestown. If I am to succeed in the creation of a Grand Lodge of South America with Les Frères Unis as its mother Lodge, my future, the future, is now with this band of patriots, these boys, so few with so little. Oh, my word, how this has all arranged itself! It is clear, I must do something to attach them to me, as de Miranda did with us in London.

François de Gurvand has now been in Europe for more than two years. I am alone. I must create an event, a profoundly patriotic event, to make an impression on these young people, to enshrine the meaning of all this, in the context of the Craft, the Great Work, as the source, the place from whence the republic has come. They must be consecrated and joined in the bond of a spiritual knighthood of initiates and perceive themselves as embarking upon a crusade, in a ritual ceremony that alters forever their lives and binds them to me. I must inspire them with courage to beat the *peninsulares*. There must be nothing frivolous or vulgar, but a mystery experienced in which I am the oracle. I am alone.

The Corsican Brethren of Les Frères Unis, almost one-third of the membership, have become Trinidad's first real gunrunners, people smugglers, and arrangers of all manner of trans-shipments to unimaginably distant places. Many will follow in their wake, but it was they who opened the contraband routes Down the Main that will exist for centuries. The Zannini, Susini, Blasini, Pietri, and Raffaelli families can see the vast profits to be made in all this. They have little use for the ideals of the Craft, the allegorical readings are lost on them, although the ritual work and the symbolism does indeed move their primitive imaginations and the notion of a secret society is very appealing, it's like the *cosca,* the family. But, they will make up numbers, fill the temple and contribute to the war chest. Money. This will require money.

In the days and weeks that followed the retreat of the patriots from Güiria, I was especially careful not to allow any conversation regarding the camp down the islands or any discussion of the war in the Atelier. There were spies aplenty on the benches who worked for the Spanish government, for the perfidious Saint Hilaire Bégorrat, the Holy Hermandad, and for the new English governor, or who were just freelancers engaging in the all-pervading habit of this place that gossips and ill speaks, there is a word for it even, *mauvais langue* and a name for such people, *macos.*

It was safer for the conspirators to meet at Mrs. Murphy's tavern and paradisal brothel near to Fort San Andres' barracks, where the English governor's general staff was quartered.

Joseph Susini said to me one morning as I was coming from the Plaza, "This young patriotess, Santiago's seester, María Concepción, is an upstanding woman." Susini could hardly contain himself. "Bella, I have seen her, hot, her face aflame, at the furnace, working the bellows. 'Put the wood in the fire,' she orders, I jump at it, Vincent, to be given the command, mamma mia, but she is good with the guns. She can take an old gun and make it new, that's the woman for you, Vincent! And Vincent, she is melting down the soldiers, thousands of them. She is turning them into balls!"

What the hell is he talking about?

"She takes the little *chasseurs à pied*, the Grenadiers, British, German—she don't care, she puts it in the pot, in the fire, they disrepair . . . what?"

"Disappear, you mean disappear, she is melting toy soldiers to be made into lead shot."

"Yes, Master Vincent, thousands of them, an army, two armies, maybe three, they become bullets, mamma mia, what a woman."

María Concepción was sending her grandfather's collection of lead toy soldiers to war—what a woman indeed. I went the next day to see for myself.

Indeed. Joseph Susini was now the chief procurer of weapons, he and Paul Pietri. There was, as well, an elderly German, Harry Meier, good with his hands. He and María Concepción had restored some seventeen muskets. Monte de Botella had become an arms factory. Under her guidance, and with a good deal of horse play, Bideau, Pietri and Piar were producing hundreds of rounds of lead shot a day. I saw Antonio de Sucre and Bernardo Bermudez de Castro taking sewing lessons, making uniforms from old drapery borrowed from the plantation house in Tunapuna, owned by Sucre's cousin, José Alcala.

It was an armed camp and a munitions factory run by a woman. A woman in her twenties. In the meantime, her brother, Santiago, recruited in Trinidad, offering ten pilar silver dollars to every man who enlisted. He paid out more than four hundred dollars. The money came from his pocket.

Their pockets. The idea that Francisco de Miranda was betrayed by Bolívar now filled Santiago with rage. His rages, his impatience with his compatriots, led to fist fights between them. In truth, de Miranda's fate, the treachery of Bolívar and the collapse of the republic, were a cause for confrontations, disputes and challenges; duels fought in the Paradise Estate's Grand Savanna, three or four a week. Much blood was shed by young men who should go to war.

The enterprise attracted many of the Free Black and Coloured men in the militia: men known to Santiago from when he served in that unit. These, several of them, were the sons or grandsons of French planters, some with aristocratic names, born from women whom the planters had either used for their pleasure in idle moments, or, in some rare cases, lived *plaçage* relationships with; not a few were educated. The Free Blacks and Coloureds joined because they were convinced that in the Venezuela that would come into existence, they would have a future better than the one in Trinidad. They would fight for more than the money.

I returned with Santiago and nine new recruits to the island, and we sat around the campfire to talk about the future.

In the morning I saw two black youngsters from the fishing village on the other side of Coco Bay, the Sanda estate, asleep in the camp.

"What's your name, boy?" demanded María Concepción, seeing the two hungrily eyeing the breakfast being prepared, the morning chill still lingering around the fire, to which they both answered "Jean". She renamed them Jean and Jean-Luis Victorie and decided that they would be drummer boys, she got them a drum, one drum, they were promised another, they practised. The camp agreed Victorie was a good name.

Then Fernando Gomez de Zaa arrived with the news that Colonel Bolívar had been successful in getting the support of the junta in New Granada and was in command of an army that he had taken into the field, fighting against Spanish positions on the banks of the Magdalena River on the other side of the continent. He had overrun the town of Tenerife and faced a strong counterinsurgency with success.

"Bolívar has captured four armed vessels on the river, Santiago, the revolution has recommenced!" shouted Gomez. "Look what he has written!" He took from his blouse a tattered pamphlet, and read: 'We were given philosophers for leaders, philanthropy for legislation, dialectic for tactics, and sophists for soldiers. Today, we have an army of fighting men. The orators have gone back to the temples, before us are fields of glory.—' This, all this is over, Santiago, now is the time for action, for strength and energy. Let's go to war!"

The news that the forces of liberty had regrouped and were on the move, that the past, an embarrassing past, was past, changed the ongoing drills and preparation for an undefined launch into an immediate plan to mount an attack on Spanish positions in Güiria. Santiago left that night for Port-d'Espagne in the *Carlota,* a sloop that his sister donated to the camp. By morning, he assembled, under the eyes of the Harbour Master James Meany, a Brother, a dozen or so of those who received the part payment for their enlistment, mostly Coloureds from the militia, and set out with them for Chacachacare. There, he found us around a blazing fire over which an ox turned. Father Domingo Bruzal came up from Saint Peter's church in Carenage to hear confessions. Myself, old Pappits and Robert joined the campfire. Pappits had contributed a goat.

Manuel Valdez, the governor's private secretary, joined us at the campfire where we were enjoying beef and freshly baked bread.

"Aah, Manuel, did you get your leave of absence from the governor?"

"No, Señor, but I have a new job now, I am adjutant to some renegade madmen who are going off to conquer what's left of the known world, and I have come to tell the Colonel and the Captain that the flotilla will await them."

I came prepared. That afternoon, with the help of Robert and Pappits, I turned the drawing room of Monte Botello into a temple. I draped it in purple and red. But first, I put up a notice above the door. It read, *"Si talia jungere possis sit tibi scire satis* - "If thou can'st comprehend these things, thou knowest enough."

I lit the room with nineteen lamps. I placed a silver seven-branched candlestick upon an altar at the eastern end of the room, which I made from a sea-man's chest draped in red velvet, to represent the Burning Bush. I laid on the dining table, also draped in red and placed in the middle of the room, the Platter of Coarse Salt, the Censer of Incense, the Sacrificial Knife, the Brazen Mirror, the Iron Bell, the Silver Chalice, the Ludovisi Ares, in bronze, and the volume of the Sacred Law.

That night at midnight I commenced the initiation of the nineteen members of Les Frères Unis present on the island, into the company of Knights of the Order of the Sword, and proclaimed them guardians of the Grand Council and Conclave of the Continent, and cautioned them, "Let no man ever lightly take a vow, be faithful and yet not unreasonable . . ." I said this remembering the poet Dante Alighieri. I alone conducted a ritual that I had created, one might say, on the spot. I proclaimed to them that they, and those who served with them in the wars to liberate the world, were to be henceforth and forever, "The Immortals."

In the flickering light I saw them kneel before me, already captured in the enigma of the ritual, as I, robed in black and red, intoned, "The earth is the Lord's, and the fullness thereof; the world and they that dwell therein.

"For He hath founded it upon the seas and established it upon the floods." I placed before them the Platter of Coarse Salt, and called each forward and bade them taste it.

"Who shall ascend into the hill of the Lord? And who shall stand in His holy place?" I incensed them.

"He that hath clean hands and a pure heart; who hath not lifted up his soul unto vanity, nor sworn deceitfully.

"He shall receive the blessing from the Lord, and righteousness from the God of his salvation.

"This is the generation of them that seek him, that seek thy face, O Jacob. Selah." Here I stopped to tell them that the word Selah meant to pause, to contemplate on what was being said, and to pay attention to what you saw being done. I passed amongst them the Sacrificial Knife, symbol of protection, power and restraint.

"Lift up your heads, O ye gates; and be ye lifted up, ye everlasting doors; and the King of Glory shall come in.

"Who is this King of Glory? The Lord strong and mighty, the Lord mighty in battle." I held up before them the Ludovisi Ares. A replacer in bronze of the youthful god of war at rest, trophies at his feet.

"Lift up your heads, O ye gates; even lift them up, ye everlasting doors; and the King of Glory shall come in.

"Who is this King of Glory? The Lord of Hosts, he is the King of Glory. Selah." I looked meaningfully at them.

"So mote it be," mumbled the disjointed chorus.

I caused them to assemble in the room in the form of a wedge pointed towards the west, with Santiago at the vertex. I brought in a blazing brazier and ordered them to come forward in threes and fours at a time and stand about it with their hands to the flame for as long as they could bear as I chanted, in Latin, something from Cicero that I had learnt as a boy. I took it that none of them understood Latin.

I then marched the lot out into the night and into the bath house where tubs of rain water were placed. I told them that, in silence and as an act of humility, they must now make themselves clean and come back into the temple dressed in the robes that I left piled upon the stair. Dressed in the white robes of the newly created Order of the Continent, I hung the blades that I brought with me around their necks, and, because time was short, I left them alone to contemplate their fate for one hour, instead of for a night. I noticed that Santiago, Sucre and some others prayed earnestly, while the rest sat upon the stools and stared at the floor. I spoke to them of the elementals. Of gnomes; the earth. Undines; the water. Salamanders; the fire. Sylphs; the air. Take deep breaths, I said, it is life itself. All this must lend itself to the legendarium that I now create, firstly, in their imaginations.

Hoodwinked, and to the ringing of the Iron Bell, I brought them into a black-draped dressing room just off the main hall, one at a time. And put them there to sit upon a high stool. I asked, "Would you give your blood for the revolution?" They invariably answered "Yes." I then placed firmly the point of the Sacrificial Knife near to the *antecubital fossa,* making a shallow cut near to where the large artery comes down the front of the arm. I then poured warm water from a tea pot down the arm, this trickled into a pan. The sounds of their "bleeding" made a few weak, others appeared on the point of fainting; on some

370

others it left no discernible impression. Santiago took it well. He said "Hold! Leave me some to die with." Very good.

I reassembled them in the now darkened room and gave them sashes embroidered with a sword and a mace, trimmed with red and purple. On the altar was the Silver Chalice filled with the blood of the bull that had been butchered for the camp. I told them it was theirs, mixed and mingled, and bade them drink so that their destiny would now be irrevocably shared. This they did reluctantly. I then related to them the heroic incidents upon which this order was founded, these I told them had occurred in 1131, during the reign of King Baldwin II, ruler of the Crusader states in the *Outremer*, and that it was more immediately connected with symbolic Masonry than any other order of knighthood. This charge ended with the words from *Psalm 4*. The message of the psalm is that the victories of sinners are only temporary and meaningless, and that only repentance can bring true happiness.

I dubbed them a spiritual knighthood, and knighted each between two lighted tapers, and hit them forcefully and deliberately across the face with a heavy leather glove and struck them with a blade hard upon each shoulder and informed them that this was the last time that they would be struck without a loss of honour. I held the Brazen Mirror before them, so that they may glimpse themselves. I symbolically placed a set of spurs upon each one and congratulated them on being found worthy to be promoted to this honourable order of Chivalry. I emphasized that it was highly honourable to all who diligently and zealously fulfilled the important obligations annexed to it.

I made sure to say the words "The Immortals" often. I noticed them pay greater attention when I did. I compared them to the founders of Rome, and told them that they were the nobility, the patricians of the new nations that would be born as a result of their work which would render them immortal.

I raised Santiago and proclaimed him Serenismo Gran Maestro del Gran Oriente Continental. His whole aspect and demeanour expressed devotion, capacity and the determination of those who are altered by a profound ceremony of commencement. I then opened the doors and allowed the others, whom I had caused to gather in the gallery, to enter and to glimpse the knights sitting on nineteen thrones, blades held high before them, covered in glory, the brazier blazing, the room full of tolu balsam, *myroxylon toluifera* incense, and ordered those who entered to stand to attention and to raise both hands high and to bow their heads and drop their hands three times before the newly made knights. I then made them file out quickly. Glory does not survive a too long or constant stare. They all reeked of the incense that had burned during the ritual, to which I had added equal parts of stacte, galbanum, and frankincense.

Subdued, perhaps even moved emotionally by the night's work, certainly reflective, Santiago and I, together with most of the company, walked down to the jetty that jutted out into the absolute black of Coco Bay. Above, the sky was a marvel of stars, so crowded together, so packed with lights of various magnitudes and intensities, that we could do little more than behold the splendour of the bright night, when as if by some magic, we all were astounded, and perhaps even terrified by hearing, suddenly coming from all around, a fantastic sound, a mellow chiming, a harp-like resonance, vibrating gently, rising all around us and seemingly descending from the starlit sky all about us, between us, an almost tactile harmonious blending of gongs, echoing against the mellifluous music of several harps that seemed to contain a chorus, holding a variety of voices, blending, calling at one time and then another in a delicate treble that was answered by a profound bass. Around and about this extraordinary phenomenon rose and fell, an eerie, sonorous orchestration strangely oriental yet familiar. The darkness thickened as the stars brightened.

The sounds seemed to come at times from the stars and to echo in the depths. Speechless, we stood and looked about us, each one moved to our innermost self with a profound sense of being in the presence of a greater power. Could this be as a result of the ceremony? Did I evoke a power? I could see two or three of our company on their knees in prayer. Santiago stood there, his gaze fixed upon the stars that filled the sky, his arms outstretched. I too was moved by this celestial music and felt that we were in the presence of a miracle, a wonder beyond our comprehension. I strained to find the source of the music that increased in volume with the added sound of bells, deep and solemn, like a tocsin that held a quality of coming from the depths, and another like a ship's bell submerged, while harps played and trumpets sounded, mellowed by distance, muted by some subtle art. About us, the night became blacker, heavier.

Then, the music stopped as suddenly as it started. This was followed by several loud splashes out in the bay, one so close that for the briefest moment I saw plainly the body of a large fish, a *grand-écaille* or tarpon perhaps, or sword fish, rise and flash iridescent in the starlight. Was that the fabled Melusine of the double fishtail, with a round shield and sword held high? Had we heard the siren's song of the femme fatale? We were all amazed, struck dumb by what was surely a wonder. Just then I heard behind us some voices coming down the hill.

"Ho there, Master Vincent."

It was Pappits and Robert with the boatmen, making their way down the hill through the manchineel forest.

"Listening to the trumpet fish? They are calling the carite and kingfish, bonito and snapper, tonight will be a good night to bank, plenty fish in the sea."

He lifted his lantern and saw the surprise on our faces. His own weather-beaten countenance cracked into a thousand lines, his lips revealed a row of blackened teeth.

"Trumpet fish, long, about two or three feet, thin like a tube, they toot and ring, call and yodel, like angels, or mermaids. Some say that they are the ghosts of dead sailors, sometimes you hear a bell coming from the deep. But we know that they are fish. Good night Master Vincent, good night caballeros."

"Fish with vocal cords?" I asked.

None answered for a while. Then Santiago said, "The siren song, a mantic truth. 'Once he hears to his heart's content, sails on, a wiser man.'"

"Homer?"

"Yes it is. I do believe, Master, that they call us to our Fate."

Whales, I thought to myself. "Look," I said, pointing at a very bright star, high in the eastern sky.

"*Canis Major*," said Santiago.

> "*Sirius rises late in the dark, liquid sky*
> *On summer nights, star of stars,*
> *Orion's Dog they call it, brightest*
> *Of all, but an evil portent, bringing heat*
> *And fevers to suffering humanity . . .*"

"Homer?"

"Yes it is."

The following evening, below us in La Tinta Bay I could see the several campfires that lit up the curve of black sand in the distance; behind us, the Paria mountains, where the sun was setting without fanfare in a seamless expanse of grey. In the bay, the dark outlines of the vessels that would take them down to the Mainland were rising in the quickening swell, rearing up at their moorings and straining on their anchor chains. The cool south-easterly picked up considerably.

"So, Sir Bideau, how many men on deck?"

"Seems like fifty to sixty, Master Vincent, we'll see who actually comes on board. I must tell you, Master, that two-thirds of those who volunteered have vanished. What you see down there, ourselves, the ones who you brought in to see the end of the ceremony, are the landing force, we are the Roman soldiers."

"And there is the Rubicon. Good luck, Jean, Santiago, Manuel."

They all stood there grinning, in the wind, offering mock salutes. We embraced with warmth and a lot of back slapping, the boy drummers Jean and Jean Luis Victorie, who created their own uniforms from remnants of Trinidad militia issue and other kit, came rattling up, grinning, all white eyeballs, running noses and hardly any teeth.

"General, Saa! It is twelve noon, time to waar!" declared Jean, as Jean Luis Victorie offered a roll. They still had just the one drum between them.

I squinted at my watch in the last of the fading dusk, it was ten to six.

"January 11th, 1813, six o'clock, time to leave, goodbye."

I turned about and set off down the hill, the silence already surrounding me, the wind taking it away to nowhere in particular.

"Master Vincent." Her voice startled me. "Up here."

She was standing at the iron railing in the gallery of Monte de Botella between two flambeaux. Their ruddiness upon her lips, wet, the wind causing disarray to her black hair and full burgundy dress. I must say this young woman is beautiful, so much so that sometimes I can hardly bring myself to look at her. This was one such occasion.

"Master Vincent, come, I must hand this to you, come, I have told your man Robert that he need not make ready to sail tonight, I hope you don't object, I think I need your company, it's a little too quiet, I suspect."

I mounted the stair, as eight or ten volunteers came by.

"So, how many sailed out?"

"I counted forty-five, Massa, and the priest and the two little boys, forty-eight, it look like to me," said Pappits. "It look like they will have rain and plenty wind." He grinned and waved, "They have a lot of rum."

We sat at an iron table illuminated by the iridescent glow of a quantity of large insects, fire-flies captured in a glass jar and spoke of her parents, buried over there, on Margarita, the revolution, her brother Santiago, their anger at Bolívar for de Miranda's betrayal, the fate of the war, the loss of their ancestral lands and fortune, and her wish that she had been born a man.

"When the English understand that it was from this house that the new insurgency on the Main commenced, you may lose all this as well."

She said nothing for some time. The rising breeze lifted the branches of the tall silk-cotton trees. Before us the Gulf of Paria, dark and ancient, exhaled the fresh water smells of its mammalian life, and from further away the delta's, and the immense Orinoco's, which gives to the Gulf its sweet water. Beyond these, unfolded the unknown vastness of the continent that her people had come out to generations ago as conquistadors, having conquered the Moors on the Iberian peninsula, now they must vanquish Spain here. I felt to harness all this. Damn it. I found that I thought of François de Gurvand increasingly. I wondered how he, they, were managing in France. What were they managing?

"I am writing an account of this," she said at last.

"I thought you would, I think I have seen you at it."

"Yes, how would you like to be portrayed, the inspiration, the invisible hand, the procurer . . . ?"

"Oh, there is no role for me, not yet, anyway. I will do what I can, here, they will need a supply route, reinforcements, I will set that up. It's too early to make me immortal."

"Yes, but I have to give you a name, a sobriquet, for the sake of the journal. What shall we call you?"

"Mr. Smith." I smiled into my rum. "It sounds English, if the governor gets hold of your journal he will think that he has another traitor on his hands."

"You are thinking of Manuel Valdez?"

"Yes, and Joseph Maingot."

"Maingot, the Crown surveyor?"

"Yes, Brother Maingot, he did the drawings of the fortifications on Don Gaspar's island for Picton, they have since made their way into 'enemy' hands."

"I have this for you," she said, handing me a roll of parchment. "It's the proclamation."

"Oh yes, I was there when your brother read it, it's quite heroic, he mentions you . . ."

"Yes, well, I wrote it, you can't trust those boys."

"Yes. Thank you, Señorita, I will treasure it."

The moon came up, bleakly, and the wind rose to promise a squall. Her jet black eyes seemed to capture all the available light as she turned to regard the rushing clouds, the severity of her profile hardly relieved by her youth and wayward hair. She picked up the insect-illuminated jar in her thin, long fingers, the wind tugging at her skirt, and we moved inside the house where Pappits had lit the candles and arranged the old mahogany table for us in a formal manner. I noticed that the settings were for three.

"Yes," she smiled her mother's smile, "José Sanda is joining us."

"And you needed a chaperon."

"Of course."

The following week the priest was back from St. Peter's Bay, he came to me directly, one could see that Magneval was no longer in town.

"Brother Vincent."

"Spare me."

"What shall I call you?"

"Monsieur Patrice."

He was very young and was not aware of the encyclicals.

"Monsieur Patrice. I was there."

"Well?"

"We made landfall at half past two, the schooner and the sloop dropped anchor in Güiria, everyone wanted to go ashore. I myself was aboard the *Carlota*, the night was as dark as in a bear's bottom, excuse me Monsieur Patrice, and the sea was rising, the pirogues could only take ten or so. Colonel Santiago and Gomez took the first boat in, I followed in the second. We came upon a fisherman, his flambeau showed his face. 'Mother of God,' he said, 'you have come for us, to save us'. He turned to shout. Colonel Santiago caught him in time.

'Shhhh, no one must know but you.'

'Yes, yes, but I must tell my father that Miranda is here.'

'This is not Miranda, this is Santiago Mariño,' said Gomez de Zaa.

'Mariño, who is that?'

In the distance we could hear musket fire and shouts, a bugle sounded. That was Bermudez and Bideau, they followed Manuel Piar and were engaging the harbour guard. Soon we were at the gate that swung open to meet us. Monsieur Patrice, the people were waiting, praise God, praise God, but the bullets were flying. And the cannon too. Manuel Piar took a cannon, he and José Brito Sanchez put it in the harbour gate and blew it away, then everybody got in. We came up the hill, some royalists were holding the Plaza and the mayor's office. Francisco Azcue and Juan Otero stood in the open, under the almond trees, and fired their muskets, bam bam, then their pistols, then took out their machetes and ran to the guardia, well, the guardia took off. I picked up the guns for them. Monsieur Patrice, it seemed that the bullets passed through them, and nothing happened.

"Boom, Piar was letting off the cannon, Colonel Santiago came to me, he said 'Father, go with Jean Bideau and Sucre, and put up the flag, our flag in the Plaza, and Father, say a prayer, eh, get some of the people together, anybody, and say a prayer, hey! hey!' he called some fellows, our fellows, 'Go with the Padre, he will put up the flag, stand in formation and present arms. See to this, Captain Sucre,' he said. Sucre said 'Captain, eh,' they laughed. But we put up the flag. The little black boys, they beat the drum. A big crowd came, people cried, the women brought arepas and coffee. At six o'clock I went to hear mass at the church of San Martino.

"By the time mass was over, Colonel Santiago formed up the men, everyone was now ashore, and we were joined by another ten young men. We needed to get shoes, everybody lost their shoes. Food, we got food. Before ten o'clock we were in Punta de Piedra, Monsieur Patrice. The people were coming, first just to see, to see who was winning, you know, but when they saw Commandant Gavazzo pulling up his tent and getting his baggage packed, they came in quantity. Well it was in Irapa that the *peninsulares* put up a fight, but we took it by storm.

"We charged, in a line, perfect, flags in the middle, the boys, remember the boys, well beating the drum. Boom-bo-Doom. 'Hold the fire,' the Colonel shouted, but you know these fellows, they fire Bom Bam Bam, the Colonel he cursed, then he say 'Charge!' By that time everybody running already, some of them firing, the Spaniards firing, but no one falls, the bullets fly by the fellows, seem to pass, how you say, between them, you know, like walking in the rain, and not getting wet, the people running, coming to see. They say, look they are not killed, it's the work of God. The Spaniards run when they see that. The Colonel he was vexed because they did not follow the command. He put up his headquarters in the mayor's house and he put the mayor in gaol. Sixty more men fell in for parade, most without shoes, but proud, very proud. The Colonel gave a speech, the town gave a fiesta, very gay, very gay. I have a letter for Monsieur Pietri, here somewhere . . ."

"Give it here."

I looked it over, he needed guns, but also needed Frenchmen, a hundred, quickly.

The following night at Harmony I gave what I thought was a very good speech and then read the proclamation.

"Well, who will come forward?"

Vincente Julia stood up, looked about him and was about to sit when Joseph Gual got to his feet, he was Manuel Gual's nephew. Luis de Limarez got to his feet and dragged Angel Benitez to his.

"Well, is that it?"

It apparently was. This Atelier had given eight more patriots to the cause. Four Frenchmen and four Spaniards. Of the four French, two were coloured, Agrical Ferney and Jean Baptiste Bideau. This made twenty-three in all. Pietri was more convincing, he was able to get eleven coloureds, six Frenchmen and an Irishman, Cassidy, who was probably drunk when he took the money, but he showed up on the quay-side. The governor was pretending to be furious, he made a big show of sending de Lopinot down there to Monte de Botella with a detachment of regular English soldiers of the line. She met them, gave them lunch and sent them away.

The governor was now quite beside himself, he had received an order from Barbados to put a halt to all subversive activities. He had made two trips to Chaguaramas, to see for himself. There was nothing to see. María Concepción had transferred some of their town properties to her great uncle William Carige and to his son Pierre.

"They have taken Maturín."

I was dining with María Concepción, young Sanda and Henriette Céleste Meany, the beautiful quadroon, at Pembroke Street. She was soon to marry Jean-Louis de Rostang, a younger brother of the celebrated Dr. Leon de Rostang, bringing a much needed fortune into that impecunious family.

"Manuel Piar, Master Vincent, is the hero."

"He has inflamed the women, Juana Ramírez, La Avanzadora and the Amazons of Maturín have chased out Monteverde."

"Santiago now has an army, it is more than five thousand and growing every day. But there is nothing, nothing in these towns. Punta de Piedra is a village, Irapa the same. Maturín, when the royalists left, they took everything. This is a design so full of accident. Master Vincent, our only hope for money is the Marquis del Toro. The in-law of Bolívar, he is with Roget in Santa Cruz. I have a letter, here, it is signed by Santiago and Jean Bideau. They need men and money."

"I will take it to him."

22:

1812–1813. Simón Bolívar,

The Liberator.

He took the passport. I must admit I was not surprised. Don Francisco Iterbe, a *peninsular*, and I, Littais L'Eau, accompanied him to the headquarters of the tyrant Juan Domingo de Monteverde y Rivas in La Guaira. He appeared miserable, haggard, hollow-cheeked, ill, unshaven, thin and short in his smart, brand new, blue and red, well-cut, too large colonel's uniform. His noodle neck surrounded by a stiff martial collar that fairly bristled with gold oak leaves, a tunic overloaded with frogs, facings, braids and epaulets. His boots were polished, his spurs tinkling. Without his sabre, he wore just a red waist-band with two long-tasseled sword knots that came down to his boot-tops. I noticed that. So did Monteverde, who did not rise. Why should he? He merely sat back in his creaking chair and raised his brows, as the Colonel stood at attention and saluted, this he did not return, his rough hands forming a triangle beneath his pointed chin. Silence. Monteverde's dark, thinning hair blown here and there by the wind that came through the office window overlooking the harbour's guns. Silence. He did not look at him, his eyes, large and black, curiously feminine, were upon Don Francisco. The slightest motion upwards of his head indicated his permission to speak.

"Captain General. This is the Commander of Puerto Cabello, Simón Bolívar, for whom I have given my bond. If he is to be punished, punish me instead. My life is pledged to his. So if the properties of Francisco Iterbe must be confiscated, I. . ."

He raised a large, hard hand.

"Alright, the gentleman is granted a passport in recompense for the service he did the King in arresting de Miranda."

The secretary, who was standing at his side, nodded and swallowed several times. I could hear his dentures click.

"I did not arrest General de Miranda in the King's service. I arrested him as a traitor, a traitor to his country." This, shouted in a high, Caribbean-accented, wild, tear-filled voice, a child's voice, brought the Captain General to his feet.

"Get out. I will deal with you, you fool, out!"

"Captain General, please, I have given my word, you have accepted it, please, as a gentleman." This from Don Francisco.

Whereupon the Captain General, after glancing curtly at the secretary, turned on his heel and left the room. Don Francisco laughed softly and, glancing at the secretary, said, "Let's get along with it, do not pay too much attention to these outbursts; prepare his passport and we will be off."

I, Littais L'Eau, in his service since that morning of betrayal now frozen in glacial time, left with him that very night for

Curaçao. That betrayal was hatched in Bolívar's imagination as a way to save face after his fall from grace at Puerto Cabello. De Miranda could not save Caracas from being sacked by the slaves, the city's only hope was the Spaniard, Monteverde. De Miranda hoped, as usual, to live to fight another day. For me, there was little choice but to follow Bolívar, I wanted to stay with history. Two months later, we were in Cartagena. He filled out, he no longer gave the impression that his teeth were about to drop out of his head. He rose early and his valet José Casablanca, shaved him and prepared his monkish breakfast. He became a caudillo before his very own eyes.

They formed an entire officer corps in New Granada, these refugee Venezuelans. Simón Bolívar addressed their Congress and moved them, stirred them, with the novelty of his words, the sincerity of his optimism and unabashed sentimentality. "I am, Granadans, a son of unhappy Caracas," he told them. Some were so moved, so overcome by acute sentimentality as he devotedly evoked the atavistic deeds executed by their long dead Conquistador predecessors, that they took rapid gulps from silver, monogrammed hip-flasks so as to steady their nerves and to alleviate the suffocation of nostalgia.

The Cartagena Manifesto, delivered in Cartagena de Indias on the 15th of December, 1812, expressed, in considerable detail and in precise phrases, what he believed to be the causes of the fall of the First Republic. It was the first of Bolívar's historic public documents. He rekindled their revolution from the ashes of his fallen hope, even as his former hero, betrayed by him to the Spanish Crown, was taken away in chains to Puerto Rico. God damn it. He was good. They sent him to the hamlet of Barrancas with a handful of regulars. He inspired the countryside and raised a brigade, attacked the brigands and defended Spanish haciendas on the Magdalena River, which altered the course of this tiring war. To his amazement he took the fortified town of Tenerife with only eleven fatalities.

We entered it with carnival bands parading, church processions with reliquaries, bells tolling, urchins running ahead, scrawling obscene graffiti on convent walls where pale nuns with delicate bones, obligated to perpetual silence, flagellate each other in pursuance of stigmata. That night, as he lay exhausted in a hammock slung so low that it almost touched the ground, a delightful smell, a compelling fragrance of sin and chance encounter, something wild and arousing, of the sort that only exists in the glandular secretions of fabulous beasts, entered, its source unseen, passing through the aroused and excited camp. The next morning he looked taller, his smile that he could not banish even when he inspected the barefoot colour-guard, revealed that she, whoever she was, had renewed the missing spaces. He may not have had a woman since his wife died.

The following afternoon at six, in glorious sunshine, we entered Guamal, the walking wounded marching alongside his bedraggled troops. The people came, young men firing salvoes, riding unbroken horses, into the dusty plaza, women holding babies for him to kiss. A fiesta with fireworks at twilight. He attended six o'clock mass, the moon and stars still visible in the cold morning air. He sat amongst the people, who rose at its end and stood silent allowing him to pass, waiting, to follow behind him as he left. We rode directly to Banco. The garrison fled. Tamalameque held out with a steady fire from disciplined troops officered by Spaniards; he led the infantry in a charge of some eight hundred elated confident patriots with fixed bayonets, a battle flag in one hand, a sabre in the other, men dropping dead on his left and on his right, across a cow pasture, through a vegetable garden and over the school wall where the garrison, overwhelmed, pleaded mercy. He gave none.

That night, overwrought by his lack of compassion, he sought comfort in the company of the grenadiers and drank rum with them to fall asleep in the horse lines, to be awakened by the changing of the guard. That day we marched twenty miles and took Puerto Real de Ocaña in the dead of night. Old men brought their grandsons to see him, experience told them that the world was ending and a new son of the soil had arisen. We fought guerilla groups and small bands that held out at staging posts and wharves in the tangled jungle along the Magdalena River and on the sandy islands that were formed during the reign of the seventh Inca, Huayna Capac in the fifteenth century. We entered Ocaña. We were repelled at Chiriguaná, but took it by trickery. We captured four vessels that were moored mid-stream. That night we slept aboard the largest and best appointed. Again the mysterious aroma came to him, but he would not receive her, and slept that night not in his hammock but under a shed on the foredeck with the sailors. Herman Diaz took the hammock and was found by the insomniac sentries obsessed with his safety, stabbed in the back with his throat cut.

We marched to Pamplona on the Venezuelan border to relieve Colonel Manuel del Castillo. He received permission from the president-governor of Cartagena to face the fifteen hundred seasoned troops on the other side. We commenced the scaling of the backbone of the continent, ascending the courses of waterfalls and following gorges to arrive at a yawning chasm, to enter into a moss-covered misty dreamworld of gigantic ferns, massive leaves like open hands, high forest, a stupefying tangle of coupling vines bursting with flamboyant orchids that appeared like huge genitalia, through which flew flocks of red and blue macaws, enormous iridescent blue butterflies and bats with the faces of daemons and wingspans of more than a yard, to find ourselves passing into the cordillera; taking the almost vertical mountain faces with a maniacal energy to cross the wide, dangerous Zulia, foaming over cataracts and hidden rocks and then to encounter a moonscape plateau, where every man slept with machetes tied to his wrists in anticipation of mountain cougars or of a sudden enemy attack.

Some deserted, more arrived, they seemed to appear out of the earth like the fabled sown men of Greek mythology. He received the news of his promotion to the rank of Brigadier-General in the predawn mists at a smoky cook-fire as he took coffee laced with rum, wrapped in a blanket, with shepherds eating tasso, and smoking a cheroot. They brought with them the uniform of his new rank. He donned it there and then and rose resplendent with the new dawn.

On February 28th, 1813, we captured the city of Cúcuta after a battle that lasted from eight a.m. to noon. He now moved in the aura of the clairvoyant. We became different men, like from a different age, who knew *la noche oscura del alma,* in an older place. The dark night of our soul made us heavy-gaited, the rigour of killing now shaped our countenance, and disciplined our moods.

He took command of four hundred men and led them to fight eight hundred seasoned troops captained by the Spanish General Rameon Correa. He lost two Colombian soldiers and fourteen were injured; the Spanish forces, realising the conviction of their assailants, abandoned their officers. The victory freed the city of Cúcuta and gave birth to the Admirable Campaign.

Cúcuta became his base. That was in April 1813. The rainy season postponed. It was a cold, clear, blue day. He and I, Littais L'Eau, sat amongst the boulders overlooking the little city with the high Andes surrounding us, rising to snow-capped volcanoes that appeared not to touch the earth, having levitated at his approach, a continent en-skied. In May we swept down like the wolf on the fold and entered the provinces of Mérida and Trujillo. We took both cities inside of one month. The smell of blood, caught, frozen in the chilly air, lingered as a nauseous aftertaste.

Mérida received him in triumph. Flowers in garlands, church bells ringing. The children, it was the children who called out in excited voices, running backwards, jumping, skipping between the cavalry, marching alongside the drums and fifes of the colour party. It was they who, calling out in shrill voices, placed the wreath of glory upon his head with the words "Look, see the Liberator! Our Liberator!" The call was taken up by everyone "the Liberator, the Liberator." The syntax of legend out of the mouths of the innocent.

I, Littais L'Eau, saw it go through him like a spear, his eyes shone and continued to shine for another seventeen years, every time that accolade was mentioned. The Liberator. He now existed in the unmatched glory of the quest fulfilled, and, even when he briefly returned to the world about him, in the silence of his solitary doubts he could evoke at will the essence and thrill of that moment.

We marched through to Trujillo where the lamentable news of atrocities committed by the Spaniards came to him. He hid and wept when he heard of the necklaces made up of children's ears and of naked women sewn together by their shoulders with cocoa bag needles and then burnt to death. He rose from his bed, half delirious with a fever that would not leave him, to issue his 'Decree of War to the Death'.

He received the welcome news of Colonel Santiago Mariño's advance from Chacachacare and of his landing on the coast of the Gulf of Paria. This would force the Spaniards to fight on two fronts. In the lengthening shadows of a premature twilight, he received the news of the Battle of Alto de los Godos. He was told by an Indian who had travelled for two weeks, that in this battle the Venezuelan patriots, led by Santiago Mariño and Manuel Piar, had obtained a great victory against Monteverde on the 25th of May. The battle, taking place in Maturín, had resulted in a patriotic victory against superior Spanish forces. A woman, Juana Ramírez, known as La Avanzadora, "The Advancer," led the final charge with other frenzied harridans as Monteverde fled. It would take five battles over a period of a year, 1813 to 1814, to occupy and pacify that city.

San Cristóbal was taken. La Grita fell. Exhausted horsemen brought him news and told of the battles fought and won in the jungles and swamps of places that as yet were nameless, by a band of men called the Immortals.

We fought the battle of Los Horcones in mid-July and occupied the cities of Valencia and La Victoria by the middle of August. The Spanish government offered surrender on the 4th of August. We entered the city of Caracas on the 6th and reestablished the republic. There was hardly a soul in sight in the deserted streets, the uncleared rubble from the earthquake, smoke rising from inextinguishable fires, evoked unspeakable memories as the smell of undiscovered corpses haunted the barefoot children, the hungry eyes of hollow-cheeked women, and of old men with broken teeth, turning away, grief bursting through their eyes.

Thank God for a joyous party of young girls and pretty women who came singing, bare-footed, with baskets of flowers and fresh bread, fruits, salt and wine, wearing white dresses with wreaths of roses and evergreens to garland the warrior-heroes and to lead their horses in Homeric processional. I saw him search their faces, some he recognised, he knew their mothers from when they were young and made their first holy communion together, holding hands and promising to be friends forever.

That Colonel Santiago Mariño did not entirely recognise the restored republic, threw him into a rage that mutated into a migraine that lasted four days, and defied both medicine and magic, only to be alleviated by the mystical appearance of a riderless black Andalusian stallion in the aluminium moonlight. Insomniac, curious and prowling the grounds of the colonial mansion that was given to him by his former father-in-law the Marqués del Toro, he approached the stallion and discovered in the crupper a note, fastened there by a diamond pin. It read "Ride the whirlwind." Against the wishes of his officers and disregarding the pleas of his majordomo, José Casablanca, he leapt atop the beast and galloped into the night, to be discreetly followed by his nephew Fernando, José Casablanca and myself with a detachment of lancers. He gave the animal its head, we, following across the diaphanous undulating countryside. We saw another rider appear coming towards him. The brilliant moon described the beauty that rode side-saddle on a mirror image of the stallion, her long black dress trailing, her dark streaming hair catching and containing the diamond stars. They collided in the phantom light and rode cross-country to a hacienda hidden in a little wood of towering windblown cedar trees. Such tryst is the fortune of the triumphant.

Heroes of classical recollection emerged from those wars fought in the east and in the west to be etched in steel in the memories of the folk; their profiles to be stamped on gold coins, military decorations, commemorative medallions, printed on the bank notes of states as yet uncreated, public parks to be ennobled by their equestrian statues, universities to be named in their honour, their portraits painted by artists who never saw them, who were not even born when they had already achieved legendary stature.

Caracas heard of Santiago Mariño, Manuel Piar, Francisco and Bernardo Bermúdez, José Tadeo Monagas, Francisco Azcue, José Gregorio Monagas, Juan Bautista Arismendi, Juan Valdez, José Félix Ribas and of course, Antonio José de Sucre who, at eighteen, was the youngest of the Immortals who sailed from La Tinta Bay, Chacachacare on a windy evening, just five years older than Jean and Jean-Luis Victorie, the black drummer boys, with whom he led the charge in the storming of Cumana.

Exaggerated stories were told of these barefoot boys dressed in invented ragged uniforms, their cheeky indifference to musket fire, the solitary drum they carried. We heard of them, of Sucre, in the capital Caracas. How they stood at Sucre's side beneath the patriotic banners, as the guns, now under his command, pounded the fortifications of Barcelona, where he took command of the fortress as it fell with the rank of Second Lieutenant. The boys, now young men, had beaten the charge as Margarita was stormed and taken; one fell there, and then there were none.

He was indifferent to the news that Monteverde was wounded in action during Las Trincheras on the 3rd October, 1813, and near the end of the same year, how he was deposed by his own officers in Puerto Cabello. The siege of that fortress saw the patriotic army repel the attempts of the Spaniards to break out. They, to the Liberator's disgust, were unable to take it despite the heroism of Colonel Girardot who fought with us in the Admirable Campaign. He fell there; his heart was placed in a golden reliquary on the Liberator's orders, and carried on his riderless charger with his boots reversed in the stirrups to the ruined Cathedral in Caracas, the seat of the archdiocese, in a triumphal procession two miles long and placed in a mausoleum where to this day it beats.

He now spoke in terms of 'the Patria' and summoned men of ability and honour, such as Don Cristóbal Mendoza, to organise a government. He told them that he was a man of conquest, they were men of government. Miguel José Sanz, esteemed by von Humboldt, and the learned Francisco Javier de Ustáriz, were the framers of the provisional government; it was they who handed supreme authority to him as the chief of the army. On October 14th, at an extraordinary meeting of the Cabildo, they bestowed on him the title of Liberator with profound solemnity and officially appointed him captain-general of the republican army.

He emerged as the first strongman of South America. The caudillo. Master of all he imagined. Jealous. Prestige manifested with a nod bestowed, with a raised eyebrow, with smartly turned-out soldiers, with resplendent officers. And the people, don't forget the people, weeping, hands clasped in appreciation of glorious victories, the Liberator, he, becoming more so with every telling. Already forgotten was the doubt, the fear, the quivering evaporation of courage as the battle flags unfurled, the bugle called, the drum, guts hardly screwed together with rum, and the camaraderie of the moment. The die was cast.

But it was from the east that the news came with every sunrise. News of Colonel Santiago Mariño and a band of irregulars increasingly described as "The Immortal Forty-five."

"Luck is with him," the Liberator would say. "He will learn fast that she is a fickle jade, more fool he who places his trust in her." The fall of Güiria gave Santiago more guns, powder, shot, and money. He attracted a force of five thousand.

We all heard that Santiago was proclaimed "Chief of the Independent Army" and that he declared the east independent. It alarmed and fascinated the Liberator to know that more than half of the east of the country was following Santiago and that a political apparatus was being created. Men spoke of Fernando Gomez de Zaa and of Jean Baptiste Bideau as well known personages in his presence, as though he was familiar with them, having known them all their lives.

If he conquered the north and the west, Santiago Mariño and the Immortal Forty-Five conquered the east, the coastal Gulf of Paria, the Orinoco delta and the hinterland. Santiago defeated José Tomás Boves, the royalist caudillo of the llanos, who participated in the unsuccessful attempts to stop his invasion of eastern Venezuela. The Second Republic was experiencing a divided, bloody, glorious and heroic dawn.

They met in La Victoria in an atmosphere made electric by their reputations. I, Littais L'Eau, served them at a table beneath a chivalric marquee in the shade of the biggest *ceiba pentandra* in the world. They were joined by Sucre who had recently vanquished the Spanish General Rosette and was the hero of Boachica, where the feared José Tomás Boves was defeated.

Outside strutted booted warriors, magnificent in royal blue and gold, some could boast of fourteen wounds received in battle, of their bravery and ardour in the vanguard, others possessed nicknames like "Resting Tiger" because of their predilection for fighting with lances, the most desperate of weapons, one in each hand, some would be remembered as the 'bravest of the brave' by the Liberator himself. Amongst and betwixt them secretaries with reams of paper were scurrying, notaries in funereal black posturing, children running, playing at war games, beautiful women with parasols, lace gloves and very nice manners, fanning themselves in contemplation of mating with these giants so as to produce heroic offspring.

Their names combined, they marched to victory at the first battle of Carabobo, where the opposing forces were evenly matched. The new captain-general of the royalists, Manuel de Cagigal, experienced the courage of men scoffed at in the royal court at Madrid. He drained the acidic cup of humiliation when he saw the Royal Standard seized by a boy young enough to be his child. In their paroxysms of defeat, José Tadeo Monagas plunged a broken sabre into the chest of the veteran of the peninsular wars and rode away with the glory of Spain, into the dust and smoke of history. In all, eight standards were lost that day, amongst them that of the Granada regiment. De Cagigal's loss that day was more than two thousand royalists killed or wounded. It was the battle flags and standards that delineated the disgrace.

The Fates, those white-robed incarnations of destiny, conspired, their winged croziers burnished by lightning, to bring these daredevils to heel. The very same José Tomás Boves, the royalist caudillo of the llanos, defeated the combined forces of Bolívar and Mariño at the Battle of La Puerta during a heatwave in June 1814, as wildfires raged across the llanos. His army of pardos, fatherless, mixed-race, abandoned men, raised by deserted mothers on dilapidated cattle farms in the trackless grasslands, routed the proud soldiery of the east and west, captured their eagles and scattered them into the as yet unwritten pages of the history books.

I, Littais L'Eau, rode like hell from that field, knowing full well that the other side of the coin of war to the death was massacre. José Tomás Boves spared none. As the walls of fire crossed the grasslands, the heroic dead and the recently executed were all consumed, their anguished, youthful souls rising, rising in the bitter brown, red and black coils of smoke, to vanish into the innocent sky.

Once more, I saw Caracas apocalyptic, plunging into bedlam as an exodus commenced, families taking to the mountains to hide in caves, in forests, to starve or be eaten by mountain lions. Others fled to join an increasing horde of the terrified to stagger eastward, pursued by royalist lancers over the vastness of the llanos, the impenetrable wilderness and through the deserted towns that were recently held by Santiago.

I rode in the baggage train in a retreating column led by Sucre and Francisco Bermudez. After the final defeat of the patriotic army at Cumana, the Liberator, I heard, had set sail for Jamaica in the company of his general staff. News, dreadful and appalling, followed us. Sucre's brothers, his sisters, his mother were all slaughtered by the rampaging royalists.

We sat together about a sputtering fire, the rain of October unceasing. We stared at Sucre as he stooped, crouched and shivered beneath a soaked blanket, examining the shards of his father's sword, broken at Cumana, in the flickering firelight. He looked like the ghost of an older person, bloodless, transparent. I could not tell the tears from the rain.

We were joined by Jean Baptiste Bideau and a small company of sailors. He appeared in crisp whites, ageless, as strong and as spirited as when we first met in Trinidad at Les Frères Unis. On the road to Güiria, we would find hunger, famine and cholera, that was his news. Our company, now under a relentless fire from artillery positions in the surrounding hills, fought its way into Güiria. We fought our way through the streets where looters and criminals defended their booty, to the devastated wharves and into long boats that anticipated our arrival. Our escape was accomplished, illuminated by the burning warehouses, the gunpowder stores exploding, burning the ships waiting to save the refugees. We boarded the ballahoo schooner, *Swallow,* owned by John Black that had been dispatched by his son to rescue the Maçons abandoned by the patriotic generals.

That night, in heavy seas and pursued by a Spanish frigate, we entered the port of Port-d'Espagne and dropped anchor in the placid Gulf. We were met by the Vénérable Master Vincent Patrice, escorted to the Atelier at Mount Moriah and accommodated in the undercroft, where Santiago Mariño had spent time before his journey from Chacachacare.

I had left Governor Munro's Trinidad; this was now Governor Sir Ralph Woodford's. We heard that Manuel Piar had come and gone; he was now in Grenada. Francisco Bermudez and Antonio José Sucre waited on the governor's pleasure. They sought asylum for themselves and for some other refugees from Venezuela, and were allowed to vanish into the bosom of their families so long as they stayed out of the town. The sailors and the marksmen on whom our lives so recently depended were turned away, and shipped back to the Mainland.

We, Jean Bideau and I, were left to fend for ourselves. The governor would have nothing to do with the patriots. I got to the island of Monos and made friends with the red howler monkeys. Jean Bideau, before he could leave for Sainte Lucie, was arrested and incarcerated in the new gaol on Frederick Street. Woodford despised black men in officers' uniforms. A crowd formed and grew outside of the prison; they said they had come to protect Bideau as the Spanish frigate, *Nuestra Señora de las Nieves,* was now in the harbour and the captain was ashore, gone to see the governor to demand Bideau be handed over to him. I heard that Sir Ralph would not risk it, because Master Vincent warned him that the town would burn before the frigate sailed if Bideau were put aboard.

At Monos I renewed my acquaintance with an argumentative Scotsman by the name of Morrison, who possessed property on the island, and befriended a wild, gypsy-like Frenchman, Honoré Tardieu. We fished and hunted the great humpback whales, drank far too much rum, and I became attached to one of Morrison's beautiful daughters, who, the following year, gave me my first offspring. I called him Santiago. Jean Bideau, I was glad to hear, was allowed to leave aboard Black's schooner, the *Swallow*, supposedly for Saint Bart. His young wife would wait for him in Trinidad. We would meet again.

This governor's harbour police, not as vigilant as Picton's, patrolled the Gulf of Paria, their gun boats driving away would-be refugees, sinking some, killing women and children alike, sending others back to the deserted beaches of the Güiria coast to starve to death. Some of these had arrived from Caracas, some of them had greeted the victor of the Admirable Campaign and led his prancing steed into the city. I once met and was entertained by them at their gracious homes in company with the Precursor, General Francisco de Miranda, and afterwards with the Liberator, Captain-General Simón Bolívar. I was to read somewhere that the bones of those returned, bleached white, still roll and tumble in the shingle at high tide on the Güiria beaches, while the Indians examine their disconnected jawbones for gold fillings.

I am not a person given to presentiment, but when I saw a few months later, a Baltimore clipper entering the second boca under full sail one February morning in 1816, my heart leaped and raced. Tardieu in his gruff Marseillais accent growled, "What's the matter, L'Eau, is someone you hate sleeping in your grave?"

I couldn't think of a word to say. I watched her, as she became illuminated by the risen sun, passed into the shallow shadow of Huevos, and shone again as her captain ordered her mainsails reefed.

The next day, being the first Wednesday in February, I attended Les Frères Unis. There, to my surprise, were Santiago Mariño and Francisco Bermudez. I, no longer an officeholder of the Atelier, joined them on the benches in the east. Now seen as old and grizzled veterans, we were held in awe and left alone, except of course by Frère Agostini, who is now truly old.

Santiago described the retreat to Carúpano, where the Liberator and he were arrested by Bernardo Bermudez, Manuel Piar and Alfredo Ripas. Naturally a fight ensued.

"I was not going to be arrested by those clowns! I struck your foolish brother hard across the face, and ran that jackass Ripas through. He fell dead, didn't say bup. But Piar was a different business, it took Bolívar and myself an hour and a half to fight him and some other idiots off. I killed two. Bolívar struck Manuel on the head with a Demerara window stick a few times before he backed out through the broken wall of the tavern."

"And my brother?" asked Bermudez.

"He was out of it, early on. Nosebleed."

"His heart was not in it."

Santiago laughed softly. "No. Nosebleed. He thought he was dying from brain damage. But Manuel Piar, that son of a bitch, he stood on the quay outside and fired his pistols at us through the windows and through the holes in the walls. He got some officers and others to fire into the place and then storm it. Well, I, your brother and Bolívar got the hell out, over a wall, into a church full of people, I hid in a confessional with a pregnant woman, as for your brother, well . . . I last saw him exchanging clothes with the priest."

"No! Never!"

"And Bolívar?" I asked.

"He managed to get to the docks, he too in disguise. He sailed out from Carúpano, the very spot where Christopher Columbus first set foot on the American continent. Ironic, eh, Frère L'Eau? Thought you would appreciate that. Well, he got aboard an American frigate bound for Jamaica. Perhaps his Brothers in Charleston sent it for him."

He regarded the Vénérable Master, who said simply, "No, it was Jean Baptiste Bideau who, aboard the *Swallow,* took him off, not an American frigate."

"Oh? Well, we named him, them, traitors. We, your brother Bernardo and I, managed to get away and into a part of the town that was still holding out against the royalists, as well as keeping out crazy people like Piar, and to bring around some officers loyal to me. We rallied what was left there in Carúpano," said Santiago, bringing his hand down on the bench. He was changed. He was now more stern, there was no more charm, just the ability to kill.

"We, your brother Bernardo and I, got to Güiria. You, L'Eau, Bideau and Sucre, had recently left. The place was in chaos. I found a printer and published a proclamation, stating that Captain-General Simón Bolívar, the Liberator, had been deposed. And I, General Santiago Mariño, as chief of the independent army, was now the supreme chief, and your brother, Bernardo, was now my second-in-command."

"Where is he, then?"

"Your brother? He joined with José María Valdez in an attempt to kill me. What do you expect? With the help of an Indian woman, I escaped to a beach outside of the town. I gave her a fortune in gold and, as if by magic, a schooner materialised, which landed me and some others at La Tinta. Where is Sucre?"

"He is with the Solis family in Naparima. Have you reported to Governor Woodford?" asked Frère Agostini.

"Governor Woodford can kiss my ass. If he as much as says good morning to me, he is a dead man, and he understands that, that son of a bitch. You know of the people dead in the Gulf, on the beaches of Güiria, eh? The ones who are starving on ships, or in the hills above Diego Martin. On the islands in the Bocas, that son of a whore."

"So what now, Frère Santiago?" the Vénérable Master Vincent Patrice, who was standing, listening, enquired.

"Live to fight another day, Vénérable Master," answered Santiago. "We are all in agreement, no matter what we say or do."

I regarded him in the candlelight, the man who had led the Immortals, he seemed to possess a doom, undecided, a destiny as yet unselected from innumerable possible futures.

"Verily. Frère L'Eau, verily," said the Vénérable Master to me—I wondered if he had read my thoughts. "Frère L'Eau, would you do us the honour of acting as outer guard tonight? Frère Sablich is unavoidably absent." I bowed. And then, quietly to us sitting there, "Comrades, assist me to open this Lodge." He smiled as he regarded Santiago, and as I left to take up my position outside the door of the Atelier, I saw the brothers Dert join them in the east and sit on either side of Santiago Mariño.

Ralph James Woodford, 2nd Baronet of Carleby, was of the opinion that he knew a great deal concerning the cargo aboard the Baltimore clipper, *Thunder*, now anchored in the stream off Port-d'Espagne. I, Littais L'Eau, recognised in him, even from a cursory examination, all the perspicuous manners of the well-educated, punctilious bureaucrat; youthful, and certainly handsome, however, possessing little of the stern daring, the terrible energies which were once necessary to control the outrageous, rebellious, indeed murderous elements that swarmed here in Trinidad in the wake of the French Revolution in the islands to the north during the years that Colonel Picton ruled the colony. He did not possess that innate enjoyment of cruelty, I felt sure, that Picton obviously had. Sir Ralph, perfidious? Never. A capacity for deceit, mendacity? No. But a cold-hearted approach to life? Yes. This was a very different man. A Protestant, even Puritan personality, as I would come to understand these prim, parsimonious, even stingy men as life went on. Cold fish? Yes. Indifferent to the suffering of others? Yes. Racially biased, in a new and insidious manner, ask Jean Baptiste Philippe, the free mulatto of the Naparimas, Saint Luce Philippe's younger brother.

Sir Ralph appeared in the eyes of the old colonists, that is those who had arrived here under the Cédula of '83 and before, as a parvenu, "a never see come see," they called him. Although his title, 2nd Baronet, disproved this. Maybe because there was about him the somewhat exaggerated attention to dress, to being the patron of new forms of leisure, style and taste: fresh interpretations of good manners, of being gracious, of cultivating only the best-bred, the need to appear dignified, polished, in such a conspicuous way that only the middle class, *le haute bourgeoisie, gentilhommes* of the *ancien régime,* aspired to be. Then, there was his conspicuous dislike for the Free Coloureds, this was awkward as many of them were well-off, even related to prominent families and certainly respectable. In this Creole society we all knew our place, but this appeared to be changing.

Undoubtedly, this governor held some purpose from the start, one could say even a directive from the War and Colonial Office and the City of London, to reform, to reshape this unruly, rebellious, disorderly, bacchanal-prone colony and to prepare it for another dispensation. He was entrusted with extraordinary powers. Undoubtedly. From the first day of his arrival, the 14th of June, 1813, Woodford set about the complete eradication of the unscrupulous, corrupt and indeed persistently seditious members of the establishment, those who grew and thrived under the military governors, from Picton to Hislop to Munro. The daily murder rate decreased.

This poor undeveloped colony, comparatively uninhabited, swarmed with foreigners, many of whom until very recently the enemies of the United Kingdom, the majority of the Catholic faith, this list included both royalists and republican French, Spaniards, as well as a legion of black and coloured fighters, all French-speaking, mostly from the islands to the north and from the Mainland, with known "trouble makers," villains and, indeed, perpetrators of massacres in their midst. All were now to benefit in the perquisites of a model English colony. I must say my suspicions were aroused.

Sir Ralph not only dismissed the current mendacious membership of the Illustrious Cabildo and the Council of Advice, but he also let go the colonial secretarial staff, including the Colonial Secretary. Colonial Secretaries, from 1803 to 1813, were important personages, whose favour the suitor at Government House found profitable to propitiate by heavy bribes. No easy task, all this, as these abuses continued for so long that they achieved an almost prescriptive right to exist.

This governor received, wrote and transmitted his own dispatches. A very secretive man. He brought along with him, from England, a coterie of very educated, well-dressed and talented young men. According to Frère Maingot, who was now the crown surveyor and often in the company of the governor, the principal one was a Mr. Philip Reinagle, a mathematician who was also an architect, whose father was a famous artist, as well as three scientists: David Lockhart (also a botanist), Graf von Schack and Richard Bridgens, who served the governor as the town's engineer. These were by far and away the most educated civil servants in the English Caribbean in the second decade of the 19th century. An academy of physics was forming at Government House, still the same ramshackle, dilapidated old wreck that Major-General Munro once lived in, but not for long. Not for long, because Sir Ralph, I understood, was negotiating with Jean de Boissière for the purchase of the Champs Elysées estate as his official residence.

I, Littais L'Eau, remained in Port-d'Espagne. Frère Maingot carried even more startling news: Adhémar de Gurvand, returned from Europe without his father, was in the company of an old and very distinguished personage, a man of considerable consequence, consequence sufficient for Governor Sir Ralph Woodford to receive them at the bottom of the front steps of Government House and escort the old gentleman inside himself. They all went directly there. Strange that Adhémar has as yet made no contact with his wife.

23:

1814: Prince Idelfonso,

Out on the Rolling Sea.

The sky, a vacant eye, stared, as the sun flared in the massive bowl of blue. The Baltimore clipper *Thunder* pitched gently, moving quickly onward, forward, westward in a brisk breeze; rising, falling, breaching the waves, swell to rolling swell; a soporific motion that put him back to sleep.

In his sleep, as always, he relived any of a multitude of lives, some were his, others were ones in which he perhaps shared a destiny. This, he knew, was as a result of his training and his practice. He was a Master of both the Art of Memory and of Time and as such, this was an occupational hazard.

At times, some dreams could puzzle or amuse him, because Time, as he knew full well, was no more than a convenience created by man's inventive mind to bring order to his affairs. "Time" was actually an elastic whole, for which no better word was yet invented, in which one could move about, experiencing it in a variety of ways, on as many levels as one's consciousness would permit. This, of course, depended on the individual. Everything was happening at that same Time.

There was no beginning, nor would there be an end, only another happening, becoming and being. These, merely because they were materially possible.

He was always curious when he went to sleep. On this occasion, immediately upon closing his eyes in the shadow of the ship's sail, he heard a person speaking in a pleasant, cultured, familiar voice, remark:– "I recently received some correspondence from the Greek historian Lucius Mestrius Plutarchus, or Plutarch, as he has become. He sends me his manuscripts from time to time before dispatching them to his scriptorum, where copies would be made *ad nauseam* for distribution. This piece is entitled *De Defectu Oraculorum,* 'The Obsolescence of Oracles'. Most interesting, in it he claims that the Delphic Oracle foretells the silence of the oracles subsequent to the coming of Christ, "the Light of the Celestial Flame." Just about thirty years after the supposed date of Jesus' death, Lucan in his Pharsalia states that "the greatest calamity of our century is the loss of that wonderful gift of heaven, the Delphic Oracle, which is silent." Then, Eusebius cites Porphyry as saying that since Jesus began to be worshipped no man had received any public help or benefit from the gods.

"Interesting fellow, Plutarchus. In his *Consolation Moralia,* which I was recently perusing, he observed: 'The soul, being eternal, after death is like a caged bird that has been released. If it has been a long time in the body, and has become tame by many affairs and long habit, the soul will immediately take another body and once again become involved in the troubles of the world. The worst thing about old age is that the soul's memory of the other world grows dim, while at the same time its attachment to things of this world become so strong that the soul tends to retain the form that it enjoyed in the body. But that soul which remains only a short time within a body, until liberated by the higher powers, quickly recovers its fire and goes on to higher things. *Corpora lente augescent cito extinguuntur.*' "

He saw himself. Youthful. He sat as a student in a vast auditorium of Greek classical proportions. The man on the podium appeared familiar, and as he looked more closely, the figure loomed larger, as if seen accidentally through a telescope. The person smiled benignly, as they recognised one another. It was he, himself. They both smiled and said, "Bodies grow slowly and die quickly." The dream faded and he became once more aware of his situation. He had been shot in the head.

Lying on a pallet in the breezy shadow of the fore-mast, canvas billowing above, he could see, on the foredeck, Adhémar, stripped to the waist, engaged in some shipboard game with members of the ship's company and some of the others who came aboard with them at Plestin-les-Grèves.

The breeze quickened, the slap of the water on the hull increased in rhythm, alternating with the motion of the ship and the irregularity of the waves. Syncopation. He tried to catch the beat but fell asleep again.

" . . . . ?"

He awoke, his face turned to one side in the pale sunlight. The benign, familiar face, smiling, faded. That episode, he felt sure, was for his amusement, although . . . you never know how the past will turn out.

It was now afternoon. The shadows of the sails under which he had slept and dreamed for most of the day had moved over and he now lay upon his pallet in the warm light of the western sun. The crew, enjoying the constant weather, as it meant little work, were engaged in their personal pursuits. Adhémar sat beside him, gazing thoughtfully out towards a horizon of hardly imagined futures. He, they, were bound for the New World, and the island of Trinidad.

It was a near fatal event. The ball fired by the Captain of Hussars, its velocity spent, had knocked him unconscious. The blow to his head which he received when he fell to the bottom of the longboat had caused a concussion, from which he was recuperating. He was now in his eighty-second year.

He was born into the Princely House of Andorra and was in direct descent from Sunifred, first Count of Urgell and Cerdanya, to whom Louis the Pius and later, Charles the Bald, had granted Charters. In 814, the Counts of Urgell and Cerdanya were created overlords of the principality of Andorra. In return, they undertook to stand guard about the passes of the Pyrenees against the Moors. His people were amongst the founders of Les Chambrés, and on five occasions in the nine hundred years of its existence, held the honour of Head.

His education, commenced at his grandfather's knee in the keep of Castle Tabernas, was furthered by Masters of the Cathedral School at Córdoba. He read languages at Oxford and, at the University of Paris, law. Having been selected for a position in Les Chambrés, he was sent to its Académie at Château de Murol in the Auvergne.

Built in the 12th century on a basalt outcrop, it held Les Chambrés' large library, its scriptorium, observatory and alchemic laboratory, classrooms and dormitories. This mountain-top fastness was to remain Les Chambrés' main centre of learning for several hundred years.

Château de Murol, surrounded by a massive curtain wall with five towers, was a large fortress opulently decorated, and would be his home for almost fifty-six years. In its classrooms sat the brightest minds of the century, who were tutored by the intellectual giants of the age. Now, in 1814, it lay abandoned, a hideout for bandits and highway robbers; pillaged, one of the many tragedies of the French Revolution.

The first lecture that he attended, which naturally was committed to memory, returned to him as he lay in the late afternoon sunlight, journeying into the west, the ship's motion already beckoning sleep and perhaps a dream. That first lecture was delivered by one of the Académie's most original thinkers, a distinguished author and erudite researcher, who rose from the benches where he had just previously assumed invisibility, and addressed his class thus:—

"Now, gentlemen, please permit me to introduce myself: I represent Aviti-Apollinares, your most entertaining ancestor. *Gloria filiorum patres.*"

All of the students present, as well as many of the Académie's professors, were related, being the descendants of the founders of the order. He continued, "not the most illustrious one by any means, but one who wrote and, in so doing set into motion vast possible possibilities. These words, when read and remembered by you, would be actualised, the possibilities of the writing and learning, that is. As you will discover, he who experiences, learns, and writing, changes everything, once it is written and read, It comes into this world. *Docendo discimus.* Remember, teach, in order to learn.

"I am a doppelgänger or 'double walker,' he continued after looking about him, his long thin nose testing the surroundings. "A living double of a person who exists in a time far distant. We are the apparitions of this rare but quite potent human condition. His name is Armentius-Apollinares, a scientist and inventor. A very, very distant relation. We meet from time to time in our imagination, and decide on what should be written, so that when read by you, it would be in this world." He glanced about the sunlit room, and managed to look each one of his eleven pupils in the eye, and smiled, lifting, and then lifting further, his thick white, unruly and very bushy eyebrows.

"Thus is the manner of the sojourners in Time. *Audaces fortuna iuvat* or *fortes fortuna iuvat!* Translate!"

"Fortune favours the brave," they all answered.

He beamed.

"Which reminds me of something that Gaius Sallustius Crispus, a Sabine, popularly known as Sallust, wrote in his *Of Gods and of the World*: 'These things never happened, but are always . . .' To fix a date, *aetatis suae,* I can do no better, than to say that this present birth of mine occurred in the 744th year anterior to the foundation of Rome by Romulus, no relation of ours, and in the 767th year of the First Olympiad. *Generalia specialibus non derogant.*"

Quickly doing the sums, Idelfonso arrived at the startling figure of one thousand and nine years as the age for the sprightly old gentleman with wispy white hair who stood before the class. Impossible.

"In an earlier existence, I, Aviti-Apollinares, was instructed at one of the best Egyptian public schools by Ra No Fer, prophet of Ptah, in all seven sciences, of the *quadrivium* and the *trivium,* and some others, *id est,* the art and practice of reincarnation, astral projection, and divination. Ra No Fer appeared in this world for the twenty-second time during the reign of the Pharaoh Menkare in the course of the seventh dynasty of Egyptian Kings at Thebes or Thebai, the Greek designation of the ancient Egyptian opet. The Karnak temple was the seat of the Theban triad of Amun, Mut and Khonsu. It was there, as the zenith of the epoch of the constellation of Taurus approached, where I was honoured to be Ra No Fer's pupil."

Here, Master Aviti-Apollinares paused, and with his overjoyed antiquarian eyes looked far and above and beyond us into another unimaginable past. *"Aut disce aut discede. Translate!"*

"Either learn or leave!" shouted several delighted voices.

"The tale that I will now relate is so old that you may imagine it as a beginning, when a fresh start was made after everything had ended. As the Master Jogavasistra observed, 'The world is like the impression left by the telling of a story.' I suppose the first question that was asked then was 'what time is it?'

"According to Herodotus, Thebes in Egypt was founded upon an idea often described as Menes, erroneously thought of as an actual person, around three thousand one hundred years before the Christian era. In truth, it is several, several thousands of years older. This would be anterior to the epoch of Taurus.

"The house of Gemini, that of the Divine Twins, is distinguished by the two bright stars, Dirah and Wasat, which represent their beautiful and terrible heads. This constellation preceded Taurus on the great cosmic wheel, which is called by the vulgar, the zodiac, Gemini is now long faded away.

"A great many things were as yet nameless. The great pyramids were brand new. The sphinx, then a huge image of the guardian god, Anubis, was already old as hell. There were parts of the world where very big lizards still lived, flew vast distances, exhaled foul breath, and laid enormous eggs.

"Most wellborn Sumerians and Phoenicians of the time, and later a few Greeks and some others, who came from the islands in the farthest west, beyond the Hyperborean, had gained their academic grounding in Egypt. Herodotus states that the priests of On-Heliopolis were the best informed of all in the seven sciences of the *quadrivium* and the *trivium:* geometry, astronomy, arithmetic, music, logic, rhetoric, and grammar.

"On-Heliopolis, as a seat of learning, more than two thousand years before the rise of the Greek city states, maintained schools that were later to be frequented by such luminaries as Imhotep the Great, Odisha, known as Kalinga, Jethro, priest of Midian, Abram, who became Abraham when graduated, Moshe Rabbenu, popularly known as Moses, Hyram Abif, the artificer, Amphion and Zethus, Orpheus the Thracian, Dionysus, Thales of Miletus, the poet Homer, the polymaths Hipparchus and Pythagoras, the philosopher Anazagoras and Archimedes the mathematician, Solon, lawmaker and storyteller, and much later, the Hebrew Prince Jesus who, along with some other past pupils, would be made into gods. It was a very good school, very good indeed, *dimidium facti qui coepit habet.*

"No great man ever existed who did not enjoy some portion of divine inspiration. I have heard the words of Imhotep and of Hor De Def, whose discourses men speak so much of, even now."

Here, he paused again, and for a moment appeared to be lost in ancient spaces. Removing his tiny gold pince-nez, he wiped them vigorously on his red silk dressing-gown, blew his nose in a saffron kerchief extracted apparently from the aether, and tried to find his place in Time.

"Well, yes. Where was I? Yes, Prince Idelfonso?"

"You heard the words of Imhotep and of Hor De Def, whose discourses men speak so much of, even now."

"Very good, Yes. *Grandescunt aucta labore,*" said Master Aviti-Apollinares, and continued:

"We were taught that from the Egyptian sciences, which may be called Isis and Osiris, was derived their religion, and, if the truth be told, all religions, from which would also descend the febrile art of politics. Osiris was portrayed as the first god to die and return from the dead. Isis became the prototype of all the goddesses, seen as mothers, lovers, sisters, aunts, wives and daughters, in roles such as child maiden, virgin, nubile woman, mother, harlot, and hag, and venerated as such.

"The Egyptians were the originators of the notion of 'sin' and, as a consequence, the doctrine of judgement after death: the transmigration of our immortal souls, the belief that after death and judgement, the souls of humans were transported to the solar system of the star *Canis Major,* Sirius, the Great Dog, later called by some, heaven: all this would be derived from the sciences of Isis and Osiris.

"The Egyptians were the source of the death and resurrection myths of Osiris, Demeter and Persephone at Elusis, and also those of Asclepius, Orpheus, Mithras, Tammuz, Zalmoxis, Dionysus and Odin and, much later on, the aforementioned Hebrew Prince, Jesus.

"These all made themselves archetypical of the zodiacal sign in which they were born. The creation of religion or politics was a necessity so as to organise government and to institutionalise order and productivity in populations of primitive farmers and herdsmen, some of whom were quite wild, so as to guarantee the continued survival of a small community of persons whose antecedents had survived the cataclysms caused by the meteors that marked the close of the previous epoch of Gemini. The religious myths of the 'gods' that have survived were, of course, the political propaganda of the time used to inform, distract and preoccupy the simple.

"The 'gods', who were a remnant of the previous civilisation, thus came to be perceived as the supernatural creators and overseers of the universe. The watchers. Future theologians who possessed no knowledge of the antediluvian sciences, and in pursuit of defining the indefinable, ascribed a variety of attributes to the many different conceptions of the 'gods'. Among the more easily accepted interpretations were omniscience, infinite knowledge, omnipotence, unlimited power, omnipresence, omnibenevolence, perfect goodness, divine simplicity, and eternal and necessary existence.

"The best minds of every epoch, which lasts approximately two thousand three hundred years, reinvented gods in their own image, to the best of their ability." The Master explained, again to Prince Idelfonso's amazement: "The quality of the gods invented speaks volumes about the best minds of any epoch. You will notice that some gods, after a thousand or two thousand years, die. Food for thought. Yes, *si post fata venit gloria non propero.* Thank you gentlemen. *Cras amet qui nunquam amavit; quique amavit, cras amet.*"

May he love tomorrow who has never loved before, and may he who has loved, love tomorrow as well. These words stayed with him all his life. Prince Idelfonso would come to idolise this teacher and seek to emulate him. As his understanding of the meaning of the lectures grew, he grasped that it was the believer who made the god immortal. When you shift your belief, the old gods die, and new ones are born, sometimes in stables.

Stimulated, curious, excited, eager for new knowledge, Prince Idelfonso became a model student and excelled in all his studies. He went on to spend seventeen years, working with the forerunners of the founders of the *Mitteilungen des Instituts für Österreichische Geschichtsforschung* in Vienna, reading in the library of the Frederick II, Duke of Legnica, in the Polish capital, travelling with Sufi initiates in caravans on the Silk Route and sitting at the feet of the Maharishis in the Varaha Cave temple at Mamallapuram, as a guest of the ghost of King Thondaiman Ilam Thiraiyar.

"Whenever righteousness wanes and unrighteousness increases I send myself forth. For the protection of the good and for the destruction of evil, and for the establishment of righteousness, I come into being age after age."

He heard these words carried on the wind as he rode across the rock-strewn plain from the ancient city of Mathura, in the shadow of the High Himalayas.

Later, he would learn from whence came the world's most precious inheritance, the only scientific device to have survived the great flood that marked the end of the world, a geometric solid called a Polyhedron, that was taken from the kingdom of Aksum and was kept for centuries, hidden in a castle in Brittany, the very one that now rested in the hold of the ship in which he was travelling westward.

The words of the Comte De Gabalis came to him in the dream. He saw the giant spheres filling the horizon. Elliptic in eclipse:— "Beyond the sun in the direction of the Dog Star lies that incorruptible flame or sun, principle of all things, willing obedience from our own sun which is but a manifestation of its relegated force. The existence of the sun behind the sun has been known in all ages, as well as the fact that its influence is most potent upon the earth during that period every two thousand three hundred years when it is in conjunction with the sun of our solar system. Then gathering to itself the power of its own source and transmitting it through our sun to this planet, it is said to send the Sons of God into the consciousness of the earth sphere that a new world of thought and emotion may be born in the minds of men for the stimulation of humanity's spiritual evolution. Such a manifestation marks the beginning or end of an epoch upon earth by the radiation of that divine consciousness known as the Christ Ray or Paraclete." Obsolescence is inevitable in this universe.

He achieved the Degrees of Master of Time and Master of Memory in 1777, his fiftieth year. He would continue to study and to organise his life around building a prodigious memory that was dedicated to one purpose, which was now at hand. He, along with the others of his cohort who attended the New Académie in the opening decades of the 18th century, was made cognisant of their diverse roles to be assumed in the immediate future, these would be crucial in the establishment of the next precessional epoch, that of Aquarius, which was expected to commence in just two hundred years. He was, however, the last to survive the revolution.

Ship sail, sail fast, he thought to himself, and out loud, *"Quod tanto impendio absconditur etiam solummodo demonstrare destruere est."* A pessimistic cloud of doubt, of fear, crossed his mind.

"Beg your pardon, your Grace?" enquired Adhémar, the shadow of the cross-trees from the swaying masts high above passing and repassing over them.

"Oh, an old proverb that translates, when a thing is hidden away with so much pains, merely to reveal it is to destroy it."

Adhémar glanced across to him and closed his eyes.

Ship sail, sail fast.

Still captured in the languor of the afternoon's torpor, Prince Idelfonso regarded his young friend, now asleep at his side, Tertullian's cryptic phrase, lingering. A great task lay before him.

The imagination of the age of Christopher Columbus was characterised by biblical geography, alchemic science and kabalistic thought. These located the navel of the world in Jerusalem where the universal constant, Pi, Infinity, became a religion. Monotheism. The Polyhedron, the gateway to another infinity, was being transported to the New World; its new home a place foretold, an island. This island wore the halo of legend, where prodigious events might take place, if, it indeed became the *axis mundi*, the next navel of the world, for another two thousand three hundred years. That event would attract the genius of the age, young people possessed of the new millennium's creative impulse. This island, which Columbus called Trinidad, a fictional place, the legendary place in the imagination of the Old World, a place of magical monsters: home of Leviathan, the great denizen of the deep, where in its Gulf of Paria they do disport themselves. This island, Trinidad, four square to the compass, just on the equator. The center of the world.

The Admiral of the Ocean Sea came upon this island in 1498, he tasted the waters in its Gulf of Paria and found them sweet and possessed of the mammalian redolence of the Leviathan. "I have found *Mar Dulce*," he wrote into the log of his flagship, the *Santa María de Guía*, "the sweet sea, where the fresh water battles with the salt."

He named the ingress to, and the egress from, the Gulf of Paria, with kabalistic terminology. *Boca de la Serpiente* and *Bocas del Dragón.* The great expanse itself: *Golfo de Ballina.* He had seen them, Leviathan. The giant whales, they formed his escort as he entered the Gulf of Paria through the channel to the south. Leviathan. *Job 41, 1* – Canst thou draw out Leviathan with a hook? The word Leviathan in Hebrew is made up of two roots, Levi and Than. ThN. Than, which is the root of Serpent or Dragon. The words of his Master came to him: "*Than* will be the symbol of transgression, but a symbol also of influence and power." This is written in the *Kabbala Denudata.* Since the root meaning of Than is serpent, Leviathan means, literally, the Than or serpent of Levi. Of this word, 'Levi', the

Kabbala Denudata states, 'The root, we may suppose, describes the coils of a serpent, perhaps the metallic gleam of its scales.'" Columbus had perceived the serpent-dragon in the different hues of the mysterious currents that appear to swirl across the surface of the *Mar Dulce*, the Sweet Sea, the Gulf of Paria, in which he sailed. It became the miracle anticipated. Where the fresh water battles the salt, this holy confluence, long sought. *Mar Dulce*. The most profound prophecies unfolded, coming to pass before his eyes, as he sailed upon the furthest perimeter of the circumference of the world.

Sirius appeared high in a pastel sky, while the other star, our own, was turning the world to fire and light, gold and bronze.

Unmoved, he saw a meteor flash across the firmament.

The fundamental philosophy of John Milton came to mind—a single material substance which is animate, self-active, and free composes everything in the universe: from stones and trees and bodies to minds, souls, angels, and God.

An island to which people from all over the world will come, have come, where various religious leaders, setting aside their historic differences and accepting concord, peace and understanding, will unite all religions with one another, thereby forming a utopian religion or a religion of humans with God being defined as science, or the supernatural force that reigned before the birth of the universe.

This island, *La Trinité,* Trinidad. Surely one of the "Fortunate Isles," as told by Ptolemy. Utopia, the ideal and imaginary island nation. Literally like no other place. *Pardes,* paradise, the ancient narrative re-told by Thomas More of Paradise Lost, and of John Milton, long ago lost, now regained. A place in waiting, surely, on the wheel of history.

The *Psalms 137:3-8* came to his mind: "For there they that carried us away captive required of us a song; and they that wasted us required of us mirth, saying, 'Sing us one of the songs of Tzion'. How shall we sing the Lord's song in a strange land? If I forget thee, O Jerusalem, let my right hand forget her cunning. If I do not remember thee, let my tongue cleave to the roof of my mouth; if I prefer not Jerusalem above my chief joy. Remember, O Lord, the children of Edom in the day of Jerusalem; who said, raze it, raze it, even to the foundation thereof; O daughter of Babylon, that art to be destroyed; happy shall he be, that repayeth thee as thou hast served us."

The horizon had achieved magnificence in the distant west.

His colleagues, in truth the remnant of his cohort—the Terror had taken a toll on his generation—had done their duty, infiltrating, then influencing to a remarkable degree, the significant interest in the City of London and the English parliament. The abolition of the slave trade was accomplished in 1807; that pernicious institution must not exist in paradise, as it would blight all and everything for all time. A real economy must be established; paradise needs working capital. Paradise also required administration. He heard a name, Ralph James Woodford, 2nd Baronet of Carleby. A descendant of a prebendary, some sort of Anglican Church administrator, a canon, he guessed, and smiled. Good.

Both the emperor and the Vatican had been avoided, but at great cost. He knew that there were powerful forces to deal with: the Freemason Vincent Patrice, whose ambition was to establish a Masonic theocracy on the continent. What did he know of our cargo? He had learnt of the death of Francisco de Miranda, Patrice's mentor and champion. The Freemason would have need of another sword to carve out from that wilderness a republic in which to establish himself.

The young warriors, Mariño and Bolívar, of whom he knew little or nothing, were Patrice's only hope at present. It was already decided even before the rise of the First Counsel, now emperor, that the future of Les Chambrés would be with the English. The emperor would die, and with him all his ambitions. France would go into decline for a hundred years, or even more, spent of men, of treasure and of minds. The rest of Europe would lick its wounds and try to recreate the past. And go to war again. The Vatican would experience the fate of the oracle centres of Rome and Greece, obsolescence, as old men stumble onto one another mumbling formulas that have lost their efficacy. England, another island, would be the future of the world, and this island Trinidad, formerly *terra incognita,* would become Utopia from where another infinity, the infinity of infinities, would be proclaimed and promulgated, deity renamed.

In medias res. . . he closed his eyes.

24:

1814–1816: Santiago Mariño,
The End of Time.

"Kairos is at hand."

"I beg your Highness' pardon?"

"Kairos is at hand. The *kairoi* are those crises in the human condition that provide an opportunity for, and indeed demand, an existential decision by the human subject, the coming of Christ being the prime example, the crossing of the river Rubicon, when Caesar cried, *Iacta alea est*—The die is cast."

"A fleeting instant when opportunity presents itself and must be grasped if success is to be achieved."

"Exactly, your Excellency."

"The appointed moment when God acts?"

"Not to be confused with chronos, sequential time. *Kairos tou poiesai to Kyrio* as it is said: it is time, kairos, for the Lord to act. This moment in history is an intersection with eternity."

They sat together in the bright sunlight on the gallery of Government House overlooking the Belmont Estate, from which rose the hot smell of the distilleries carried on the morning's easterly breeze. Before them the Polyhedron, unpacked. Now in the brilliant light it looked like a large, hugely large, and clear crystal, an enormous gemstone, some five feet high, nearly three across the base, multifaceted, carved *mezzo-relievo*. A complex, convex Polyhedron, a geometric solid, within which could be gleaned by the sun's light, curious angular rhombic, dodecahedral, honeycomb facets, other shapes and angular forms. He heard it described by one of the erudite young men, whose voices could be heard coming from within the house. That it seemed to be two objects, one inside of the other. Notwithstanding the bright morning light, it appeared to possess a source of brilliance of its own, emitted from its depths.

Lying upon a sheet of white canvas laid out on the grass in the shimmering sunlight, it revealed itself once more as precious and original in Adhémar's eyes. His father died to save this thing, this thing, that had lain, had been kept in their house for centuries. It belonged to him, not to these Englishmen. No matter what the Prince thought or said. His father had died defending it, and was rotting in that field, to make sure that it did not fall into the hands of the Vatican or the emperor. He looked at it. Taking up its own unique space, distinctive, so separate and complete, neither connected to, nor dependent on him or anybody. It was so old, yet it looked new. He couldn't help it, he stepped forward and put his hand on it. It felt hard and hot.

"Fallen from heaven according to the myths," said the governor.

"Not at all," replied Prince Idelfonso Tiburcio Burgundofara. "It may be described, possibly inaccurately, as an advanced type of rhombic triacontahedron. A solid, containing within its depths subtle aspects of the dual of an Archimedean Polyhedron as well as, yet unknown, aspects of the golden rhombus and other geometric theories. As a solid it is a mathematical description of Time. It is an equation, a door to another infinity. It was once described as 'The Gates of Aksum,' the entrance to the forever lasting.

"If a learned mathematician were to write a description of the formulae that it describes, he would require a blackboard about one hundred and forty feet long. It is said to be made of tchãm, a rare crystal-like, or crystal-appearing material found only in meteors. It antedates anything that we know to have been made by human hands. It is said by those who know about these things, of which there are very few, that it is antediluvian and comes from a time when a civilisation flourished on this earth, millennia before the biblical flood."

"Is it possible to know why such an object was made, or how the sculptor gained the inspiration, or the knowledge, to produce it?" enquired the governor.

"Impossible to say," replied the Prince. "The parchment scrolls which accompanied it out of Ethiopia describe it as a scientific tool that, if used properly, will afford us a glimpse into a different perception of Time, the discovery of a new understanding of eternity." He smiled and looked at Adhémar and continued, "It seems that something of its existence was known by the early Arab polymaths. Hassan-i Sab' h, for example, in his *Sargozasht is-Sayyidna*, discusses the first understanding of God as the infinite, and foretells that in the next interpretation of divinity, which will surely come when humanity has attained a higher level of consciousness, the next secret name for God, as infinity, would have thirty-six letters, if that is of any help to you, your Excellency."

"Not to me, Sire, but most likely to young Graf Anselm von Schack, who has been sent to us by his colleague Johann-Carl Gauss, known for his work on the heptadecagon discussed in his *Disquisitiones Arithmeticae*, and of course to Phillip Reinagle, who I understand is foremost in the study of topology, graph theory and calculus.

"Indeed, both these young men have written and presented advanced work on differential geometry, geodesy and complex analysis, the limits of mathematics are being explored, most fascinatingly the rigorous treatment of the notion of infinity with particular reference to work on number theory. We are very lucky to have them."

The governor rose and took Adhémar by the arm so as to conduct him. Preceded by the Prince, who was also on his feet, they walked towards and into Government House.

"Come, Mr. de Gurvand, come join His Serene Highness and myself. Let us meet these bright and ingenious young men who will unravel the secrets of this ancient mathematical marvel. I believe that they are gathered in the sitting room. Charming house, wouldn't you say, Your Highness?"

Adhémar followed discreetly, crossing in their wake the creaking, rotting floorboards of the front gallery, into the sparsely furnished, now freshly painted white, somewhat dilapidated sitting room that was dominated by a large oil painting, framed in gold-leafed rococo, of the Prince Regent, and a massive, sepulchral sideboard, where a company of young men were gathered around a long table covered with heavy books and shiny brass instruments. All were elegantly attired in morning wear and speaking animatedly. He longed to leave, to see Marie Eugénie and Alain.

It was not until after *petit déjeuner*, and after Adhémar had told the story of defending their precious cargo and its contents several times over, receiving polite but heart-felt condolences from the governor and the other young men, and gently aided by Prince Idelfonso, who was well aware of Adhémar's feelings with regard to the loss of his parent, the destruction of his ancestral home and his yearning to see his beloved wife and son, that Adhémar was able to make a graceful exit.

To home, to the house on the grass market. A compulsion draws me there to my father's house. I feel that I must stand in the place where he once stood, for a moment. The last in a lifetime. The town is being rebuilt. The heat of midday. Cocoutes, standing at the gate. The dilapidated house, small, old, grey, empty.

"Cocoutes."

"Massa Adhémar, all ya reach home!"

There is no more "all you" I tell him, just me.

He nods and nods.

"Yes, Massa."

We ascend the creaking outside staircase, leaving the smells of the store rooms and stable behind, into the living-room and open the doors to the little gallery. Home. Everything is here. Except him.

"Massa Adhémar, you want to know? Missee Marie Eugénie is by she family, you want me to call she?"

"Oh yes, Cocoutes, yes please, go quick."

She comes, they come. My wife, my son. My anxious eyes can hardly contain her, them. I hold her close, we kiss. She has changed. I smell her, familiar, sunshine. She is the same. I am different. I am the same. I look at her. She is different.

"Marie Eugénie, Marie?"

"Yes, oh yes."

She is golden in the afternoon's sunlight, her eyes, her loveliness. I feel like a stranger. She smiles and kisses me with her smile. "Alain, kiss your father." This boy, so tall, so dear. I hold him close. "You came on the Baltimore clipper, Papa? We saw her in the stream, not so Mama?"

"Yes darling, we saw her."

The others, her cousins, her cousin Mi Mi, stand around, blushing, awkward. Why do I feel different?

"Am I different, do you find me different?"

"Yes, you are, you have been there and back, you've been away, and now you have come back, welcome home my darling Adhémar."

We must find a place to blend these differences and match the similarities. I know that she knows that. Símon Agostini comes, he is an old man, and bustles about. The trunks arrive, bags and baggage. He takes charge of the household.

"Thank you, Símon."

"Your father?"

My anxious eyes, terrified, they tell him. "Yes."

"Yes?"

I nod, "Yes."

"My dear boy, I am sorry. Please, whatever you require."

We embrace. He is so small.

"Ah well." He sighs.

Marie, I hold her close, we kiss. Oh, sunshine. The others come close, I put my arms around them all. The boy, my son, my son. I kiss them all. I know that I will cry now, . . and I do, I do.

"Your father, Adhémar?"

I tell a story, a version of the story that I will tell over and over several times. Everyone comes now. The house slaves, neighbours, Jean de Boissière, I greet him fraternally and hug him, we look into each other's faces, I nod and so does he. Others stand in the doorways, crying, and as if by magic, Néolise and her mother Julienne, and Jean-Paul.

"Your father? Massa François? . . . Massa Adhémar?"

I take her by the arm into his room and seat her on his chair, and tell her, I can't remember what. She weeps and weeps, so do I. I reassure her that everything will be alright. She is older than I remember, her red and cream madras kalinda tied with the knots of a spoken-for woman. My father's woman. Thin, yellow-olive skin taut, her features now finer, a quantity of small brown moles on her cheeks and neck, her brown intelligent eyes, sharp, sunken, dark rimmed, overflowing. I hold her close and kiss her cheeks, her tears. The smell of wood-smoke and of toil upon her. I look into her face, my father loved this face, knew this face.

"Massa Adhémar, your father dead? Is that true? You have come home? Ohi, Ohi. Yes. Praise God."

Jean-Paul comes to us, to her, my brother, my father's son. Almost as tall as I. We shake hands, awkwardly, he starts to cry. I look into his face, searching it for resemblance, our resemblance, and look across the room, as I take him in my arms, straight into the long mirror and see us three there, reflected, standing in the afternoon sunlight. Alain comes to us, I put my arm around his shoulder. This is my family.

"Come home with me to La Pamplona, Adhémar, the house in town is not in good order. We have been with Papa."

427

Then, to her lovely eyes I turn again. "Yes, Marie Eugénie."

I say her name, just to say her name.

We leave in the afternoon's sunlight. By dusk we are riding through shadowy Maraval, later the risen full moon's pale light finds us above Moka, ascending the hilly bridle path. The slaves are running ahead and around us with flambeaux. We climb and cross the Saddle, the full moon bright, illuminating the valley below with a cool, clear light, and we descend into misty Santa Cruz. Me and Marie Eugénie.

In returning to Trinidad, I have a sense of not knowing it at all. In a great many ways I can hardly recognise myself in these settings, in this life here. Marie's parents, Pierre-Louis Roget and his wife Jeanne, who is my cousin, my father's cousin, through their shared grandmother, are kind to me and listen to everything I have to tell them. Prodigious events, he tells me. Pierre-Louis treats me differently, he says that the fight where I did everything to save my father makes me a man. Now I must have more children, sons, and settle down. His wife Jeanne cautions patience, Marie Eugénie is happy to see me well and alive. She advises that I should rest, sensing my inability to find myself, locate myself anew in Trinidad.

I take pleasure in riding out with Alain. He is quite polite, I notice, and never takes his eyes away from me. We glance at each other frequently, and smile. I find that I speak of his grandfather often, telling him of Brittany and Beaumanoir. The days and weeks go by.

Jean de Boissière has come to see me. I find him in Pierre-Louis' front office. He now dresses more like an English country squire. The rough-neck Frenchman, the importer of second-hand slaves, the grasping money-lender who charges ruinous interest is now eclipsed, he is like those I saw at

Government House. We talk. He is discreet. I tell him the version of the story that I have told everyone, the visit to the family home, and how we found it in a ruined state, the nature of the destruction caused by the revolution in France, the war in Europe, the roving bands of highway robbers, the attack on our party, my father's death. He has his own news, his father, who has survived the revolution, is now Mayor of Bergerac. I mention nothing, as promised, of the Polyhedron or of its capabilities to anyone.

The important visitor who is presently with the new governor as his honoured guest? A charming shipboard acquaintance. Learned, a Spanish prince, no less, I tell him. He gives me news of the battles on the Terra Firma. And speaks of the heroism of Santiago Mariño and the death of Francisco de Miranda, the terrible plight of the Venezuelan refugees, the callous nature of the new governor as displayed in his treatment of respectable, proper people, wealthy people. Then jokingly, perhaps maliciously, of the coterie of elegant gentlemen who now surround Sir Ralph and the new and refined tone being introduced to the colony. A bachelor, the ladies of the town now take long walks up Belmont Hill and twirl their parasols for Governor Woodford's notice. Towards the end of his visit, he has declined to stay to lunch, he makes mention of Frère Vincent, the Vénérable Master for yet another term in the Chair. "Come, and dine with me, Adhémar, I am meeting Maingot, Henri de la Bastide and, perhaps, Louis Rochard, who has just returned from France, at Mrs. Murphy's on the first Wednesday of next month, after the meeting of the Atelier." I say yes, as it would be good to see friends.

Santiago Mariño felt a temper rise, that surprised him, as a state of breathlessness came upon him, sending the blood pounding in his ears, when he saw the governor ride by the Atelier wearing a straw hat as if he were a peasant, a Negro slave or a fucking tourist.

Now he was hearing that this man, this fancy English gentleman, did not just turn back the waterlogged schooner in which the remnants of Eugenio María Trujillo y Pazos' family were travelling, but gave the order to bombard it, sink it, so that it would serve as an exquisite example to the worthless Venezuelans who were leaving in waves, seeking refuge from massacres now taking place on a biblical scale in cities all over the country.

Every day Santiago Mariño was reminded of his helpless state by the perpetual lamentation of misfortunes droned by his fellow emigrés as they argued over the vagaries of ingratitude, the disillusionments of victories and the hopelessness of hope. He ranted against Bolívar. And prayed for redistributive justice. And wished that he, wherever he was, was equally impotent, jailed behind the iron bars of regret, shackled and sightless and friendless, while atrocities were being committed against the womb that gave him birth.

But the bitterest pith returned to in every acrimonious conversation, had to be the heartless nature of this pompous, dandified, womanish fop of an Englishman.

I, Littais L'Eau, looked at them sitting beneath the big, naked Indian tree that grew next to the Tuileur's cottage above Piccadilly Street.

"Oy! Ralph! *Eres marica!*" he shouted as the governor's entourage rounded the bend in the road beneath the Atelier that would take it to the Royal Road and thence, to San Juan de Aricagua.

430

"Santiago! Shut your mouth! You want to get us thrown out of this fucking place? Eh?"

Francisco Bermudez, who was standing behind him, drew back behind the trunk of the tree on whose root Santiago was sitting. A black hen with a dozen clean-necked chicks pecking around in the dirt at his feet was making clucking sounds, to which the chicks responded with squeaks and peeps.

"I feel to kill him when I see him."

"Not today, while the world is falling apart."

The rooster came up importantly, the hen and her brood scuttled away.

"He has something hiding up in that house on Belmont Hill, Maingot is saying to anyone who listens."

"What the hell is it, a new scheme to kill innocent people? That son of a bitch. I will wring his neck before I leave this shithole of an island."

He got up abruptly and kicked the rooster in the arse, this sent it flying, squawking down the hillside, which raised a shout of laughter from a party of Maçons who were making their way up the hill to attend a meeting, it was the first Wednesday in September of 1816. The Atelier was working a First Degree initiation that very evening and already the candidates were sequestered in the grotto at the foot of the hill.

Later, after the First Degree I, Littais L'Eau, joined them at Mrs. Murphy's tavern to celebrate with the new Entered Apprentices.

It was a rousing rumbustious time: a full of rum, women and music fiesta. The rumbling strum of guitars in major key, with Santiago, dressed in black, leading the seguidilla's offbeat start, a false start that signalled the interludio. His voice rough, his red head thrown back, sweat running down his neck, he shouted a croaking chant and clapped his hands, setting the pace, the guitars went in at it, he stamped the rhythm deep into the floor boards with his steel-heeled gaucho's boots, tossing the Colombian whores who now appeared as beautiful gypsies, creating hysteria, flambeaux flaming. The salida, the guitars, the castanets, he singing, rapido, making the music louder, quicker, hands clapping, he singing the interludio, high-voiced, short, interrogations, clapping, triple-time, now just the castanets alone, this, a very old Castilian folk-song, how did he know that?

Flashing skirts, stamping heels, the smell of rum, women and fire. More guitars, dancing on tables, on the bar. Castanets, maniacal rhythms. His voice, hoarse, coplas, shouted off key, his face ablaze, his fiery red hair flinging sweat fastened to his arrogant rooster face in flaming curls, magenta ringlets, a warrior at his rest. His piercing blue eyes, lowered now, chin tucked in, his glance fiercer, daring all comers, his body straight and taut, arms and hands in motion shape the algebra of the arabesque, streaming sweat, flying droplets, wet, the women licking the perspiration, drinking the hero. The other Venezuelans not far behind, but he outdistancing them, with interludios, out-shouting them, coplas now, outraging them, haranguing them, daring them, challenging them—everybody, the brothers Dert, joining, tall, Basque, hard men, terrible people. I watched Adhémar de Gurvand as he withdrew into a corner with de Boissière and some others, our eyes met.

Crescendo! Repeated. They did the entire thing over again. Fandango now, many bottles of rum raised, drained, the torchlight flickering red, redder, clapping, singing. He was shouting something into Bermudez's ear, they laughed and bounced their foreheads together, Maingot joined them, arms about shoulders they danced, stamping together, the three, round and round, then they made a dash for the door. I expected that. Outside I heard horses neigh, I saw the brothers Dert make for the door, Mrs. Murphy called something, I jumped to my feet and followed. Already they were mounted upon the stamping, rearing, whirling stallions, I grabbed hold of a big black mare and hurled myself onto the saddle, she leapt into the night, I followed the drumming hooves, the wild shouts up Frederick Street and into and across the Paradise Estate's Grand Savanna. We were leaving the town behind, riding, galloping abreast wildly through the night, through Paradise, and swerving eastward to Belmont. Maingot, the brothers Dert, Francisco Bermudez, Santiago and me, Littais L'Eau.

We took the Belmont road at a gallop past the grove of silk cotton trees, and followed a rising, winding carriage way. Where were we going? Government House! We leapt the low garden gate and thundered across the sloping lawn toward the old house, which shone in the moonlight, white and phosphorescent. The sentry shouted, I could hear him running, another shouted, a bell was ringing, a whistle.

Ahead the house loomed, bright, alight with candlelight, the regiment's band played "Where ere you walk," there people, men, women, a garden party, we, they, rode into them, the crowd, shouting, scattering, whirling horses, people falling over each other. I saw him and Bermudez silhouetted against the brilliant interior as they mounted the gallery steps and rode into the house, there was something large and glass-like on a table, he snatched the canvas that it was upon, and dragged it towards him, Bermudez was on the other side of the table. The horses were neighing, stamping, sliding, huge in the room, the candelabra swinging above, people scampering, a white-

433

liveried house slave lifted a woman up and away from the horses as they kicked and slid upon the polished floor, another tried to take hold of Santiago's, he slashed the man across the face with his riding whip, blood down his white blouse. They, he and Bermudez, they both grabbed hold of the canvas from either side and pulled the thing between them across and off the table and charged through the crowd holding the canvas between them and tossed it into a buggy. Santiago leapt inside and lashed the startled horse, it bolted forward, we rode, we all followed each other down the hill.

"What's that?" I shouted at him.

"The governor's fucking balls!" And into Paradise Estate's Grand Savanna we went, howling, laughing, shouting Spanish profanities. Already we were being followed, a shot was fired, another, we raced across the Savanna, the horses breathing hard, the thunder of hooves, shouts, the buggy bouncing, flying, over tufts and mounds, he standing, reins in hand, lashing the horse with a whip, howling Venezuelan obscenities into the night, and down Frederick Street we went.

"Where are you going, you madman?"

"To the jetty, Bideau is waiting with a boat."

The jetty? Bideau? I spurred my beast and rode ahead. In the distance I could see a crowd about the waterfront, in the light of several torches there was a melee of people, men, soldiers. I arrived, we arrived. "Take it to the boat!" he shouted, and the brothers Dert took hold of the thing and dragged it out of the buggy, it fell and rolled, I looked, it was a big glass object, a sculpture of some sort.

"Throw it in the longboat!" he bellowed. People, Negroes were fighting with the soldiers, there were shots coming from the barracks, more soldiers came running. Some blacks were throwing torches into the barracks building. This place, all it takes is a moment of confusion and hell is let loose. The barrack was ablaze, at the back, I could see that, some soldiers ran back into the burning building.

Already, the pursuers were almost upon us. De Gurvand was fighting with Dominic Dert, who was directing the sailors to put the object into Bideau's ship's longboat. They were armed with sabres, my God. Now Vincent was on the scene. He tried to restrain de Gurvand, who shoved him away. Dominic Dert was wounded in the neck, now de Gurvand's blade went through his chest, two wounds, he's a goner.

An English officer and two troopers were trying to prevent the object from being put into the ship's longboat by the sailors who were fighting them off. Bideau came to Santiago and shouted something and pointed to the street. I could see horsemen arriving, with torches held high, other people with torches all around, some were pushing carts into the street to form a barricade. I must get out of here, another building was ablaze, the crowd was looting. My pirogue was tied to the jetty, I ran towards it. Bermudez was with me.

"Let's get to hell out of here now!" he shouted.

"Right away!" I answered.

We untied the pirogue, Benoît Dert also jumped in, I pushed off. Shots were being fired from the shore, we rowed out towards a schooner that I recognised was Bideau's *Botón de Rosa*. I looked back, I could see Vincent defending himself with his ebony cane out of which flashed a long thin blade, as an officer with a drawn sword moved towards him. Vincent was barring the officer's way as the sailors from Bideau's schooner were lowering the thing into Bideau's longboat. The Englishman staggered away, for a brief second I saw blood spurt red from his neck, the jugular.

"Leave the bloody thing!" shouted Bermudez.

"Forget it, let's go."

De Gurvand intervened, he was fighting off another officer and another who cornered Vincent. One fell holding his stomach as de Gurvand leapt over him to attack the other. Even in the hurly burly it crossed my mind that he was saving Vincent's life. I watched their fight, the boy has become a swordsman, he was gaining on the officer, another joined, Vincent ran him through.

Bermudez and Dert were rowing with all their might, the pirogue swung about. I lost sight of de Gurvand, the longboat with the thing in it was now away, two soldiers jumped into the water and swam towards it, no luck there, two buildings were alight, aside from the barracks, one must have been Mrs. Murphy's, what a loss, more shots, de Gurvand was on his knees. The officer raised his blade. Vincent was running past them, running on the jetty, he leapt into the sea, splash! His tall hat was floating away, he was swimming hard. Santiago was standing, shouting, shouting something, the longboat stopped, the rowers raised their oars, Vincent was dragged aboard, what the hell?

We were now alongside the schooner, sailors on the deck, they opened fire, a salvo, at the shore where a boat was being readied, the *Botón de Rosa's* foresails were being hauled up, the mainsail was already, a breeze, just a whisper, they hauled the anchor, she leaned and barely moved, we scrambled up a knotted rope, I kicked away the pirogue.

"Oh! Shit! I am going abroad."

"So it would appear," Bermudez said, scrambling past.

The longboat was alongside us, they scrambled up too. Santiago was standing in it, he was commanding a net. A net! A net was thrown. The thing was bundled into it, a rope, a rope! A davit swung out, they winched it up, it was swung aboard, we were moving. The boat with soldiers was gaining on us, one stood and fired, a bullet whizzed by my head, wack! Benoît Dert gave a gasp and dropped dead at my side. Another soldier stood, a sailor fired from the deck of our ship, and the soldier fell, we were moving. The foresail was up, she leaned away in the breeze. I saw the waterfront ablaze, reflected in the black water, shimmering red and yellow, I tried to discern de Gurvand, no luck, I made out Maingot, he was talking to the governor.

Boom! From the harbour fort. A whizzing whine swished overhead.

"Chain-shot!"

Boom!

"Sail away, sail away, sail away."

"Where to, Captain?"

It was Santiago Mariño standing with Vincent.

"To Haiti, to bring home the Liberator," shouted Captain Jean Baptiste Bideau.

"Drop me in Güiria, comrade."

"To Cartagena, my friend," I, Littais L'Eau, said.

"Fernando Gomez de Zaa is raising men there and building fortifications, he is assembling an army," said Vincent, he looked very shaken and old. Wet, and shivering in funereal black. The brothers Dert were dead. They were close to him. He had killed two English officers, there was no going back, that was now out of the question.

The wind picked up, we were underway. The *Botón de Rosa* had been equipped for war, she was a floating arsenal. That thing we brought aboard was now stored below. What the hell was it? Nobody knew.

"A trophy," said Santiago.

By morning we sailed in a rolling, windswept sea for the Boca Grande, beating up towards the Venezuelan coast, the sky looked very wild. To the east, aft, I could see a storm coming up, with several squalls racing each other across the Gulf of Paria, pouring rain out of grey, blue-black clouds in sheets that slanted this way and that, illuminated in the remnant of the sunlight, already huge drops were splattering onto the decks and against the sails.

By afternoon we were in the middle of it, Bideau ordered a reef taken on the mainsail and the foresails lowered as she heeled with the force of the wind. The *Botón de Rosa* plunged full speed ahead. I stood behind Bideau, he at the helm, I held on to the backstays with both hands. I enjoyed this sort of weather, the thrill of speed and the motion of the ship, the sense of danger, the sheer excitement of being under sail in a storm. Ahead the waves rose and ran before us, dark grey green, from which schools of flying fish leapt. Suddenly, in the midst of it, I saw for the briefest moment what looked like someone, a head, an arm, the palm of a hand that waved and then was gone. I grasped his shoulder and shouted, "Look, something out there to starboard, look there." I pointed. "Look!" He leaned out as best he could, the ship was pitching in the wind, the wheel under pressure, to broach was not what we needed now.

"Look. There."

"Yes."

He bellowed above the wind as she rose up and pitched.

"Hey Ramón," he shouted to a sailor at the mast.

"Look, in the water, look to starboard, throw a rope, quick sharp man, quick, we could never go around, we will never find him if we did." This to me. Ramón stood balancing on the heaving deck and flung a coil of rope towards a man holding on to a box, the rope fell short.

"Makefast. Leave it, leave it." Bideau shouted as the man was obviously swimming vigorously to it, we came almost abreast of him, I looked at him. "My God, it's Sucre!" I shouted into Bideau's ear. "It's Sucre!"

"Yeah, throw another line, Ramón, throw it now, you idiot, I am going to put her in irons. Helm's a lee!" he shouted and swung the wheel and everything spun around, the boom on the mainsail swinging about to be made-fast, the bow now headed into the wind, as the ship shuddered and seemed to have stalled, unable to manoeuvre, as she rose up in the water and rolled.

"Take the wheel, L'Eau," he said, grabbing my hand and putting it on the wheel, which immediately felt alive and moving.

"Hold her steady, L'Eau. Don't mess around."

With that said, he was down on the deck at the gunwale, hauling at the second line. The man, Sucre, grabbed that as well as the other and was already falling behind us. I looked straight ahead, as the ship broke through a huge wave that sent a vast rush of water over, down and across the deck, not daring to look over my shoulder.

"Haul, together now, Ramón, haul! Jacques, drop the main, just drop it!"

Other crew came to their aid, and with several hands at it, the man was soon athwart us and being hauled up and aboard. "Look! Another man there," I shouted, "Look! Look! There are people in the water!"

"You there, you jackass, help him, Marcello!" shouted Bideau.

"Steady as she goes L'Eau, L'Eau, steady! Do nothing! Take the helm from him Jacques, move it. I've got him. Get that one Ramón. Help him, Ramón. We'll bring her about soon, Jacques, easy, easy, keep her head in the wind, to the wind, easy, throw that line, now, throw another, this one, this one! Come on Ramón, throw it."

In a matter of a few minutes we hauled two more on board. "Alright, we are going about, Jacques. Now! Up with the main, up, up! Put your back into it, up, up. Marcello! the gaff vang! she is sagging away to leeward." Bideau was now back at the helm, the *Botón de Rosa* lurched forward, heeling over, "Too much sail, take a reef, Jacques, take it now, haul in that halyard, take up the number one. Alright, away we go."

Below, we got the story. Sucre, who was studying English in Trinidad, had received word that the Liberator was coming back to Venezuela and decided to join him, and was on his way to Güiria in a yacht when they were overtaken by the storm that sank them. This had happened just two or three hours before. They, he, and a crew of five were in the water in no time at all and more or less came to the conclusion that they would be dead by nightfall. They saw the sharks, big like hell. He was glad, very grateful, to be with us.

"Güiria is behind us comrade, we are for Cartagena, to join up with Gomez."

"Güiria will soon be under attack, the patriots' army will fade away unless we get there," said Sucre.

The argument went backward and forward well into the night. Then it was decided that it was to be Güiria, and Antonio de Sucre was named General Santiago Mariño's Chief of Staff. We put about and a day later we dropped anchor in Güiria.

"Hold there Mr. Piggot!" The governor's voice rose above the tumult. "Spare de Gurvand, I will need witnesses to tonight's events, see to that arm of yours Mr. Piggot! Mr. Maingot, what is the meaning of all this?" he demanded.

It was from Joseph Maingot, who was known to Sir Ralph to be a Freemason, that the governor now demanded an explanation of the night's events, to which Maingot naturally pleaded innocence and ignorance, blaming it all on exuberance and the Latin temperament. Sir Ralph of course was unaware that it was Maingot who had informed Santiago Mariño of the strange object kept at Government House.

Captain Bradshaw, in the meantime ordered the guns at Fort San Andres to open fire on Bideau's schooner, as well as the making ready of *HMS Scorpion* to pursue the schooner with a company of harbour police on board. But the confusion caused by the night's events and with the barracks on fire, interminable delays accrued, with the result that the *Botón de Rosa* was well underway, taking advantage of the evening's light air and the surrounding darkness by the time the sloop of war commenced pursuit.

Prince Idelfonso listened carefully to what Joseph Maingot explained. "Your Grace, Master Vincent has no knowledge of the value or the scientific significance of the stone that you describe, neither does Santiago Mariño. To Mariño it was a method, a means he employed to insult Governor Woodford, and to take revenge for what the Venezuelan patriots see as cruel and senseless acts, the preventing of helpless people, women and children, being given succour and solicitude on this island. As for Master Vincent, he sees in Mariño a way to fulfil his own ambition, which is to dominate the Craft of Freemasonry in the southern hemisphere."

With anguish the Prince regarded Joseph Maingot. "Sire de Surgères, how can we regain what is on that ship, where can we reach them, we will pay whatever price they ask. I want back what is mine."

The old man was severely affected by the loss of the Polyhedron, to a degree that he became ill and was taken to bed at Government House. "I will pay in gold a fortune to any man who will bring back to me what cannot be replaced," he said. He grew so weak that the doctor would lift him like a child and prop him against the pillows.

"Find them, Adhémar, find them, Sire de Surgères. This fair land, *La Trinité*, must not be Paradise Lost. John Milton must not have the last word. Lucifer's hoards must be forever chained. They are now in Hell, in Tartarus. Adhémar, *La Trinité* must not become Pandæmonium, the High Capital of Satan, the capital of Hell! *Listen!* Satan exhorts his followers; he will be supported by Mammon and Beelzebub, *here.* Belial, worthless men, and Moloch, too, child sacrifice, beware— *Leviticus 18:21* '. . . thou shalt not let any of thy seed pass through the fire to Moloch'. These two will be present, at Satan's side. Save *La Trinité*. Adhémar. If only for the memory of your father."

They gave the old man what comfort they could. His ravings, incomprehensible to them, seemed to foretell nothing but tragedy, unless his lost treasure was found. Indeed, the hunt for the *Botón de Rosa* commenced on the very night that the Polyhedron was stolen from Government House in Belmont and the fracas on the wharf left five dead in Port-of-Spain, as the town was now called. Sir Ralph would have to answer to London as to why an important scientific experiment was not treated with the care that it deserved.

Prince Idelfonso refused to believe that the treasure which his order had kept for some six hundred years, indeed one that

442

became its very raison d'être, somehow was now lost, vanished in the fog of war. He spent vast sums dispatching fortune hunters, in search of this millennial treasure, and as he regained his strength, would often be seen on the jetty interrogating sailors and travelers, but to no avail. In the hope of receiving news from the Venezuelan wars and the whereabouts of the Polyhedron, he became a member of the Atelier Les Frères Unis. He died some years after being raised to the Sublime Degree; he was one hundred and two years of age when he passed away in July of 1839, and was buried in the Atelier's graveyard beneath the giant naked Indian tree in the regalia of a prince of the House of Andorra, and wearing the jewels of his rank as a master of his order. His tombstone inscription reads, "THE MAN WHO THINKS, WILLS TO KNOW." As quoted from the Comte de Gabalis, by the Abbé N. de Montfaucon de Villars.

As for Adhémar de Gurvand, he experienced a deep sense of remorse with the Polyhedron's vanishing. A profound melancholy, that could mutate into a fit of depression would overwhelm him at times, caused by knowing, remembering that his father, François, had given his life in vain to save this object, this stone, unique and of incalculable value, that in a very real sense belonged to their family, that was now irretrievable lost.

Adhémar would live to a great age, surrounded by an ever increasing circle of descendents. He did become, "the master of men," in much the same manner as his father-in-law, Pierre-Louis Roget once was, and even be the leader of the French Creole Catholic party, on the island. The memory of his father, their adventurous story and, the "stone that fell from heaven," became the stuff of legend in his family, increasingly told with the proverbial grain of salt.

I, Littais L'Eau, would spend the duration of the Venezuelan War of Independence with General Santiago Mariño. We conquered, and held, virtually all of eastern Venezuela more than once. Then, there was in 1835 a violent and bloody military coup, which was known as the *Revolución de las Reformas*, led by Santiago, during which he actually took power for a while. He had become a revisionists. He would have established military control, and control of the religion of the state, with a view to reforming it. Vincent Patrice, Vénérable Maître, certainly had a hand in all of this, and very nearly realised his ambitions. Santiago held the Masonic Grand Rank of Serenismo Gran *Maestro* del Gran Oriente "Nacional"— not "Continental" as was hoped—fulfilling at least part of Vincent's master plan until his death on the 20th of November 1854, in La Victoria.

And the fabulous trophy, the mysterious object stolen so dramatically from Government House that night in Trinidad? Apocrypha has it that it accompanied Santiago Mariño on all his campaigns and was present at all his victories and triumphs. He kept it by him, as well through his darkest times and would be seen sitting by it in periods of despair and disappointment. It became much more than a trophy of youthful adventure, it assumed the nature of a talisman. Having to go into hiding, after that brief period when he actually held power, it was placed in the trusted hands of his sister María Concepción and her husband José Sanda at their home in Caracas. But, like the winds of the sea, the winds of fate often decide for us not just our destination, but our destiny. In the maelstrom of war that followed Santiago's rise to power and his fall into ignominy, the Sanda family was forced to flee Caracas and to return to Trinidad, leaving behind Santiago's lucky charm hidden in the basement of their house. The family's financial situation after José Sanda's death caused the property to change hands. Ironically, a Freemason's hall was built over the site and a Lodge erected, consecrated and named Lodge George Washington. To the best of my knowledge, Santiago's trophy is still there, in the abandoned basement, which is now covered over by a close tiled black and white checkered floor. Interestingly, Caracas is also at 10° north of the equator.

FINIS

Gérard "Jerry" Besson was born in 1942 at 50 Hermitage Road, Belmont, Trinidad and Tobago, W.I. He has worked in advertising as a Creative Director in all media and as a writer, publisher and social historian, he has specialised in the history and folklore of Trinidad and Tobago. In 2007, he was awarded a National award, the Hummingbird Medal (Gold) for Heritage Preservation and Promotion, and received the Lifetime Achiever Heritage Preservation Award from the National Trust of Trinidad and Tobago also in that year.

He has authored *Tales of the Paria Main Road*, *A Photograph Album of Trinidad at the Turn of the 19th Century*, *The Book of Trinidad* (with Bridget Brereton), *Folklore & Legends of Trinidad and Tobago*, *From Colonial to Republic* (with Selwyn Ryan), *History of Scotiabank*, *History of Ansa McAl*, *The Angostura Historical Digest*, *The Cult of the Will*, and *The Voice in the Govi*.

www.ingramcontent.com/pod-product-compliance
Lightning Source LLC
Chambersburg PA
CBHW030926020726

47498CB00001B/135